Murder Is a Must

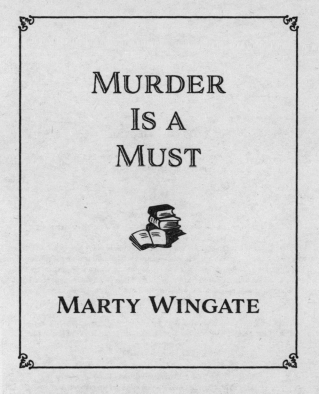

Marty Wingate

BERKLEY PRIME CRIME
New York

BERKLEY PRIME CRIME
Published by Berkley
An imprint of Penguin Random House LLC
penguinrandomhouse.com

Copyright © 2020 by Martha Wingate
Excerpt from *The Librarian Always Rings Twice* by Marty Wingate
copyright © 2020 by Martha Wingate

ISBN: 9781984804143

Berkley Prime Crime hardcover edition / December 2020
Berkley Prime Crime mass-market edition / September 2021

Printed in the United States of America
1   3   5   7   9   10   8   6   4   2

Book design by Laura Corless

To Leighton with love

1

The taxi drove west away from the rail station, avoiding the Monday-evening commuter traffic on Manvers Street. Instead, we encountered it along Green Park. Skirting Queen Square, we swung round the Circus, where lights twinkled in the austere Georgian terraces that formed the circle—doing their small part against the January darkness. No quicker a journey than walking, and certainly not cheaper, but I'd had no energy for the hike from the train up to Middlebank House. Perhaps I should've done. Nervous excitement had built up during my afternoon journey from Liverpool to Bath—my tummy atwitter at the thought of the First Edition Society's inaugural literary salon. It would be my first official public event as curator, and would go live in only twenty-four hours.

Nerves were the order of the day. When I walked into the entry, Mrs. Woolgar, Society secretary, shot out of her office and, dispensing with formalities, said, "Ms. Burke, a man delivered six cases of wine this afternoon. I had him leave them in the kitchenette, but—will we need that much?"

"I tell you what," I said, dropping my case next to the hallstand and hanging up my coat. "If they don't drink it all during the salon tomorrow evening, you and I can finish it off after everyone's left."

Behind her glasses, Mrs. Woolgar's eyes grew large. "Well, I hardly think—" She caught herself.

"Or we'll keep it until next week's salon," I said. "And the next or however long it lasts. We saved fifteen pounds with a large order."

"And Professor Fish? You're certain he'll arrive early enough tomorrow—and Mr. Moffatt knows to collect him?"

Actually, Arthur Fish wasn't a professor—he was a tutor at a college in London. But as he was our lecturer for the inaugural salon, I thought it better not to press the point. Titles and position meant a great deal to Mrs. Woolgar.

"Mr. Fish will come down on the train and arrive by midday, and Val will meet him." I'd been over this with her, but repeating it helped me as much as I hoped it helped her. "I've a cold lunch arranged"—or would have, as soon as I did the shopping in the morning at Waitrose—"and he'll have a quiet afternoon to sort himself out over a cup of tea."

While she tried to think of another potential disaster— my reading on the situation—the secretary smoothed the cutwork collar on her dress. She wore her usual-style frock, a narrow skirt and wide lapel, this one navy with matching belt. I admit to a bit of envy at Mrs. Woolgar's 1930s wardrobe. Narrow skirts didn't suit me.

"Still," she said, "I'm not entirely comfortable with the title of his talk—'Fifty Ways to Murder.' Rather sensational."

I might've conceded her point but for the fact it was also the title of his popular book and that Middlebank was home to the First Edition library, a stunning collection of books from the women authors of the Golden Age of Mystery.

It had been the lifetime passion of Lady Georgiana Fowling, who, through her élan and generous nature, had garnered the love and admiration of the people of Bath and the worldwide membership of the Society. Her ladyship had died almost four years ago at the grand old age of ninety-four and, sadly but inevitably, during the last few years of her life, the Society had diminished and the world's attention had turned elsewhere. This is where I came in.

"The title did its job, though, didn't it?" I reminded Mrs. Woolgar. "The entire series of salons was sold out in a fortnight even though we had only this first title to announce."

Mrs. Woolgar sighed, and I knew this indicated she could think of no other argument for the moment. "That arrived by hand for you this afternoon," she said, nodding to a brown envelope on the hallstand.

Comic Sans font had been used to print out both my address—Ms. Hayley Burke, Curator, First Edition Society, Middlebank House—and the return address—Make an Exhibition of Yourself! James Street West, Bath.

"Thank you," I said. "I believe I can leave it for the morning."

"Well, then," Mrs. Woolgar said, "I'll say good night. Tomorrow will be an eventful day, I'm sure."

"Yes, it will be—in the best possible way."

Without another word, she walked to the back stairs and descended to her garden flat on the lower ground floor. I understood her restraint—to a point. Glynis Woolgar had been personal assistant to and dear friend of our founder for many years and, as directed in her ladyship's will, had become secretary in perpetuum for the Society. Mrs. Woolgar had seized this duty and interpreted it to mean nothing should happen unless it had happened while Lady Fowling had been alive. Devoted as that made her look, the secretary's love of the status quo was seeing the Society slowly grind to a halt.

Just let me introduce a new idea, and I was met with a

heavy sigh and a raised eyebrow—her way of reminding me that I had been curator for not quite six months, had never met her ladyship, and had only recently read my first detective story. And so, what did I know?

I knew my responsibilities and I took them seriously. Job one—resurrect the First Edition Society to its former glory, even if I had to drag Glynis Woolgar along kicking and screaming.

But at this moment, I needed my bed, and fortunately, it was quite near. We were self-contained at Middlebank—Mrs. Woolgar's flat on the lower ground floor, our offices and a kitchenette here on the ground floor, the library up one flight of stairs on the first floor, and my flat above that. An attic and a cellar completed this typical Georgian terrace house—built up instead of out.

I picked up my case, but set it down again when Bunter appeared.

He came sauntering out of my office, his tortoiseshell fur groomed to perfection and his tail straight as a rod apart from the question-mark curve at its tip. After she had been widowed, Lady Fowling had always had a tortoiseshell cat, and he had always been named Bunter—this one, number seven, had come on board as a kitten not long before she died.

He stretched, digging his claws into the Persian entry rug and retracting them before pausing at the bottom of the stairs that led up to the library. He twitched his tail with reproach, and I knew why—I was late. An entire day late. I spent weekends with my mum in Liverpool, but usually returned home on Sunday evening.

After a pause—perhaps deciding he'd looked at his calendar wrong—the cat approached, arched his back, and rubbed against my leg. I made a show of rummaging in my bag before slowly pulling out a catnip mouse and dangling it before him. After we'd gone through the ritual of presentation, I said, "Right—you know the agreement. Get a fresh mouse, give up a manky mouse."

We headed upstairs. On the first-floor landing, I opened the library door, switched on the lights, and made straight for the fireplace, the cat on my heels.

Sticking my hand in the coal bucket, I rummaged round. I'd brought Bunter a new mouse each week for several months now, and only recently had I instituted the one-for-one rule, and so it wasn't as if his cache of toys would ever diminish.

Now I pulled out not a lump of coal, but a sorry specimen of catnip mouse, stiff from dried drool and its catnip long since gnawed away. "Ewww," I said, holding it gingerly between thumb and forefinger. "Would you like to say any last words?"

But Bunter, mouth full of fresh prey, only watched as I carried it out. At the library door, I looked back to see him drop the newest addition into the bucket.

I put my hand on the newel to continue to my flat upstairs, but turned back to Lady Fowling—her full-length portrait, that is—hanging on the library landing.

"I wish you could be here tomorrow evening," I said, confident that no one could hear me talking to a painting. In her enigmatic smile I read that, come time for the literary salon, she just might listen in.

At last in my flat, I dropped my case, kicked off my shoes, and pulled the band out of my ponytail as I moved into the kitchen, phone in hand. I tapped an icon with a red heart labeled *Val* and switched the kettle on, but changed my mind and reached for a wineglass instead.

"There you are," he answered. "Are you home? How was the train?"

"All right. Crowded. The fellow across from me made it through several cans of Tennent's Lager—he must've started his journey in Glasgow. He offered me one—at least, I think that's what he said. And your day—all four classes plus office hours?"

"I had a student ask me today did a novel need a protagonist or could it be peopled only with secondary characters."

"Well, that's a fine way to begin the week. Everything all right with Mr. Fish?" It was Val who had secured our first speaker, having heard Arthur Fish once speak at the Chiswick Book Festival. Arrangements had worked out perfectly when the author had graciously waived his fee in exchange for selling his own books at the salon. "You reminded him that there will be only twenty people there?"

"He hasn't had a new book out in two years," Val said. "We're doing him a favor as much as he is us. So, coffee tomorrow—the Pump Room?"

"Perfect. I'll be close by looking at that space near the Gainsborough."

"Pump Room it is, then," he said. "Good night. Sweet dreams."

Dreams were all we had at the moment, and so I took them to bed with me, drifting off as soon as my head touched the pillow.

The next morning, Mrs. Woolgar popped into my office first thing. "Shall we, Ms. Burke?" Her eyes fell on the corner of my desk where sat a pristine, rose-red file folder marked *Exhibition*. "Are we discussing that?"

"No—that topic is for tomorrow's board meeting." I gathered a notebook, papers, and my mug of tea, and followed the secretary out to the entry and into her own office, where our morning briefings were held.

Why? Why did we meet in Mrs. Woolgar's office instead of mine? True, she had a comfortable space with oak bookshelves and desk, a floral Axminster rug, and a view of the street. But my office was larger with a wingback chair for my guest, plus two chairs and a tea table in front of the fireplace, and a Victorian desk—walnut, highly polished to show off its swirls and bands. And, I had a view of the garden. My office—the curator's office. And yet, I didn't protest. One of the first things I had learned about working with Mrs. Woolgar was to choose my battles carefully.

We kept the meeting brief—that evening's literary salon our only concern.

"I've written up the agenda," I said, pushing a paper across Mrs. Woolgar's desk, and tapping a finger at the starting time, seven thirty: *Remarks by Hayley Burke, curator.* I did so like the look of that. "We have two young women to serve the wine. Pauline is sending them over from the Minerva—they work for her at the pub. I'll introduce our speaker. Apart from that, there's little to do. He's in charge of his own book sales."

"I wonder will he approach murder methods by discussing the author or the detective?" Mrs. Woolgar mused. "Will it be Sayers's choice in *Unnatural Death*—"

I kept my face in neutral as I scanned the cheat sheet in my head—*Dorothy L. Sayers; detective, Lord Peter Wimsey. Yet to read* Unnatural Death.

"—or Inspector Grant's intellectual ways in *A Shilling for Candles*—"

Inspector Grant, let's see—yes! Josephine Tey. Have yet to read any of hers.

"—or examine only methods. What would he say about laburnum seeds?"

Wait now, that sounded familiar—I think I saw the movie.

I felt sure Mrs. Woolgar's mention of specific Golden Age of Mystery authors was not meant to trip me up—we'd at least got that far in our professional relationship—and I should've been able to add some coherent thought to the discussion. But, put on the spot, I came up with nothing, and so carried on with business.

"Once Mr. Fish is taken care of this afternoon, I will start on my assessment of the books we have on the shelves in the library," I told her. "And study the list of the rare books that are in storage. I want to get an idea of the direction we'll take for the"—breaking my own promise that we would not discuss this topic this morning, I half swallowed the last word—"exhibition."

The glow of the computer screen reflected in Mrs. Woolgar's glasses and masked her eyes. Still, I thought I detected a look of displeasure.

I popped up from my chair, excused myself, and fled.

As I gathered my coat and bag, I rehearsed my introductory remarks for that evening's lecture, but by the time I headed out the front door of Middlebank and into a chilly January morning, my mind had shifted to my new venture—and the topic for the Society's board meeting the following afternoon: the exhibition.

The six-week series of literary salons—debuting that evening with Arthur Fish—had been booked out before Christmas, and so I'd had bags of time to concentrate on another project. I knew exactly what that should be—to mount a show focusing on our founder and her accomplishments. I called it *Lady Georgiana Fowling: A Life in Words*.

We had no shortage of material. Not only the contents of the library, but also the more valuable volumes at the bank, which I had not yet fully investigated. Could one of them be worth as much as the Dorothy L. Sayers book I'd seen in an online auction going for six thousand pounds? I was unclear if all the stored books were signed editions, but I knew that many of the volumes at Middlebank had been inscribed with charming comments from the authors, such as *To Georgiana, Albert thanks you for your support, and so do I!* That from author Margery Allingham mentioning her amateur sleuth, Albert Campion. On my to-be-read list, of course.

Enriching the library, we had her ladyship's notebooks—three cartons full of everyday school exercise books, the kind with the marbled covers. She had kept them throughout her life, beginning with her marriage at twenty to Sir John Fowling, a baronet, seventy. Sir John had died ten years later, after which Lady Fowling's casual interest in the Golden Age of Mystery became a lifelong obsession. Her notebooks teemed with the everyday—shopping lists, recipes—as well as thoughts on writing, her favorite authors and characters, and memories of her marriage.

We also had Lady Fowling's own novels to display. She had written fan fiction—borrowing a sleuth here and there from established authors—but her light shone brightest when she wrote about her own detective, François Flambeaux, a wealthy landowner from Dorset who disguised his serious, crime-solving nature by acting the gadabout.

What we didn't have was a venue. Middlebank itself was unsuitable for the sort of event with freestanding glass cases, scenes reconstructed, displays both lifesize and intimate. We didn't have the space. The ground floor of the terraced house comprised the entry, two offices, and a kitchenette. The library itself took up most of the first floor—shelves, books, enormous table, chairs. My flat was on the second floor, and so that was certainly off-limits—as were Mrs. Woolgar's accommodations on the lower ground floor. No, we needed a purpose-designed site.

We also needed an exhibition manager.

When I'd announced my firm intention to go forward with the exhibition, Mrs. Woolgar acted as if I were mad as a box of frogs. The board of the First Edition Society lined up on their usual sides. Mrs. Jane Arbuthnot and Ms. Maureen Frost stood with the secretary—although I sensed Maureen edging toward the fence. On my side were Mrs. Sylvia Moon and Mrs. Audrey Moon, who were both in their eighties and game for almost anything, and my good friend Adele Babbage—by far the youngest board member. In Lady Fowling's later years, she and Adele had enjoyed an affectionate mother-daughter-like relationship—or more accurately, considering the decades of difference in their ages, grandmother-granddaughter. This was something Adele had never known growing up. But on the subject of an exhibition, even Adele thought I might be doing too much too soon.

At least they'd all agreed to attend a meeting about the exhibition, and so I'd scheduled one for the next afternoon—Wednesday. When it came to meetings at Middlebank, the agenda hardly mattered to the board members—they looked forward to a jolly good time with tea and pastries and the sherry decanter on the table. It reminded them, so I was told, of when Lady Fowling was alive and they spent many an afternoon laughing and sharing stories either in the library at Middlebank or at the Royal Crescent Hotel.

Tomorrow afternoon's board meeting would be my second go-round on the exhibition. The Society was on a roll, and we needed to follow up the salons with the announcement of an exciting event in order to keep everyone's attention. I admitted—with great reluctance—that it was possible I still felt the need to prove myself. I'd got the job as curator when the Society had desperately needed someone—anyone—to fill the role, and I'd not yet shaken the thought that I had been only a stopgap measure.

Work had to begin immediately—it would take a year to mount a show of even a modest size, and when I considered the scope of the undertaking, I couldn't breathe. Scheduling enough time for move-in and buildup, handling of delicate books, protective lighting, promoting the event through the right channels, coming up with ideas for the actual displays—signage that read *Here's a Book* wouldn't cut it—those jobs were only the tip of the iceberg.

Val was in on the planning, of course, and he brought with him the backing of Bath College, the adult education school in the city. We were a good team, Val and I—in the business sense as well as personally, although that side of the relationship hadn't moved quick enough for either of us. Still, his support meant the world to me.

But we couldn't publicly announce the exhibition until we had secured a venue. I was reminded of this now as I walked down Julian Road and stopped alongside the Assembly Rooms. The building's entrance did not face the road, but sat at a ninety-degree angle, the doors opening onto a large courtyard where tour and school groups could gather as they waited to go in. A popular and exquisitely kept historical venue, but the spaces within—the Great Octagon, for example—were hired for weddings and receptions and the odd two-day trade show. It was the same all over Bath. We needed a place that could accommodate us for a two-week run. We needed the Charlotte.

The Charlotte sat just across the road from the Assembly Rooms and at the corner of a terrace block. It had been created by combining two houses. On the ground floor, the wall between had been knocked down, providing a comfortably large event space with offices up on the first floor. Parts of the second house—the corner one—had not been refurbished.

The exhibition area had been restored in the Georgian style so loved in Bath. When I had worked at the Jane Austen Centre, we'd held a week-long show there—*Jane and Siblings: The Austens at Home*—and so I knew the place well. For a long-term event, it was perfect. Sadly, it was perfect for many other organizations—its calendar booked solid for the next three years. Unavailability only made it all the more desirable.

And so, instead of the Charlotte, I had an appointment to look at rooms with an address along the Lower Borough Walls, above a mobile phone shop.

Turning my back on the Charlotte, I hurried along St. Andrews Terrace before dashing across George Street and striding down Milsom into Union Street—I always made better time going downhill. As I passed Lush, my phone rang, and I saw it was a call from my daughter.

"Dinah, sweetie, how are you?"

"Hi, Mum, just running to class, but I wanted to find out about Gran's appointment with the surgeon yesterday."

"Promising. He said she'd definitely walk better when he finished with her. She's down for surgery." My mum had been in a car crash almost three years ago. She now used a walking frame in her flat, and a wheelchair elsewhere. She'd had a fall in November—no broken bones, but her doctor had referred her to an orthopedic surgeon, and he had given her hope. "But it's not life-threatening, so she's on the bottom of the list. How are you? Your job isn't distracting you from classes, is it?"

My daughter, just shy of her twenty-third birthday, studied the history of everyday life at Sheffield. We never brought up what job she might get when she graduated—after all, what sort of a role model was I with a degree in nineteenth-century literature? And yet I had turned out all right. Finally, at age forty-five.

"It's only pub work, Mum, and it's only every other weekend—studies are fine." I heard a nanosecond of hesitation—a length of time only a mother could detect. "Dad says he can get me on answering phones at some car-hire business, and I'd get double the pay."

"Did he?" I asked brightly, silently cursing my ex.

"Apparently, he knows someone."

"Well, you wouldn't want to give up your pub job before you knew for certain he could do that, would you?"

"You're right," she said with relief. "I'll stick with this. He does get a wild hair sometimes."

With my job as curator and Dinah's ever-so-part-time pub work, I'd only just got on an even keel financially. Now, with the promise of my mum's leg being sorted, came the realization that although the cost of Mum's surgery would be covered, there would be other related expenses. I didn't need Roger's weak, empty promises to lead our daughter astray.

"Look, sweetie, I'd better go. I've an appointment and just arrived."

"An appointment with Val?" she asked, a bit of tease in her voice.

"No, it's work. Although—"

"I'm off, Mum. Class."

I made short work of viewing the potential venue—narrow stairs for access and a decidedly dreary look to its two small rooms, which showed remnants of a previous exhibition on the history of felt markers. No storage, no kitchen, no loo—no thanks.

Leaving the Lower Borough Walls behind me, I heaved several huge sighs. I needed something concrete to present to the board the next afternoon, and not only about the venue. What of an exhibition manager?

"What about you?" my mum had asked when I'd told her my idea.

"Me?" I laid my hand on my chest and felt my heart race. "Manage the entire exhibition—design and all? No, Mum, I couldn't do that. We need a proper person. Someone with qualifications and experience."

Mounting this sort of show was a job for a professional with specific talents. I, as curator, would be there every step of the way, of course, and perhaps someday in the future I could do it myself, but not now. *Lady Fowling: A Life in Words* was too important for a first-timer. A truly impressive event required a person who could see a space, know the material, and build a visual experience that would draw the public into Lady Fowling's world.

Exhibition managers were thin on the ground, I could tell you that. I had an appointment with one the next day here in Bath—Zeno Berryfield, whose company was called Make an Exhibition of Yourself!—the exclamation point his. I swallowed hard, hoping and praying he hadn't been the one to put on the felt-marker event.

When I turned up Bath Street—quiet and empty—my spirits rose. There was Val standing in the shadow of the colonnade with his hands stuck in the pockets of his duffel coat. I hurried over, and he wrapped the coat round me as my arms circled his waist.

"We've got to stop meeting like this," I said.

The corners of his eyes crinkled as he smiled. "Oh, I'm all for that."

We kissed and kissed again, the warmth of his lips spreading down to my toes. I drew one arm out and brushed my fingers through his chestnut hair.

"I could use a bit of good news," I said. "Do you have any? Doesn't matter what it's about—has one of your students been offered a publishing deal, or is Waitrose carrying a new line of ready meals?"

"As it happens," he said, "I do have good news. I've booked us a place for next weekend."

It was an announcement of some import. Val and I had met in October, and there had been no denying our mutual attraction, but our timing wasn't the best. Life had intervened—beginning with my daughter, who arrived in Bath unannounced for a week's visit. To say we were surprised would be an understatement. I had invited Val to dinner that evening, but five minutes after he arrived, we had decided dinner could wait. Two minutes after that, there was Dinah, waiting downstairs at the door.

The three of us had shared the lasagna—yes, it was from Waitrose—and Val had left soon after, wanting to give us mother-daughter time. Dinah had thought him sweet and "quite taken with you, Mum."

After that week, Val's twin twenty-four-year-old daughters arrived for a visit—I had yet to meet them, because my mum had had her fall and I had gone to Liverpool for a week, followed by Christmas and all that entailed, and then

Dinah had come back to Bath for a few days—the obstacles to getting on with my relationship with Val seemed never ending. Finally, we'd given up.

Not totally, but we'd decided to act like adults and plan a proper weekend away, just the two of us. Things like this mean more at our age, and so with the prospect of a romantic getaway, we remained celibate. And frustrated.

We had redirected our energies into collaboration of another kind, focusing first on the salons, and now, the exhibition. And we were doing all right. Fine. After all, that weekend was less than a fortnight away.

"Where are we going?" I asked, thrilled that I'd had no hand in the planning.

"Woolacombe—North Devon."

I gasped. "Woolacombe?"

"We've got a room on the second floor of the hotel that looks out to the seafront."

The seaside—January or no—was where I most wanted to be, and he knew it. I kissed him again. "Did you do that for me?" I asked. "A deluxe room?"

His green eyes twinkled. "Yes," he said, and I laughed. "And because if we can look out at the sea any old time we want, perhaps we can spend a bit more of the weekend in the room."

For a moment, we looked deep into each other's eyes, and then it became too much.

"Coffee."

Morning coffee in the Pump Room, with its high ceilings and white tablecloths, was the perfect place to calm my nerves about that evening's salon while, at the same time, I came to terms with my disappointing venue search. Our orders arrived and we dived in—Val spread brown sauce on his bacon roll while I slathered my Bath bun with cinnamon butter. I licked a finger and, while I stirred the foam down in my cappuccino, described the space above the mobile phone shop.

"So," I said, "we can tick that place off the list."

"Admin at the college regrets turning Wood Hall into offices now."

Val had done his part to search for a venue, and we had both come up empty-handed. But I pushed those troubles to the side. For the moment, I wanted to think happy thoughts.

"Which author should I read next?"

I had asked Val, a writing teacher who specialized in genre fiction, to guide me in my quest to learn about the Golden Age of Mystery authors and their detectives.

"Well, you've got Christie under your belt," he said. "You might move on to Sayers."

"Ah, Dorothy L. Sayers—her sleuth is Lord Peter Wimsey. On one of my paperbacks, he's wearing a monocle."

"His trademark."

"Why? Does he have poor eyesight, or is it because he wants to look like a toff?"

"Or could there be another reason?"

"Hmm," I said, picking up the second half of my Bath bun. "Yet another mystery to solve."

When we were nearly finished with coffee, our phones pinged with texts. As Val dug in his coat pocket, I saw my message.

"What?" I fumbled my password, hurrying to reread what I hoped I hadn't seen.

Val got to his message first—but it was the same as mine. "Bloody hell," he said.

The text came from Arthur Fish.

Paddington Station shut down. I don't drive. Don't think I'll make it for this evening.

2

Shut down?" I shouted. Heads turned, and I dropped my voice to a furious whisper. "They can't shut down an entire train station. Can they? Wait, you don't think it's a—"

A man at the next table leaned over. "Electrics."

"Sorry?" Val asked.

"No trains out of Paddington, because a high-speed test train damaged overhead power cables." The man lifted his phone. "I've got the National Rail alert app."

Val and I looked up the news on our own mobiles. I couldn't take it in. No trains, no speaker. Our inaugural literary salon canceled? With a lurch, my mind began moving again.

"What are we going to do?" I asked. "Who is next week, I can't remember? Could we switch?"

"It's the American on Poe."

One of the international members of the Society—and the only week she would be in the country. "No, that won't work."

Silence again. I swallowed hard against a rising sea of tears and slapped my hand on the table. "Well, we're not canceling. We must begin as we intend to continue—with quality lectures or readings that suit our audience and our mission. I don't suppose we can ask Maureen Frost to act out all the parts in *The Mousetrap*?"

"She'd be dead keen on that," Val said, and I saw his green eyes harden to jade. "No, we'll book her for another time. This evening, we are going to hear Arthur Fish. I'll go fetch him."

"You what?"

"What can it be—two hours there and two back? He lives in Richmond—at least it isn't central London. Look, it's eleven now. I'll drive up and collect him and bring him down, and we'll arrive in plenty of time. I'd already arranged for another lecturer to take my afternoon class, I might as well put myself to good use."

"Val, no," I said, "that would be a terrible day for you." I frowned. "I should go with you. And I would do, but . . ." I glanced at my watch. "What time can you leave?"

With Paddington Station closed, hundreds of thousands of people who would normally take a train turned to cars, clogging not only the Great West Road into and out of London—but also every other major and minor route. It took Val three hours to get to Richmond, and after a quick turnaround, he and Mr. Fish started the journey back through thick traffic.

I had spent the first half of my afternoon unable to settle on anything, while attempting to keep a positive outlook as I made pointless trips up to the library and down again, talking to myself. Bunter sat on the Chippendale chair on the first-floor landing—out of the fray—and watched. Twice Mrs. Woolgar came out of her office, thinking I had spoken to her.

I had to admit, she was taking this turn of events better than I thought she would. "Ms. Burke, what else can we do but wait and hope Mr. Moffatt and Mr. Fish arrive in time?" she asked. "Now I believe I'll go down to my flat and rest. You'll let me know if you hear anything—one way or the other?"

"They'll be here, Mrs. Woolgar, I know they will."

Val rang at four o'clock when they stopped for coffee at a roadside service on this side of Reading.

"He's got two cartons of books," he said in a quiet voice. "I don't know how he was going to manage those on the train."

More to the point, who did Fish think would buy them all?

I went up to dust the shelves in the library, knowing they didn't need it, and then distracted myself by admiring the many different editions Lady Fowling had acquired. Perhaps I would read the first page of a few of them—that would keep my mind off Val and Arthur Fish and the long journey from Richmond to Bath.

Bunter busied himself with the contents of the coal bucket while I shifted the short library ladder over and climbed its two steps to reach the top shelf but one, where I found part of the Dorothy L. Sayers collection. I ran my finger along the spines and thought, yes, Lord Peter Wimsey would be my next read—and why not a book from our own library instead of one of the musty old paperbacks I'd gleaned from charity shops around town? I skimmed the titles in front of me. Here were three editions of *Strong Poison*, each with a different cover. Farther along the shelf, *The Nine Tailors*—in English and the German translation, *Die Neun Schneider*. Next, *Murder Must Advertise*. Being careful not to pull it out by its spine, I slid this one off the shelf. It had a yellow dust jacket—many Sayers books did—and at the top of the cover in words almost as large as the title itself: *4'6 Cheap Edition on thin paper.*

"Four and six, not a bad price," I said. "Must be a wartime edition."

When I opened the cover to check the publication date, a folded sheet fell out the back of the book and drifted to the floor.

With a quick glance at the door to make sure Mrs. Woolgar hadn't seen and wouldn't accuse me of damaging the goods, I retrieved the paper that had fallen out of *Murder Must Advertise*, sat down, and unfolded it.

> *Dear DLS,*
> *How can I ever thank you enough for this incredibly generous gift you have given me? To think that I now possess a book signed by all the members of the Detection Club from 1933, when your entertaining Lord Peter story* Murder Must Advertise *was first published. You know of my great respect for all of you, and my growing library of books by you and the other authors, especially the women, whom I greatly admire for their strength, perseverance, and talents. You are kind to speak well of my François Flambeaux—knowing, as you would, that he is a particular creation of mine imbued with qualities I borrowed from my dear late husband. I don't mind that so few readers know François, because he is still dear to me.*

Where was a tissue when you needed one? Thoughts of Lady Fowling's marriage to Sir John always touched me—she had written about him with such tenderness. I wiped my eyes with the back of a sleeve and continued.

> *Please know that this book will be treasured and kept safe, as I am sure it is quite valuable. What a*

lovely gesture for you to give it away. I look
forward to a time I can share it with others.
*   Yours kindly,*
*   Georgiana*

*   P.S. I recently saw your photograph in the*
newspaper, taken at your previous employers, SH
Benson's. You were unveiling a plaque near the
staircase at their place of business—the "site" of
the death in your book Murder Must Advertise.
What a jolly idea for them to make the connection
between your story and the actual place that
inspired it. This makes your gift all the more
special!

DLS? Dorothy L. Sayers. A thrill ran through me at the personal nature of the letter.

The Detection Club? The name rang a vague bell. More research was needed, but it must have been unusual for club members to all sign a book written by only one of them.

Where was it? Where was this rare, signed, first edition of Dorothy L. Sayers's *Murder Must Advertise*? I would need to conduct a search of the library, leaving no book unopened, and if I didn't find it, I would bring the cartons out of their secure storage and examine each one of those.

Look how important this made Lady Fowling. She wasn't only a fan—she had been considered an equal by Dorothy L. Sayers, one of the great names from the Golden Age of Mystery.

A worm of a question wriggled its way into my elation. Why was this letter that Lady Fowling wrote to Dorothy L. Sayers never sent, and instead, stashed in a book here at Middlebank? Had her ladyship imagined a friendship that didn't exist?

"Ms. Burke?"

I leapt out of my chair at Mrs. Woolgar's sudden appearance.

"It's past six o'clock," she said, her voice laced with reproof.

"What? How can that be . . . I didn't think . . . I must change my clothes—people will begin arriving soon. But where are Val and Arthur Fish?" Then I looked down at the letter in one hand and the book in the other, and remembered what I was about. "Mrs. Woolgar—see what I've found!"

She approached, and catching sight of the letter and her ladyship's spidery handwriting, she smiled. "Oh my, now where has that been?"

"Hidden. Stuck in the back of this book—the wrong book. It's a letter Lady Fowling was writing to the author, Sayers. But it looks as if she never sent it."

"Nonsense," Mrs. Woolgar said, glancing at the letter before handing it back to me, "this is only her first draft. She always wrote a letter out and then copied it over onto proper stationery before posting it."

I could've hugged the secretary on the spot for this bit of information, but I knew my place, and instead gathered up letter and book. "This is fantastic—wait'll I tell you more. But now I must hurry. Hang on, where's my phone? Oh, there. I'll text Val and be down in two ticks." The front door buzzed. "That'll be the servers. Mrs. Woolgar, would you—"

"I will let them in."

"And the chairs?"

"Yes, I'll bring in the Chippendales. And I'll light the fire. Now off with you."

We should have enough seats for everyone, as long as we had no surprise guests. If need be, I could perch on the ladder. I left Mrs. Woolgar talking to Bunter—"Come now, boy, dinner"—and flew up the stairs to my flat. As I unlocked the door, a text came in from Arthur Fish.

Just off m4. Plenty of time.

Plenty of time—was he mad?

I changed into my dress for the evening—geranium pink with a ruched waist and, most importantly, a bit of give. Next week, I would wear it with a jacket and the week after that with a floral scarf. Long ago, I'd learned to squeeze as much use as possible out of my wardrobe. Pulling the band off my ponytail, I combed my hair, twisted it up, and secured it with a spring clip, and then, carrying my shoes, I went downstairs, stopping at the library to greet our two servers before arriving at the front door out of breath and with mere seconds before the door buzzed.

Mrs. Audrey Moon and Mrs. Sylvia Moon—both co-cooned in layers of wool—beamed at me. Behind them, I saw Jane Arbuthnot's ramrod posture, and Maureen Frost's steel-gray pageboy with Adele's mass of red curls in the far back. The board. They had been invited early to meet our speaker, and here they were. Where was he?

"Oh, Hayley!" Audrey Moon exclaimed. "We're so proud of you."

I blushed and greeted the Moons with kisses on their cheeks, shook hands with the next two, and received a hug from Adele.

"Well," Mrs. Arbuthnot said, "where is our illustrious speaker?"

"Minutes away," I said. "Mrs. Woolgar, would you—"

The secretary escorted the group upstairs, but Adele hung back.

"Here it is," she said, "your first outing. You all right?"

"Fine. Fantastic. Fabulous."

"What's wrong?"

"No trains from Paddington and Val drove up to collect Arthur Fish. They turned off the M4 about twenty minutes ago."

"Oh, the trains—I didn't realize."

"I'm sure they'll arrive," I said. "But what if they're late?

You know the others will say I was too ambitious with these literary salons, and then they'll never agree to—"

"Look"—Adele tore off her coat, thrust it at me, and adjusted the purple tunic she wore over red leggings—"you wait here for them. I'll go up and make sure everyone has a glass of wine, and then I'll ask Audrey and Sylvia about their cruise. That'll be good for half an hour at least. Everything will be fine."

I made a choking noise that was meant to be assent.

Two early birds came to the door next, and after that, others began to drift in. I knew one or two, but most were strangers to me. Nevertheless, I welcomed them warmly and sent them up to the library. "Do have a glass of wine," I called after.

Keeping the door ajar meant there would be no incessant buzzer as people arrived, but the cold air would do me in. I paced, rubbing my bare arms and panting from the stress. Finally, I'd counted everyone in, closed the door, and stood facing the stairs, wondering what I would tell them all. The buzzer went off behind me and my heart leapt into my throat.

There they were—Val with bloodshot eyes, and our speaker, a slender man with thinning hair, round wire-rimmed glasses, and rosy cheeks. Each carried a carton of books in his arms.

I could've kissed them both, one more than the other.

"What a cock-up," Arthur Fish said after brief introductions. "I'm terribly sorry, Hayley—it was awfully good of Val to be my driver. Look now, I'm ready to go—point me in the right direction."

Adele looked down from the landing.

"Mr. Fish, is it?" she asked. "Welcome to Bath."

"Adele Babbage, board member," I said, "meet Arthur Fish, our speaker for the evening. Adele will see you up." He moved toward the stairs. "Hang on." I took the carton of books from Val and put it on top of Arthur's. "Now then, off you go."

Adele hurried halfway down to retrieve one of the boxes and led our speaker away.

I returned to Val, took his face in my hands, and kissed him. "Thank you, thank you."

He pulled me close and whispered, "I'm at your service."

Giggly with relief, I said, "Oh, I like the sound of that."

Mrs. Woolgar loomed at the top of the stairs. "Well, I must say, that was close. Ms. Burke, why don't you join our guests in the library, and we'll give Mr. Moffatt time to change his clothes."

"He's perfect just as he is," I replied.

"It's all right," Val said. "I've at least got a jacket and tie."

"Good, well, I'll go on up—but we won't start without you."

"No, don't wait. I've already heard his entire talk on the way here."

I flew up the steps and entered the library with a smile on my face, breathlessly greeting people that I had just greeted at the door. "Good evening, hello, so wonderful of you to be here." I looked for our speaker, and spotted him chatting with Mrs. Moon and Mrs. Moon. Whatever he said had sent them into peals of laughter. As I approached, I took two glasses of red off a tray that passed by.

"Mr. Fish, glass of wine?"

"Thanks, Hayley," he said, "just what I need."

Adele came up behind and spoke in my ear. "That's his second."

In one smooth movement I took the glass away from Mr. Fish and passed it off to Adele. "Here, let us take care of that for you while you get yourself settled." I led him to the fireplace and turned to the room. I felt the comfortable warmth behind me, heard the merry crackle of logs, and smelled that hint of woodsmoke—along with another odor. I sniffed. Burning herb of some kind. I glanced behind me into the fire, where a small lump with a leather tail smoked and then burst into flames. Thanks, Bunter.

I took a deep breath and straightened, raising my voice over the murmur of conversation. "Good evening, everyone, and welcome to the First Edition Society's literary salon season."

3

". . . and that's why," Arthur Fish said, wrapping up, "you'll never find death by Morris Men in any of her novels."

Generous applause broke out around the library, accompanied by smiles and chatter as the servers circulated with more wine. I made sure our speaker got that second glass he so well deserved and stood back to admire the scene. We had done it—pulled off a winner for the inaugural literary salon in the First Edition library.

A queue began to form in front of Arthur Fish as he settled at the end of the table with a stack of his books at his elbow and a pen in hand. Time for me to mingle.

I didn't get far—a stocky fellow not quite my height appeared in front of me. He had a shaved head, and I caught a glimpse of a tattoo behind his left ear, peeking up from his wool scarf.

"So," he said, "Middlebank opens its doors at last."

"Hello, good evening," I said, taking a step back. "We're delighted to welcome you. Have you come far this evening?"

It was one of those questions the Queen asked people when they lined up to meet her, and I now could see how handy it was to have that query ready.

"Just up the road. What are your plans? Will you be adding to the library? Taking away?"

"Selling? No," I said, "we wouldn't sell any volume Lady Fowling herself had—"

"Came across a *4.50 from Paddington*. Boot sale. Saturday last. Near Beaulieu. Crime Club Choice edition. 1957. Near fine. Two quid. Worth seventy-five."

I flinched as he peppered me with details. "Did you now? I do so love a good Miss Marple."

"*Appointment with Death*. 1938. Orange cloth. Sunning on the spine. Still, ten pound. Boot sale. Leicester. They didn't know what they had." He nodded as if confirming the truth of the matter.

"That's a Poirot story, isn't it?" I asked, proud at how well versed I was in Agatha Christie's work.

"*Endless Night*. 1967. Gilt-lettered spine. Three-pound fifty at a house clear-out."

Dear God, someone save me. My gaze flickered round the library—I saw everyone else in congenial conversation while I stood there listening to the deals of the century.

"Well," I said, in that *let's wrap this up* tone of voice, "you obviously have an eye for it, Mr.—"

"Bulldog!" Arthur Fish called from across the room.

The fellow turned his head, and now I could see the detail of his tattoo. It was a stack of books—five of them, I thought—and quite intricate work. I could almost read the titles.

"Hayley," Arthur said, walking over to us, "do you know Bulldog Moyle?"

"We've just met," I said. "Mr. Moyle—Bulldog—was telling me about his collection."

"I can imagine he was," Arthur replied. "Listen, Bulldog, did you see those bound volumes of *The Strand* that came up for sale—"

Leaving them to it, I backed away and into Val.

"The evening's a success," he murmured in my ear, and the tingling that shot down my neck had nothing to do with literary salons.

I snuggled against him and turned to whisper, "I suppose I'd better buy one of his books."

Thank you, Arthur, for such an enjoyable lecture," I said. The book signing had ended, the servers had cleaned up, and our inaugural crowd for the literary salons had left. I now stood at the open door, shivering slightly. "I hope we made it worth your while."

I'd say we had. Handing him his remaining carton, I could tell it was practically empty, and thought he'd sold more books than people attended.

"My pleasure," Arthur said. "And thanks to Val for going the extra mile—literally—to get me here. The best of luck with your exhibition. I look forward to seeing it."

I'd been flying so high by the end of the evening—and on only half a glass of wine—that I'd blithely shared the news of our next project. A bit too blithely, apparently, from the look Jane Arbuthnot now threw me as she buttoned up her coat.

"Yes, well," I said to Arthur, "we certainly hope that the exhibition will become a reality, although, of course, there are many details to work out." I flashed Jane a smile.

The board members departed, and then Val gave me a sweet and lingering kiss on the cheek and left with his carload—he had offered to take the Moons home and drop Arthur Fish at the rail station for a late train back now that Paddington had reopened.

I had not had one second to tell Val about my discovery—

Lady Fowling's letter indicating the existence, but not the location, of a well-signed first edition of *Murder Must Advertise*. That news must be given in person. I would do it tomorrow, before the board meeting.

Only Adele, Mrs. Woolgar, and I remained. The secretary murmured something that may have been a compliment about the evening—or not—and retreated to her flat.

"Good show, Hayley," Adele said, wrapping a paisley scarf round her neck. "I'd best be off. I told Pauline I'd stop in at the Minerva on my way home."

I stuck out my bottom lip. "Good that someone has time for her significant other."

"Isn't Val coming back?" she asked.

"No."

"You two need a little less work and a little more play."

"Agreed." I recovered my spirits. "We're off to the seaside—not this weekend, but next. And no one can stop us."

I had Wednesday completely under control. We held no morning briefing, as I had an appointment with exhibition manager Zeno Berryfield. I'd booked his only available time, which meant he must be in high demand.

Bath College's modern black building lay just to my right when I reached James Street West, but I turned away and headed east to Berryfield's office. Val would have no time for a visit—he had classes all day and only a half hour to get to the board meeting at four o'clock. Bless him for finding another teacher to cover his last class. He and I were well prepared for the meeting, and if Mr. Berryfield was the right man for the job of manager, the board would see our proposal in a new light. Even if we did still lack a venue.

I located the right building number, but there was no sign for Make an Exhibition of Yourself! Regardless, I rang the bell. No one answered, but I heard the *snick* of the lock as it opened, and I entered to find my only option was a staircase. Two flights up I came to another door with *Your Business Here, Ltd.*, painted on the glass panel. Inside, I saw a large room with rows of desks and men and women busy on phones and computers. I stepped inside for directions.

"Ms. Burke?"

A man appeared in front of me. A large man—he towered over me, blocking the light and casting himself in silhouette.

"Mr. Berryfield?" I asked.

"Heigh-ho." He took my hand and shook it vigorously. "Come through, will you? Tea or coffee?"

"No, thank you."

He took off down an aisle, and now I could see him in full color. He wore a teal blue business suit and high-shine black oxfords, his black hair just long enough to comb. I hurried after him, and he held up at a desk by the window that was clean apart from a laptop and a mobile phone. When he turned, I saw his wide tie sported large, multicolored polka dots, reminding me of a package of Smarties.

"Please sit down," he said, gesturing toward an empty space. "Oh, sorry; now, who's taken that chair?"

He wandered off. I took a closer look at the other people and overheard a nearby woman on the phone say, "We export to Africa as well as EU countries."

"Do you share this office?" I asked when Berryfield had returned with a chair from two aisles away.

"It's called hot-desking," he replied as he sat down, pushing a worn black satchel under his feet. Leaning forward, he clasped his hands. "Have you heard of it—hot-desking? You book a desk for a day. It's quite handy for me, as I am in the middle of relocating and want to test the potential of Bath Spa for my new headquarters. Put my toe in the water, so to speak."

He pushed his mouth to the side as if to show he knew how lame that little joke was. He had a pleasant face that was rather long but suited his build, and he had a helpful look. Rather like the fellow who worked behind the fish counter at Waitrose and was always so patient with me while I chose between Dover sole and plaice.

"How long have you been in Bath, Mr. Berryfield?"

"Not long—a fortnight. Building a business can't be rushed, Ms. Burke. And speaking of business, I have done my research and looked into the First Edition Society, Lady Georgiana Fowling, and this world-famous library. I didn't want you to waste your time getting me up to speed. Better for us to talk about this magnificent event you have in mind."

I'd been carrying around a knot of worry inside my chest for days now—the closer the board meeting came, the tighter the knot. But now I felt it begin to loosen. Mr. Berryfield may have chosen a silly name for his company, but that didn't mean he wouldn't be a fine exhibition manager. And what was wrong with hot-desking? The general chatter in the room added to the atmospheric energy—it probably boosted business.

"And," he continued, "as my own website is currently undergoing redesign, I will take a moment to explain myself. Yes?"

I, too, had done my research and taken a look at the leaflets he'd sent over to Middlebank as well as what he had to offer online. Both resources contained only the sketchiest of details, and now I knew why—he was in transition. Perfectly reasonable.

"Yes," I said, "thank you. Please do tell me about your previous work."

"Immersive events, Ms. Burke—those are my specialty and what I would bring to you at the Society. You don't want people shuffling through rooms half asleep, reading boring signage, wishing it would all be over so they could get to the tearoom. You want excitement! Activity!"

He hit his fist on the desk. I jumped.

"The Golden Age of Mystery. Murder. Detectives." He lifted his eyebrows. "I see great potential."

"Oh, well—" I hadn't thought we'd need activities.

Berryfield continued. "I'm probably best known for my one-sixty-fourth-scale replica of the Giant's Causeway inside the lobby of a coastal museum on the Isle of Man. Why merely walk into an event—how boring is that? There, you had to leap from basalt column to basalt column, and as you stepped on each stone pillar, a selkie song rose up."

"My." I cleared my throat. "Celtic legend comes to . . . er . . . life."

His face flushed and his eyes shone.

"But the Giant's Causeway is on the coast of Northern Ireland. It's the North Atlantic," I said. "How did you give the impression of the sea?"

"It was easy enough. We lined the lobby, flooded it, and used a wave machine."

Wait—this was beginning to sound familiar. "Is that where a man was—"

"That incident," Berryfield cut in, "was blown out of all proportion." A shadow passed over his face. "Yes, there occurred an unfortunate leak in the lining, and the electrics in the building were blown, and there was that one fellow who did come in contact with a—"

"You electrocuted someone!"

"The charges were dropped!" Berryfield took a sharp breath and let it out slowly. He put his pleasant smile back up. "But, heigh-ho."

"Well, Mr. Berryfield, I believe—"

"Now, as I see it, for your exhibition, we'll need a great deal of blood."

I shot out of my chair. "Thank you so much for taking the time to talk with me this morning. Of course, we are in only the initial stages of planning, and so I'll need to get back to you with more details. Good-bye."

Racing down an aisle, I found Zeno Berryfield on my

heels, talking the whole while. "I'm sure you'll love the idea once you know more. It will be no problem getting the blood—I know a fellow with a pig farm. Wait—don't you want to hear—"

I made it out the door and down the stairs before he could tell me what he intended to do with the pig's blood. On the ground floor, I paused—panting, sweating, and near tears.

Outdoors, I took a deep breath of cold January air and started up Stall Street as I faced facts. Apart from the idea of an exhibition and a well-thought-out budget, what did we have to tell the Society's board at the meeting that afternoon? I had promised details. How could I expect them to rally round such a project if we had neither manager nor venue?

I pulled up at the Minerva, a tiny pub in Northumberland Place, thinking I might chat with Pauline to take my mind off things. Pauline had been our cleaner at Middlebank—during which time she and Adele had met, so I took credit for their relationship. She'd sold that business to manage the pub, but she wasn't working at the moment, and so I ate a packet of crisps and drank a glass of orange squash and stared unseeing out the stained glass windows. When I left, I still couldn't quite face returning to Middlebank—what if Mrs. Woolgar asked how my meeting with Zeno Berryfield had gone? Instead, I wandered aimlessly through the city, more miserable by the second. I had no conscious destination, but when I lifted my gaze from the pavement, I found myself in front of the Charlotte, the best—and most unattainable—exhibition venue in Bath.

Currently, a show of local watercolorists was on, and so, thinking I couldn't feel any worse, I handed over a five-pound note, took a leaflet, and walked in, joining the few others in attendance this midday. While they studied the art, I took in the rooms and their lovely Georgian decor—

the high ceilings, the symmetry in paneling, and the pea-green walls accented by white cornices. I admired the fireplace with its ornate pilasters and central frieze of an urn with foliage. Instead of paintings of the Mendip Hills, I imagined a lighted glass case displaying the first edition of *Murder Must Advertise* signed by members of the Detection Club in 1933.

As I wallowed in my misery, a woman passed behind me, and I heard her say, "No, I completely understand why you must cancel, but as it is such short notice, you must understand the Charlotte cannot issue a refund."

I froze, and she continued, "April may not seem short notice to you, but no one else would be willing to take on the space with dates barely three months out."

Her voice faded as she moved away. I whirled round and saw her. She had short dark hair and a ring of keys and looked official. I pursued—dodging freestanding paintings and running into her when she stopped.

"I'm so sorry," I said, grabbing her arm to steady her. "It's only that I happened to overhear you say—I wasn't eavesdropping, really I wasn't, but . . ."

"No worries," she said, gently removing her arm from my grip.

"I'm Hayley Burke from the First Edition Society," I said, hurrying on. "Are you Naomi Faber, reservations manager here at the Charlotte? Didn't we speak on the phone? Did I hear you say you've had a cancellation?"

Thirty minutes later, I stepped out onto the pavement, turned, and shook Naomi's hand—a woman who had either saved my professional life or helped me dig a hole so deep I would never climb out.

"Thank you so very much," I gushed. "I'm sure I can get the deposit to you by tomorrow afternoon—the Society's board will be thrilled, really they will."

"What luck that you stopped in, Hayley," Naomi said. "I never would've thought to tell you of the cancellation. Are you sure you can handle these dates?"

"Mid-April—absolutely. We've got a crack team assembled. Tell me, do you know the manager for this water-color exhibition?"

"The artists did it themselves. I won't let that happen again, I can tell you. Slipshod planning, tatty display boards that had to be re-covered at the last minute, and an ancient lighting system. Plus, they couldn't agree on anything. As I'm sure you know, an exhibition is only as good as its manager. Cheers, now—see you tomorrow."

I nodded and smiled and nodded again and was still nodding after she went back inside the building and left me on the pavement. Yes, we can do this. But although I was flying high, I balanced on a thin tightrope with a seething swamp beneath, because I knew what it meant to take advantage of this windfall of dates for our exhibition—it meant I would be stuck with Zeno Berryfield as manager. Fine. I tugged on my jacket with resolve. I would take him on, but he would work under strict oversight. I would watch him like a hawk lest he try to sneak in a vat of pig's blood.

"Hayley. Hayley. Hayley. Hayley. Hayley."

I turned at my name and saw a fellow across the road in front of the Assembly Rooms.

"Dom!" I called, trotting over and rushing up to him.

His arms locked at his sides. "No hugs!"

"No." I shook my head and took a step back. "No hugs—I remember."

Dom Kilpatrick had been an office mate of mine at the Jane Austen Centre. He was a lanky fellow in his midthirties who wore his curly, dark brown hair short on the sides and back. His black-framed glasses always sat slightly askew, and he had a smile to match.

"I haven't seen you in ages," I said.

"Seven July of last year at your leaving do held at the Garrick's Head," he said. "Fifteen of us were there from the Jane Austen Centre plus your friend Adele. There were six plates of filled crusty rolls—two each of beef, chicken, and pork, but you made certain they brought out another plate of cheddar and chutney for me and for Margo. No one left until half past eleven. It was a party."

"Yes." I laughed. "I do remember a bit of a sore head the next morning. How are you?"

"I still work on the customer database at the Centre, but two days a week I come here to the Assembly Rooms and run a virus check on the computers for the Fashion Museum. On Wednesdays I arrive at eleven o'clock and go into the café and have a coffee and a McVitie's chocolate Penguin, and on Thursdays I arrive at three o'clock and have tea and a fruit scone." Dom stopped abruptly and coughed. "I'm fine. How are you?"

I sensed the hand of someone teaching Dom how to be socially acceptable. He was a whip-smart fellow and had a fantastic memory, but he could be a bit awkward in conversation, although he and I had always got on well.

"I'm doing fine, thanks, and enjoying my new job."

"You're the curator for the First Edition Society's library at Middlebank House."

"I am indeed. So, Dom—about Margo." I recalled Margo— a young woman on a work-study program from a local school who had started not long before I left the Centre.

Dom's face turned a blotchy red. "Margo is my girlfriend now," he said. "She doesn't mind how I am."

"Oh, I believe that any woman would consider herself lucky to call you her boyfriend."

Dom's face grew blotchier as he gave a nervous laugh and pushed his glasses up the bridge of his nose.

"So," I said, "you've just finished at the Fashion Museum—had your coffee, too?"

Dom threw a look over his shoulder to the door of the Assembly Rooms and stuck his hands in the pockets of his jacket. "I won't have coffee today. When I went in the café . . . I couldn't."

"Is it closed?"

His eyes grew wide, and I saw fear in them. "No. I saw Oona."

4

❦

"Oona Atherton?" I breathed, and glanced over to check the entry to the Assembly Rooms just as Dom had. "She's here?"

He nodded, his head bobbing up and down. "And so, I'd better not stay, because . . . you know."

How well I did. Anyone with any sense would know to steer clear of Oona Atherton. But although Dom said goodbye and left, I didn't move.

I had erased Oona from my mind, but now all those memories came flooding back and I saw myself once again her personal assistant and general dogsbody during the exhibition she'd mounted for the Jane Austen Centre five years ago. Held at the Charlotte. She was brash and arrogant and had run roughshod over everyone—the word *demanding* didn't come close to describing her. I had ended many a day in tears—days that didn't end until nearly midnight.

The trouble was, she worked miracles, mounting the most spectacular exhibitions. And, to be fair, she never asked more of the people under her than she was willing to give herself. If we were there until the wee hours adjusting lights and reconfiguring freestanding, enclosed Perspex boxes of letters, lace sleeves, and quill pens, then Oona was there, too. That's what made it so hard to hate her—she stuck in and never let up on herself or anyone else.

Oona worked freelance, but her name had never occurred to me as I started planning our own exhibition—that's how completely I'd obliterated the memory of her.

But I had come a long way in five years. I had risen in my profession and built up confidence in my own abilities. *I* ran the First Edition library and *I* would be in charge of the exhibition—the manager would work for me, not I her. And after all, if it were a choice between pig's blood and Oona—well, better the devil you knew.

Keeping that thought, I made my way inexorably into the Assembly Rooms and then to the café, where the doors stood open.

I did not go in, but instead ducked down behind the chest-high stand that displayed the menu and, unobserved, peered over it into the room. The café—a wide-open space—had a smattering of people at the tables, but I could've spotted Oona in the middle of a heaving crowd. I saw her now, sitting near the windows looking at her mobile. She hadn't changed one whit—her thick brown hair scraped back into a bun high on her head, and wearing a tailored navy business suit and low heels. To those who did not know her, she might not look the tyrant, but even the sight of her made me break out in a cold sweat. And yet . . .

Throwing my shoulders back, I stepped into the room, and as if she sensed a change in the energy field, Oona looked up and her face broke out in a wide smile.

"Hayley Burke," she called as she stood. "How the hell are you?"

Her voice echoed in the room and heads turned, but Oona took no notice. I scurried over.

"Oona, what a surprise," I replied in a low voice. We performed one of those awkward half-hug, air-kiss routines.

"Do you have a few minutes?" she asked. "Let's catch up. What can I get you—coffee? Tea?"

"Oh no, let me. What would you like?"

I hardly had to ask—her usual order was tattooed on my brain.

At the counter, I said, "One Earl Grey, please—but not in a bag. If you don't have it loose, would you please tear the bag open and empty it into the pot? Make that two bags. With a slice of lemon, but only if you cut it fresh. And raw sugar. Do you have raw sugar? If not, Demerara will have to do. Also, one normal tea."

The woman behind the counter gave me a look that was oh so familiar.

The tray of tea things rattled as I carried them over, but Oona didn't seem to notice. That's an odd thing about her—she could spot a plate one-eighth of an inch out of alignment in a display of the Austen family's Wedgwood dinner set, but be oblivious to the feelings of people round her.

"Curator at the First Edition Society," Oona said as we sorted out cups, saucers, and teapots.

"Oh, how did you know—"

She nodded to her phone. "Looked you up this minute. I see you're starting off well—a series of literary salons. I always knew you had it in you—to build a top-notch organization out of a well-meaning gesture."

"The Society is entirely Lady Fowling's creation," I said, "and it's only since she died that things have . . . slowed down."

"Regardless," Oona said, pouring her tea through a strainer, "you were obviously the right woman for the position."

"Well." I blushed. "And not only do we have the literary salons, but"—*Don't say it, Hayley. Yes, go on, tell her. No, don't*—"we are now planning an exhibition."

I gulped my tea, the liquid searing my throat. Slowly, Oona took a spoonful of Demerara—no raw sugar available— tilted it over her cup, and watched the crystals sift into her Earl Grey like light brown snow.

"Is this exhibition about detective fiction—Christie, Sayers, Tey, Allingham, Marsh?" she asked.

"It's called *Lady Fowling: A Life in Words*. She was an amazing woman, Oona, and left behind a world-class collection of first editions from those authors and more."

"The exhibition is next year?"

"No, April."

"April?"

I could hear the scorn in her voice, but in for a penny, in for a pound.

"Yes, April. The Charlotte just became available, and I've booked it. I see no need to wait."

Oona took her time, lifting her cup and letting the steam drift round the contours of her face before she took a sip.

"You must have a crackerjack manager to be able to take the paraphernalia of Lady Fowling's life and showcase it for all of Bath—for all of Britain and the world—to see in such a short time."

A thrill of fear shot down my spine. "Yes, it *is* a short time, but I am confident it can be done. We're speaking with a local person for manager."

"So, you've filled the post?"

"We haven't quite reached an agreement yet." The silence at the table screamed in my ears, and to put myself out of my misery, I added, "So, how long have you been in Bath, Oona?"

"A few days—a week."

"On a job?"

"Holiday," she said. The fact that Oona continued to

dress for work while on holiday did not surprise me. "I'm waiting for the tap on the shoulder from the British Library," she continued. "They have a position opening up this summer—it's only a matter of time before I hear."

Enough of this cat-and-mouse game—it was too stressful not knowing which role I played.

"As we haven't actually hired this local fellow," I said, "if you are at all interested, I'm sure the board would listen to your ideas on our exhibition. That is, if you didn't mind interrupting your holiday."

Only a twitch in her firmly set mouth betrayed her nonchalance. "I suppose I could—that is, if you wanted to set something up."

"As it happens, we have a meeting this afternoon at four. If you arrive at half past, they'll be ready for you."

"Done."

When we'd finished, I glanced at the time and panicked—two o'clock. Oona had spent more than an hour interrogating me about the collection and the Society. I rushed down to New Bond Street and into the Bertinet bakery, where I swooned at the scents of butter and sugar and savories. Five minutes later, I carried away what they had left of Portuguese custard tarts, petit fours, and macarons and hurried off while wolfing down a ham-and-cheese croissant. I paused in a shop doorway only long enough to text Val.

News on venue and manager. See you soon.

Dropping my phone in my bag and stuffing the last bit of croissant in my mouth, I hiked up to Middlebank, thinking about what I'd done. Oona's eagerness to consider the managerial post disconcerted me, but I quashed any worry by telling myself she didn't seem the type for a holiday and that I put her quick agreement to appear at the board meeting down to wanting to stay busy.

Mrs. Woolgar came out of her office the minute I walked in the front door. She had already made her opinion clear when it came to the exhibition—how could we even think of putting her ladyship's life on display?—but would attend the board meeting because she was the First Edition Society's secretary, and that was her job.

"I've some lovely pastries for the meeting," I said, hurrying up the stairs with my two boxes. "See you at four."

By three thirty, the library table had been laid with a platter of delectables, and nearby, the kettle sat ready. In my office on the ground floor, I had just finished printing out the agenda for the meeting that I had amended to include *Interview with potential exhibition manager* when the front door buzzed.

Val wore his good suit, ready for battle.

"Come in, come in." I pulled him across the threshold.

"You've had a busy day if you've found us a venue and a manager, and"—he brushed a finger across my mouth and pastry flakes fell onto my sweater—"you managed to have lunch, too?"

I laughed. "I have even more news than that. Come up to my flat and I'll show you."

On the coffee table, I'd laid out Lady Fowling's letter about the first edition of *Murder Must Advertise* signed by all members of the Detection Club in 1933. "According to Mrs. Woolgar, this is a draft of her ladyship's letter to Dorothy L. Sayers," I said.

While Val examined it, I hovered. "And it was stuck in a book on the shelves?" he asked. "How many years has it been there and no one knew it? And where did Lady Fowling hide the signed book?"

"Mrs. Woolgar may know more, I haven't had a chance to ask. But wouldn't this be an enormous draw for the exhibition—with all those signatures? Although I suppose we should find the actual book before we start shouting about it."

"Yes, better to have it in hand. And now, what other news?"

I began at the beginning, telling of my appointment with Zeno Berryfield.

"Do you remember when that fellow was electrocuted on the Isle of Man?" I asked, going into my bedroom to find a different pair of shoes and calling back to Val. "I shudder to think what Berryfield would come up with for us. But we don't have to worry—now there's Oona."

I related the highlights of my association with her, and thought I did a fine job at sounding entirely neutral.

"What aren't you telling me about Oona?" Val asked, standing when I walked back out to the sitting room. "How was it working with her?"

I collapsed on the sofa, holding one shoe. "It was hell. No one was safe from her fury. She barked orders, demanded the near impossible." I pointed a shoe out the front window in the general direction of the Charlotte. "I rewrote the interpretive signage at least a dozen times; she was never satisfied. We worked all hours, and it was just when Dinah was studying for her GCSEs and I should've been at home helping her."

"If it was that awful, why put yourself through it again?"

"Because she's brilliant." I held the shoe up in surrender.

"You wouldn't consider managing it yourself?" Val asked, echoing my mum.

"No, how could I do that? But I could learn from her. Oona has a way of seeing the subject and bringing it to life. The Jane Austen exhibition won an award."

"Yeah," Val conceded. "It was amazing. I took two of my classes over and went again on my own."

"Did you? I worked the exhibition every day."

For a moment, we were quiet, drifting away in what-ifs.

"We were that close," Val said, "and didn't even know it." He rubbed my arms and kissed my forehead. "Right; if she's that good, she's the one."

* * *

While the board settled at the library table exclaiming over the pastry selection, Bunter sashayed in and curled up in one of the fireplace chairs. I poured the tea. Although I had proposed the exhibition at a previous board meeting—complete with budget—a review would do no harm. And so first, Val spoke about Bath College's commitment to support the venture through promotion and staffing, and I continued with other details. Then Maureen Frost unknowingly provided a setup.

"This is still all speculation, isn't it, Hayley? I don't see the point in going over the idea without any concrete way forward."

"Indeed," I said with conviction, "what *would* be the point? Fortunately, I do have an update. The Charlotte has become available in April."

The board and everyone else in Bath knew that the Charlotte was the best, and so I let this news sink in. Jane Arbuthnot spoke up first. "But that's barely three months. How can that be enough time to do Georgiana's life justice?"

"If anyone can do it, Hayley can," Sylvia Moon said.

"And with her second-in-command, Val," Audrey Moon added, and Val gave her a wink.

"Mr. Moffatt has his own work," Maureen said, "and it wouldn't be fair to require too much of him." She had softened toward Val since he'd arranged for her to do a dramatic reading of an Agatha Christie short story for one of his writing classes.

"Hayley understands Georgiana," Adele said, and I smiled, grateful she'd decided to back the event. "Who better to help us share her with the world?"

"Still, April . . ." Mrs. Woolgar said.

"I would like to point out," I said, "that with the week of setup beforehand, the opening gala for the exhibition would fall on the twenty-first of April."

I watched the faces round the table, and after two seconds, I heard a catch in Mrs. Woolgar's breath. "Her ladyship's birthday," she whispered.

"Yes—what would've been her ninety-eighth," I said. "And what better way to honor her?"

I'd left the library door open, and the sound of the buzzer gave us all a start. I looked at the time—twenty-eight minutes past four. Val went down to answer, and I moved swiftly and surely into the next step.

"As you can see on our agenda," I explained, "I've asked a potential exhibition manager here today to give both you and her a chance to chat about the possibilities." I heard voices on the stairs, and when Val arrived at the door with our interviewee, I rose.

Oona entered, portfolio tucked under one arm. She was a picture of calm, undisturbed even by Bunter's tortoiseshell form streaking past her and out the door.

"Hello, Oona," I said, "thanks so much for finding the time to meet with us today. First Edition Society board members, may I introduce Oona Atherton." I went round the table with names.

"Oh, Adele—good to see you again," Oona said.

"Yes, hello, Oona," Adele replied, her face as red as her hair.

"And Glynis Woolgar. Mrs. Woolgar was Lady Fowling's personal assistant and is now secretary to the Society."

"How do you do?" Mrs. Woolgar said.

We settled at the table. "Tea, Oona?" I asked with dread.

"No, thank you," she replied as she took papers from her portfolio and waited.

Good. I gave the board a précis of Oona's work, and she passed round copies of her CV. Board members asked about previous events. I provided feedback on the exhibition she had managed for the Jane Austen Centre—sans the "hell" description. Eventually, I gave Oona the opportunity to interview us.

She began with that wide smile of hers. "I have only one question. I would like each of you to tell me one memory you have of Lady Fowling—or, if you never met in person, the first thing you think when you hear her name."

The silence that followed worried me, until Jane Arbuthnot piped up. "She listened and heard everything you said."

Next, Maureen Frost smiled. "Do you remember the fancy dress ball here at Middlebank when she came as Lord Peter Wimsey—monocle and all?"

"She put Sylvia and me in one of her detective stories," Audrey Moon said, two red spots on her cheeks. Her sister-in-law laughed and added, "We were music-hall dancers!"

"I think of her great generosity," I said, deciding I shouldn't tell them I had regular conversations with Lady Fowling's portrait on the landing.

"She welcomed discussions with other writers," Val said. He had told me about the time—donkey's years ago—that Lady Fowling had spoken to one of his genre-fiction classes.

"She saw beyond the surface and understood what a person needed," Mrs. Woolgar said, and then dropped her gaze to her lap. Jane Arbuthnot reached over and patted the secretary's hand, and—not for the first time—I wondered about Mrs. Woolgar's personal history.

Adele took her turn last. "She was the best Cluedo player I've ever seen." We ended with a gentle laugh.

"Before I go," Oona said, "may I paint a picture for you—a picture of what a visitor might see when she takes that first step into the exhibition? Tell me, Mrs. Woolgar—did Georgiana have a desk?"

"Queen Anne. A lovely burled walnut, highly polished with cabriolet legs."

"Yes," I piped up. "I've seen it—it's in the cellar." I'd spent a fair bit of time poking round there a few months previous.

Oona nodded. "In your minds, walk into the exhibition with me," she said in a gentle, low voice. "A trifold panel covered in a dark green fabric blocks the view of the rest of the room and forms a small study. An antique floral rug covers the floor, and against one wall is a low bookcase filled to overflowing. In the middle sits Georgiana's Queen Anne desk. On the desk, we see more books—*Whose Body?* by Sayers, *The Daughter of Time* by Tey, *My Cousin Rachel* by du Maurier—along with loose sheets of paper and a fountain pen left uncapped, as if she had only that moment stepped away to make a cup of tea. And without realizing, we pause, waiting for her to come back. That's the Georgiana Fowling I see."

In the stunned silence that followed, Oona gathered her things, stood, and said, "Thank you for this opportunity. Good day."

I saw her out, and at the front door, clearing the emotion from my voice, I said, "Thanks so much for stopping by. I'll let you know what they decide as soon as possible."

"Great, Hayley," she replied in a breezy manner. "I look forward to it."

When I returned to the library, it was to see Mrs. Woolgar dabbing the corner of an eye with a lace handkerchief and Sylvia Moon clasping her teacup and staring out into space.

Jane Arbuthnot looked up at me and said, "When can she start?"

5

Before the meeting wrapped up, the board members made it clear that in hiring Oona Atherton as exhibition manager, money was no object and, to prove the point, earmarked a 10 percent increase to the offer if need be. They were caught up in the emotion of the moment—Oona was that good—but I knew to keep an eye on expenses, and as the group descended the stairs and gathered coats and bags, I promised I would not go over the budget.

"You do whatever it takes," Maureen Frost said, turning up the collar of her coat and heading for the door with the rest of the board.

"Adele," I said, "hang on."

She had been slipping out just ahead of the Moons, but I tugged on her coat sleeve, and she came back into the entry. I closed the door and we were alone for the moment— Val had carried the tea tray into the kitchenette, and Mrs. Woolgar had retreated to her office and closed the door.

"I didn't realize you knew Oona," I said, and watched Adele's face redden.

She shrugged. "Oh yeah—don't you remember I brought a group of girls through the exhibition? That was my first year teaching."

"That part I remember. And what else happened?"

"Nothing."

But I waited, and at last Adele wrinkled her nose and shook her head. "I recall Oona and I met for a drink one evening."

"Recall anything else?" I asked.

"Ms. Burke?" Mrs. Woolgar emerged from her office.

"See ya," Adele said, making her escape. "Bye, Glynis."

I watched Adele's mass of red curls disappear. I sensed the cover-up of a good story, but I could wait. Now, I turned to face the secretary, ready for whatever might come.

"Perhaps I was too hasty in dismissing the idea of an exhibition," she said, her hands clasped in front of her. "I see now that what you want to do is commemorate her ladyship's contribution to Bath as well as the worldwide literary community. I will assist you and Ms. Atherton however I can."

"Thank you, Mrs. Woolgar," I said, touched at her confidence in my decision. Due, of course, to Oona. "But first, I must contact her and see if she will accept our pay package—"

"But the board did approve an increase if need be. Please keep that in mind."

"Will do," I replied.

"Well, have a good evening, and I'll see you at our morning briefing."

Off she went, downstairs to her flat—never-never land. Known thusly to me, because I never went in and never knew what she did after her workday finished. Danced the night away with the Society's solicitor, Duncan Rennie? Fell asleep in front of her telly watching old *Coronation Street* reruns? Mrs. Woolgar's personality was conservative—the only excessive trait as far as I could tell was her need for privacy.

Val came out of the kitchenette. He took my hands and our fingers entwined.

"What did you think of Oona?" I asked.

"She knows how to work a room."

"Mmm. After the meeting broke up, did you hear the Moons and Jane and Maureen telling each other stories about Lady Fowling? I think we should record them—set up proper equipment in the library and make sure the sherry decanter is full and let them go at it. We can use their memories somewhere in the exhibition. Maybe you could go through the old photos we have and make a video. We could run the audio over it."

"That's a fine idea," he said, pulling me closer.

We kissed, and with his lips on mine, the idea of an exhibition slipped from my mind—and from his, too, if I read the signs correctly. We came up for air only when I felt a pressure against my ankles.

"Bunter," I said. "Is it time for your dinner?"

Bunter gave a throaty reply and Val said, "I should go."

"No, don't. You should be here when I phone Oona and make the offer." And speaking of offers. "Then after that, would you . . . do you want to stay to dinner? I could cook something. Upstairs. In my flat."

Because it had just occurred to me our romantic getaway next weekend was eight days off, which seemed like forever.

He nuzzled my neck and murmured in my ear, "Dinner. But don't cook—why don't we phone out for pizza. Later."

We followed Bunter into the kitchenette, where I opened a tin and gave the cat his meal. I found it difficult to concentrate on business, and had to take a quick, sharp breath—the air heavy with the aroma of fish-in-gravy—to bring me back to the duty at hand. I took a notepad, and Val and I settled at the table. I made the call with my phone on speaker, and when Oona answered, I presented the offer and we waited.

"This is quite an undertaking, as I'm sure you both realize," she replied. Right—now for negotiations. "But as manager, I would not impinge on your or Val's normal work schedule for all the little things that need to be done. I would prefer to have my own PA with me."

Oona had her own personal assistant?

"Of course, perfectly understandable," I blathered. "I certainly hope we can work something out." I wrote the amount budgeted on the notepad, added the 10 percent allowed increase and a note—*borrow from staffing budget?*—and showed it to Val. That might barely pay for the PA. Perhaps I'd contribute part of my own salary—anything to keep from being at Oona's beck and call.

"She's Clara Powell," Oona said, "and she lives with her grandmother in Shepton Mallet, so there won't be any trouble for her to get here. And she is actually more an intern, so I'm sure whatever you can arrange will be fine with her."

Poor Clara. Val did the sums and came up with a new number that included both manager and PA, and when I read it out, Oona agreed for both of them.

"Look," she said, "we should get started ASAP. How about dinner this evening—the three of us can go over a general schedule and do a bit of brainstorming. We've no time to lose."

"Er . . . well—"

"We are getting to this a bit late," she reminded me.

Val scribbled something on the notepad and pushed it toward me. *Next weekend.* I grabbed his hand and gave it a squeeze.

"Yes, of course," I said. "Let's meet."

"Good. We've a great deal to do and very little time to do it."

We met at the Ask Italian off Broad Street—about halfway between Middlebank and Oona's temporary digs just across the Pulteney Bridge. Six o'clock—we had our pick of tables.

"It's early," I said to Val. "Isn't it? We may be finished in an hour or two."

He smiled and played with my fingers, but Oona walked in and we had to attend to business—greetings, offers of congratulations, comments about looking forward to working together, and choosing a large table in the back. We ordered our food, and Val and I asked for wine, but Oona requested a bottle of fizzy water without ice. "I want to keep a clear head." That should've told me.

Our shared starter—mushroom crostini—arrived, and we each reached for one. Oona must've swallowed hers whole, because the next moment her mouth was clear, and she began her interrogation about the collection.

"We've five thousand or so books in the library at Middlebank," I said. "Some first editions, but many reprints, foreign editions, new covers, that sort of thing. The rare volumes are at the bank. None would fetch a mint, but to a collector they'd be treasures. We'll need a new valuation for insurance purposes, so I'll contact Bath Old Books tomorrow about that."

"We need a writer's point of view to show how the Golden Age of Mystery affected Lady Fowling. Are you a writer, Val?"

"Well, I—"

"Yes, he is," I said.

"Are you published?"

I kept quiet, even though I knew the answer. He had told me during a cozy chat on a cold winter's night after Christmas while Dinah had been staying. She'd gone out with friends, but I expected her back at any moment—it was just the way Val's and my luck had been running—and so we were on our best behavior. We had turned out the lights in my flat and sat at the window, the room glowing from the full moon, and exchanged a secret or two. That's when I'd learned he'd written one book and it had been published not long before his wife—estranged, almost divorced—had died. The girls, not even five years old, had needed a father with a steadier job than writing, and so he had turned to teaching. I said I wanted to read his book, but he swore there were no copies left. "It was rubbish, chucked in the bin long ago." But I've been known to have the occasional mooch around the charity shops of Bath, and so now when I did so, I kept an eye out on their bookshelves for *Too Late for Regret* by V. Moffatt.

But Val's reply to Oona made no mention of his own credits. "I have a few former students who are published. I could ask one of them."

"Good," Oona replied, not seeing the smile I sent Val's way. "Next, we'll need a good angle—a connection between her and the authors she collected. Perhaps something she had that no one else did."

Val lifted an eyebrow.

"Well, as it happens," I said, a frisson of excitement zinging through me, "I've just come across evidence that Lady Fowling was given—by Dorothy L. Sayers herself—a first edition of *Murder Must Advertise* that was signed by members of the Detection Club in 1933."

Oona's eyes widened. "All of them?"

"I'm not quite sure—we haven't located the actual book yet. It's possible her ladyship carried out a bit of subterfuge to keep it safe."

"Now"—Oona sat back and threw her arms wide—"that is the sort of thing that will turn heads."

"Although," I hurried to add, "it's probably better not to mention it until we have the book in hand. Don't you think?"

"Bollocks," she replied.

Our meals arrived. Val stuck a fork in his lasagna, causing a plume of steam to issue forth. I inhaled the aroma of my carbonara, before catching and twisting strands of linguine onto my fork. As I stuck the wad in my mouth, I noticed Oona had already finished a third of her risotto.

"Who runs the Charlotte now?" she asked.

The pasta seemed to swell in my mouth. I chewed furiously, attempting to shove the rest of it into my cheeks like a chipmunk. Val touched my hand and replied slowly, "Let's see now, what is that woman's name? I know that Hayley has done them an enormous favor taking those empty dates in April, and I'm sure that—"

"Naomi," I answered with a cough. "Naomi Faber. She wasn't there for the Centre's exhibition you managed."

"Naomi." Oona seemed to roll the name round in her mind for a moment, and then shook her head. "No, don't believe I know her."

We returned to eating, and I shoveled food in as quickly as I could, but it wasn't long before Oona dropped the spoon into her empty bowl and pushed it aside. I left my carbonara to congeal.

"Now," she said, "I've got a few questions for you."

It was the nightmare of being on *Mastermind* and unprepared as she quizzed me about the minutiae of detective stories as they would relate to the displays. I spoke about Miss Marple and ventured a vague comment about Sayers's *Murder Must Advertise*, which I intended to start reading that night. Then Val stepped in and headed her off in a different direction—Lady Fowling's notebooks.

Throwing him a grateful look, I added, "They'll help us create an aura of her presence. I see the exhibition as a personal look at Lady Fowling—her strength after being widowed so young, the way she made literature her life. Women writers dominated the Golden Age of Mystery, and her ladyship championed them. That's worth bringing to the world's attention and celebrating."

"It's perfect," Val said.

But had I said too much? I shouldn't tread on Oona's toes—exhibitions, after all, were her business.

A quietness settled on her as she looked off into the middle distance. I opened my mouth to apologize, but Oona spoke first. "I'll want to read through these notebooks—can you have them ready tomorrow?"

Without waiting for an answer, she shifted to logistics—furniture moving, display cases, and signage.

"Signage will be your department, Hayley," Oona said, and my stomach hurt. "I believe we can do this, but I see a solid three months of work ahead."

I saw three months of sleepless nights—and I had no one to blame but myself.

The cleaner had started to mop the floor before we left the restaurant, and a lone server stood sentinel by the front door, waiting to lock up.

Out on the pavement in a chilly drizzle, Oona said, "I'll see you at eleven tomorrow. I'll have Powell with me."

She strode off, and Val put his arm round my shoulders as we watched her go. "Steady on, Hayley Burke, curator of the First Edition library," he said.

6

D^{eath.}

    "His name is Death?" I said, unable to keep the
incredulity from my voice. I'd set my phone on the counter
and had Val on speaker—it was the next morning before
work, and I was in my kitchen fishing a tea bag out of my
mug and pulling the milk from the fridge.

    Val laughed. "Ah, *Murder Must Advertise*. How far have
you got?"

    "Well, the murder happened before the book started. This
'Death' fellow has just started working at the ad agency, and
I can't quite tell if he thinks it's murder or not. It's quite en-
tertaining. Sayers could really turn a phrase, couldn't she?"

    "She wrote the tag line 'Guinness is good for you'—
that'll live on."

    "The victim in *Murder Must Advertise* died in a fall
down a staircase, and there was a staircase at Sayers's old
ad agency," I said. "That's what Lady Fowling mentioned
in her letter."

"A writer uses everything in his or her memory and experience to come up with a good story. Sayers was no exception. Lunch?"

"Yes—I'll let you know when I can get away. First day, you know."

I was far more apprehensive on Oona's first day than I had been on my own at the Society—and my nerves were not helped by Mrs. Woolgar's sudden appearance at my office door fifteen minutes before our nine o'clock morning briefing.

"Good morning, Ms. Burke. I've just seen an item in the *Chronicle* about the exhibition," she said. "Not the print edition, but online."

Scrambling to get my laptop open and find the right web page, I stammered, "I haven't . . . wait now . . . I thought we agreed it was a bit early to . . ." At last, I located it—a short item headed MYSTERIOUS RARE BOOK SURFACES—about the first edition of *Murder Must Advertise* signed by *the most famous mystery writers of all time.*

"I didn't think Oona would . . . Oh dear, Mrs. Woolgar, you don't know the details, do you? It's about the letter I found—the one Lady Fowling wrote to Dorothy L. Sayers. Will you sit down?"

She perched on the edge of the wingback chair across the desk from me—Bunter curled up behind her—and I explained, ending with, "I wanted to ask your advice on the matter, but it's been a whirlwind two days. As we don't yet know where the book is, I thought it best not to say anything, but apparently Oona thought differently."

Mrs. Woolgar's shoulders relaxed. "You've put your trust in Ms. Atherton—she must know best. And the book?"

"I'm conducting a thorough search."

The front door buzzed. We both walked into the entry, and as she retreated into her office and closed the door, I called after her, "I'll be in directly."

Please don't be Oona. Not yet—it's too early.

Certainly not Oona—she didn't have a tattoo of books behind her left ear.

"Mr. . . . Bulldog," I said. What was his surname? And surely he wasn't really Bulldog. "Moyle. Mr. Moyle."

He peered out from under a wide-brimmed hat. "Do you know how much a first edition signed by the entire Detection Club would be worth?" he asked.

Behind him, a steady rain fell. I opened the door farther.

"Please come in," I said, reminding myself this was what the First Edition library was for—people. "Would you like a coffee?"

"Can I see it now?"

"No, I'm sorry—"

"Will you have an early viewing?"

I swallowed a snort—I wasn't a funeral director.

"The exhibition is in April," I replied. "Did you read about it in the *Bath Chronicle*?"

"Alerts set up on my computer. Saw it early this morning and got the train."

"Where do you live?"

"Chippenham. Am I on the list?"

"What list?"

"Who's in charge?"

That's it. "I'm in charge, Mr. Moyle," I said, putting on my mum voice as if I were talking to a truculent teenager. "Details will go up on our website just as soon as they are available. You are signed up to receive our newsletter, aren't you—under your actual name? What is your first name, by the way?"

He hesitated. I gave him a slight frown. He stretched his neck to one side, and I heard it pop. "Stuart," he said.

"Fine, Stuart. We're delighted you've stopped by, and be sure to keep an eye out for further information about the exhibition and our other events. Is there anything else I can do for you?"

Apparently not. When he'd left, I walked into Mrs. Woolgar's office saying, "I don't know what he thought he would accomplish by coming all this way to—"

The front door buzzed again, and I pivoted on the spot, ready to tell Stuart "Bulldog" Moyle that harassment was not the way to get on my good side, but when I flung the door open, I found instead Zeno Berryfield.

"Hello, Ms. Burke," he said with a smile. "Good morning."

He held up a clear, see-through umbrella, over an orange mackintosh that covered his teal suit, with the Smarties tie peeking out at the top. His high-shine black oxfords glistened with rain.

"Mr. Berryfield, what a surprise." I glanced past him to the pavement, hoping Oona wasn't on her way in. "I'm afraid I—"

"I'm only checking back to see if you need any further details before you make your decision about manager for your upcoming exhibition."

"I'm sorry I haven't been back in touch," I said, and then realized I'd only seen him the day before. "As it turns out, we have hired someone else. I so appreciate your giving me the time, and I've no doubt you will find many other opportunities here in Bath."

He kept the smile on his face, but I saw a light go out in his eyes, leaving them small and dark. "Yes, yes. Well, heigh-ho. I thank you for your consideration. Can you tell me who is your first choice?"

"I'm not sure we're ready to—"

"I see. Yes, I do see. I wish you luck with this first choice, and I hope that if she does not work out, you will give me a call."

When I closed the door, I stared at it for a moment. It must be sparsely populated, I told myself—the world of exhibition management. I returned to Mrs. Woolgar's office and sank into a chair.

"Now. Right," I said. "We need to arrange payment to the Charlotte."

"I've already been in touch with Mr. Rennie," Mrs. Woolgar

said. "He'll have the check ready for you to collect by twelve o'clock."

From then on, it was business as usual. We chatted about choosing a new font for the newsletter, after which I returned to my office and rearranged my desk for the next half hour, keeping one eye on the clock as it crept closer and closer to eleven.

Buzz!

"Hello, good morning," I said, stepping back from the open door.

They looked like winners of a mother-daughter dress-alike contest. Oona, as usual, wore her navy suit, low heels, and hair in a high bun. Next to her, but a head shorter, stood a young woman not much older than my Dinah, dressed in a navy suit, low heels, and with her black hair scraped up into a matching bun. She held a large umbrella over both of them, her arm stretched straight up to clear Oona's head. Each had a satchel slung over her shoulder.

Coats were shed and hung on hallstand pegs and the young woman shook the umbrella on the doorstep before inserting it into the stand as Oona made the introductions.

"Hayley Burke, Clara Powell."

"Ms. Powell," I said, holding out my hand.

"Clara, please." She pulled a pair of large, heavy-framed glasses out of a pocket and put them on, then gave my hand two firm pumps and smiled. Her glasses wobbled.

"Hayley," I said with a smile. "Lovely to meet you."

"This is terribly exciting," Clara said. She pulled a tablet from her satchel, as if she might begin taking notes on the spot. "We did a production of *Busman's Honeymoon* at school for leaving—I played Honoria Lucasta, Lord Peter's mother. My nana loves mysteries and remembers Lady Fowling. She's terribly impressed Oona's taken me on."

"Enough," Oona said, and Clara clammed up. "Found her

at Taunton College," she continued, as if her PA were a stray puppy, "doing the office administration course and in desperate need of some real-world experience. She has great potential."

"Good morning," Mrs. Woolgar said from her office doorway.

After I made the next introductions, Clara admired the secretary's 1930s-style outfit—cherry red narrow skirt, white blouse with a wide lapel, and a narrow gold belt. "A timeless classic," she said.

Mrs. Woolgar beamed.

"Right, where shall we begin?" Oona asked.

I led the way to my office, where my desk became the manager's. Bunter, who had taken up his post as ceramic cat on the mantel, watched Oona with large, dark eyes and whiskers at attention.

"Is that a cat?" Oona asked.

"He's Bunter," I said. "Lady Fowling always had a tortoiseshell cat, and she always named him Bunter."

"We should find a stuffed cat for the study display," Oona said, and carried on without noticing Bunter had narrowed his eyes to slits. "Hayley, I've decided you should transcribe Lady Fowling's notebooks."

"All of them?"

"Certainly, beginning with the fifties. Date each entry and categorize it—household, personal, Golden Age of Mystery. She may've left a clue to that book's whereabouts. Plus, it'll get you started on signage."

"I intended to search the library for the book."

"I'll put Powell on it. Show her up, will you?"

Such a lovely place," Clara said, her head turning this way and that as we climbed the stairs. "Oh, is that Lady Fowling? She's beautiful. Look at this library—it's everything Oona said and more."

"It was Sir John's house first, of course—her ladyship's husband—but I feel as if she brought her own spirit to Middlebank. Now, it's your choice how to work the search for *Murder Must Advertise*. Oona explained about how it's signed?" Clara nodded. "So, do you prefer to start with the bottom shelves and work your way up or go from the top down? Most of the Sayers collection is up there. I think you'll be able to reach just fine with the ladder."

Clara's enthusiasm flagged.

"Doesn't look terribly safe," she said.

The ladder had only two steps and a top cap—it wasn't as if she'd be climbing to the roof. But I thought Clara had enough to endure, being bossed round by Oona, and I wouldn't add to her burdens.

"I tell you what," I said. "Why don't you start on arranging the notebooks by date. I'll bring them up for you—and I'll take a look at the books later."

"Yes, if you think that's best," she said with relief. "After all, you are in charge."

I don't know where she got that idea.

I returned downstairs to find no sign of Bunter. Oona had cleared my desk of my things and was now emptying the contents of her satchel—notebooks, drawing pads, laptop—onto my desk.

"Just taking Lady Fowling's notebooks up to the library," I said, creeping round her to retrieve a carton.

"Mmm," she replied.

I also snatched my laptop from under a stack of sketchbooks Oona had deposited on the floor and scooted out. When I returned an hour later, she barely looked up.

"Naomi at the Charlotte is waiting for our payment," I said, brave little soldier that I was, "and so I'll collect that and run it round. I may be out an hour or two. Could I bring you lunch?"

"No," Oona muttered, "I'll send Powell out for something."

* * *

"A nd that makes it official," Naomi said, slipping the check into her desk drawer and handing me a copy of the agreement. "You certainly have your work cut out for you the next twelve weeks, don't you?"

We sat in her office on the first floor, and out the window I could see the Assembly Rooms across the road and the Mendip Hills in the distance. I thought of my office being occupied for the next twelve weeks, and not by me.

"Naomi, what about that space you have on the other side of the Charlotte? We used it for offices and storage while getting ready for the Centre's exhbition."

When the Charlotte had been created by knocking through the walls between two terrace houses, a vertical slice of it from ground level to second floor had been left untouched.

"It's been sitting untouched for years—I don't think it's in a fit state to be occupied."

"Oh, please," I asked, with feeble hope, "it's only that it would be easier on all concerned"—*me*—"if we gave the manager and her PA room to spread out." I wondered what Oona would say about hot-desking, but promptly dismissed the idea.

"Well . . ." Naomi drew out the word as she thought. "I suppose I could let you have the space on the second floor. You have to climb an old, windy staircase. It might do—at least you'd have your own entrance off the street and wouldn't have to come through the main door every day." She appeared to brighten up at that thought. "Do you want to take a look?"

She led me back through a door to an area of the building that had not been refurbished. It was as I remembered, only more so—shabby, with stained and peeling Victorian wallpaper and a decided smell of damp. A dusty wooden staircase went down to the ground floor and the door out to the pavement. Leading up to the storage-cum-office was a wrought iron spiral staircase. It might once have been white, but what paint hadn't chipped off had yellowed. I followed Naomi, and we climbed to the second floor.

"Sorry," she said at the top, pushing a stack of cartons to the side, then brushing her hands together and coughing.

She pulled keys from her pocket and opened the door to reveal a dark storage closet stacked with file boxes, several old computer monitors, and a few broken chairs. "Here we are. It isn't awfully large. I believe there's a desk in the back. Could your manager make do with this?" she asked.

My nose itched from the dust damp. I thought it would take a fair amount of work to transform the musty closet into something resembling an office.

"Perfect," I said.

"Who is it you've hired?"

"Oona Atherton. Do you know who she is? She didn't think you'd met."

Two pink spots bloomed on Naomi's tan cheeks. She crossed her arms tightly. "She said that? Oh, well, difficult to remember the little people, I suppose. Look round if you like—if it suits, you can take the keys with you."

I'm so glad you've branched out into Sayers," my mum said. "She had such a mind. And you've no idea where Lady Fowling may have hidden this particular first edition?"

We sat over coffee in the kitchen of her flat in Liverpool on Saturday morning. Weekends with my mum were a restorative for me, sort of a mini-holiday and therapy session rolled into one.

I licked my finger as I finished up a Chelsea bun and said, "It's most likely in the cartons at the bank—I'll start on those next week when things settle down."

The coffee revived me. I had fallen asleep on the train to Liverpool that morning, almost missing my change at Birmingham New Street. I should just dismiss sleep from my daily schedule until after the exhibition.

Thursday evening and all of Friday had been given over to cleaning the former storage closet to make it inhabitable for Oona and Clara—I had been determined to get them moved into the Charlotte and out of my hair. True, they would be only a ten-minute walk away, but even that distance would give me breathing room.

Oona had done her share of work, whereas Clara had seemed to see her job as representing Health and Safety, and kept reminding us to hold on to the railing as we went up and down both the wooden staircase from ground to first floor and the spiral steps up to the second. At ten thirty Friday night, Val and I had left Oona and her PA arranging the meager furniture. He walked me back to Middlebank, pulling a cobweb from my ponytail before kissing me good night.

"How can she fault you for wanting a proper two days off?" Val had asked.

"'We've very little time and a great deal to accomplish,'" I had intoned. "How many times will I hear that in the next three months?"

Oona hadn't been best pleased upon hearing I'd be visiting my mum Saturday and Sunday. I'd followed that up by telling her I would be away for three days the following weekend. At this second piece of news of my skiving off work, she'd picked up her pencil and started sketching a display layout. No bark, only silence.

"I'd rather have the bark," I now told Mum as I swirled the dregs of my coffee. "At least I'd know where I stood with her."

"I remember your Jane Austen exhibition," Mum said, "and Dinah studying for her exams. There were quite a few tears—and not all of them from your daughter. But just you remember"—Mum touched my cheek—"this time is different."

* * *

Was it?

"We'll need to shift that portrait of Lady Fowling from Middlebank here to the Charlotte the week before the exhibition," Oona said to me Monday morning. "That large painting on the library landing. We'll install it as the last thing people see on their way out, as if she's bidding them good evening. Here, Powell"—she handed her satchel to Clara—"I want to go down to look at the space before the watercolorists arrive."

I stood blocking the doorway, too stunned to move or reply. I couldn't let Oona take Lady Fowling away—she belonged at Middlebank.

"Surely some facsimile of the painting could be made," I suggested.

"Do you think we could just ring up the Royal Academy and have them send down a young artist who is eager to copy the masters?"

"No, I didn't mean—"

But Oona wasn't listening. She picked up her sketchbook, pushed me aside, and bolted out the door, her feet clanging on the metal of the spiral staircase. Clara chased after and grabbed hold of the railing.

"Oona, please do be careful," she shouted down. She returned to the office, shaking her head. "She won't listen. Well, Hayley, are you here to look over the press releases?"

That had been my intention, but now I had other issues. I must think of an acceptable alternative to moving Lady Fowling's portrait. I couldn't let it be shuttled about as if it were merely canvas and paint—it was the embodiment of the woman herself. And if it were gone, to whom would I talk?

At some level I knew that I did not carry on actual conversations with a painting—even though Val had heard me murmur a comment or two on my way up or down the stairs—but I felt her ladyship's presence at Middlebank, and I attached that feeling to the portrait. Moving it would be like tossing Lady Fowling in the boot of a car and carrying her off.

From that Monday morning, I crammed eight days of work into my four-day workweek, including two briefings a day. First at Middlebank with Mrs. Woolgar—we carried those off without a hitch. I reminded the secretary about my impending three-day holiday, and she told me that she would be gone overnight Thursday to visit a friend in Tunbridge Wells. As this meant Bunter would not be left alone, we were both satisfied.

Next, the morning briefing at the Charlotte, ostensibly run by me. On Tuesday when I arrived, it was to hear Oona finishing a story she'd been telling Clara.

"So, I was stood there, and he didn't even notice until the fellow behind me said, 'Oi, Berryfield—trouble with your posh coffee order? Move along.'"

Clara snickered in response, and Oona acknowledgd my arrival with a wry smile. "It was Zeno, wasn't it?" she asked. "The other manager you were talking with about this job?"

"What? Who?" Was it a good thing that I was such a terrible liar? "Oh, Zeno Berryfield?"

"Count your lucky stars I was here to save you. Isn't that right, Powell?"

"Heigh-ho," Clara said with a grin, and her face reddened.

"Heigh-ho, indeed."

I continued to search the library for the signed copy of *Murder Must Advertise* while also transcribing a decade's worth of her ladyship's notebooks. I dated every page of entry, beginning with February 1950. I felt sure one of those assignments had been Clara's, but she was no longer at Middlebank and so I carried on. I didn't mind—I felt as if I understood Lady Fowling and had a better idea of how to sort her musings, although many defied categorization. What was I to make of this string of nonsense from September 1950?

> *Quiet Anticipation Despite*
> *Wiley Detective Beckons Death*
> *Betrayal Deemed Quintessential Appraisal*
> *Marvelous Merchants Appropriate Quietly*
>   *Authentic Deception*

I suspected the phrases related to Lady Fowling's Dorset detective, François Flambeaux—she had a penchant for flowery language when it came to her own sleuth. Perhaps he'd gone undercover as a newspaperman in one of her stories and had to write headlines, just as Lord Peter had become an adman and created jingles. I listed those odd phrases on a page all their own and left it to Oona to decide how to handle them.

Our second literary salon was remarkable for its lack of drama—unlike Oona's moody performance the next morning.

"They're like midges," she complained to me, huddled over her desk. "Impossible to swat away. Interest in the exhibition is one thing, harassment is another. If you see any of them hanging about, Hayley, send them on their way."

By *them* I thought she meant Stuart Moyle or his ilk. A second brief item had appeared in the papers about the first edition signed by the Detection Club—this one with a quote from Oona. If she kept planting these bits of gossip, how could she be annoyed that they generated interest?

On Thursday morning, I edged into Oona's aerie at the Charlotte with coffees from across the road as a peace offering. Clara, in the corner, set her tablet on a tea table and, with a distracted air, thanked me for her cappuccino.

Oona had not spoken about my upcoming three-day weekend, but her displeasure was palpable, hanging in the room like a miasma. To prove myself worthy of a normal life, I had printed out what I'd done to date and brought the file folder with me. I eased it onto her desk.

"I'll drop the final pages off tomorrow morning," I said. "And I will have finished searching the library by then, so on Monday, I'll start on the cartons of books from the bank."

Oona muttered something and pushed the thick folder to the side. I hurried out, my swift exit prompting Clara to remind me to be careful on the stairs.

Late Thursday afternoon, Val and I met at the Waitrose café. We kept to business. He had finished up his own preweekend task list—contacting next week's lecturer and putting out a call for bids to print the exhibition program. It was difficult to stay focused—my mind kept trying to move further away from the exhibition and closer to Woolacombe and the seaside.

My phone vibrated on the table—a text from Oona.

I know where it is! Death is the clue. Murder must

And there it broke off.

"She knows where it is?" I asked. "The signed copy? Or is this a ploy to get me to go through another decade of notebooks before I'm allowed to leave town?"

"You don't need her permission," Val reminded me.

"Too right, and I'll tell her so. It's all well and good if she's discovered the location of the book—it's quite exciting—but I don't need to write signage for the display this very second." I tapped a finger on the tabletop and then composed my reply.

Happy dance! Will stop by to take a look.

"But I won't stay long," I told Val. "I'll acknowledge her find, locate the book, and take it off to Duncan Rennie so that he can store it securely."

"I'll go with you."

"Thanks," I said, grateful for the support in case Oona put up a protest. "I wonder how she figured it out? Well, I'm sure she'll tell us the whole story."

And yet, we did not leap up from the table and rush away. Instead, we finished our tea and held hands and looked out the window as a shaft of sunlight fell across Walcot Street. Nothing else came in from Oona, and at last, I sighed and said, "Better get this over with—and then I can go pack for the weekend."

"You don't need much," Val reminded me with a wink, and I grinned and blushed like a schoolgirl.

Just gone four o'clock, we zigzagged our way to the Charlotte—cutting across Saracen Street and up Broad, dashing across George Street when the traffic had stopped, and then up Bartlett and Alfred, where we reached the wide paved area outside the Assembly Rooms and ran into a crowd. My first thought was a tour bus had unloaded, but then I saw Dom standing to the side. Then I noticed the reflection of blue lights flashing in windows across the road.

"Hiya, Dom," I said. "Is it an ambulance? Did someone in the Assembly Rooms collapse?" Medical emergencies at popular tourist spots were not unheard of.

"You hired Oona," Dom said.

"Yes, I did. For our upcoming exhibition. It's because, although she may be difficult, she's—here, Dom, let me introduce you to Val Moffatt."

"You teach writing at Bath College," Dom said. "Margo says you're Hayley's boyfriend."

Val confirmed the statement with a smile. "And I hear you work magic with computer systems," he replied.

"Dom," I said, "how did you know I'd hired Oona?"

"Margo told me. She said Sarah in the shop talked with Terry, who saw Adele at the Minerva." He pushed his glasses farther up the bridge of his nose.

Good to know the grapevine was alive and thriving.

"I know Oona's difficult, Dom, but remember how good the exhibition was."

Like a curtain, the crowd in front of us parted, revealing the street to be filled with blue-and-yellow-checkered police cars. So, not a pensioner in need of medical attention. Instead, across the road at the Charlotte, PCs in yellow high-vis vests were stretching crime scene tape across the door. Not at the Charlotte's front door, but at the site around the corner—the door that led up two flights of stairs to Oona's temporary office.

My mind went numb. And then I saw several people emerge from the building wearing blue paper coveralls and booties and gloves and—

"SOCO," I whispered. "Scenes of crime officers."

Val and I pushed forward, but a woman PC stepped in front of us and said, "Move along, please."

"I'm Hayley Burke, curator of the First Edition Society at Middlebank House." My voice shook and I had a flash of déjà vu—identifying myself to police like this. "This is Val Moffatt. Our exhibition manager is working on the second floor, what's happened?"

The PC turned away and spoke into the radio attached to her shoulder strap, received a crackled reply, and said to us, "Would you follow me?"

Val grabbed my hand. We crossed the road and made it to the Charlotte just as the blue-and-white crime scene tape across the doorway was lifted and out came a face

I recognized—Detective Constable Kenny Pye, his sleek black hair and dark skin set off against the pale Bath stone building behind him.

"Ah, Ms. Burke," he said. "And Mr. Moffatt. We need to talk."

He led us inside, where the dusty and formerly dark entry was awash in floodlights. Plastic sheeting covered the floor and the staircase.

"Where is Clara? Where is Oona?" I asked. "Was there an accident?"

"Oona Atherton was found at the bottom of the spiral staircase that leads to the second floor. She's dead."

7

B ut . . . dead?" I clutched at Val's arm. "I can't believe it.
Clara was right—Oona should've taken care."

"That's Clara Powell you're referring to, Ms. Burke?"

It was Detective Sergeant Ronald Hopgood speaking as
he came down the steps. He reached the bottom of the staircase and swept a finger under his salt-and-pepper, push-
broom mustache.

"Sergeant Hopgood," Val said, "was this an accident?
And if so, why are you here?"

"Mr. Moffatt, Ms. Burke—how is it that you knew Ms.
Atherton?"

"I hired her—she's." Full stop, and it took me a moment to
go on. "She was an exhibition manager and worked on an
event five years ago at the Jane Austen Centre. The First Edition Society engaged her to put up a show here at the Charlotte.
Bath College has endorsed the event, and so Val is involved."

Hopgood's caterpillar eyebrows twitched, but he didn't
look surprised. "When was the last time either of you saw
her?"

"Monday afternoon for me," Val offered. "I dropped off a list of college donors for the program."

"I came by this morning—well, almost midday."

"Here?"

"Yes, here. I dropped off a folder, but I didn't stay."

"Both of you, follow me—but watch where you step."

We obeyed, Val and I creeping up the wooden staircase behind Hopgood. As we neared the top, I swallowed hard, preparing myself for the worst, but when we reached the first-floor landing, it was to find a businesslike atmosphere—paper-coveralled officers examining, chatting, pointing, and photographing. At the bottom of the spiral staircase a dark tarpaulin had been spread over a small, indistinguishable mound. When a SOCO team member pulled away one corner, I caught a glimpse of Oona's shoulder and a hand. I took a sharp breath and looked away, and Val caught me round the waist.

"Oona sent me a text," I said, pulling out my phone to show him. "It was only an hour ago. All this happened since?"

"Pye," the sergeant called over, "do you have the mobile?"

The DC held up a clear plastic bag with a phone inside.

"Where's Clara?" I said, my voice hoarse.

"She's next door with a PC," Hopgood said, "in Ms. Faber's office."

Could I assume the watercolor exhibition had closed early for the day?

"Sergeant," Val persisted, "this can't be an accident—you must suspect something. Could you not just come out and say it?"

Hopgood's eyebrows lifted and dropped like drapes being raised and lowered. "At first glance that's just what it may look like—an accident. Perhaps Ms. Atherton lost control, dropped what she was carrying, and tumbled down. I can't take you upstairs at the moment, but I will tell you that the office in which she and Ms. Powell worked has been turned over."

"Turned over—a robbery?" Val asked.

"And if it were a robbery," the sergeant said watching me, "what might they be after?"

A first edition of Murder Must Advertise *signed by every member of the Detection Club in 1933.*

But, at that moment, another, more pressing thought occurred to me. "Was Clara here when it happened?"

I had a sudden fear for her—she didn't seem strong enough to weather such a terrible event. She was too young.

"Ms. Powell tells us she was out and returned to find Ms. Atherton dead. She rang 999 and here we are."

I pictured my daughter, Dinah, stumbling upon a dead body and I felt light-headed. Then, one of the papers on the floor caught my eye. I leaned over and read the date—May 1954. It was part of my transcription of Lady Fowling's notebooks.

When I straightened, I saw DS Hopgood give his constable a slight nod.

Pye said, "Ms. Burke, why don't we go next door and have a chat?"

Oh yes, the chat.

"Mr. Moffatt," Sergeant Hopgood said, "would you remain here?"

I fumed as I followed Kenny Pye through the door that led from this older, shabbier side of the Charlotte into the refurbished event-space offices. Did Hopgood separate Val and me so that we wouldn't have a chance to "get our stories straight"? Did he think we were the guilty parties? And guilty of what—being so irritated with Oona that we would throw her down the stairs?

The detective constable pushed open the door to Naomi's office—there was no sign of her, but a female PC stood in the corner, and sitting in a small heap in a large chair was Clara. Her bun had come loose and hanks of her dark hair hung lifeless. She gripped her glasses in one hand, and she looked up at me with surprisingly wide eyes in a pale face.

"I lost my phone," she said. "I lost my phone and came back to look for it."

Behind me, Pye said, "That's about all we've got from her so far. Do you know her well enough to—"

"Tea."

Another uniform came through the door carrying a tray and, under his arm, a stack of paper cups. He set it on Naomi's desk and left, so I poured two cups, one for Clara and one for me. I'd seen her put a spoonful of sugar in her tea—I added an extra for good measure and even stirred one into my own.

I pulled up a chair next to Clara's and handed over her cup. She took a drink, shuddered, and gulped another. Then she said, as if answering a question, "I had to use Oona's phone. I lost mine. That's why."

I glanced at DC Pye, who nodded me on.

"Where had you gone, Clara?"

"Oona needed a fresh set of sketch pads and pencils—from that place next to the pub, the Green Tree. She's quite particular about materials."

"So, you were away at the art supply shop?"

"I started and was almost there, but Oona hadn't told me which size sketch pad and I went to text her, but I didn't have my phone. I looked and looked through my bag, but it wasn't there. I couldn't buy the wrong-size sketch pad. So, I came back to ask her."

"Do you have a key to the outer door?" DC Pye asked.

Clara stared at him for a moment, a vague look in her eye. "No," she said, "Oona has the key. The door was unlocked. I came up the stairs and—" She grabbed my arm and squeezed. "I told her to be careful, but she wouldn't listen. I lost my phone. I saw hers"—Clara flung her arm out—"in the corner. I had to ring for an ambulance."

Kenny Pye picked up the questioning, but Clara didn't

seem to have any more useful details—she hadn't noticed anyone, couldn't remember the route she'd walked or just how long she'd been gone. I admired his patience, especially as every answer ended the same—"I lost my phone."

Although I had a fair idea of what the police were thinking might've happened, I wasn't sure that Clara had cottoned on to the theory that Oona's death had not been an accident. Should I tell her? Was it my responsibility?

Hopgood appeared at the door. "Ms. Powell, we're ready for you to go up to the office and have a look round. Shall we?"

Clara began to tremble, and I took her cup away before she spilled what remained of her tea.

"Up those stairs?" she whispered. "I don't think I can."

I would need to explain to the sergeant about the library ladder and Clara's fear—no doubt compounded by Oona's death—but for now, I had my own question.

"Has the landing been . . . cleared?"

Clara made no indication she knew what I meant, but Hopgood understood and his face softened, giving me a glimpse of the kindly-uncle side of him. "It has," he said. "Right, Clara. I'll go with you. Shall I be in front or in back—which is better?"

I followed Sergeant Hopgood, pulling Clara behind me—she clenched my hand like a vise—then a PC, and finally DC Pyc, and we climbed the spiral staircase like a train chugging round and round up a mountain.

"Where is Val?" I asked as we shuffled up.

"Out on the pavement, giving one of my officers a description of your movements," the sergeant said as he reached the landing and stood aside for us to go in.

Oona's office had indeed been turned over—drawers pulled out, file boxes opened and spilled, papers scattered across the floor.

But it wasn't only papers that had been tossed about—there were books, too—copies I had lent Oona from the library at Middlebank. Sprawled open in a corner and lying facedown, I saw one of her ladyship's own stories starring François Flambeaux. A lovely book with tooled leather binding and gold lettering. A fury rose in me.

"How dare someone do this," I said, my voice thick.

"Oona would be terribly annoyed at the mess," Clara said in a weak voice. She had remained behind me in the doorway, but glanced over her shoulder down the spiral stairs as if caught between the devil and the deep blue sea.

"Couldn't have been more than two hours ago now," Hopgood said quietly, and then snapped to attention. "Pye, we'll need to comb any nearby CCTV for all comings and goings, including Ms. Powell here. Get traffic on the blower."

"Yes, boss."

I could almost smile. For a moment I did not see Hopgood, but his alter ego—a 1920s PI named Alehouse, the main character in short stories written by Kenny Pye, who took Val's evening classes at Bath College.

"Also, we'll need to see all the incoming and outgoing calls and texts on the victim's mobile."

Clara lifted her gaze from the floor. "I lost my phone."

Val came up the stairs and saw the devastation. "Bloody hell."

"Did Ms. Atherton have enemies?" Hopgood asked.

"Enemies?" I echoed, staring at him blankly, my mind whirring as it assembled a suitable phrase or two in response.

"Enemies?" Clara shouted. "Certainly not! Oona's skill and experience might've been envied by some who aspire to her level of interpretive excellence, but surely no one would resort to . . . to . . ." She petered out with a puzzled look, as if wondering what she was about to say next, and instead got busy twining her hair back into its bun, searching her jacket pockets, and coming up with a pin.

The sergeant kept his eyes on me as he said, "If any of

the three of you think of a person who might've had even the slightest altercation with the victim, you will tell me,"

How long would that list be? I wondered.

"Sir," said one of the coveralled officers. With a gloved hand, he held up a half-eaten roll—that and an unopened sandwich next to it were the only things remaining on the desk. Hopgood noticed the food and turned to Clara.

"Oona's," Clara said, and blinked several times before continuing. "I went down to Pret."

The sergeant's eyebrows met in the middle. "You told us you hadn't left until your errand to the art supply store."

"Did I?" she responded. "Well, it was only lunch."

"You went all the way to Pret A Manger?" I asked. There were a dozen sandwich shops between here and there.

"Oona prefers their jambon-beurre baguette. The other one is mine."

"Take both in for testing," Hopgood instructed the officer, who bagged the food.

Val glanced round the room one more time and then cut his eyes at me. "Do you see it anywhere?"

I shook my head. Nowhere in the heap of books that the police were now sorting through did I see what looked like a first edition of *Murder Must Advertise*.

"And 'it' would be—?" Hopgood asked.

The reply would take more than a few words, and so Hopgood, Val, and I headed back down the spiral staircase toward Naomi's office, leaving Clara with DC Pye, identifying the bits and pieces strewn about the office. On the first-floor landing, the detective sergeant called down to the ground floor, where a woman stood stripping off her paper outfit. She was, I seemed to recall, the medical examiner.

"Anything, Frankie?"

"Broken neck for starters," she said. Hopgood moved on,

but she added, "Ronnie! Head trauma, too. It doesn't look like she hit it on the way down—no blood or tissue on the railing—so my guess is a cosh of some kind. Right temple. Perhaps she turned when her assailant was about to strike her from behind."

"Don't forget stomach contents," he replied.

The ME threw him a wry smile and said, "Thanks for telling me my job."

Back in Naomi's office, I took a few deep breaths as I rid my mind of blood and tissue and broken necks. Inside the offices at the Charlotte, it was as if I were in another world, unattached to the everyday reality of my flat and my job and my life. Shock—easy to diagnose, difficult to suffer.

We sat on chairs pushed against the wall, and Val and I took turns telling Detective Sergeant Hopgood the entire story—Lady Fowling's letter to Dorothy L. Sayers, the indication that a quite rare book existed, signed by the Detection Club. Thankfully, Val took over at that point, describing the club and the book.

"Murder Must Advertise," Hopgood said. "I'm not familiar with that one. How does the victim die?"

My shoulders slumped. "In a fall down a spiral staircase."

8

Detective Sergeant Hopgood must've noticed my waning energy because he cut our interview short. "I'll post a foot patrol at Middlebank—even if the book isn't there, you never know what'll get into people's heads. Your secretary—"

"Mrs. Woolgar. She's away." She had reminded me of her plans that morning, and I had promptly forgotten. "She left this morning to stay overnight with a friend who had minor surgery. She's in"—I searched my brain for details that I hadn't thought important—"Tunbridge Wells. She'll return tomorrow afternoon."

"Duly noted, Ms. Burke," Hopgood said. "We aren't finished, of course. I'll want contact details on every person you've told about the book, a better picture of what this exhibition entails, and further background on Ms. Atherton. And anything else you may be able to shed light on. After that, you and Mr. Moffatt will need to sign your statements. So, shall we say the station at tenish? It looks to be a busy weekend."

Not that I hadn't already suspected it. The dream of my carefree, romantic getaway with Val had begun to fade as soon as I'd seen those flashing blue lights. I couldn't expect the police to say, *Sure, you go off on your little holiday— we'll stay here and investigate the death of a woman who was murdered while doing the job for which you hired her.* How would it look to the board if I told them of Oona's death and then scarpered?

And what of Oona herself? Such a life force—whether or not she had been easy to get along with, she was passionate and talented. And now gone.

My eyes welled with tears as I said, "Yes, Sergeant. Ten o'clock tomorrow."

It was past eight o'clock by the time we left the Charlotte. We hadn't seen Clara again—a PC had taken her back to her grandmother's in Shepton Mallet. Nor had we seen Naomi. Hopgood told us she'd been occupied pacifying the watercolorists, who were annoyed that the last weekend of their exhibition had been marred by murder.

As Val and I walked to Middlebank, the cold air seeping into my bones, I said, "I'll have to tell Mrs. Woolgar when she returns tomorrow. I'll need to explain to the board. I wonder will Naomi give us our deposit back for the exhibition." I sniffed, caught a whiff of woodsmoke, and longed to be sitting in front of a warm, crackling fire with the sound of the sea outside the window.

Val stopped, caught my arm, and turned me round to face him.

"Hang on," he said. "It's a bit early to decide that, don't you think? Let's give it a day or two."

"I suppose," I said, but with little energy and no enthusiasm.

Middlebank was quiet and dark. Bunter met us at the door, walking on tiptoes and weaving figure eights round our legs. I picked him up, and he rubbed his face against my chin, and then, when Val leaned in, against his, too.

Bunter is usually one for only a quick cuddle before he needs to be on his way, but now he snuggled against me, and his purring vibrated through my chest. Val's arm circled my waist, and for a moment, the three of us stood like that, until Bunter had had enough. He jumped down, and we followed him into the kitchenette.

"Well, cat," I said, "here's your chicken and liver." He gave the fresh dish of food a sniff and then trotted off to his bed in Mrs. Woolgar's office. "Cuppa?" I asked Val, and silently we headed upstairs.

I paused on the first-floor landing outside the library door and regarded Lady Fowling—the portrait—and then took Val's hand and we continued to my flat. Perhaps I'd come back later and have a chat with her.

Inside the door, I dropped my bag, pulled off my coat, and made for the kitchen, filling the kettle and switching it on. I turned on the hot tap, grabbed the soap, and scrubbed my hands as if I were Lady Macbeth.

"It's my fault she was here," I said as Val joined me. I handed him the soap without thinking. "If I hadn't hired Oona, she wouldn't be dead."

"We don't know that's true. We can't be sure why someone would want to kill her. Was it about the book or something else in her life?"

I splashed water on my face and dried it with a tea towel, which I passed to Val. The kettle began to rattle as it heated.

"Look," he said. "I only wanted to make sure you got home all right, but you probably want to be alone, so I'll go now and we'll meet up tomorrow."

"Stay." I sucked in my breath, surprised at my own plea. But it came to me what I wanted—needed.

Val hadn't replied, and so I continued. "Please stay. I know it isn't a seafront room at the Grand Hotel in Woolacombe, but even so—"

"Of course I'll stay," he said. "I'll stay to keep you company. But I don't want you to think . . ." His gaze darted round the kitchen and into the sitting room, and he added, halfheartedly, "I can sleep on the sofa."

"You will *not* sleep on the sofa."

Slowly his green eyes crinkled at the corners as he smiled. "Ah well," he said. "If you insist."

He made me laugh and I felt a world better. For a moment, we looked at each other, and then I drew close and our lips brushed. I reached over to the counter, switched off the kettle, and led the way.

The lamp in the sitting room spilled light into my bedroom, keeping us in semidarkness—quite enough to see, but not too much. We took our time, slowly peeling off layer after layer, and attending to detail. I became momentarily annoyed at the tiny buttons on men's shirts, but we got over that and at last we were down to nothing. The band holding my ponytail was the last to go, and when my hair fell to my bare shoulders and Val kissed the hollow place at the bottom of my throat, things began to move along a bit quicker.

When at last he pulled the covers up over us, we ended where we'd started, staring into each other's eyes.

"That was better than the seaside," I said.

"What?" His voice was full of mock incredulity. "Better than ice cream and tide pools and eating fish and chips with those annoying little wooden picks?" He gave me a squeeze. "We'll get there—just not this weekend."

We snuggled and were quiet. After a few minutes, I felt Val's arms round me relax and could hear his breathing even out as he drifted off. But I was wide awake. My mind had cleared, and I thought I could see a path forward. When he stirred and stroked my arm, I said, "What about that cup of tea?"

"I don't need anything," he said, but I heard his tummy protest.

"Come on, I'll do us an omelet."

Val pulled on his trousers and went to start the kettle while I dashed into the loo to make sure I didn't have rings of mascara under my eyes. I had two dressing gowns on the back of the door and quickly dismissed the idea of wearing my favorite—a thickly matted chenille number—and instead grabbed a thin, peacock blue silk robe I'd got from a charity shop—a small spot of embroidery on one shoulder had come unstitched, but it was practically unnoticeable. I dropped the ball, however, when it came to my feet, and padded out to the kitchen in woolly slippers.

"Hiya," I said, kissing him behind the ear. He'd already laid the table, and so I took over and cracked eggs into a bowl. As I whisked, Val ducked out and returned wearing his shirt, too.

I looked down at my robe and tightened the belt. "I should put some clothes on."

"Oh, please don't," he said, and added, "Unless you're cold."

"No, not cold. You took care of that." And central heating, too, but no need to mention it.

"Here, let me cook," he said. "I'm a dab hand at eggs. One of my few mealtime successes when the girls were young."

"Have you heard from them lately?" I asked.

"Bess rang. I thought it was time I asked them for a visit so you could meet."

Val already had been introduced to my Dinah, but I had yet to be face-to-face with his twins, Bess and Becky, aged twenty-four. He had been a single parent from the time they were barely five, after his wife had left them and then died quite suddenly.

Not that I was worried about meeting his daughters.

"I look forward to it," I said, my heart jumping into my throat. "You told them that, didn't you—that I look forward to it?"

"Yeah, of course I did."

"Good, that's good."

We ate in silence—only exchanging the occasional silly smile. "All right, now," I said, scraping the last bits of egg from my plate, "you're going to think this is a daft idea, but if we're going to continue with the exhibition, we should hire Zeno Berryfield."

Val frowned. "Could we trust him? What would become of the event if he gets hold of it?"

"The thing is, we could get him to sign an agreement that he couldn't make a move without our say-so."

"You could do it, you know," Val said, waving a fork. "You could mount the exhibition yourself."

I shook my head. "No. It's too much—the scope. It's that all-encompassing view that's needed, as well as a load of practical knowledge. And even if he is a bit odd, at least Zeno's had experience. I can learn all the good bits and leave off his . . . eccentricites. He'll be a name and a source. I don't think we can keep the Charlotte otherwise."

Val remained skeptical, but I saw the hiring of Make an Exhibition of Yourself! as a way to continue—it would be difficult enough to tell the board and Mrs. Woolgar what had happened. At least we'd still have a manager.

I found a toothbrush for Val—Dinah had forgotten hers at Christmas, and we had bought a three-pack at Boots—and we got ready for bed proper, switching off the lights and leaving only a soft glow coming from the front window. Val's hand slid down my back and hips, and he pulled me closer and kissed my hair and we said good night.

9

I've two pieces of bread for our breakfast," I said, and opened a cupboard. "Or cornflakes?" The thought settled on me that I would need to start shopping for the occasional—or even regular—overnight guest. I smiled.

"Tea," Val said, drinking the last of his down. "I'll go home and shower and meet you before we go to the police."

Oh yes, that's right—despite the blue sky and my morning-after-sex euphoria, we had more somber business to attend to. Oona was dead, the police thought it murder, and the exhibition was in danger.

"The Bertinet by the rail station?"

"I'll see you there in an hour." Val cupped my face in his hands and kissed me softly.

"Bye," I whispered, but he didn't move. "Bye?"

"Yeah, right—bye."

I dashed into and out of the shower and wandered my flat with my hair in a towel and a cup of tea in hand. I needed to impose order on my day, and so I started a list.

Tell Mrs. Woolgar. But she wouldn't be back from Tunbridge Wells until the afternoon. Should I send her a text? Leave a note on her desk? No, wait—I thought of another way to get word to her.

I would let Duncan Rennie tell her. As the First Edition Society's solicitor, he would also be the one to arrange for the cartons of rare books to come out of storage and be delivered to Middlebank. After all, I needed to continue searching for the rare copy of *Murder Must Advertise*.

Next on my list—prepare a solemn statement for the board. I would end it on a sad, but positive note, and say that we must go on with the exhibition.

Talk to Adele. At the board meeting last Wednesday week, Oona had recognized her and Adele had been flustered. I should've insisted Adele tell me details then, because now I was unsure how she would react to Oona's death. But as Adele was teaching and wouldn't be free until the afternoon, I'd send her a text and we could meet after school.

Zeno Berryfield. Would he be hot-desking today? Had he been hired elsewhere? Would he accept our offer with its restrictions?

Naomi—I must make certain she kept hold of our April dates.

I added Mum and Dinah to my list, but perhaps I could wait until tomorrow to tell them—I didn't think Oona's death had grabbed any headlines.

And now, to Oona herself. What happened? Was it—as I feared—someone willing to murder to get hold of a one-of-a-kind first edition of *Murder Must Advertise*? Someone who knew the plot well enough to toy with police by making it look like a copycat murder, using a detective story written nearly one hundred years ago?

On the way to meet Val, I nipped into the Charlotte to have a word with Naomi—to assure her we were still on. Just inside the front door, a cluster of watercolorists stood with steaming mugs in hand, speaking in low voices and glancing over their shoulders. At the sight of me, their eyes widened and faces paled.

"Hello, good morning," I whispered. "Is Naomi in, do you know?"

"Not until twelve," one of the men said.

"Right, well—I'll stop back by later."

"Are you police?"

"Me?" Had Sergeant Hopgood been interviewing these people? Did he suspect a watercolorist of Oona's death? "No, I have a bit of business to sort out. I'll send her a text."

The group heaved a sigh of relief. One of them even smiled and waved as I left, calling out, "Cheerio, then."

On my way to the Bertinet, I worked on a text to Naomi.

Wanted you to know we are committed to the exhibition regardless of—I paused and considered my words—**the terrible event of yesterday. Let's talk.**

I admired the text—it acknowledged what had happened but stated my determination that life must go on. Just not for Oona. I didn't want to gloss over her death, but I couldn't help thinking if roles were reversed, Oona would forge ahead.

Hitting send, I walked into the coffee shop, and was greeted with the sight of a full case of pastries and a gentle kiss from Val—as close to heaven as I'd ever come.

Over breakfast, we divvied up our day. Val, naturally, would take over explaining to the people at Bath College our current circumstances and reassure them the exhibition was not in jeopardy. We would visit the board together— the Moons loved Val, and Maureen Frost had a professional respect for him, so no trouble there. Jane Arbuthnot, however, could be temperamental and easily swayed by the secretary's opinion on the matter.

"I've asked Duncan Rennie to talk with Mrs. Woolgar."

"Good to have a solicitor on hand."

"Yes, good for the Society—and for the secretary." With scant evidence and no courage to ask questions, I had formed the idea that Glynis Woolgar and Duncan Rennie were an item.

"Why don't we wait until she's been apprised of the situation before we talk to the board?" Val suggested.

"Right, that would be better. I'll catch Adele this afternoon when school ends and take her to the Raven. Maybe you could meet us there later."

I finished my almond croissant with a light dusting of icing sugar on my cardigan and a stickiness around my mouth. Val, sensibly, had eaten a ham-and-chutney roll and looked none the worse for wear. I did my best with a damp tissue before we headed the short distance up Manvers to the police.

At the station, we gave Sergeant Hopgood a detailed account of those who knew about the first edition of *Murder Must Advertise*, signed by the Detection Club. We piqued his interest for certain with our tale of Stuart "Bulldog" Moyle.

"Have you seen him since?"

We shook our heads.

"I'm in touch with Arthur Fish," Val said, "the lecturer from last week. They seemed to know each other. I'll leave you Arthur's details."

Oh God, the literary salons. My mind jumped ahead to next week. Margaret Raines—a retired detective chief superintendent to talk about the Metropolitan Police in fact and fiction. Raines now wrote novels, police procedurals, and so could cover the topic from both sides.

"And so, Sergeant"—I thought there was no harm in asking again—"you're absolutely certain Oona truly was murdered? She didn't have an accident?"

"It doesn't look as if she went over willingly," Hopgood said. "But was it planned or a violent act in the heat of the moment—a knock on the head and a shove? The prints in the office and on the stairs are turning up nothing unusual."

"When can we get back into the office?" I asked, hoping I didn't sound cold and calculating. "The thing is, when the Society finds another exhibition manager, we will need that work space."

"We'll be finished at the site by the end of today," Hopgood said, "but we've gathered a great deal of material—books and papers—and we're not ready to release them yet."

"Oona made a lot of sketches about displays and such," I said. "They'll be useful as we continue. And also—those books belong to the First Edition library."

"They will be returned, Ms. Burke, all in good time." Hopgood placed his open hands palms down on the table as if bracing himself. "Now, I don't need to remind the two of you that this is a police enquiry, and as such, we will brook no interference on the public's part."

My jaw dropped. "We haven't done anything."

"No, of course you haven't," the sergeant said. "Let's keep it that way. Mr. Moffatt?"

"Does that mean you don't need Arthur Fish's contact details?" Val asked, a thin veneer of innocence over mischief.

Hopgood's eyebrows quivered, then smoothed out into a single thick line. "As I'm sure you remember, we consider the gathering of evidence a one-way street. Ms. Burke," he said, "as you are the most familiar with the papers and such that we've recovered from the site, I would like you to—shall we say—interpret them for us. Tomorrow morning? We'll give you your own room and provide as much tea as you can drink."

Police station tea? Less a lure and more a deterrent.

"Yes, all right."

"And the rare book—I'll have an officer search your library."

I envisioned police parading up and down the staircase at Middlebank. I thought we had done with that.

"Must you? I've almost finished searching the library and, really, I don't believe it's there. And we are well and truly secure now," I reminded him. "Not like in October."

Hopgood acknowledged that fact with a nod. "I'll send Pye over."

Oh well, that's all right then—I liked Detective Constable Pye. Maybe Val could be there, too, and as we searched the books, I could listen in on the two of them talking about fictional detectives. I might learn something.

The sergeant glanced down at the short list of people we'd given him. "Is there anyone else?"

With Oona's treatment of those who worked for her, her past was probably littered with possible suspects, but as that included me, I decided not to call attention to it. "We haven't got far enough into planning for many people to be involved," I said. "And I know little of Oona's private life. Wouldn't Clara have information on any recent jobs?"

"We'll see. Pye is with Ms. Powell at the moment," the sergeant said.

"He went to Shepton Mallet?" I asked.

"No, she's at the flat here in Bath where Ms. Atherton was lodging."

Once we were outside the station, I said to Val, "I need to check on Clara. Why is she here? And at Oona's flat? She's a girl, she shouldn't be alone talking with the police."

"She's not been cautioned," Val replied. "They only want to know if she has any more information. And she is an adult."

"I think about Dinah in Clara's shoes," I said. "Bess and Becky are adults—how would you feel about them being questioned? Even if it is Kenny Pye?"

Val frowned. "All right—you go. I'm off to talk with the department head at the college. But after that, I'll go with you to see Berryfield."

"Good. But prepare yourself—he's a case."

We parted, and I headed up and across Pulteney Bridge and down William Street to a long, straight terrace and Oona's temporary digs. The building had a keypad entry, but all I could do was press the button for her number. I identified myself and heard the lock *snick* as it released.

I took the lift to the second floor and I encountered another keypad at the door of the flat, but one of the women PCs stood ready to let me in. The flat had a compact entry with a narrow hallstand and a screen—a live camera showing the downstairs entry. Within, DC Pye occupied a chair and Clara teetered on the edge of the sofa with tea things on the table between them.

The constable stood. "Ms. Burke—the sarge thought you might pop by."

Did he indeed—Hopgood the mind reader. "Hello, good morning," I said. "Clara, how are you?"

Vestiges of her job clung to the PA. Although she had dressed in trainers, denims, and a long sweater, she had pulled on her suit jacket, and her hair remained in a high, Oona-style bun.

"Hello, Hayley, good morning," she said, taking her glasses from the table and putting them on. "I'm terribly glad you stopped in. Won't you sit down? Would you like tea?"

"No, thank you." But Clara looked crestfallen, and so I said, "Oh yes, why not. I could just do with a cup."

"The kettle's not long off the boil—it won't take me two ticks," she said, and hurried into the kitchen.

I glanced about the place—sparsely furnished, but pleasant and airy with a view south toward the rugby pitch.

"Had you visited Ms. Atherton here?" Pye asked.

"No," I said, settling on the sofa, "but of course I had her address for our records. That's how I knew where to find you."

"There now," Clara said, returning with the pot. "I'm sorry I've only Maries to offer."

I eyed the plate of thin biscuits on the coffee table. As far as I was concerned, Maries—and their doppelgänger, rich tea biscuits—were good only for crushing and mixing with a great deal of melted chocolate to use in a tiffin.

"Lovely," I said, taking one, "thanks."

"Well, Ms. Powell"—the constable stood, flipping his notebook closed—"you'll be into the station this afternoon, won't you, to sign your statement?"

"I will, Detective Constable." She followed him and the PC to the door and held it open. "I'm sorry not to be of more help. I'm afraid I'm one of those people who never looks at her surroundings. My nana says that I could walk by her on the pavement and wouldn't even notice."

Once the door had closed, Clara returned to the sofa, poured out our tea, and set the milk and sugar closer to me.

"Clara, why did you come back here—couldn't the police have talked to you at your nana's?"

"I need to go through Oona's things," she replied, stirring her tea. "She has no family to speak of."

"What will you do with it all?"

But, in truth, I couldn't see much to worry about—the place looked more like a hotel room than a dwelling. Didn't Oona have a real home? Exhibition managers didn't earn rock star wages, but she must've made at least a "comfortable" living at what she did and could afford a little cottage in the Cotswolds. No, on second thought, that wouldn't suit her—a flat on Hampstead Heath, perhaps. But I couldn't recall if she'd listed a permanent address on her CV.

"Clara, about Oona—"

"I'd rather not talk about it, if you don't mind, Hayley." Clara took off her glasses and began cleaning them with the hem of her sweater. "You see, it's rather difficult for me to think about. That anyone would do such a thing—why, it beggars belief." She put the glasses back on and straightened up. "Hayley, could I ask you something?"

"Of course."

"May I stay on—as personal assistant?" When I didn't answer, Clara rushed on. "It's only that I'm sure you won't want to give up on the exhibition—it's such a terribly worthy cause to bring Lady Fowling's life to people today who are clamoring for—and . . . and . . . I would carry on with whatever jobs you give me. I know it's a temporary position, and I wouldn't want to be in the way, but you see, I've told my nana I had this terribly lucky break, and how it would help me find real work and she would be proud of me and I told you that she remembered Lady Fowling and . . ."

At last, Clara had to pause to breathe. I put my hand over hers and found it icy cold. Poor sausage—set adrift in such an awful way.

"Yes, you can stay on. We are determined to continue with the exhibition, and so of course we will need help no matter who is in the lead as manager."

"Oh." Clara's face flushed a rose red. "Oh, thank you so much. Does that mean you've hired someone already?"

"I'm working on it. So, why don't we schedule you for two days a week—I wouldn't want you to spend every day traveling to and from Shepton Mallet."

"I won't need to—I'll be staying here. Oona got this flat on a five-month let, and it's all paid up."

"Five months?" Maybe Oona didn't have a real home at all—perhaps she was one of those people who constantly hopped round the country. It would suit her work.

"Are you settled in?" My gaze went to the single bedroom, and Clara's followed.

"I'm not sleeping in Oona's bed," she said, as if Oona still laid claim to the space. "No, there's plenty of room—

my bed is just there." She nodded to an alcove in the pass-through between the bedroom, bathroom, and kitchen.

"Is that a camp bed?"

"It's quite cozy," she said.

The sofa looked more comfortable. "Well, if you're certain you're all right here, then, that's sorted, isn't it?" I asked. "But you'll go home to your nana for the weekends, won't you? I'd hate to think of you knocking round this place just waiting for work to begin on Monday." And it would save me worrying about her.

Before I left, Clara gave me her new mobile number, and I promised to update her on our schedule. Then I marched off to find Zeno Berryfield, fretting along the way. Would he think a ready-made PA a benefit to accepting the job as manager, or would he be unwilling to take someone else's leftovers? And if so, what would I do with her? The First Edition Society didn't need a full-time PA.

I paused in the middle of the Parade grounds to ring Zeno, and he picked up in one.

"Ms. Burke"—he sounded breathless, and I could hear traffic behind him—"what a surprise. How may I be of service?"

"Mr. Berryfield, I'd like to have a word. Are you at your desk today?"

"I am, for my sins." He chuckled. "I'm catching up on several proposals that have come to me recently. The director of"—on his end, the sound of a bus rumbled over his next words—"is particularly waiting for me to respond."

"Oh, well then—I wouldn't want to take up your valuable time."

"Not at all, it will be a delight to see you again. Shall we say, fifteen minutes?"

That's the time it would take me to reach James Street West—I looked at the people around me just to make sure he wasn't among them. Over the phone connection, I heard a horn. At his desk? I didn't think so.

"Yes, perfect." Next, I rang Val. "Zeno in fifteen—can you make it?"

"I can't. It's what I get for showing my face on campus. I've been asked—seeing as I'm not out of town—if I could take a meeting on student numbers this afternoon. The implication being if I want the college to stay firm with the exhibition, I need to give something back. Can we wait until Monday for Berryfield?"

"No, I'll be fine."

I rang off before he could detect the gaping holes in my confidence.

10

Zeno Berryfield came out on the first-floor landing to meet me. He wore his teal suit—the uniform of Make an Exhibition of Yourself!—and looked unruffled, as if he'd been beavering away at his desk all morning and not wandering the city. He took me to a dark corner of the vast room of hot-deskers and, once again, left me standing while he scared up a chair.

"Well, now, Ms. Burke." He took his black satchel and dropped it on the floor, then placed forearms on the desk. Leaning forward, hands clasped, with what looked like a smug smile on his face, he continued. "How are all the preparations for your First Edition library event proceeding? Had enough of Oona yet?"

"I didn't realize you knew Oona had taken the job."

"Come now," he said. "Do you think she would pass up the opportunity to crow through her social-media outlets? Exhibition management is a small field populated by a group of people who all know each other and keep an eagle eye on the pulse of the profession."

I ignored his mixed metaphor, because it occurred to me at that moment I'd have to give him the news of Oona's death before I offered him the position. My mind had deftly leapt over that necessity, and it caused me to stumble.

"I'm sorry to have to tell you, but—" I glanced round the vast room. Even though the desks near us sat empty, I lowered my voice. "Oona is dead."

Zeno stared at me blankly for a moment. "What—what do you mean, dead?"

"Dead, Mr. Berryfield. Oona died yesterday afternoon, quite suddenly and under suspicious circumstances." What a useful phrase—helping me to avoid repeating the word *murder* ad nauseam.

He frowned and cocked his head as if trying to get the words straight. "She . . . are you certain this isn't a publicity stunt, Ms. Burke? Because I can tell you firsthand that if you think my schemes for immersive events are out there, they are nothing compared with what Oona can conjure up."

"This is not a publicity stunt! I saw her myself. It looks as if she were pushed down a set of stairs and . . . and I can tell you the police are involved and an enquiry has begun."

"Well, blow me down."

"Yes," I agreed, "it's an awful thing. Oona had already begun planning the exhibition—well, of course, if you knew her, you would know what a dedicated worker she was."

I remembered Oona and Clara sharing a laugh over Zeno, and so thought I might be on thin ice trying to imagine a friendship of any sort.

"The thing is, Mr. Berryfield, as dreadful as Oona's death is—and let me say again, the police are working diligently and I'm sure are close to finding the responsible party—we at the First Edition Society plan for the event to go on as scheduled. And, to that end"—I cleared my throat of nothing—"I am here to ask if you would be interested in stepping in as manager."

There was a pause—a silence as thick as treacle—before

Berryfield said, "Are . . . you . . . mad? Do you actually believe I'd want to step into that dog's breakfast? How many people has Oona riled already? How many has she treated as if they were serfs and she their feudal lord? Take over from Oona? I have my reputation to consider, Ms. Burke. I'm sorry for you, but not so sorry that I'd try to clean up the mess you've got yourself into." He ended with a snort. "Do me a favor."

Thusly turfed out, I stood on the pavement in shock at both Zeno Berryfield's reaction to Oona's death and to my offer. I had doubted his bravado about other work coming in, but it seems I had been wrong—he didn't need the job as the First Edition Society's exhibition manager. Now what were we to do?

My mind felt as ransacked as Oona's office, and without a single coherent thought to be had, I retreated to my only refuge—the café at Waitrose. I trudged up the stairs with heavy feet, joined the queue, and when I reached the till, ordered the first thing I saw on the menu board and took a seat. When the server brought a plate of poached salmon and broad-bean salad to my table, I asked, "Is this mine?"

Apparently it was.

While I ate, I moved to the next item on my list and sent Adele a text.

Let's meet when you're through with your day.

Five minutes later, a reply came.

Aren't you in Woolacombe?

Oops.

No. Will explain later.

Her next text came swiftly.

Raven at five. You'd better have a good excuse.

Yes, I had a fine excuse.

When I had chased the last few broad beans across my plate, I left.

Mrs. Woolgar had returned to Middlebank. I could hear voices coming from her office as I stood in the entry— the Society's solicitor, Duncan Rennie, was with her. As my hands were full of shopping bags—before leaving Waitrose, I'd remembered I was short on everything—I pushed the front door closed with my bottom. Time to face the music.

When they saw me, the solicitor stood, but the secretary remained seated behind her desk.

"Hello," I said, standing in the office doorway. "Mrs. Woolgar, I'm sorry you've returned to such news."

She nodded, her mouth a thin line. "Do you have further details?"

"Please, Ms. Burke," Duncan said, gesturing to the chair, "do sit down."

"No, thank you, Mr. Rennie. I only wanted to explain further to Mrs. Woolgar."

I tried, but my explanation sounded like a load of nothing even in my own ears. I ended with, "It's . . . it's dreadful what happened to Oona, and it isn't that I believe we can be all 'business as usual,' but I do feel we must carry on and so I've revived my search for a manager. We should not let go of the dates at the Charlotte. I feel sure we can find someone to fill the role. Clara Powell, Oona's personal assistant, has offered to stay on."

Mrs. Woolgar gave a faint nod. "Perhaps she has insight into what Ms. Atherton expected to create for the exhibition."

A thin glimmer of hope shone in the distance. "So, you agree that we should continue?"

"I do," Mrs. Woolgar said. "I'm sure the board will feel the same. Even though we had only a glimpse of Ms. Atherton's vision, I believe we could see what was possible."

I had expected more of a fight, yet here was Mrs. Woolgar agreeing with me. Then the penny dropped. The secretary was not putting her trust in me, but in our deceased exhibition manager's incredible ability to capture people's imagination. The Oona Effect continued beyond death.

"Good, that's good. Thank you." How petty of me to be upset at the very outcome I had wanted. "Have you spoken to the board members?" I asked.

"Mrs. Arbuthnot has been informed."

Yes, of course she has.

"And Ms. Frost—just before she left for a short holiday."

All right for some.

"The Moons?" I asked.

"I'm sure Mrs. Sylvia and Mrs. Audrey Moon will be receptive to you."

At least she left me the easy ones. "And I'll explain to Adele, too."

"That's settled, then, isn't it?" Duncan asked with a relieved smile. "Ms. Burke, ten cartons of the rare books will be delivered this afternoon. Would you like me to stay?"

"No, thank you, Mr. Rennie. I'll have them taken up to the library and begin the search."

"I'm sure you'll run across it. This is quite a prize that you've discovered," he said.

Yes, but was it worth a life?

I paused, the shopping bags growing heavier by the second. "Oh, and Mrs. Woolgar—I won't be going away for the weekend after all."

* * *

The afternoon took care of itself. I had a brief, but compassionate, phone conversation with Audrey and Sylvia Moon, who comforted me with "She was so full of life, wasn't she?" I exchanged texts with Val to catch him up while I unpacked one small carton at a time on the large library table, looking for the elusive treasure.

The books had been packed away well—each wrapped in acid-free tissue paper, not too many per carton, and all lying flat so as not to break the spines. These first editions had been published beginning in the 1920s—well before Lady Fowling had started collecting—and many included an inscription to the original owners. *Happy birthday, nephew! . . . A Christie for Christmas . . . Albert Campion to the rescue!*

Halfway through the second carton, my heart thumped in my chest when I spotted a yellow dust jacket that read *Murder Must Advertise*. The book had all the signs of a Dorothy L. Sayers first edition from her publisher, Victor Gollancz—bold Art Deco–style font, none of the artwork that decorates books today. But, although a first edition, it was unsigned. I took it out onto the landing and held it up to Lady Fowling's portrait.

"So, not this one. But it's somewhere, isn't it? Oona thought she knew, although she never got the chance to tell me."

Lady Fowling regarded me from her painting, and her brown eyes seemed to flash with a knowing gleam. *Keep looking.*

"What if it isn't in one of these cartons?" I asked. I paused and—as if I'd heard her counter with a question of her own—added, "No, I haven't read to the end of the book yet, but I will. I was busy last evening."

Oona found the clue. You will find it.

"Ms. Burke?"

I dashed to the railing and called down. "Yes, Mrs. Woolgar?"

"Did you need something?"

"No, thank you. I was only . . ."

Better not finish that sentence.

By five o'clock, I had changed clothes and stood on the pavement outside the Raven, looking up Quiet Street and waiting for Adele. But she caught me out by coming from the other way.

"You'd better have a good excuse for not going to the seaside," she said by way of greeting. "Is Val all right?"

My mind took a swift turn away from murder and back to the previous evening—the good part of it. The best. I took a sharp breath and focused.

"Fine, yes, it's only that something's happened. Let's go upstairs and get our drinks."

Adele squinted at me out of the corner of her eye. "What is it, Hayley? Oona hasn't run off, has she?"

"Oona is dead." Too abrupt, but I couldn't stop it from popping out. I should get cards printed up and hand them out to all and sundry. *I regret to inform you that . . .*

Adele's face paled, setting off her wild red curls, and emphasizing her Celtic-goddess look.

"What? How?"

She wouldn't move until I explained. I kept it brief so that we could get indoors before she sank to the ground. Once finished, I took her arm. "Now—come on."

Upstairs, I left Adele in our usual corner and bought a bottle of red at the bar. I asked for three glasses, although I had a feeling Val might need to buy a second bottle by the time he arrived.

Adele took a sizable gulp of wine and then peppered me with questions, which I fielded as best I could, ending with "Clara's a trouper. She wants to stay on and she's eager to learn, but it's obvious this is tough on her."

"And you think the murderer is someone who wants the book?"

"Possibly. What else?"

I splashed a bit more wine into our glasses and cut my eyes at Adele. "You haven't told me about you and Oona."

"Are you thinking I'm a suspect?" she blurted out.

"Adele!"

"Do your police contacts want to question me under caution or something?"

"You know that isn't what I meant."

"Good thing I have school as an alibi, isn't it?" she asked hotly. "And Suffragette Club after. There's CCTV all over school—I'd be easy to spot."

I crossed my arms and leaned back against the bench. "Yes, well, lucky break for you. We'll tick you off the suspect list, then, shall we?"

She sucked in a breath and let it out like a kettle, then offered a sad smile.

"Sorry," she said. "It's just a shock to think of someone with such a strong life force suddenly gone." I waited for her to continue, and finally, with a sigh, she added, "The difficult thing to remember about one-night stands is that most of the time they should be regarded as just that."

"The exhibition was five years ago," I said. "You never heard from her again?"

"No, and really, just as well, don't you think?"

"Yes, I certainly do." I couldn't imagine Adele and Oona as a couple. "So, will you explain it to Pauline?"

"Pauline's heard about Oona—well, apart from this. She's heard about mine—and I hers. We decided warts and all would be the best way to proceed."

"Sounds serious."

This time her smile was not sad. I gave her a kiss on the cheek. "Good on you, girl. And to think I can say that I introduced the two of you."

Adele laughed. "Just because we met on your doorstep. But I'm sorry about Oona—and sorry you had to cancel your weekend."

Val appeared at the top of the stairs and paused to give me a smile, and I could feel its warmth across the room. I leaned my head toward Adele and murmured, "We didn't cancel everything."

Two pies—one steak and ale, one chicken and ham—and a plate of sausage and mash. And that second bottle of wine. We pretty much solved the problems of the world, the three of us, although we didn't solve Oona's murder. That was, after all, the job of the police.

"I'm glad for you that Glynis took it so well," Adele said as we stood, stretched, and reached for our coats.

"It has nothing to do with me, it's only that Mrs. Woolgar and the entire board were so taken with Oona."

"Don't underestimate yourself," Val said.

"Never—I can move mountains," I said. "I wonder—if I shifted the Mendip Hills a few hundred miles, would that impress Mrs. Woolgar as much as Oona did?"

"You'll let me know when you need help?" Adele asked as we headed downstairs. "Listen, Hayley—you wouldn't want to be the exhibition manager, would you?"

"Not my job," I replied.

"Well, it had better be someone's."

Once we were on the pavement, Adele walked off in the direction of the Minerva—where Pauline was behind the bar—and Val wrapped his arms round me.

"Say . . ." I paused, and our breath came out in puffs as if we were steam-train locomotives. "Why don't you go back to your place and pack a few things and come to mine."

He grinned. "I . . . er . . . didn't want to presume, but as it turns out, I have a bag in the boot of my car."

I threw my arms round his neck. "Good—we'll have the most important part of our seaside weekend—each other."

"I tell you what," he said, and I saw a sparkle in his eyes. "You get out your pail and shovel and I'll have a load of builder's sand delivered to Middlebank. We'll spread it all over the entry."

"Better not—I don't want to give Bunter any ideas."

When I stepped out of the shower the next morning, Val was on his phone.

"Yeah, love, of course . . . No, it'll be perfect . . . No, this doesn't really have to do with us—with Hayley or me. It's a police matter . . . Hardly—I met her only once or twice . . . Right, give your gran my love, and we'll see you and your sister tomorrow. Cheers."

"Tomorrow?" I asked, toweling my hair.

"Tomorrow," he confirmed. "Dinner. Is that all right?"

Meet the Daughters Evening. "Of course—perfect." But my voice had jumped an octave.

"Come on," Val said, guiding me into the kitchen. "You look like you could use a cup of tea. I know I could."

"I'm delighted they're coming and that we'll finally meet," I said, splashing milk into my mug. "I really am. You know that, don't you? It's only that . . . I want to make a good impression."

"They'll love you. There wasn't a problem with Dinah, was there?"

"We didn't have time to be nervous," I reminded him. "She surprised us."

Val laughed. We sat at the table, and a sudden chill came over me. I held my tea close and contemplated what was to come. Dinah had taken to Val immediately—because he was kind and she could see how much I cared for him, and because she was a daughter meeting the new man in her mum's life. Mums and daughters were one thing, but dads and daughters something entirely different. Did Val understand that?

His smile faded a bit.

"You aren't worried, are you?" I asked.

"No, of course not," he said in a hurry. "Are you?"

"Certainly not."

"Good, good." He rubbed my arm absentmindedly.

We had the decency to exchange embarrassed smiles, and then began to sort out the details. Dinner at his house, of course—the family home. I would be a guest, not the hostess. Best to take these things slowly.

What did they like to eat?

"Fish fingers?" Val offered. "At least, that's what they liked when they were seven. I don't remember them eating as teenagers."

We settled on roast chicken—at least he knew they weren't vegetarians. At the moment.

After breakfast, Val left to clean his house in anticipation of the following evening's dinner. He lived in a modest but comfortable family home in an aging semidetached south of the river. It had two bedrooms upstairs and, on the ground floor, a small kitchen, the family room—which had been turned into Val's study—and a tiny sitting room that looked out to the back garden. Val mentioned something about getting the strimmer out. A bit extreme, I thought. After all, it was the dead of winter—weren't gardens supposed to be all sticks and brown grass?

Meanwhile, I would be spending the morning at the police station. Before I left my flat, though, I rang my mum to explain about Oona, and in return, received a loving dose of sympathy mixed with *Carry on, Curator*. After that, I told her about dinner with Bess and Becky, and she looked on the sunny side. "They can't help being lovely young women—they have a fine father. Just as you did."

A shrewd move on my mum's part, distracting me like that. My dad had died when I was twelve, but I had fond memories of him, and I now exchanged my worry for pleasant thoughts.

Then she added, "Don't anticipate problems."

Too late.

By the time we'd finished our conversation, I was out the door of Middlebank and headed for Manvers Street. Next, I texted Naomi, who had yet to reply to my previous message.

Confirming our dates. Can we chat?

Please don't write us off.

Sergeant Hopgood put me up in my old stomping grounds, Interview #1, where three fat binders waited for me on the table. He gave me a notepad, pushed the compulsory cup of tea on me, and left. I set the cup on a small table next to the mirror-that-wasn't-really-a-mirror—even I knew that—and opened the first binder. These were the papers that had been scattered about Oona's office. Police hadn't attempted any organizing, but they had inserted each sheet in its own plastic sleeve. My transcriptions of Lady Fowling's notebooks were here as well as Oona's sketches for the exhibition. She had made notes and marks on my work, and although her comments were practically illegible, it pleased me to see that she had read through.

Was it here—in the material from her ladyship's notebooks—that Oona came across the key to the location of the rare book? I stared hard at each page, hoping to decipher her marks. Words were circled, paragraphs boxed, and loopy pen doodles adorned many margins.

Wait. Loopy doodles that looked like . . . a spiral staircase. Yes—some of them even had lines with knobs on the ends, just like the iron newels at the top and bottom. The spiral staircase was the scene of the crime in *Murder Must Advertise*—was she using it as a way of marking clues without knowing she foreshadowed her own death? I shivered at the thought.

But try as I might, I could not see a pattern or clue. Oona's loopy doodles appeared random—next to a poem Lady Fowling titled "Ode to Bunter," and running alongside her ladyship's shopping list for a dinner party in the winter of 1955.

Then it struck me. There was no significance in the loops—it looked as if Oona's pen had been running dry and she had scribbled in the margins trying to get it going again.

I turned the last page in the third binder—Lady Fowling's jottings about her own detective, François Flambeaux, uncovering a plot to steal the Rosetta stone—and I slumped in my chair. It had just gone two o'clock. I stuck my head out the door of the interview room, caught the nearest uniform, and asked for Sergeant Hopgood.

When he appeared, I said, "I'm missing something—I must be. Let me go through them again. It's only, just now I need a break."

"Right you are, Ms. Burke—let's leave it until Monday, shall we? Now, about this Mr. Moyle." Hopgood's eyebrows lifted. "He has form."

"He's stolen rare books before?"

"No, it was a punch-up at a car-boot sale in Melksham two years ago—not even over a sale, but an argument about the author of a 1954 book called *The Detective's Companion*. Still, we are trying to get in touch with him now to have a few words about Ms. Atherton."

"Can't you look at CCTV to find out who went in and out of the Charlotte?"

"Would that we could," Hopgood replied. "But there are no cameras on that side of the building. The closest are over

the road at the Assembly Rooms—pointed the wrong way—
and further along at the top of the Bartlett Street shops."

"Did Oona's mobile have any . . . vital clues?"

Hopgood's eyebrows did a little dance before he said,
"All work-related calls and texts, it appears. Apart from
that last call Ms. Powell made. No, for this enquiry, what
we need are eyewitness accounts of comings and goings.
I've sent out a team to doorstep up and down the road."

There had been a mob of people watching police arrive
Thursday afternoon—after Clara had found Oona and
phoned—but they were mere passersby after the fact.
Would police also try to find every one of them? What a
job.

I cut over to Marks & Spencer, ducked in, and walked out
eating a sandwich. I paused in Quiet Street to finish the
last bite and ring my daughter, expecting to leave a message. Miraculously, she answered.

"Dinah, sweetie, how are you?"

"Mum, Gran phoned earlier and told me about your exhibition manager—how creepy the way she died. Are you
involved? Will the police let you solve the case again?"

"Let's not get carried away—I did not solve anything, and
I'm an innocent bystander here. I only wanted to tell you I'm
all right. We'll let the police sort this out—I have enough to
do. But it was lovely of your gran to ring, wasn't it?"

"Yeah, Mum. She's a grand gran."

I picked up a tone in her voice. "Is there someone with
you, Dinah? Am I disturbing?"

"You're not disturbing," she said in a rush. "It's only
Dad—he popped by this morning."

"Did he?" I did my best to keep the acid out of my voice.
"And he's there now?"

"He is. We went out for breakfast—we had a lovely time.

He'd heard of this new place in Sheffield that some posh London chef had opened, and he thought it would be great to try out."

I gritted my teeth—I'd wager a pound to a penny it was Dinah who had paid for that expensive meal and not my ex. Roger was awfully good at spending other people's money.

"Sounds like a perfect Saturday morning."

"Mum, do you know what Dad said?"

I steeled myself. Over the years I'd learned to take that phrase of hers as a warning Roger had come up with another of his mostly useless and often expensive—for me—ideas. Dinah loved her dad, and I would not stand in the way of that—he did have many good qualities, although I'd be hard-pressed to rattle off a list on the spot. But she recognized his shortcomings, too. These days, she used *Do you know what Dad said?* as a signal.

"No, sweetie, what did he say?"

"That he and one of his mates could upgrade the electrics here and save my housemate and me loads of money."

Even ignoring the fact that Dinah and her friend only rented the house, this was still an incredibly bad idea—what did Roger know about electrics? Nothing. "Sweetie, would you put your dad on the phone," I suggested mildly, saving my ire for its proper target.

"Dad—Mum wants to talk with you."

I heard Roger's voice. "Why don't you put her on speaker so we can all talk?"

Coward. "Sorry, Dinah sweetie, I have to run," I said, temporarily abandoning what I knew would be a futile attempt to ask my ex to act like an adult. "You tell your dad I'll talk with him later. I love you—bye!"

Dropping my phone in my bag, I came round the corner of the Assembly Rooms, where thirty or so students stood in a mob of a queue, chattering in Spanish. I navigated round them, and when I had a clear view across the road to the Charlotte, I saw a man standing outside the door that led to Oona's office. He had a shaved head and a scarf wrapped round his neck, and—although I couldn't see it from this distance—a tattoo of a stack of books on his neck. Stuart "Bulldog" Moyle.

11

I gasped and jumped back, knocking into the students.

"Sorry, so sorry, very sorry," I said, sinking deeper into their midst. At last hidden from view, I went for my phone, which had disappeared into the depths of my bag. Cursing, I came up with it at last and rang Detective Sergeant Hopgood.

"He's here," I blurted out in a strained whisper when the DS answered. "Stuart Moyle. Bulldog is here."

"Where are you, Ms. Burke?"

"I'm at the Assembly Rooms, and he's across the road at the Charlotte—in front of the door that leads up to Oona's office. Just standing there looking at his phone!"

My protective coating of Spanish students began to disappear as they filed in, and I leaned up against the wall of the entry for cover, straining to listen for Hopgood's reply. After a muffled exchange, he said, "Ms. Burke, please do not approach him. Stay out of sight, and let us take care of this."

Relief washed over me. "Yes, yes, good. Thank you. I

won't move." I didn't think I could. My hands were shaking—
my entire body was shaking. It was over—the police would
scoop up Moyle, find the evidence they needed that he was
the one who had murdered Oona, and we could all get on
with our business. I clicked my tongue at him. All this for a
book? Murder must never be a means to an end. Murder
must . . .

I was too full of nervous energy, and my curiosity got the
better of me. I eased my head round the corner and peered
across the road just in time for an open-top tour bus to pull
up and block my view. People got off, people got on, and
the bus departed. When the new tourists had drifted away,
the street was empty—including the pavement in front
of the Charlotte.

Empty. Where was he? Where had Stuart "Bulldog" Moyle
gone? I eased forward along the building until I reached the
corner so that I could look to my right—in the direction of
Lansdown Road—then left toward the Circus, and again
straight ahead up the road that had no CCTV.

Only after I was certain no one lay in wait did I make
my way across the road. The blue-and-white tape was gone
from the door, and so I assumed the police had finished
searching inside. Now what?

Moyle had gone. Now I would need to convince the police I truly had seen him, and they would probably search
the entire area. Sighing, I resigned myself to wait, and while
I did so, I gazed up at the building as a scene played out in
my mind.

On Thursday afternoon, this door had been unlocked.
Someone—Stuart Moyle?—had walked in off the pavement
and climbed the wooden steps to the first-floor landing. He
had paused, listening, and then slowly tiptoed round and
round the spiral staircase until he reached the top. Oona's
door had been open, and he saw her at the desk. But she had
taken no notice of him—too chuffed at having solved the
Murder Must Advertise treasure hunt.

Did he demand the book? Did they argue? Did she brush him off and stride out of her office while tapping out a text to me? He had caught her, knocked her over the head, and thrown her down the stairs. Did he then go back into the office and search for the book? Did he check if she was even alive before he fled? Was he so callous he could take a life only for the benefit of adding one more book to his shelves?

"Ms. Burke?"

I whirled round. Stuart Moyle stood in front of me—and no police in sight.

Murderers return to the scene of the crime—everyone knows that.

"What are you doing here?" I asked, my voice hoarse with fear.

I judged my chances. He wasn't tall, although a bit stocky. Still, I wondered if I could give him a good shove and run for it. Why is no one out on the street? If I called for help, who would hear?

"Appointment."

It took a moment for the word to make sense—and then I noticed the phone in his hand.

"You have an appointment? With whom?"

He glanced down at his phone. "Oona Atherton. The one in charge. Your exhibition. Saw her name online. I rang. She said we'd chat."

"When?" My voice was weak. "When did you make this arrangement?"

"Wednesday." He held out his phone, and I glanced at the text exchange between him and Oona that proved his point. In the distance, I heard a police siren.

I haven't done anything!" Stuart complained as he stood surrounded by police. "I didn't know she was dead until you told me this minute."

"But we have been trying to reach you, Mr. Moyle," Sergeant Hopgood replied mildly. "On a number Mr. Arthur Fish provided, and we have had no luck."

"That isn't my fault. Arthur probably doesn't have my new number. My old phone was stolen, you see, and I lost all my contacts."

An epidemic of lost mobiles. Did Stuart's run away with Clara's? I didn't make this observation aloud—I was trying my best to fade into the solid wall of Bath stone behind me, unnoticed by police and especially by Bulldog.

"Nevertheless," the sergeant said, "now that we have told you what has happened to Ms. Atherton, I'm sure you won't mind coming to the station and answering a few questions for us."

"But I didn't know her." Bulldog eyed the uniforms on either side of him. "I'd never even met her. I'm sorry for what's happened, but it's nothing to do with me. Why would I know anything about her murder when I'd never even met her and we'd only exchanged messages?"

"Well, our chat won't take any time at all, then, will it?" Sergeant Hopgood held open the door of one of the blue-and-yellow-checkered police cars. Moyle shrugged and got in.

"Ms. Burke," Hopgood said, "we'll be in touch." He gave me a nod before getting into his own unmarked car, and I watched as the two vehicles pulled away.

What I thought most notable about Bulldog's encounter with the police was that he spoke in complete sentences. Did fear do that to him? What did we really know about Stuart Moyle? Little—but Arthur Fish, our inaugural literary salon lecturer, knew him. It occurred to me that I needed to give Arthur a ring—to thank him for his lecture, ask about book sales. That sort of thing.

But first, as I was already here—

I walked round the corner into the main entrance of the Charlotte, and one of the watercolorists recognized me. "Looking for Naomi? She's a busy one today."

One flight up to the first floor, Naomi Faber sat in front of her computer with a frown clouding her brow.

I tapped ever so lightly on the doorpost. "Hello. I hope it's no bother that I've popped in."

"No, certainly not, Hayley. I'm terribly sorry I haven't got back to you. Here, sit down." She pulled a chair closer to her desk. "Tea?"

"Ah, no thanks. It's about what's happened—"

"Dreadful," Naomi replied. "But it looks as if the police presence has been confined to the . . . er . . ." She nodded her head in the general direction of Oona's office. "Now, as to your question. There's no problem with continuing as long as you can find a manager—I can't have another exhibition run by committee. I was a fool to let the watercolorists try that on me."

"Yes, we'll certainly have a manager." Just not Oona. Nor Zeno. Who? "And so, I hope you don't mind, but I'll need a new key to the street on our side. Police have kept all of Oona's things as evidence at the moment." Naomi paused long enough for me to worry. "We'll be keeping that door locked from now on."

She nodded and opened a desk drawer that housed a small, built-in combination safe. I looked away as she twirled the dial. When the door popped free, she rummaged through a loose collection of keys, and over the clattering of metal, I added, "Now that I think about it, I'll need two—one for the . . . manager and one for me."

Naomi's hand hovered over the jumble before it dived in and came up with two keys on the same ring and handed them over. There was one thing out of the way.

"Clara Powell came to see me this morning," Naomi said.

"This morning?"

"She, too, seemed quite confident that the exhibition was a go. But I got the impression she was casting herself in the role of manager. Really, Hayley—she's quite young. What sort of experience does she have? You can't expect her to do it all."

"Clara isn't our exhibition manager. She probably gave you that impression because she's eager to get on with things."

"Yes, such enthusiasm," Naomi said, but with a smirk I didn't care for.

"When was it you worked with Oona?" I asked.

That did the trick—the smirk disappeared to be replaced by a hard line and a flushed face.

"A year or so ago. In Plymouth—an exhibition on gin sponsored by a distillery. Oona created one of those living paintings—*tableaux vivants*, they call them—out of Hogarth's *Gin Lane* print. Caused a bit of controversy, but it turned out a huge success."

"But, only a year ago—and yet she didn't remember you?"

Naomi shrugged and turned back to her computer screen. "I was one of many. As a manager in high demand, Oona couldn't keep up with every worker, I'm sure. So, Hayley, you'll let me know if you need a hand with anything. Once you have your own manager in place, of course."

I returned to Middlebank with nothing to show for my day. The dates for the exhibition were safe, but only until Naomi discovered I couldn't find a manager. Could we get one lent to us? I had worked at the Great Western Railway museum in Swindon until Dinah and I moved to Bath eleven years ago—perhaps someone there could help. If anyone remembered me.

No clues had jumped out at me from the binders at the police station. I would need to go through them again. Oona's death had something to do with the signed first edition of *Murder Must Advertise*—didn't it? The book was key, not only to solving Oona's murder, but also to our exhibition's success. A rarity. No—a one-of-a-kind. Oona had found a clue and so I should be able to find it, too.

I worried about Clara. What was she doing in Bath at the weekend when she'd agreed to go back to Shepton Mallet until Monday? She *had* agreed to that, hadn't she?

At Middlebank, I made myself a cup of tea in the kitchenette and took it to my desk. Bunter hunkered down on the arm of the wingback chair and watched me, his radar ears turning this way and that. We were both out of sorts, and eventually I realized what was wrong—it was Saturday and I wasn't meant to be at work. I should've been visiting my mum in Liverpool or—this weekend—away with Val at the seaside. As far as I could see, the only good thing to come from staying put was the chance to meet his daughters, who were due in for dinner in twenty-four hours. I wondered how the housecleaning was progressing.

"Polishing the floors?" I asked when Val answered my call.

"Squirrels," he replied, his voice weary. "I haven't got to the cleaning yet, because I noticed a corner by the window in the girls' room had been gnawed straight through. And only since Christmas. Didn't take them long, the little buggers. I've been plastering."

"Housecleaning tomorrow, then, and I'll help. When you've finished with repairs, come straight over and I'll cook us a meal, and you can have a bath."

"Don't you want a bath, too?" he asked, his voice brightening.

"Oh, so—not as knackered as you're making out to be, is that it?"

I lit a small fire in my office, which Bunter thought a fine idea. He stretched full out, tummy turned to the heat, and I tucked my toes under him and picked up my copy of *Murder Must Advertise*. Still no sign of the murderer in the book. Sayers's sleuth-in-disguise—known as Death Bredon at Pym's Publicity Ltd.—had certain ideas in his head, which he wasn't terribly forthcoming about. I was sure to find out who did it in the end, and so instead of trying to follow his line of thought, I read for enjoyment.

The door buzzed, and to save Mrs. Woolgar dragging up from her lower-ground-floor flat—if she was even home— I put down my book, slipped my toes from under the cat, and padded out to the entry.

I opened the door to Zeno Berryfield in his teal suit, Smarties tie, and high-shine black oxfords. This dapper attire stood in direct contrast to his sagging shoulders and woebegone look.

"Please, Ms. Burke," he said in a rush with his hands up as if to ward off a blow. "You have every right to slam the door in my face, but I beg you, give me one moment to offer an abject apology for my uncalled-for, unprofessional, and unfeeling reaction to your plea for help yesterday."

I had more manners than to slam the door in his face— although it had been my first inclination. But if he wanted to apologize, then I would let him have his say.

"Fine. Come through, Mr. Berryfield."

In my office, Zeno deposited his bag and unbuttoned his jacket as he took in the room. Bunter had retreated to a corner, but now crept forward and sprang to the mantel, where he wrapped his tail round his legs and regarded us with golden eyes.

"Oh, look, a cat," Zeno observed. "And, you've taught him to hold still just like one of those statues—that's a good trick."

"Cats don't do tricks, Mr. Berryfield," I said, gesturing to the wingback chair as I sat at my desk. "Not unless it's their idea."

For a moment, Zeno watched Bunter watch him. Then the man blinked and the cat, having won the staring contest, yawned and licked the back of a paw.

I rested my arms on the desk and with a kind and attentive, but businesslike, look said, "Now."

"Yes, right." Zeno sank into the chair and looked at the floor. With what appeared to be great effort, he raised his gaze and only then did I notice his red-rimmed eyes. "Well, there's nothing else for it, Ms. Burke, but to apologize wholeheartedly for my behavior. It is not usually my way to be caustic or unfeeling. I can only blame my reaction on shock at hearing such horrendous news about Oona. Dead." He sighed. "I still can barely take it in. After all we shared."

Had they jointly managed an exhibition? I didn't see that as likely—not the way Oona had reveled in ordering people around. I remembered her mocking comment about Zeno. Perhaps he had started as her PA.

"Had you and Oona worked together?"

"Worked together?" His dark eyes were vacant. "I suppose you could say we did—and we didn't. Oona was my wife."

12

Your what?"
    A totally inappropriate response on my part, but it burst out before I could stop it. Oona Atherton and Zeno Berryfield married? I couldn't comprehend.

"That is," I rushed on, "I had no idea. You weren't—married—five years ago when Oona put on the exhibition for the Jane Austen Centre. Were you?"

"No . . ." He dragged the word out like a moan. "We met barely three years ago. But, although our life together may have been brief, it was all-consuming." He looked up to the ceiling of my office and waved his arm in an arc. "We were like two bright objects in the sky, colliding in a fiery explosion and burning hot and fierce until we had consumed each other's energy and fell back to earth, mere shells of our former selves."

I tried to imagine Oona devastated by the ending of a relationship—any relationship—and I have to say, I couldn't quite picture it.

"And so, Mr. Berryfield, the two of you are still married—were married—when Oona was killed?"

"No," he said, rolling his shoulder to adjust his jacket. "We divorced six months ago. There was nothing left of us— apart from our physical relationship." He smiled and gave a quick nod. "Never anything wrong in that department."

For a moment, I wondered how I had managed to get into a conversation about Oona's sex life two days in a row, then I shook myself free of all that and said, "Yes, well, I'm sorry for your loss. And thank you for coming to explain. I certainly understand now how the news could've hit you."

"And for me to turn your offer down in such an abrupt manner," Zeno said, as if picking up on a previously unfinished sentence. "*Tsk.* How rude. But I have recovered from my shock, Ms. Burke, and so now I am perfectly capable of having a reasonable conversation about your exhibition— *Lady Fowling: A Life in Words.* A lovely title, I may say— so evocative."

"Are you saying you want the job after all?"

"What I'm saying is"—Berryfield offered a chagrined smile—"in my emotional state yesterday, I may have over-looked your need for a swift and effective solution to your difficulty, and so if you are still seeking to fill the post, please do consider me." He bowed his head.

What an act. Of course he wanted the job—he always had. How much did he want it? It occurred to me that I'd better check on his whereabouts on that particular Thursday afternoon. The police, that is—the police should check on his whereabouts. Would they consider him a suspect? Did I?

Hiring Zeno would solve a few sticky problems on my end—namely, Naomi Faber's insisting we have a manager in order for the Society to keep the exhibition dates at the Charlotte. And, apart from his crazy ideas for displays, Zeno knew the basics of exhibition management, some-thing I needed to learn. I could use him for my own pur-poses. Until Sergeant Hopgood told me otherwise, I saw no reason why I couldn't take advantage of the situation.

"Yes, Mr. Berryfield, we are still looking, and as you

know, time is short—although that doesn't mean I don't have time to check your references. But I do want to make it clear that if you join us, you would be working for me, and I would have the final say on all decisions."

"I would have it no other way, Ms. Burke. Quality is what you seek, and quality you shall have." The gleam returned to his dark eyes, and once again he turned into that friendly man behind the fish counter at Waitrose—both competent and accommodating. "And may I say that you are gaining quite a reputation as curator of the First Edition Society and its library. I hear good things. Heigh-ho!"

No need to overegg the situation, Zeno. "The board will need to be notified," I continued, "but I'll take care of that. And so, barring any unforeseen complications, shall we say you will be here Monday morning at ten?" I shifted papers round my desk as a signal the interview was finished. "Oh, and one more thing. Oona had hired a young woman as her personal assistant. We'll be keeping her on the project."

"A PA?" Zeno asked. "My, my—Oona was flying high, wasn't she?"

As I saw him out, I asked, "Remind me when you arrived in Bath, Mr. Berryfield."

"Oh, a fortnight ago. Three weeks? It's been a whirlwind—one day blending into another as I consider my options."

"Had you seen Oona since you've been here?"

"No." He shook his head, and there was a catch in his voice. "That will be one of my great regrets. Our last parting was full of emotion, of course, but also frustration and a sense of something left undone. If only we'd had one more chance."

There—an exhibition manager. Of sorts. Zeno Berryfield had better beware, though, because I would brook no funny business when it came to this event.

"It was perfectly reasonable of me to ask him if he'd seen Oona," I told Bunter upon returning to my office. The cat had dropped back down to the hearthrug with his back to the dying embers. "Sergeant Hopgood can't accuse me of sticking my nose in where it doesn't belong. I'm hiring Zeno, I should know what he's been up to."

I left myself a reminder to tell Hopgood about Zeno, Arthur Fish about Bulldog, and the entire board about our new exhibition manager, and then gave up for the day.

"Right, cat, I'm quitting work. Mrs. Woolgar will give you your dinner, won't she?"

An ear twitched in response. I took my copy of *Murder Must Advertise* and went up to my flat, where I dropped it on the coffee table, stretched out on the sofa, and promptly fell asleep, waking at six. I stretched, brushed my hair out, and had the minced beef simmering in a tomatoey sauce by the time Val knocked.

I called that it was open, and there he stood in the kitchen, already cleaned up and with a bottle of wine under his arm. The aroma of the spaghetti Bolognese filled my flat, and I saw him hesitate, caught between kissing me or lifting the lid on the saucepan, but—fortunately for him— kissing me won out. He set the wine on the table, drew me close, and pulled up the hem of my loose shirt. He slipped a hand underneath, massaging the small of my back.

"Hello," he whispered. "How was your day?"

His lips, warm and soft, worked their way down my neck, and I could not think of a single thing about my day before the present moment. I reached down and tugged at his belt buckle.

"Oh, you know—this and that. Yours?"

"It was . . . er . . . what?"

So much for good conversation.

Later, as the pasta boiled and we drank wine, I did actually remember details about what I'd been doing, and as Val wasn't really moved to discuss squirrels, I laid out my day.

"Back to the station on Monday," I said. "A second time through those binders should do the trick—there's got to be something there."

"Do you want me to go along? Two pairs of eyes on it?" he asked.

"Not with your Monday," I said. He had classes all day and into the evening on Mondays and Thursdays. Although my entire job was as curator of the First Edition Society, Val already had a full-time job as a writing teacher at Bath College to which he added the Society's projects. The college was happy with the arrangement. Our collaborations were good publicity and cost them little.

"I've got Monday morning well in hand," I told him. "Nine o'clock briefing with Mrs. Woolgar, during which I'll explain I've selected a new exhibition manager. I'll ask her to contact the board—except for Adele, because I can tell her. Tomorrow, I'll text Clara and ask her to arrive at Middlebank at nine thirty. That way, I'll have thirty minutes to go over the situation with her before Zeno arrives at ten. Then, I'll take an hour with the two of them to lay out our timeline and prioritize tasks, after which I'll walk them over to the Charlotte and introduce Naomi. After that, I will hie me to the police station."

"Leave Tuesday's salon to me," Val said. "The retired DCS from the Met. I'll meet her when she arrives that afternoon, get her sorted, and you only need to show up. Right?"

On Sunday, I gave up any thoughts of murder, exhibitions, and my responsibilities as curator of the First Edition library and instead helped Val clean his house. I then left him to dinner preparations and returned to Middlebank, made an apple crumble, and began to worry about the evening to come.

Val and Jill had married young, as had Roger and I. The twins came along after only a year of marriage, and by the time Bess and Becky were nearing five, Jill had become unsettled. After a difficult period, she had left her family behind—husband and daughters—to move north with another man. A few months after that, she had contracted bacterial meningitis and died two weeks later. It had left everything unfinished, and Val had been forced to leap into the breach, giving up his own writing career in order to teach full-time and provide a home for his twin girls.

Twins. Would I be able to tell them apart? I'd seen photos, of course, although the most recent was a year ago Christmas. Bess and Becky had thick dark hair—from their mother, I thought—which they both wore shoulder length, although they had their father's smile that made their eyes crinkle up at the corners. But they were identical. How would it look if I got them mixed up?

We were laying the table when they arrived, bursting in the front door, bringing with them cold air and a great deal of laughter and chatter, and I could see at once that, although identical, they were each their own person.

Their new hairstyles—Bess's bob and Becky's layered cut—would be an easy visual aid, but there were other tangible signs of difference. I could see that Bess possessed that quality of being sure of everything. She gave her dad a hug and a kiss and, upon introduction, offered me a politely confident handshake. It's all right, I didn't mind starting that way. She then drew a bottle of white wine out of her bag and began looking in a drawer for a corkscrew.

Becky's turn. She was just as happy to see her dad and she had a polite greeting for me, but an air of uncertainty hung about her, and she had a slightly softer outline. Her arms were full—she presented Val with two massive leeks pulled from her allotment in Devon and me a pot of snowdrops dug that morning.

"I didn't know if you had a garden where you live," she said.

"Yes, we do, a back garden." Which Mrs. Woolgar maintained, but surely she couldn't object to snowdrops. "I know just the spot for them. They're lovely, thank you."

Under the guise of getting ready for the meal, conversation was easy—easier, at any rate. The weather, the neighbors, the grandparents. The girls would be staying over on a Sunday night, which may have seemed like nothing on the surface, but signaled to me the significance of their visit.

We gathered in the sitting room with glasses of wine. The girls had taken the sofa, and Val and I were in facing armchairs. I asked about their work.

"Mondays are fairly quiet," Bess said. She had charge of the booking office for a hall in Cheltenham that housed the opera, symphony, and theater.

"Your job sounds like a great deal of work, keeping everything straight," I commented.

"It does take a firm hand," Bess said.

"Bess is older by three minutes," Becky pointed out, "and she got all the organizational skills."

"Yes, but you're the creative one," her sister replied, and in only one exchange, I saw that bond, strong as steel, between them. For a fleeting moment, I wished Dinah had had a sister. Not a twin, though—I don't think I could've managed that.

"Your work is wonderful, Becky," I said. "Those beets look quite real."

Becky, who lived in Devon close to her grandparents, painted and taught art. Val displayed his daughter's work proudly—beets, cauliflower, aubergine, and broccoli hung up the staircase, and a large, heavily framed picture of a bunch of carrots took pride of place in the entry.

"Dad's got my entire veg series," Becky said. "I'm beginning an experimental stage now—using saturated color blocks for landscapes."

"Hayley, is your job dangerous?"

Bess's question—offered politely—sliced through the conversation. I noticed Becky drop her gaze.

"Not terribly," I replied, and attempted a smile.

"It's only . . . that woman was killed, and she was working for you."

"Yes, and that was dreadful. But it didn't happen at Middlebank."

"Not this time," Bess said.

Val stirred, but I jumped in before he could say anything.

"I work with books and they are hardly dangerous. We do have a ladder in the library, but it's only three steps and I'm unlikely to fall off." Unbidden, my mind went to Clara and her fear of heights. Was she still here in Bath?

"Do you think she was murdered?"

"Bess!" Val said.

"I'm sorry she's dead," I said, and had to take a breath before continuing. "But I really do not know the details—it's a police matter now."

"Such a lot of things go through your mind when someone dies, don't you think?" Becky asked, at last looking up from her wineglass. "When it's someone you know, I mean."

Bess twitched an eyebrow at her sister, leading me to believe Becky wasn't following the script. Becky's gaze returned to her wine, Val gave Bess a warning look, and I saw that I would need to stay on my toes for the rest of the evening.

But the meal turned out to be a pleasant affair, making me hope I'd managed to clear the evening's only hurdle. At the table, Val told stories about the girls, who laughed and blushed and said, "Oh, Dad, we were only ten, what did you expect?" I offered tales of Dinah growing up, and Val told them about our first official date. He'd taken me to the seaside in November, and I'd spent so long poking round in the tide pools, my fingers were numb with cold and I couldn't hold my hot chocolate. He didn't mention he'd sacrificed his own warmth and let me slip my hands in under his shirt. I glowed with the memory.

Becky asked me to name my favorite mystery writer. I knew it was an innocent question, but it struck a nerve, reminding me that as curator of a library full of detective stories, I should know more than I did. I began hemming and hawing, when Val came to the rescue.

"Lady Fowling painted the Golden Age of Mystery with a broad brush," he said to the girls as if he were lecturing a class. "For example, she included Daphne du Maurier, who is usually put on the romantic suspense list. But I think she's a good addition."

"Yes, her ladyship championed women writers," I said, relieved for the few extra seconds to think. "And she was a writer herself—her detective was named François Flambeaux. There are so many choices, I'm not sure I can think of a favorite."

"How does a detective decide who the suspects are?" Becky asked.

"Well, there's motive, of course," I said. *Who were the suspects in Oona's death—who had a motive?*

"And opportunity," Val said. *Yes—did all the suspects have an alibi?*

"And method," I popped in, realizing I did know something. "Agatha Christie was awfully fond of poisons."

"Is that how your friend died?" Becky asked.

"No, it was a violent death."

The conversation had taken a turn I didn't like. Perhaps neither did Bess, because she had risen from the table during the last exchange and now called out from the kitchen, "Is there ice cream? Wouldn't it be lovely to have ice cream with the crumble?"

"Sorry, love—" Val began.

"That was my job," I said. "Shall I pop out and get a tub?"

"No, you don't need to do that," Bess said, reappearing in the doorway. "Dad'll go—won't you?"

"Ice cream?" Val asked.

"Just down to the shop. Won't take you two ticks," Bess said.

"I will, sure, although it'll take me more than—" He rose and started for the door, then stopped and said to me, "Fancy a walk?"

"No, I think I'll stay here. You go on." Because I felt certain that ice cream was not Bess's actual reason for sending her dad out on a cold January night.

His eyes flickered from daughter to daughter to me, and I believe he cottoned on. "Sure?"

"Yeah," I said, and gave him what I hoped resembled a reassuring smile. "I'm fine."

Val left and the three of us cleared the table, after which we took our wineglasses—almost empty—into the sitting room.

"What else do you have in your allotment, Becky?" I asked.

She had been watching her sister and, at my question, blinked.

"Oh, er, only cabbages and leeks now. I had half of it in a cover crop for the winter, giving it a rest, and so end of March, I'll—"

"How do you think Dad's doing, Hayley?" Bess cut in. She leaned forward, hands clasped, elbows on her thighs. "It's only that we worry about him."

"He seems to be doing fine," I said evenly.

"He takes on too much, doesn't he, Becky? Always has." Becky nodded. "But he seems really happy, Bess."

"He brought us up on his own, you know—since our mum died. I suppose he's told you about that."

"Yes, he told me."

Bess's eyes scanned the tabletops in the room—a cursory search. "Has he taken all her photos down?"

To my annoyance, I felt myself going red. I knew the implication here—Bess was accusing me of wiping the memory of their mother from the house.

"Have you seen her photo?" Bess asked me. "Becky, do you have one to show Hayley?"

Becky reached over to her jute bag and brought out a snapshot in a heavy metal frame—not exactly the thing one carries around all the time. She held it out to me, and I dutifully took it.

Jill looked disheveled but happy, as she sat on the same sofa I sat on now. She had a toddler in each arm, and it looked as if both girls were kicking their legs out in all directions against their confinement.

"How lovely," I said, softening toward the girls. This was all they had of their mother, I told myself, and so why wouldn't they be extra careful about what happened to their dad?

Also, the photo reminded me of Dinah at that age. I could still feel her resistance against being held and remembered her overwhelming desire to be free. "How old were you—eighteen months?"

Bess's smooth demeanor faltered. "Yes, that's about right. The thing is, Hayley, Dad can be so trusting, and Becky and I have learned we need to look out for him. We don't want him disappointed."

"He seems really happy," Becky said again, as if her sister would hear it the second time.

"That's not the point," Bess replied sharply. She went no further. The front door opened, and she snatched the framed photo from me and stuffed it back into Becky's bag a second before Val appeared, holding up a tub of ice cream.

"Right," he said, panting slightly. "Who's for pudding?"

13

As Val drove me back, I chatted about the dinner and the girls' jobs. I admired my pot of snowdrops and fiddled with the heater. Val stayed quiet until he'd pulled up in front of Middlebank, switched off the engine, and turned to me.

"How was it? When I was out?"

"Fine," I said. Not fine—but not his responsibility, either.

"Did she keep it up—Bess?"

I took his hands. "They want you to be happy."

"Oh God, she did. The two of them? I'm sorry."

"Nonsense, there's nothing to apologize for."

"This is down to Bess, and where she goes, Becky follows—it's always been that way. The older sister. How can three minutes make so much difference? Well, I'm going to have a talk with them."

"You will do no such thing," I said firmly.

"I *will*. They're my daughters, and they know how to behave. They know better than this."

"Ah," I said lightheartedly. "Did it end badly the last time they tried?"

He blushed and started to speak and exhaled and inhaled, squeezed my hands, and started again. "They really were girls then, and I let it go, because it didn't matter. But this time, it does."

He locked his green eyes on me and I thought, well, there it is—as close as we'd come to acknowledging what was between us. It was enough for now. I cupped his face in my hands and brushed his lips with mine.

"Do you think I'm going to let Bess and Becky scare me away?"

"God, I hope not."

"You're going to have to let go of this," I said. "I know you want to make everything right for everyone. It's what you've spent your life doing for your daughters—trying to make up for them losing their mum." *To the exclusion of your own life.* "But this time, it's out of your hands. Bess, Becky, and I will sort this out ourselves. All right?"

Val responded with half a nod. I hoped that I sounded more confident than I felt.

Y ou have reached Timeless Productions." The man's voice on the outgoing message had a touch of cockney blending into what was known as an Estuary English accent. "Looking for a company to showcase your dreams? You've come to the right place, but at the moment, we are away with the fairies"—a chuckle—"so go on, you know what to do."

I left a message for this last of the three references Zeno Berryfield had provided. Did no one work on a Monday morning? Checking the time, I realized it was just as well no one answered, because the rest of my day was about to begin. I headed into the secretary's office for our morning briefing with one goal—for Mrs. Woolgar to approve of our new hire. Or, at the least, to keep her reservations to a minimum.

She remained silent through my explanation. "And so, you see," I said, wrapping it up, "it really was our only option. Not that Zeno is a bad option—I'm making quite sure of that. I've got calls into the references he gave me, and when I hear back from them, if what they say causes me any alarm, I will pull the plug on the offer."

I sat with my hands in my lap in the chair across the desk from the secretary, whose large glasses did, as always, a fine job of disguising her feelings.

"Do you believe that his association with Ms. Atherton"—I'd been vague about that, sticking only to the professional side of their relationship—"was a benefit to Mr. Berryfield's work? Will he be able to carry on as she had begun?"

There it was again—the Oona Effect.

"We have her notes, and we have her notes on my notes. And her sketches. They will guide us as we go along."

Oona's notes on my notes—her scribblings on the transcriptions of Lady Fowling's writings—were why I had to go back into the police station instead of just reading over the files on my own computer.

"Will Ms. Powell be of any help?" Mrs. Woolgar asked.

"I'd say she will," I said, cautiously optimistic about how our morning briefing was proceeding. I stole a glance at the time. Nine twenty—only ten minutes until Clara arrived. "And so, here's what I plan to do."

By the time the front door buzzed eight minutes later, Mrs. Woolgar had agreed to contact the board and our solicitor, Duncan Rennie, with the news and ask them to tea that afternoon. The load on my shoulders lightened, to be replaced with the job of buying tea cakes and a new bottle of sherry.

"When he arrives, I'll be sure to bring Zeno in for introductions." I pulled the secretary's door closed and went to answer the buzzer.

Clara, back in her Oona-style suit with hair in a tidy bun, looked ever so put together, down to her large glasses, which perfectly framed her bright eyes. She blinked hesitantly, her tablet tucked under an arm. She should've been wearing a coat—it was too cold for a suit jacket only.

"Hello, Hayley. Good morning."

"Good morning, Clara, do come in. You must be freezing."

As she prepared to enter, two uniformed police officers strolled by.

"Oh, hello," I said, remembering Sergeant Hopgood's promise of a foot patrol. "Good morning."

Clara glanced over her shoulder, saw the police, and scurried over the threshold.

The uniforms nodded and continued on their way, and I closed the door against the cold.

"Go through to my office, Clara. We have a great deal to talk about. I have what I hope will be good news."

"Yes, all right." She hurried before me and perched on the edge of the wingback chair, her back straight as a rod.

I settled at my desk. "How are you, Clara?"

"I'm fine, Hayley. How are you?"

Not exactly what I meant. "I'm fine. Clara, where did you spend your weekend? Did you go back to your nana's in Shepton Mallet?"

Clara hesitated, her lips forming a word that might've started with the letter *w*. Nothing came out for a moment, until she coughed slightly.

"Well, you see, my nana thinks I have my accommodation all sorted here in Bath. I may have implied it had been arranged for me as part of my pay package. At this point, I thought it best not to confuse her. And there is Oona's flat, you see. All paid up. I have the receipt." She leaned forward. "You don't mind, do you, Hayley? That I'm staying there?"

"No, certainly not. Why would I mind? It's only that I was worried about you being alone."

"Oh, I can take care of myself," Clara said with a sharp nod. "And I wanted to be ready for my first morning—I was so very happy to get your text about getting back to work on the exhibition today."

"My text," I repeated. The words jogged my memory. "That reminds me; any sign of the phone you lost?"

Her face went blank.

"Clara?"

"I lost my phone," she said.

"Yes, it's just that I thought it might've turned up. You know how they do—you think something's gone for good, and then there it is under the sofa cushion or in a shoe, and you wonder how it got there."

"In my shoe?" she asked.

"Never mind." I had wanted to ask her about visiting Naomi, but our time was running short. I would bring that up later. "Well, on to my news. I wanted to let you know that we have hired a manager, at least on a trial basis. Let me explain—"

Buzz. What—the front door? It can't be Zeno. Please don't be Zeno. Not yet.

Mrs. Woolgar came out of her office and reached the front door just ahead of me. She opened it, and took a step back when she saw Zeno wearing a coat so thick with fleece, it looked as if he might've pulled the entire sheep on over his suit.

"Hello, good morning." He beamed at the secretary. "I am Zeno Berryfield, the exhibition manager for your upcoming event. And I believe you must be Glynis Woolgar—am I right? Lady Fowling's longtime friend and associate?"

Had I mentioned Mrs. Woolgar to Zeno? I didn't think so, but then it couldn't be difficult to glean the information from the Society's website.

"Good morning, Zeno," I said. "Please do come in." I introduced the two, and Zeno took Mrs. Woolgar's hand, which she took back again fairly quickly.

"Pleased to meet you, Mr. Berryfield," she said. "I won't keep you now, as I'm sure you and Ms. Burke have a great deal to do this morning. However, I do need to tell you, Ms. Burke, about Mr. Berryfield's tea with the board. Maureen Frost is booked for this afternoon, and Mr. Rennie would have to shift his schedule to attend. Shall we proceed with the others?"

"No, Mrs. Woolgar, I wouldn't want to . . ." *Have to go through the whole thing twice.* "We could try for tomorrow afternoon. No, wait, we have the literary salon tomorrow evening."

"God, I love a good literary salon," Zeno said with enthusiasm. "I quite admire your lineup for the season. Is this the one with Margaret Raines from the Met?"

"Yes, well, of course you are invited," I said, wishing Zeno would be quiet so I could think. No, wait, perhaps I'd just spoken the solution. "I tell you what, Mrs. Woolgar—the board arrives early to meet our lecturer for the evening, why not use the time to have them meet Zeno as well? Over a glass of sherry."

"Yes, fine," she replied. "I'll take care of it." She left, closing her door firmly behind her.

"Thank you," I called after. "Well, Mr. Berryfield, why don't we go to my office? I want to introduce you to our PA."

Our being the operative word here. I didn't want Zeno getting proprietary over Clara.

She stood when we entered my office. I took a breath to start the introductions, but before I could, Clara said, "Hello, Mr. Berryfield. Good morning."

"Have you two met before?" I asked.

Their answers came on top of each other.

"Yes," Clara said.

"No," Zeno said.

Then he looked abashed and put a hand to his chest.

"Oh, I'm terribly sorry. *Have* we met?"

Clara's face had turned bright pink. She nodded. "Yes, we have. It was—"

"No, wait, don't tell me. Were you working for Oona at the show in Carlisle? I did stop in to say hello at that event. But, you know, Oona had a way of filling a room to the exclusion of others, didn't she? Again, I'm terribly sorry about that—not remembering. It's unforgivable."

Clara turned even pinker. "Oh, it's nothing."

"Heigh-ho, Ms. . . ."

"Powell," I said. "Clara Powell."

"Ms. Powell."

"We'd better get started, hadn't we?" I said. "I do want to go over the schedule and review how far we've come before I take you over to the Charlotte. I told Naomi Faber—the booking manager—we'd be there at eleven. That should give us plenty of time."

Zeno carried a fireside chair over to my desk and the three of us sat. I opened a file folder full of everything I had on the exhibition—I had printed it out that morning at five o'clock, because if you can't sleep, you might as well work.

"First, let me say that I'm sure our professional relationship—the three of us—will be fruitful, but I do want to point out that you, Clara, are to report to me."

"Yes, Hayley, of course."

The front door buzzed.

I hesitated for a moment, but heard nothing from Mrs. Woolgar's quarters, signaling to me that she was done with answering the door for the morning.

"I'm sorry for the interruption," I told Clara and Zeno, "but let me see to this."

I sprinted to the entry and pulled open the door to find Becky on the front step.

"Hello, Hayley."

At that moment, my life split in half. Work waited in my office, while here on my doorstep, one of two people with whom I knew I had another sort of business.

I prayed she didn't notice my moment of hesitation. "Becky, come in, please. How lovely to see you. I'm glad you didn't have to leave first thing this morning." *As both you and your sister said you would.* I checked the pavement, but there was no Bess lurking behind her.

Becky wore one of those coats with a multitude of zippered pockets, which she now used to occupy her hands— *zip, unzip, zip, unzip*—as she looked round the entry.

"You did say stop in anytime, but perhaps you're busy this morning."

"Not so busy I can't take a few minutes to visit." What else was I supposed to do—send her on her way back to Devon? In my mind, I tried to move us all round Middlebank like chess pieces, but couldn't figure out how I could be in two places at once.

At that moment, Mrs. Woolgar emerged from her office—possibly intrigued by a voice she didn't recognize— and I introduced Becky.

"Lovely to meet you, Ms. Moffatt. That was a fine pot of snowdrops you gave Ms. Burke."

I took Becky's coat and hung it on a peg as she replied, "They make a good show of it in winter," and then added, "What a lovely dress," nodding to the secretary's thirties-style frock with its purple appliqué at the shoulder. "Do you sew your own clothes?"

Mrs. Woolgar smiled—actually smiled. "Thank you, I do, yes. Now, Ms. Burke, would you like me to take Mr. Berryfield and Ms. Powell up to the library so that you and Ms. Moffatt have some time to youselves?"

Not everyone could charm the secretary so easily, and I would love Becky for that if nothing else.

"Thank you, Mrs. Woolgar," I said, resisting an urge to hug her for this kindness. I put my head in my office and quickly explained to Zeno and Clara the benefit of perusing the collection—"it will help you get a sense of Lady Fowling's tastes"—and handed them off to Mrs. Woolgar, who escorted them up to the library. I gave Becky a quick tour of the ground floor.

"Now, why don't we go up to my flat and have a coffee?"

Up the stairs we went, pausing for a moment on the first-floor landing. Inside the library, I heard Mrs. Woolgar say, "No, Mr. Berryfield, I don't believe I have heard about the time you created a one to one-hundred-twenty-eighth-scale papier-mâché replica of Ben Nevis."

Oh God—I should take over before Zeno starts talking about pig's blood. I should be emphasizing the quality of the exhibition, the need to coordinate, the imperative to remain true to the First Edition Society's mission and the library's far-reaching influence. I became short of breath and fought against dashing in and giving orders.

"She's lovely, isn't she?"

Becky stood admiring the full-length portrait of Lady Fowling, who was looking at me as if to say, *Here's your business now. Pay attention.*

I took a deep breath. I could do only one thing at a time, and at the moment that one thing was find out why Becky had stopped by Middlebank instead of going home to Devon.

"Lady Fowling," I said. "Yes, she is lovely. We never met, but I feel as if I had known her—so many of her friends share such wonderful memories."

"Did she leave any family?" Becky asked.

"A nephew," I replied. "He isn't involved in Middlebank, however."

"Family is very important," Becky said, with her eyes still on Lady Fowling.

Right, better get on with this. We continued up another flight to my flat, where I put the kettle on and got out the cafetière while Becky stood nearby looking down into the back garden. We took our coffee out to the sofa, and Bunter trotted in the door and hopped into Becky's lap.

"Bunter!" I said.

"Oh," Becky cooed, "aren't you a love?"

She scratched the cat under his chin and tugged lightly on his tail. When Bunter put on his starved-for-affection act, a session like this could go on forever.

"It was lovely to spend time with you and Bess last evening," I said, hoping to jump-start the conversation.

Bunter, at last sated, shook himself and sauntered off to the window, where a patch of low winter sun offered the false promise of warmth. Becky picked up her mug of coffee.

"Our dad is the best," she said as openers.

"Yes, he is."

She took a shortbread finger off the plate and tapped it on the rim of her mug in an absentminded fashion. "I don't really remember our mum. I should, I know—we were nearly five when she left—but I just don't. Bess remembers. Bess remembers everything—at least, she says she does, although I wonder if that's true or if she's making it up so that we don't lose—"

Downstairs, the buzzer sounded. Becky stopped, and her gaze shot to the open door of my flat as her eyes grew large. I heard the faint sounds of Mrs. Woolgar greeting someone.

"Let me just nip down," I said to Becky. I had recognized the visitor's voice, as I'm sure she had.

When I reached the library landing, I could hear Zeno pontificating about an exhibition as a microcosm of life and saw Clara taking notes on her tablet. *Focus, Hayley.* I turned my attention to the entry below.

"Hello, Bess," I said, walking halfway down the stairs. "You've met Mrs. Woolgar? Why don't you come up?" Bess shed her tailored coat, thanked the secretary for taking it, and followed me as I rabbited on. "I'm so glad you had time to stop, instead of rushing back to your job. Coffee? It's fresh. We'll save the tour for after—I'd love to show you Middlebank before you leave."

In my flat, Becky had moved to the window next to Bunter, and greeted her sister by saying, "I thought you had already left for Cheltenham."

"I thought you had a lesson to give midday in Torquay."

"Look, Bess—Hayley has a cat. His name is Bunter."

"Hello, Bunter," Bess said, and approached, offering a hand to sniff. With the cat between them, the twins stood facing each other in silhouette against the window, and at that moment, even with the different hairstyles, I would be hard-pressed to tell them apart.

I retreated to the kitchen for another mug, and heard Bess's stage-whisper. "I told you to leave this to me."

"She invited us—that means me, too."

They're girls, I told myself, *and I've frightened them.*

No, wait—not girls.

"Mum," Dinah would often say to me, "I'm not a girl any longer." "Sorry, sweetie," I would always reply. "I know you're not—you're a young woman."

Bess and Becky were young women. Still, Val had been their protector their entire lives, and they felt the need to return the favor. Could I blame them? No. But how was I to convince them they weren't about to lose their father?

"Just let me take care of things," Bess whispered to her sister.

"Bess, what is it? Why are you—"

When I stepped out of the kitchen, they jumped apart and froze.

"I'm awfully glad to see both of you. But I have a feeling this isn't just a social call. Why don't we all sit down?"

I poured Bess's coffee, and as she stirred in milk, I wondered how long we could keep silent before someone—not me, I vowed—would speak.

Bess broke first, casting her eyes about my flat.

"This is a lovely place. And your accommodations are included in your job?"

I smiled. "You know, that's just about the first thing your father said to me when we met." And I had reacted badly—we laughed about it now.

Bess frowned, probably trying to decide if that was a good thing or a bad one. "Of course, if you live on the premises, I suppose it means you never really get away from your job."

"True."

"Dad's never had it easy, you know," Bess said, causing me a bit of whiplash as the subject changed. "Bringing us up by himself. I'm sure we were a handful."

"I've never heard him complain."

"He's the best dad," Becky said.

Bess persisted. "So, now, at this stage of his life"—I swallowed a protest that she was making forty-five sound like eighty—"we feel it's our responsibility to keep an eye out for him."

"What are you afraid I'm going to do to him?" I asked.

"Leave."

They saw more clearly than I had thought. They saw perhaps even better than we did ourselves that Val and I had moved beyond a casual relationship. Smart girls. Women.

"Why would you think that? Why would you let that worry you?"

"Do you think our mum loved us?" Becky asked.

"*Don't,*" her sister whispered.

"Of course she loved you," I rushed in.

"How would you know?"

"Because she was your mother," I replied, and my eyes filled with tears. "And because I could see it in her face in that photo."

"She left us," Bess pointed out.

"She didn't think she was leaving you forever." I wanted to put my arms round them, but knew better, and instead clasped my hands in my lap. "Even with your parents divorced, she would always have been your mum and loved you."

How many times had they heard that through their lives, and yet still needed to hear it again? The air between us quivered, but the moment passed, because, inevitably—today, at least—the front-door buzzer went off.

14

The new arrival had nothing to do with me—it was board member Jane Arbuthnot, coming for morning coffee with Mrs. Woolgar. Nevertheless, the twins beat a hasty retreat, and I hurried down the stairs after them. They gave me a polite good-bye, but spoke not a word to each other. I closed the front door and put an ear to it, wishing I could hear through the thick oak. What were they saying out there on the pavement? Why this extra visit? I understood they could feel protective of Val, but now I sensed another issue lurking just below the surface. Did it concern Bess? Did Becky even know what it was?

Zeno's voice drifted out from the library. "No, Ms. Powell, when I create an exhibition, it's a visceral experience."

I raced up to the library. Enough of the Berryfield lecture—it had just gone eleven o'clock, and we were late for our appointment with Naomi. I hustled my crew off to the Charlotte, usually a ten-minute walk, which we made in five. We paused at the door, and I tried to catch my breath.

"Clara," I said, "the police have finished in the office,

but you will let me know if you feel uncomfortable working there. I could try to make other arrangements."

"No, Hayley," she replied, jutting out her chin. "I will be fine. We must get on with things. Don't you agree, Mr. Berryfield?"

"Well said, Ms. Powell, that's a fine attitude. I'm sure Oona would want us to carry on."

Inside the Charlotte, chaos reigned. It was moving-out day for the watercolorists, and so we maneuvered our way through a sea of easels and paintings flowing past until we reached an islet of calm near the edge of the room. A sign tacked to the doorpost listed the dates for the next exhibition, which was called *Druids Then and Now*.

Like in an old film, I saw calendar pages flying off a wall, and I realized February was upon us and our April dates were breathing down our necks. We had yet to make a single decision about theme or high points or layout. We'd yet to secure the loan of any display boxes or paraphernalia. What materials would we use? What about lighting? Signage! What about—

"Hayley, good morning. Sorry if I've kept you waiting."

Naomi approached us, but backed up a step when a man called, "Coming through!" as a Perspex display box was carted by. One of the watercolorists—the man I now recognized from my other visits—approached.

"Listen, Naomi, I've left that framed painting of the Box Tunnel as I said I would, all wrapped and labeled. It's back in the alcove, won't be in anyone's way, and I'll return for it next week. Cheers, now. See ya."

Naomi acknowledged him with a nod, and when traffic had cleared, I said, "Good morning, Naomi, may I present Zeno Berryfield, our exhibition manager?"

"Mr. Berryfield, yes." Naomi offered a hand for a brief shake. "Pleased to meet you. Shall we go up to your office—I'm afraid I've got a Druid in mine at the moment."

We took the stairs to the first floor and then walked

down a corridor to the door that separated the newer, refurbished Charlotte from the older space, where up one more flight waited Oona's office. That is, Zeno's office.

Clara had been leading the way, but stopped abruptly, staring at the spiral staircase. Naomi cut her eyes at me. Meanwhile Zeno, apparently oblivious to the hesitation, glanced round at the peeling wallpaper and stacks of cartons.

I leaned over to Clara and said, "Would you rather—"

"No!" She jumped as if I'd pinched her, and took off up the stairs at a trot. I hurried behind to provide assistance if needed. She made it to the top, but then pressed her back against the wall and looked at the floor.

Naomi opened the office door, and I breathed a sigh of relief—things had been put back in as much order as possible, although that couldn't have been difficult, because every scrap of paper had been removed by police. With a jolt I remembered I was expected at the station. *Right, let's get this thing moving.*

"Thank you, Naomi, I appreciate your help. Oh, look, you've brought in extra chairs." Four office chairs, taking up entirely too much space.

"I thought it might be a good idea for me to attend your first meeting back here since . . ." Naomi pulled out one of the chairs and sat down. "To represent the Charlotte's interests."

"You have a Druid in your office."

"He can wait."

Fine, let her listen.

We shifted round the room awkwardly, trying not to bump into one another's knees. Clara opened her tablet, Zeno crossed a leg, Naomi clasped her hands, and I pulled a file folder out of my bag.

"Well," I began, "I want us to remember that this is very much an exhibition about Lady Fowling and the First Edition library. Oona, of course, had many good ideas, but—"

"I've just been remembering," Zeno said, staring off into the distance, "the time Oona and I created a pop-up display for a Dalí exhibition in Cambridge. I persuaded her to think big, and so in the middle of Market Square, we installed an enormous, silicon melted pocket watch. People could walk right up and touch it."

"That sounds quite compelling," I said, handing out the three copies of my agenda I'd brought. I'd have to look over someone's shoulder. "Now—"

Naomi cut in. "When we staged the *Gin Lane tableau vivant*, Oona left it to me to sort out the baby. We obviously couldn't have a real child in danger of tumbling off its mother's lap, and so I—"

"Sorry," I said. "I really do need to get to the business at hand. Another appointment, you know." Would Sergeant Hopgood be drumming his fingers and tapping his toes while he waited for me?

"Yes, Hayley," Clara said, "of course we must get to work. Oona knew I understood the importance of a competently run meeting and the necessity of staying the course, so if you ever need me to—"

"Thank you, Clara. Now, everyone, please can we get started?"

The air was thick, making my mind sluggish. I longed to fling open a window for a blast of winter, but sadly, there was no window in the room. I fanned myself with my phone and continued.

"Although several ideas have been tossed about, we have yet to settle on the focus of the exhibition."

"You do have that lovely name," Clara reminded me, her fingers poised over her tablet.

"Yes, thank you. I certainly hope we can keep *Lady Fowling: A Life in Words*, but it will depend on that one-paragraph description we come up with and, of course, having the material to support it."

"I can see it now," Zeno said. "An immersive event

where the focus will be the life of a single woman left lonely, bereft of affection, and struggling to carve out a niche in a changing world, finding that refashioning herself in the image of an age gone by was her only solace."

"That is not only incorrect, it's patronizing," I replied. "Lady Fowling was a strong woman. You cannot remake history."

"It's the direction I feel certain Oona was heading," Zeno said, and I was about to ask how he knew anything about where Oona was heading, but Naomi took over.

"Oona would've been far more concerned with what attracted Georgiana Fowling to the Golden Age of Mystery. Revenge. All those murders in all those books. Oona would want to showcase that aspect. Was it vicarious pleasure for Georgiana? Who was it that she wanted to murder?"

"That's preposterous," I snapped. "Lady Fowling did not want to murder anyone. The mystery genre is a framework to tell a story. It's a convention."

"The thrill of the hunt," Clara said, and all eyes went to her. "It's what Oona mentioned—that Lady Fowling spent many happy years in pursuit of a good book, a rare book. She must've collected many, but none like the first edition of *Murder Must Advertise*, signed by the Detection Club in 1933. The person who can find it will go a long way to making the show a hit."

I agreed—it would be a feather in the cap of any exhibition manager.

"About this book, Ms. Burke." Zeno leaned forward in his chair. "You're keeping it safe, I assume?"

"We haven't actually located it, Mr. Berryfield, but that is only because I have yet to find the time to search through the entire collection."

"So, yes. I see." He cast his gaze about the room and then out onto the landing. "It was the book."

I refused to allow him to wrest the meeting from me so that he could talk about Oona's murder, and so I ignored his comment. "Well, this is a start, but as you know, we have a great deal to do and little time." And now I wanted my employees and my exhibition to myself. I smiled at Naomi. "Thank you so much for your enthusiasm, but we'd best let you get back to your Druid. I have a few specific tasks for Zeno and Clara to attend to this afternoon."

Naomi rose, brushed her skirt, and—in a slightly miffed tone—said, "Of course. You will let me know if you need anything. Perhaps I'll stop in at the end of the day just to make sure."

"No need," I said, herding her out the door and bumping into chairs as I did so. "I'll shoot you a text if there are any questions. Bye!"

I pushed the extra chair out onto the landing and watched as she made her way down the spiral staircase and through the door that led to the other part of the Charlotte. Yes, that's right, I reminded myself. There are two ways to get to Oona's office—on this side, from the door off the street, which had been left unlocked on the day of her murder, or through the Charlotte's main entrance, up one floor, past Naomi's office, and through the door that divided the building. Again, I wondered if Naomi had told the police she had known Oona. Something else to check. I turned back to my crew.

"Clara, do you still have the room dimensions on your tablet?"

"I do."

"And the built-in cases are indicated with their height and area?"

"Yes."

"Zeno, I'd like to see three examples of what you envision as the focal point for the exhibition."

It was a test, as far as I was concerned. We had Oona's idea for the entry, but there could be a display in the center of the room that would tie the entire show together. I wanted to see what Zeno could do—without blood. I checked the time—nearing one o'clock.

"I'm away, but before I go, let me remind you that we must be true to who Lady Fowling was. There's no need to make up things about her. She had a long and rich life, and that's what we must focus on. Remember, we have a wealth of primary sources at our fingertips—not only her notebooks, but the people who knew her."

Zeno and Clara looked at me blankly. Had they heard anything I had said? I gave up. "I'll stop back at five o'clock."

I hurried down the stairs—half expecting Clara to call out to be careful— and trotted down Julian Street thinking about lunch. Did I have time? No. Instead, I dashed into the newsagent on the Paragon for a packet of crisps and a Cadbury Dairy Milk, and as I paid, I heard myself telling a nine-year-old Dinah, "No, sweetie, chocolate is not a proper meal." As it turned out, sometimes it was.

I'd finished the crisps and made it through half the chocolate bar by the time I reached the police station on Manvers Street and so stashed the rest in my bag as I walked in, prepared to state my name as usual. But the desk sergeant caught me by surprise and said, "Hello, Ms. Burke. Shall I ring back for you?"

Just as well we were on more familiar terms. With the briefest of glances at his name tag, I said, "Yes, please, Sergeant Owen."

Detective Constable Kenny Pye came to retrieve me.

"Sarge is on a community-engagement course today," he explained as he led me to Interview #1.

"How . . . er . . ." Professional-development workshops, connect-with-the-public meetings—I may not be a police officer, but I knew what these things could be like. "Did he go voluntarily?"

Pye laughed. "I'll get the binders for you. Tea?"

"Oh please, no. Water?"

The DC returned with a glass of water, left, and came back again with his arms full of the three binders. He deposited them on the table and turned to go. "Just give a shout if you need me."

"Actually, there is something. I have further information about the case."

"Right." Kenny Pye sat down across from me, pulled out his pocket notepad, and listened while I explained about Zeno.

"They were married?" His black eyebrows shot up—a poor imitation of the caterpillars above his boss's eyes, but a valiant effort.

"Married and divorced," I said. "I learned this on Saturday."

"And now he has her job?" Pye asked.

"Yes, I hired him, but you see, it's because we needed a manager, or the Charlotte wouldn't let us keep our dates for the exhibition in April. Time is short and we're already behind."

"April seems like ages away."

"No, not ages." An enormous black cloud looming on the horizon.

"Right, I'll take his contact information. Does he live locally?"

I had only a box number attached to the hot-desking company where Zeno had let space by the day. We had his bank details, of course, and his mobile number, but no physical residence. "I'm not entirely sure. He's been in Bath for about a month, so perhaps he's found a short-term let. But at this very moment, he's working in the office upstairs at the Charlotte."

"Is he, now? Well, perhaps I'll stop in this afternoon and have a chat. Was that it?"

"No. Naomi Faber—she directs the bookings at the Charlotte. Did you talk with her?"

Pye flipped back a few pages in his notepad. "Mmm. What about her?"

"Did she tell you she knew Oona?"

"Knew her from where—and when?"

"An exhibition in Plymouth. Oona created one of those living pictures where people dress up and pose as a famous painting. Look, I know it's probably nothing, but you need every detail. When you spoke with her, where did Naomi say she was the afternoon Oona was killed?"

"What did she tell you?"

I should know better than to expect an exchange of information from the police.

"I haven't asked. There's one more thing. About Bulldog—that is, Stuart Moyle. I'm sorry if I led you to believe that he looked as if he was waiting for me on Saturday—but then, you were looking for him, weren't you? Did he tell you or Sergeant Hopgood anything useful?"

Pye hesitated, and I wondered what could push him just far enough to speak. "I should know, shouldn't I?" I asked. "In case I should be wary of him."

The detective constable seemed to consider my question before saying, "We are confirming his alibi, but let's just say he isn't a priority for us."

So he wasn't their prime suspect, but he was still on the list.

"Right, well"—I tapped the stack of binders—"better get to work."

Here's what you get from a poorly carried out task—poor results. My assignment to look for clues by once again examining the transcription of Lady Fowling's notebooks—annotated by Oona—along with all the other papers gathered from the murder scene fought for importance in my mind with the exhibition itself and the location of the signed first edition of *Murder Must Advertise*. Murder, exhibition, book—I couldn't seem to hold all three in my head at once, and had to backtrack time and again.

When the exhibition took over my brain, I concentrated on Oona's early, sketchy thoughts for displays, hoping to glean a few ideas to throw to Zeno. On one page, she had dashed off an arrangement of what might have been an old typewriter alongside a fountain pen. Either that, or it was a slowworm creeping past the cliffs of Dover. She had scribbled an illegible title across the top of the page.

Then I would remind myself to look for clues to her murder, and once or twice I traced Oona's drawings with a fingertip, hoping that the movements would bring forth one tiny bit of extremely important information about the case. Or the book. Nothing. Another few hours wasted. Perhaps I wasn't missing something—perhaps what I hoped to find just wasn't there.

15

I finished my Cadbury Dairy Milk as I walked back to the Charlotte, where Zeno stood in the empty exhibition space talking with a man in a gray three-piece suit. His silver hair was cut quite short on the sides and back, and the rest gathered into a tiny ponytail right at the top of his head.

"We're more than Stonehenge," the man was saying, "and we mean to prove it."

"Zeno?" I asked.

"Ah, here she is now." Berryfield threw an arm out toward me. "Hayley Burke, curator of the First Edition library."

The man grabbed my hand and shook it with vigor. "Tommy King-Barnes, Folkstone." He may be from Folkstone now, but his accent said London. And his voice sounded familiar. "Very pleased to meet you. *Druids Then and Now*—that's me. We start move-in tomorrow."

I tried to picture him in Druids' robes or whatever they wore. No, couldn't do it.

He cocked his head at me and added, "I dropped into the

Charlotte today just to make sure we'll have enough space for the human sacrifice," and then he burst into riotous laughter at the look on my face.

Zeno joined in. "God, Tommy, you are such a one for the wit."

"No worries there, Hayley," Tommy said, giving Berryfield a playful punch on the arm. "We Druids will be dull as ditchwater compared with what Zeno here will come up with for you."

And the penny dropped.

"Hang on," I said. "Are you Timeless Productions?"

"The very same! Have you seen one of our shows before?"

"Zeno listed you as a reference. I left you a message this morning."

"Did you? Awfully sorry about that, but I haven't had one second in this dimension or the next to answer. Well, no time like the present. I'm happy to tell you that Zeno will not let up until he gives you the exhibition of a lifetime. You'll have all of Bath if not the entire country talking about it. You should be confident in your choice."

Tommy gave Zeno a wink. Zeno beamed. I needed to sit down.

The muffled strains of Mick Jagger singing "Satisfaction" started up nearby. Tommy patted a jacket pocket, pulled out a phone, and shook his head. He dropped the phone back, and as the music continued, he pulled a second phone out from the other pocket, put it back, and finally pulled a third phone from an inside breast pocket. All the while Mick Jagger continued to wail.

Third time's the charm. Tommy answered, "Timeless Productions, how may we be of service?"

"Heigh-ho," Zeno whispered.

The Druid waved as he walked off, saying into the phone, "No, we ordered four hundred cutout masks, not four thousand."

Zeno cleared his throat, threw on a serious face, and

narrowed his eyes at me. "Ms. Burke," he said. "The police were here."

Why did that sound like an accusation?

"Oh," I replied coolly.

"It was a Detective Constable Kenny Pye wanting to talk with me about the inquiry into Oona's murder. I wonder how did he know of my association with her."

"I told him."

The corners of Zeno's mouth turned down. "I see. Well, I don't know what he expected me to say. And it saddens me that the police would come here, to my place of work, and interrogate me as if I were a common criminal."

His place of work? Interrogate him?

"It's what police do, Zeno—talk with everyone who had even a passing knowledge of the victim. In an enquiry, one piece of information leads to another, and I'm sure they—" I stopped. Who was I to say how the police built an enquiry? Longing to ask what he'd said to Kenny Pye, but knowing I would sound like a nosey parker, I looked for another subject. "Clara—is she upstairs?"

"Ms. Powell is gone," Zeno replied.

"Gone? But it isn't five yet."

Zeno shrugged. "Detective Constable Pye knocked on the office door, and the next thing I knew, Ms. Powell had taken flight, so to speak. Something about wanting to talk to the local press in hopes they would run a series on fictional detectives and their connection to Bath."

"She shouldn't pursue her own ideas without consulting me first."

Zeno stuck his hands in his trouser pockets. "I am not Ms. Powell's keeper, you made that clear. The two of us are your responsibility, Ms. Burke, but I agree, we shouldn't make more work for you. Is there anything I can do to help with the matter?"

"No, I'll have a word with her. Starting tomorrow, there's no need to report to Middlebank—your workdays will begin here unless you hear otherwise. I'll be by at eleven, and we'll begin a list of displays."

I walked out and took a gulp of cold air as an icy mizzle began to fall. I should ring Arthur Fish. I should try again to contact Zeno's other two references. I should figure out what to do about Bess and Becky. I should have a talk with Clara. I should find that first edition. I should suss out who murdered Oona. But couldn't I do all of that in the morning? Quite happy to see the end of the day, I decided I needed an easy evening, and with Val teaching until nine, I knew just the person and the place. Adele at the Minerva—she could often be found there nursing a pint while Pauline worked behind the bar. I texted to let her know I'd show up.

See you at Minerva?

Her reply came quickly.

Raven

No, this wasn't a pie evening.

Burgers. Minerva. 7

k

That settled, I committed myself to one more task before I clocked off: I bought a bottle of sherry. When I reached Middlebank, Mrs. Woolgar's office door stood ajar, and so I looked in.

"All ready for tomorrow?" I asked. "The board members know they will be meeting Zeno before the lecture?"

The secretary nodded. "Maureen Frost thinks she remembers hearing his name from some theatrical . . . oh, let's see, what word did she use?"

Travesty?

"Festival. A festival in Suffolk celebrating the spoken language of the Iceni." And what touch had Zeno added to that event? I wondered. Did he dress someone as Boadicea and have her ride in on the back of a bull?

"She may want to speak with you about it," Mrs. Woolgar added.

Great, another task for my Tuesday morning.

The secretary shut down her computer, stood, and brushed off her skirt.

"Mrs. Woolgar, thank you for being so kind to Bess and Becky this morning. I wasn't prepared to see them, and your help smoothed it all over."

"You're welcome, Ms. Burke," she said, in a voice one or two degrees softer than usual. "They seem like lovely young women."

There now—she got it right. Young women. "I didn't realize you sewed your own clothes."

"Yes, I sew," she replied, those two degrees of softness gone. "Where did you think my dresses came from—a time machine?" She clasped her hands at her waist. "When I was young, I altered clothes as my living." I detected a gleam in her eye behind those thick specs.

This grain of personal information was more than I'd got out of her in my first six months at the Society. I seized it and attempted to shake loose another morsel. "Did you have a shop?"

"A shop, no—well, of sorts. The front room of my maisonette."

Was that pride I heard in her voice?

"How lovely. And this was . . . ?"

"A lifetime ago." She threw back her shoulders. "Now, Ms. Burke—what does Mr. Berryfield mean by an 'immersive event'?"

From sewing to pig's blood in record time.

"He believes that activities will draw more people to the exhibition. Don't worry—I won't let it get out of hand."

* * *

The Minerva had only six tables—plus a few outside, used in winter only by hardy smokers. I was early, and so had no trouble spotting Adele in her usual corner with her usual pint, but with an unusual look so glum that even her mass of red curls drooped. Behind the bar, Pauline polished the brass cask handles with such vigor I feared she might break one off.

"Shall I order?" I asked Adele, who shrugged.

I stepped up to the bar and said, "Hiya, Pauline."

"Oh, Hayley, hello," she said airily. "Lovely to see you. What can I get you?"

"Two burgers, please, extra chips. And a glass of red wine. A large glass." I cut my eyes at Adele, who had turned away from us and appeared to be studying a pane of the stained glass window beside her. "Better make it a bottle, and two glasses."

I took my purchase to Adele's table and plopped down across from her.

"What's this about?"

"What is what about?" she asked in her own airy tone.

"Did you two argue?"

Adele took the last swig of her beer, pushed the empty glass aside, and reached for the bottle of wine.

"I didn't argue," she said. "Pauline has got the wrong end of the stick about something and won't let go."

"And that would be about what?"

Adele heaved a sigh and said, "She thinks I'm mourning Oona's death."

Oona—I could not leave her behind. "Are you?"

"No, I am not," Adele snapped. "I had something on my mind, and Pauline misinterpreted my preoccupation. I said she was jumping to conclusions and, well—it went on from there."

I couldn't believe my ears. All this for a one-night stand five years ago? "Are you breaking up with Pauline?"

"That's just what she said!" Adele's voice rose. "Won't anyone hear me out?"

I waved my glass of wine. "Carry on."

"I was a bit nervous, that's all. I wanted to tell Pauline that I thought perhaps it was time she and I moved in together." Adele's lower lip stuck out. "But I didn't have the chance, did I? She stormed out and I haven't seen her since Friday. And she didn't look best pleased to see me walk in the door this evening, I can tell you."

Nothing like a good old-fashioned misunderstanding. "You two are mad about each other," I said. "And also, just plain mad." I took a drink of my wine, and then another. "Wait here."

I stalked up to the bar. "Pauline, you and Adele need to talk. To each other."

"I know what this is about," Pauline said, keeping her eyes on the glass she was polishing. "Look at her over there—she's mourning."

"That isn't a look of mourning, Pauline—it's a look of being cheesed off with you for not listening to her. Do you remember exactly what Adele said that started this?"

Pauline frowned at my question. "Something about time . . . time to . . . to make a decision. I thought she was breaking it off." She glanced at Adele, who had turned her attention directly on us. "Have I been thick? Oh, Hayley, will you ask her if—"

"Yes, Pauline, you've been thick, and no, I will not— you talk to her when you've finished your evening. I'm going to eat." I nodded to the two plates just put through from the kitchen. "Hand me those burgers."

I took our food to the table just as the evening crowd began to drift in.

"Yeah, so?" Adele asked.

"I should've been an agony aunt." I glanced over to see

Pauline smiling at Adele and turned back to find Adele making googly eyes at her girlfriend. "Oi!" I snapped my fingers. "Let the woman do her job, and hand me the brown sauce."

We got busy with our burgers under a much lighter mood.

"I haven't talked to you since Friday," Adele said. "Tell me what's been happening."

Where to begin?

"We've hired a new exhibition manager—the fellow I told you about before. Zeno Berryfield."

"That was awfully fast," Adele noted.

"There's no time to waste," I said.

"A quick hire. In *Murder Must Advertise*, Death Bredon got on with Pym's Publicity immediately after that fellow fell down the spiral staircase." She held up her burger and looked at me over the bun. "You've finished that one, right?"

"Not quite." Not by a long shot. "Listen, there's something you should know about Zeno. He and Oona had been married."

Adele's eyes widened. "Blimey," she said, her mouth full of burger.

"He just told me on Saturday. They met two or three years ago, married, and divorced last year sometime. Brief."

"How very interesting," Adele said, barely concealing a snicker. "What's he like?"

"He's . . . You'll meet him tomorrow before the salon. Six o'clock. Sherry with the board."

"Did he know you'd given Oona the job?" Adele asked in a speculative way. "Did she know that he knew? Were they still in touch?"

"There can't be that many exhibition managers in the whole of Britain—I believe they had been keeping tabs on each other. Perhaps Zeno had his sights set on that post at the British Library that Oona thought was hers. Oh, do let's talk about something other than Oona. Tell me a story about Lady Fowling. I hope I can find that first edition to use in the exhibition. Tell me what she thought of Dorothy L. Sayers."

Adele dragged a chip through a pool of ketchup and bit off half of it. "You know that her detective, François Flambeaux, was partly inspired by Lord Peter? Georgiana admired Sayers—her life as well as her writing. I know that some of the elements in *Murder Must Advertise* are dated, of course, but the way Wimsey got onto the right trail was spot-on. Perseverance and pluck."

I took a large bite of burger and chewed and thought about my resources at hand—the things I had that could help me find the book. "Do you think Lady Fowling left me clues to where she'd hidden it? No, wait, I don't mean *me*—"

"I know what you mean," Adele said, and grinned. "You feel as if you can talk to her, don't you? Now, about the book—Georgiana did love a puzzle. Once, Flambeaux went in disguise to uncover a sinister plot to capture the market in English oak memorabilia. The plot revolved around a system of numbers written in ink visible only on the first night of the waning full moon that told of . . ." Adele frowned. "Well, the solution was a bit convoluted, but quite inventive. With her imagination, I'd say it's possible Georgiana laid a trail directly to that book."

"I may never find it," I said.

Adele patted my hand and, channeling Lady Fowling herself, said, "Of course you will."

I didn't deserve such confidence. Not when I continued to flail. The first edition may have nothing to do with Oona's murder, but finding it would certainly put the oomph in the exhibition that we needed.

This need for energy became all too apparent when I arrived at the Charlotte on Tuesday morning.

"Good morning, you two," I said.

Clara sat in a corner with her tablet, and her chair turned at an angle so that she didn't quite face me when she offered a smile and said, "Hello, good morning, Hayley."

Zeno sat at the desk, his laptop open and a spiral-bound notepad in his lap, and he wore his uniform. Did he have a wardrobe full of teal suits?

"Ms. Burke," Zeno said. "What news?"

"What news?"

"My official introduction to the board—all set?"

"Oh, yes. Six o'clock."

I'd had a callback the evening before from one of Zeno's other references, but I'd been in bed and on the phone with Val, finding a way to tell him his daughters had dropped in for a visit, without getting into how they wanted to manage his life. "I had invited them to stop in, remember," I had told him, "and I was delighted to see them, even though they couldn't stay long. We'll consider it a step forward." He seemed mollified, if unconvinced.

I had let Zeno's reference leave a message. I listened later and again that morning, but still caught only the gist of it. A breathy woman from Exhib, Ltd., said Zeno had been an "ever-so-reliable and just plain fun fellow" during the buildup to an exhibition called *Anne of Cleves: I Like Her Much Worse.* At least wife number four of Henry VIII hadn't lost her head—no telling what Zeno would've made of that.

"Well, what do you have for me this morning?" I asked brightly, hoping to overcome the feeling of ennui in the room that made me want to curl up and take a nap.

Not a great deal, as it turned out. Zeno presented two ideas for displays: signage on the history of the monocle and a list of the word counts for each of Lady Fowling's Flambeaux stories.

"It's the essence of writing, isn't it?" Zeno asked. "And suits your title, *Lady Fowling: A Life in Words*, perfectly."

I'd never heard anything so boring in my life.

"I need to make this clear," I said through clenched teeth. "Time is short, but not so short that I couldn't look for another manager if appropriate and engaging ideas for the exhibition are not forthcoming."

Clara's eyes grew wide and darted from me to Zeno and back. My face felt as if it were on fire. Would he call my bluff?

Zeno pulled himself up and took it on the chin.

"Yes, Ms. Burke, I completely understand. I'm sorry that I've been distracted when it comes to the creative side of management, but you see, we have a duty of care to the items we display. I've just come across information that relates directly to Lady Fowling's impressive collection. Were you aware of the new lighting recommendations for fragile paper in exhibitions? The last thing we want to do is use the wrong sort of lights and damage the things we love the most. It's an issue that's been uppermost in my mind."

Was he having me on? Before I could react, he continued.

"Let me forward you the article from *On Display Today*, a scholarly magazine that helps us keep up on the latest trends and issues in exhibition management." He took out his phone, his fingers flew over the screen, and he said, "There we are."

I heard my phone ding.

"Thank you, Zeno, I will certainly take a careful look. And now," I said, from a weakened position, "what of a central focal point display?"

"Yes." Zeno smiled and tapped the side of his nose with his forefinger. "I've an idea, but I'd rather keep quiet on that front at the moment. Working through a few details with a chap out on the Locksbrook Road. Now, if we're finished here, Ms. Burke, I'd like to dash downstairs and take a look at how high that ceiling is in the main hall. Would you excuse me?"

I stared at his departing figure. Why did he need to know the ceiling height, and what business would he have out on Locksbrook Road, a place lined with industrial estates?

"Do you know what he's up to?" I asked.

Clara had been following the exchange, but at my question, she flinched as if caught eavesdropping. She glanced down at her tablet, and then up at me.

"He hasn't said, but he seems quite excited about it."

"We can only hope for the best," I said, which elicited a faint "heigh-ho" from her. "Clara, you're very welcome to come to the salon this evening. In fact, why don't you arrive at six so that I can introduce you to the board, too?"

"Thank you, Hayley, that's so very kind of you."

"Now, I did want to have a word with you about going to the *Chronicle* and suggesting a series on fictional detectives." Clara looked up expectantly, and a good part of my annoyance fell away. I continued in a gentle tone. "It sounds promising, but you should've come to me first so that we could discuss it. Remember, every decision goes through me."

A look of surprise swept over her face like a cloud scudding across the sky, followed quickly by distress. "But, I thought . . ." she began, and then dropped her head and muttered something about "never point the finger." She looked up at me again and said, "I'm terribly sorry, Hayley. It was unprofessional of me to take action on any matter without permission. I do know that you need to approve our activities, and I have no excuse whatsoever. I hope you can forgive me and will allow me to continue as your PA."

"I'm not about to fire you," I said. The poor girl had gone so pale I thought she'd faint on the spot. "I'm only reminding you that it's important to go through the proper channels before—"

I heard footsteps on the landing below, and apparently, so had Clara, because her eyes cut to the door and back to me.

"Hang on," I said. "Was it your idea to go to the paper before talking with me, or was it Zeno's?"

The footsteps rang on the metal staircase.

"No, no, mine," Clara said quickly.

Zeno appeared on the landing.

"You know," he said, leaning an elbow on the doorpost, "I could've sworn that was a fifteen-foot ceiling at the entrance, but as it turns out, it's only twelve."

I leapt from my seat. "Zeno, I need to have a word with you. Come downstairs and out to the pavement with me, will you?" I turned to Clara. "I'll see you at six."

She opened her mouth, but Zeno cut in.

"Outdoors?" he asked. "Are you mad? It's absolutely frigid out there."

"This won't take long. Let's go."

As I marched off, Zeno said, "Would you like a coffee while I'm out, Ms. Powell?" Clara looked ready to answer when Zeno added, "Fine. I'll bring one back for you."

Down the spiral staircase, down the wooden steps, and out onto the pavement. I stopped there, pivoted, and put my hand up. Zeno took a step back and raised his eyebrows. "Couldn't we go across the road to the café? So much more civilized."

"Whose idea was it for Clara to go to the papers about a feature?"

Like time-lapse photography, Zeno looked affronted, then confused, followed by red-faced, and finally abashed. "Entirely mine, Ms. Burke, and I want to apologize unequivocally for that. Please do not hold Ms. Powell in any way responsible. She is an eager young woman who wants to make her mark, and it wasn't fair of me to even bring the subject up without considering that her enthusiasm, her drive, might lead her to—" He shook his head. "I'm afraid I was distracted by the arrival of a member of the Avon and Somerset constabulary or I would've realized my mistake. Although that is no excuse." He bowed his head.

Zeno appeared to be taking the blame for Clara's rash action, but she had taken the blame herself. Why were they both so eager to take responsibility? And was it so important in the long run? It was, after all, not a bad idea.

"Hayley. Hayley. Hayley."

Across the road stood Dom, wool coat buttoned up to his chin and knit cap pulled down to rest on the frames of his glasses. He held his arms straight at his side, his hands flapping slightly.

"Hello, Dom!" I called, and crossed the road. Zeno trailed after me.

"Zeno, this is Dom Kilpatrick. We worked together at the Jane Austen Centre."

"This isn't my day," Dom said. "I shouldn't be here on Tuesday at twelve. Wednesday at eleven o'clock and Thursday at three o'clock I come to the Fashion Museum at the Assembly Rooms. I run a virus check. But I had to come today because there's been a crash on one of their systems. This isn't my day."

"Well, good to see you no matter the reason," I said. "Zeno is our exhibition manager."

"Pleased to meet you, Dom," Zeno said, and stuck out his hand. Dom looked at it, but made no reciprocal offer. Zeno didn't seem to take offense, and said, "Well, Ms. Burke, I do want to get back to work on the entry display. I'll just nip into the café here and take Ms. Powell back a coffee as promised. I'll see you . . ."

"At six. Yes."

"Heigh-ho."

Dom and I watched Zeno continue into the Assembly Rooms, and then Dom said, "He worked with Oona."

"No, actually he—well, yes, but not here."

"I saw him," Dom said. "I saw him going into the Charlotte."

16

I carried out a quick translation of what Dom had said and reinterpreted it to suit the prevailing truth.

"You saw Zeno go into the Charlotte yesterday? Because that's when he started work."

"Yesterday was Monday. I don't come to the Assembly Rooms on Monday. Wednesday and—"

"Yes, Wednesdays and Thursdays are your days." I inhaled deeply and steeled myself. "What day did you see him?"

"Wednesday."

Wednesday was the day before Oona was murdered.

"Dom, this is extremely important. I need a detailed description of what you saw on Wednesday. All right?"

"There's a crash on one of the systems," Dom said. "I shouldn't be here on Tuesday. Wednesday is my day." He took off toward the Assembly Rooms.

"Dom, hang on." I chased after him. "I really need to know about this. Listen, how long will you be?"

Dom checked his watch, pressing the stem to light the dial even though it was broad daylight. "Thirty minutes."

"I'll buy you a coffee when you're finished—how's that?"

"It's Tuesday," he said, but then added, "I have a coffee and a Penguin."

"And a Penguin. Please—I'll meet you in the café after you sort out the computer problem."

We parted in the entry, Dom to the Fashion Museum offices, and me to the café, where Zeno was coming out with two coffees.

"Oh, Ms. Burke, I didn't realize. Should I have got yours as well?"

I skirted him as if he were radioactive, running into the menu stand as I did. "No, no—I've some work to do before I need to be at . . . and thought I might as well do it here. I'll see you . . . later." I backed into the café. Only when the swing door closed did I breathe a sigh of relief.

Ring the police, a voice inside my head told me. Ring and tell them what? No, better to wait and get the facts and present them in a calm and sane manner. So, I made myself as comfortable as possible in the café while I waited for Dom. I ordered a fruit scone and a cappuccino, took a table at the back, and stared at the door. Thirty minutes was an eternity, but at last he appeared, wearing his coat and knit cap as if he might be ready to leave. I leapt up.

"Here! Now, have a seat and I'll get your order. Won't take two ticks."

"I drink filter coffee," he said as I dashed up to the counter.

"Yes, I remember."

Only after his coffee had been sorted—two sugars, no milk—and he'd unwrapped but not taken a bite of the chocolate-covered biscuit could I get a word out of him about what he'd seen.

"Wednesday, I leave the Centre at ten fifty and walk up to the Circus and then turn the corner onto Bennett Street. There was a crowd waiting for the tour bus, and I had to

walk into the road to get round them. I saw him—Zeno
Berryfield—coming down and walking into the door on
the side. I remember that door."

He would. We were in and out of the Charlotte that way
during both the planning and execution of the exhibition for
the Jane Austen Centre.

"Was he alone?"

"Yes." Dom glanced at the Penguin.

"Did he seem in a hurry or upset or happy or in a mood
of any sort?"

Dom only stared at me. I should've known better—
emotions were not easy for him to track.

"No, never mind. Thanks, Dom, I appreciate your help.
Give Margo my regards." I'd taken two steps, but turned
back and said, "Remember we ran into you last Thursday?
That was the day Oona died. Did you see Zeno go into the
Charlotte on Thursday?"

Dom had taken half the chocolate biscuit in one bite and
stopped chewing, his mouth full. He paused and then shook
his head.

D S Hopgood, please, Sergeant Owen. This is extremely
important."

"Right-o, Ms. Burke," the desk sergeant said, and looked
down at his computer screen.

"Or DC Pye?"

"Doesn't look as if you can have either of them at the
moment—they're out on a call."

I sucked in my breath. "Is it about the Oona Atherton
enquiry? No—never mind." I'd seen the look in his eye,
and I knew I wouldn't get an answer. "Do you know when
they'll return?"

"Why don't I send DC Pye a text, and we'll leave it with
them? I'm sure they'll be in touch when they can."

"Thank you. I think I'll wait."

I paced, sat down for a few seconds, and paced again. I composed a single-word text to Val—**Developments**—but deleted it immediately. What good would that do when I knew so little? Also, I remembered he would be collecting our speaker for the literary salon and taking her out to lunch. Retired detective chief superintendent Margaret Raines, author of police procedurals, would address us on the Metropolitan Police in fact and fiction. That evening's lecture had almost slipped right out of my head. Again. I needed to pay more attention to my job, and I would do so as soon as this bit of business had been sorted.

Zeno had lied. That was the only conclusion to be drawn from this, because Dom did not lie—he didn't have it in him. Zeno lied about seeing Oona in Bath, which means he could be lying about so much more. We may have him. The murderer. I shivered.

"Ms. Burke?"

I gave a little yelp and swung round to see Sergeant Hopgood at the front desk, his eyebrows sky-high.

"Steady on," he said.

"You were out," I said.

"'Were' being the operative word, Ms. Burke," he said. "Come through."

I followed on his heels through the door and down the corridor.

"Did Constable Pye tell you about Zeno?" I asked. "That he and Oona had been married? Have you found out where he was on Thursday? What did he tell you? Because I know more now. I know something that may shift your entire enquiry and—"

Hopgood stopped at Interview #1 and I nearly ran into him.

"Why don't we discuss your concerns in here?"

He nodded me in and I took a chair, dropped my bag, and sat on my hands in hopes it would keep me grounded.

"Now," Hopgood said. "Zeno Berryfield, ex-husband of

Oona Atherton. He is also an exhibition manager by profession and is now seeing to your own event. You hired him Yes?"

"Yes. Zeno told me he had not seen Oona since coming to Bath. Did he tell Kenny—Constable Pye—the same thing?"

DC Pye entered at that moment, and the sergeant repeated my question.

"They'd had no contact," the constable replied, "and Berryfield said he was sorry about that. 'Devastated' was the word he used. He's . . . er . . ."

"Yes, he certainly is," I said. "And he's also a liar. I've got an eyewitness who says Zeno was seen going into the Charlotte last Wednesday at eleven o'clock in the morning." It didn't escape my notice that my statement made it sound as if I were in a detective story myself. I hoped I got the words right.

The two men glanced at each other, and then began to pick apart what I had said. Witness? Time? Reliability? They asked for Dom's contact details.

"So," I said, "let me just say I know Dom Kilpatrick. He's highly intelligent, unable to lie, and a really great fellow. But he can be a bit fragile."

"Will he need an advocate?" Hopgood asked. "Someone to be with him?"

"Certainly not. He isn't—wait, yes, he will need someone. Me. I think it would put him at ease if I were here. Shall I ring him?"

"We'll let you know, Ms. Burke," Hopgood said. "First, let us confirm Mr. Berryfield's alibi for Thursday. We'll get to Mr. Kilpatrick after that."

"Where did Zeno say he was?" And why hadn't I asked Zeno that question before coming here?

The detective sergeant nodded to his DC, who replied, "Up to Bristol by train, where he spent the day."

"Are you certain?" I asked.

"It's a difficult thing to lie about," Hopgood said. "There's CCTV everywhere. But we will certainly do our due diligence and make sure we can locate Mr. Berryfield at both Bath Spa and Bristol Temple Meads stations when he says he was there. Pye, get a uniform on it."

"I would do, boss, but we've only got Evans working on CCTV, and he's out sick."

"Blast," Hopgood said. "Well, Ms. Burke, we'll get to this as soon as we can. In the meantime, mind how you go."

What was that supposed to mean—that I was in danger, or I was to keep my nose out of police business?

"Of course, Sergeant. Always."

I left before I could blurt out that I'd be spending the evening with Zeno. There would be loads of other people around. It wasn't as if I planned to confront him about his alibi for Thursday. Given the chance, of course, I would ask him about seeing Oona the day before the murder, which I saw as entirely within my remit as curator of the First Edition library.

Outdoors, I hurried down the pavement. Gone three o'clock, and I fought with myself about my next move. I should go back to the Charlotte and find out what Zeno had got up to and if I needed to rescue Clara from one of his "I once staged an exhibition in which I—" lectures, but a text arrived from Val.

Lunching at the Gainsborough. Join us for coffee?

He'd taken the literary salon lecturer to the Gainsborough? We hadn't budgeted for that—was it what a retired detective chief superintendent expected?

I walked into the restaurant ten minutes later to find it mostly empty apart from a cluster of people standing around a table in the corner. A woman's voice rose and flowed toward me—one of those rich, throaty voices that sounded as if it had been steeped for a great many years in a single malt. The cluster parted when I arrived at the table.

She must've commanded quite a presence during her years at the Met—not tall, but stout with short gray hair brushed back off her face. Now well known as an author of police procedurals, she had garnered a fair-sized fan base including the Gainsborough's chef, several dishwashers, and three servers, who now waited to get an autograph from our speaker.

Val rose and began to introduce me, but he got no further than "Margaret, this is Hayley," when she rose and took over.

"Margaret Raines," she said, pumping my hand. "Delighted to be in your lovely city. You'll have coffee?"

"Oh, coffee, yes, but I wouldn't want to take up—"

"You might as well sit down," Val said, as if he'd already given in on any afternoon agenda.

"Have you had your lunch?" Margaret boomed. "We'll take a round of sandwiches here, along with coffee."

The restaurant staff nodded and scurried off to their work. I heard one young woman say, "I have all her books—wish I'd known to bring one for her to autograph."

Those sandwiches went down a treat, and the entertainment was top-notch. Margaret embodied a combination of beloved nanny and steely policewoman. As she told her stories, I tried to imagine myself one of her suspects. No, wouldn't want to be in their shoes.

"Who stands to gain?" she asked in the middle of discussing the anatomy of a crime. I should've been taking notes, but instead I reached for another triangle of sandwich. "That isn't always so obvious. For some people, the thing most desired is not to be flaunted, but hidden away and cherished. Remember that," she said, shaking a forefinger at us. "Or the crime could've been committed for status. But then, of course"—she shrugged—"there are those criminals who cannot even give a reason for their violence. What then?"

Nearly half past five, my hands had begun to shake, and it had nothing to do with the three cups of coffee I'd drunk. Nerves. For the last hour, I'd been worrying about the time, and Val had caught on. Margaret, lost in gripping stories, took no notice of anything, including my and Val's feeble attempts to wind up the afternoon so that the evening could begin. We exchanged looks, attempted interjections of "Well" or "Now," and rearranged the empty coffee cups and plates. Nothing worked. The board would arrive at Middlebank at six for sherry with not only our speaker, but also our new exhibition manager, Zeno. I had responsibilities. If I could get to my phone without being noticed, I could call Val. The ringing of a mobile would be just the thing to break up the session.

Suddenly Margaret shot out of her chair and said, "My goodness, the afternoon got away from us—how did that happen? I'd say we'd better leg it, shall we?"

We shifted into top gear. I settled the bill as Val and our lecturer hurried out to his car. They had an intermediary stop before arriving at Middlebank—Margaret had only just remembered she needed to collect copies of her books from a cousin's house in Twerton. I couldn't take that detour; I needed to go directly back. I had no worries about the sherry hour or the wine service at the lecture—I had left those details to Mrs. Woolgar and the two young women servers we hired from Pauline—but I needed to smarten myself up. I could make it back in twenty minutes, couldn't I? I left the Gainsborough just as Val stowed Margaret in his passenger's seat. He took my hand and said, "You all right?"

It all came rushing back to me—the meeting at the Charlotte. Zeno, Naomi, and Clara trying to out-Oona each other. Learning that Zeno had lied. Spending yet another afternoon at the police station.

"No," I said. "Yes. But I have so many things to tell you, it'll have to wait. See you soon." I gave him a smile that I hoped looked reassuring and a peck on the cheek.

I trotted the first stretch, making it only as far as Marks & Spencer before I slowed to a fast walk, the thickening crowds on the pavement doing their best to get in my way. Wheezing by the time I hiked up to Middlebank's door, I greeted Mrs. Woolgar with a nod and pointed upstairs. "Change," I mouthed, and then pulled myself up two flights and into my flat, where I collapsed on the bed with my feet dangling off the end. I heard a *thunk* as one of my shoes dropped to the floor.

17

Although I had been a hairsbreadth away from falling asleep, I still made it to the library by ten past six wearing my literary salon geranium-pink dress with ruched waist. For this evening, I'd accompanied it with a floral scarf—as if no one would be the wiser to my wearing the same dress three weeks in a row—brushed out my ponytail, and put on fresh lipstick. I felt a world better and more than ready for that sherry.

The board members hadn't waited—when I walked into the library, Adele was circulating among them, pouring refills. Even Val and Margaret had arrived before I did. No one gave me a second look. Mrs. Woolgar had taken charge of Margaret, giving her a tour of the collection, and Zeno had cornered Jane Arbuthnot in an animated, albeit one-sided, conversation. Mrs. Audrey Moon and Mrs. Sylvia Moon had taken Clara under their wing, and when he saw me, Val excused himself from Maureen Frost and handed me a brimming glass. I took a sip and then a deep breath.

"Good evening, everyone," I said. "You may've already

had an opportunity to greet our lecturer for the evening, but let me officially introduced her." Once that formality had been taken care of, I continued to the next order of business. "And now, about our exhibition." I turned to Zeno, who obediently came to my side, looking as fresh as ever in his teal suit.

"There is no need to go into detail about the circumstances, because I'm sure you are quite aware of what's happened. But as sad as we are about Oona, I think we all realize that for the sake of the Society, we need to push on with the exhibition about Lady Fowling. To that end, we're delighted to welcome Zeno Berryfield as manager."

Who was the liar now? I smiled as I said the words, but behind them doubts crowded in about Zeno's whereabouts the previous week and the tales he'd been telling.

But I had to push that aside to concentrate on the evening. After a smattering of applause, we ended the presalon hour, and small conversations broke out. I knocked back the rest of my sherry and headed for the entry to greet guests.

The first one was Bulldog Moyle.

"Hello, good evening," I managed. I'd forgotten that he had bought the series because he hadn't attended the previous week. Behind him, another surprise—Arthur Fish.

"I rang Bulldog the other day," Arthur said, "thinking he might give me his ticket for tonight—I'd hate to miss Margaret. He persuaded me that I should just come along regardless. I hope you don't mind."

"You're very welcome," I said, thinking with the addition of Zeno and Clara—and now Arthur—perhaps I could perch on the mantel like Bunter. "After all, you were our inaugural speaker. Please go up." Arthur headed for the stairs, and I stepped in front of Bulldog. "Could I have a word?"

After a glance up to his friend's disappearing figure, Moyle shrugged.

"I want to apologize again for ringing the police on Saturday," I explained. "I'm sure you can understand how unsettling it would be for me to see someone waiting on the pavement at the very place where a murder had been committed two days earlier."

Bulldog stretched his neck to the side as if his collar were too tight. The top of the book tattoo winked at me above his scarf.

"Yeah," he said. "Well. Got it sorted."

"Good. I hope you enjoy the lecture," I said, and then added, "Oh, there's just this—Arthur said he rang you. Didn't you tell the police that you'd lost your mobile and he didn't have your new number?"

Bulldog stared at me a moment, and then his eyes darted past me to people drifting in the open front door.

"He has it now."

We had more than a full house, but no one seemed to mind the close quarters once the lecture got under way. Just as Margaret had captivated the staff at the Gainsborough, she caught up everyone attending the salon in her stories of the Met, the true ones and those in popular mystery and crime fiction. When she'd finished, a book-buying queue quickly formed, and for another three-quarters of an hour, Margaret's voice could be heard above the general chatter in the room.

Another successful evening for the literary salon series, but I could remember little of what she'd said, because my attention had been elsewhere. I had spent far too much effort trying not to stare at Stuart Moyle. What's this about Arthur Fish having—or not having—Bulldog's mobile number? I should ask Arthur what sort of a collector Moyle was. Avid? Rabid? Was he the sort who kept his most valuable items a secret? In the art world, stolen paintings could disappear entirely into a "private" collection. Would Bulldog murder Oona in order to get his hands on that first edition and then hide it away?

But he didn't get it—Oona's last text indicated she knew where it was, not that she had it in hand. Had he tried to force the information out of her? And even now, did he have plans to conduct his own search?

I'd yet to finish going through the boxes of rare books Duncan Rennie had sent over from secure storage, but we'd needed the library space for the lecture, and so, that morning, I had shifted the lot into the library storage area, which amounted to locked cupboards behind one section of wood paneling. I would keep my eyes on Bulldog, and if I caught him trying to case Middlebank before he left, I'd give him a boot to the bum.

When I hadn't been stewing about Stuart, I had watched Zeno, who, after the lecture, enjoyed himself entirely too much chatting with anyone within easy reach. He'd charmed Audrey and Sylvia Moon, and even Jane Arbuthnot and Maureen Frost had thawed a bit. Mrs. Woolgar remained decidedly uncharmed, but then she was well known to be a hard sell. And Adele? Every time she looked at Zeno, I saw her stifle a giggle.

The crowd dribbled out of the library, heading to the entry, where Mrs. Woolgar handed out coats. Like a sheepdog with her flock, I deftly cut Arthur Fish off from the herd before he could make it to the stairs.

"Oh, Arthur," I said in all innocence, "I wanted to tell you about the great feedback we've received from your lecture."

Bulldog paused and so did I. After a moment, he nodded at Arthur. "I'll wait downstairs."

When he was out of earshot, I continued with Arthur. "Everyone loved your talk, really. What a way to start the series. Also, there's just this one more thing. You gave the police Bulldog's mobile number, but apparently it was a phone he'd lost."

Arthur chuckled. "Is that what he told them? Not really lost, I gave them the wrong number. He's got more than one mobile—one for general use, one for his books, and one for his miniature-army-figure collections."

"Toy soldiers?"

"Yes. He won't answer the book phone unless he recognizes the number—I must've given the detective constable that one by mistake."

Maybe Bulldog recognized that number as police, and that's why he didn't answer.

"Seems like it could cause confusion having three mobiles," I said. "I hope Bulldog didn't blame you for giving them the wrong number."

"Sorry, Hayley—"

It was Clara, holding a carton of wineglasses. She'd volunteered to stay behind to help the servers pack up.

"Can I give you a hand?" Arthur asked, taking the box from her and heading downstairs behind the servers.

"Thank you, Mr. Fish," Clara called.

We followed. On the way down, I said to Clara, "You didn't have to help tidy up—you were a guest this evening."

"I didn't mind," Clara said. "It's all part of a PA's remit—pitch in where needed. Thank you so much for inviting me, Hayley. What an inspiration Ms. Raines is."

"I'm glad you could make it—are you all right to get back to your flat?"

"Oh, yes, thanks."

Zeno came out onto the library landing, looked down, and called, "Good night, Ms. Powell. See you bright and early."

"Yes, Mr. Berryfield, good night," Clara replied, but in a whisper, as Zeno had gone back into the library.

Arthur and Bulldog were out the front door just ahead of the servers and then Clara left. I turned to Mrs. Woolgar, who hovered near the stairs to her lower-ground-floor flat. "Ms. Raines is a fascinating woman," she said to me. "And this was a successful evening. Well done."

"Thank you, Mrs. Woolgar, thank you." I gushed as if she'd just congratulated me on winning Wimbledon—compliments from her were that rare. "Of course, it wouldn't've been possible without your help. See you in the morning."

I was alone in the front entry when my phone rang. The jangle echoed in the space as I fumbled to answer—late-evening calls were so rarely a welcome interruption. My heart skipped a beat when I saw the caller: DS Hopgood.

I answered, "Yes, hello?" as I dashed into my office and closed the door but for a few inches. Zeno was still in the library with Margaret and Val.

"Ms. Burke? I hope this isn't coming at an inconvenient time, but I did think you'd want this news sooner rather than later. It's about Mr. Berryfield's alibi for the day Ms. Atherton was murdered."

I braced myself against my desk. "Yes? Did he . . . was he . . . ?"

"We have located him here at the Bath Spa station leaving at 10:37 and arriving at Bristol Temple Meads at 10:49. We can track him as far as a building on Temple Quay. We find him returning just at the time he said, 18:30 from Bristol Temple Meads arriving at Bath Spa 18:41. He isn't difficult to spot, I'll say that for him."

An appropriate response was called for—I had enough sense to know that—but my mind had gone numb, as if cushioning me against a great swell of emotion.

"Ms. Burke?"

"Yes, Sergeant, thank you," I managed to choke out. "And so, Zeno is no longer a suspect?"

"His alibi is confirmed for well before and past the time of the murder. We got a good look at his face on the platform, both going and coming, because he'd stopped to ask a question at the ticket barrier." When I didn't speak, Hopgood added, "I thought this would ease your mind."

"Yes, indeed it does. Thanks for ringing. Good night."

"Good night."

I looked out of my office to see Val and Margaret coming down the stairs followed by Zeno. As they landed in the entry, I threw open the door and stalked out. It had been building inside me, this uneasy fear of Zeno, along with annoyance at him for not coming clean about seeing Oona in Bath. With Hopgood's news, these two emotions coalesced and swelled into a fiery fury that demanded release. I could not blame him for the former, but I could certainly blast him for the latter.

"Well, a successful evening," I said to the three of them. Zeno had paused on the last step but one. I looked up at him now. "Zeno, could you stay just a moment longer?" I asked the question in what I thought sounded like a pleasant and congenial voice.

Val looked from Zeno to me as he helped Margaret on with her coat.

"Of course I'll stay, Ms. Burke," Zeno said. "I've learned that in exhibition management, our hours are not our own, especially as time grows short."

"Do you need me?" Val asked with a slight frown.

"No," I said, and waved a dismissive hand, "it's just a quick question for him. You go on and drive Margaret to her cousin's."

"A lovely evening, Hayley," Margaret boomed. "Please do keep me informed about the Society. I daresay I'll be down for this noteworthy exhibition."

"Thank you, Margaret, we'll look forward to seeing you again," I said, shepherding them out the door and, just as it closed, adding, "Good night."

I turned back to Zeno, who smiled and said, "Shall we talk in your office? Turned quite cold again, hasn't it? Is the fire going?"

Not a chance. This wasn't a settle-down-by-the-fire sort of conversation. This was more of a stand-in-the-front-ontry-as-if-you-were-in-the-dock confrontation.

"We won't be long," I said quietly. "Zeno, you told me you had not seen Oona since arriving in Bath."

"Yes. Well . . . yes." His eyes flickered round the entry.

"But that isn't true, is it?"

"What do you mean?"

"I mean that you lied. The day before Oona was killed, you were seen going into the Charlotte."

"Who would say such a thing?" he blurted out, his face going scarlet. "How can you believe such a fabrication?"

"It's no 'fabrication,'" I said, my voice rough with anger. "It happened, and when asked, you lied about it. Did you see her more than once? Did you go back to the Charlotte or meet her somewhere or go to her flat? And forget to mention those encounters, too?"

His face, immobile for a moment, began to crumple like an avalanche, which then traveled down through his entire body, and when it hit his legs, caused him to sink to the step, holding on to the railing with one hand.

"I'm so ashamed," he said to the floor. "Look at me— even now, confronted with the truth, I did not have the courage to admit my failure. Yes, Oona had already contacted me about her new project. We met once or twice. She was so proud and I wanted to be happy for her—at least we still had that. I went to her on Wednesday. I had hopes. Such hopes. One last chance for us to reconcile our differences and perhaps find the common ground we had once held. It was an emotional meeting, but not a happy one."

"And how was it you forgot to mention all these encounters?"

"What good would it have done apart from dredging up my failures?"

I had an overwhelming urge to punch him in the face for lying to me, and—as irrational as it sounded—for not being the murderer. Before I realized it, I moved toward him with my hand balled into a fist.

The knock on the front door, brief but urgent, jerked me back to reality. I answered to Val.

"Margaret got a taxi," he explained as he peered round me into the entry.

Saved from being charged with grievous bodily harm, I opened the door wide to let him in.

Zeno popped up off the step. "Ms. Burke, I understand my transgression, I really do. And you have every right to send me packing this minute. I only hope you won't—for Lady Fowling's sake, of course, but also for Oona's. I beg you, let me mount an exhibition she would be proud of."

I considered my options. Keep Zeno—which satisfied Naomi's requirement of having a proper manager—or keep my sanity.

"Also," Zeno said, "I realize this may not be the right time to mention it, but I hope you are as concerned as I am about the relative humidity in the Charlotte. Lady Fowling's books and papers are priceless, and we mustn't do anything to harm them. It so happens, I've written a paper on the qualities of the various types of silica gel, and I'd be happy to share it with you so that we may . . . that is, if there is a 'we.'"

Fear and anger had drained away as I imagined spots of mold appearing on her ladyship's favorite books. Did I have time to delve into the world of silica gel? I gave up. "Yes, all right," I said. "But this is it, Zeno—no more lies."

He raised his hand in a silent oath.

I sighed. "I'll see you in the morning."

He flew past us, grabbing his sheepskin coat on the way and saying, "Mr. Moffatt, a pleasure to meet you this evening. I look forward to a good long chin-wag about your courses. 'Anatomy of a Scene'—a vital skill for any writer. Ms. Burke, I am in your debt. Good night to both of you."

I'll say this for Zeno, he had the good sense to leave

before I changed my mind. When he was gone, I threw both locks, set the alarm, and slumped against the door.

Val took my hands and pulled me to him, lacing his fingers through mine and giving me a much-needed kiss.

"You have impeccable timing," I murmured. "Two seconds later and I'd've laid him flat."

"What was his transgression—wearing shoes so shiny he can see himself in them?"

"Even worse," I said. "He told me he hadn't seen Oona here in Bath, but he had—Dom saw him go into the Charlotte last Wednesday. That lie led me to believe that he might be the murderer. It seemed logical, don't you think? But Sergeant Hopgood rang just before you came downstairs to say they'd confirmed Zeno's alibi. So, that's off."

"Did you want him for the murderer?"

"I shouldn't. If they had arrested Zeno for Oona's murder, we would be out an exhibition manager again, and then what?" I put my hands on Val's chest. "I've had enough of this day. I hope you're staying."

Val and I had spent so few nights together that we'd yet to have that lazy morning after that we so deserved. When it would come, neither of us could guess—it certainly wasn't the next day. I saw him off early and got myself dressed.

Just before leaving to check on my two charges at the Charlotte, I rang the last of Zeno's references again, this an outfit called Tartan Affairs, apparently run by a Scot. I left another message. I wanted to be thorough, although I knew that applicants give only those references that will put them in the best light. And actually, I had to admit Zeno couldn't even be considered an applicant any longer. No, like it or not, he was our exhibition manager.

But it seemed securing the post had given him a sort of complacency, because although he had started like a house afire, he had since slowed to a crawl. I had asked for three ideas for a focal point display—a central exhibit within the show that would either grab those attending and propel them through or turn them off and send them out the door—and Zeno had yet to come up with a single usable idea.

Instead, he continued to offer thoughts on individual displays that were so lacking in interest as to be banal. Worse than banal—soporific.

Wednesday morning, Zeno sprawled in the desk chair in Oona's office, checked his notes, and offered the idea for a display with signage titled *Sir John Fowling and the Tins Market*, accompanied by examples of early-twentieth-century tinned tomato soup.

"You said, didn't you, Ms. Burke, that was how Sir John made his fortune, which led to Lady Fowling's generosity in later life?" Zeno asked, apparently trying to lay the blame at my feet. I crossed it off the list.

Another idea he called *How to Build a Library* sounded promising at first glance, until I saw that what he meant by it was how to build a library—choosing the wood, the depth and width of the shelves, the hardware to hold them up. Then there was *Middlebank Refurbished*, which could find a home at an event for builders and developers, but as I told Zeno through clenched teeth, "Building restoration would not be appropriate for our audience. Also," I continued after I'd unlocked my jaw, "these are hardly ideas for a focal point."

"Yes, Ms. Burke, you asked for a knock-their-socks-off display," Zeno replied. "And I can tell you that I have something in the works, but"—he tapped a forefinger on the side of his nose—"mustn't say too much just yet."

I stood and took my coat from the back of my chair. "I'll be back by this afternoon. Where is Clara?"

Zeno shifted in his seat, leaned forward, and with an unaccustomed serious air, said, "I've no idea, but I'm glad you've brought up the subject. Is Ms. Powell all right, do you think?"

I sat down again. "What do you mean?"

He shook his head. "I can't explain it exactly, but she seems distracted, occasionally combative, and generally missing that spirit of a young person new to our profession. Also, I have heard her speak quietly but with intensity, as if she's having an argument with herself."

"Perhaps it's her style to work aloud," I said.

"Yes, of course, that must be it," Zeno said with that kindly fish-counter smile. "I'm sure you're right."

At the bottom of the spiral staircase, I took the door that led to the refurbished side of the Charlotte. Naomi's door stood open, and as I passed, I heard Clara's voice, but high-pitched and anxious. I hovered for a moment but couldn't make out any of her words, so I reached round to knock lightly on the doorpost before looking in, so I wouldn't be such a surprise.

Clara leapt out of her chair. I could've leapt, too, at the sight of her—her face washed of color and her bun ever so slightly askew.

"I hope I'm not disturbing you two," I said, trying to think of a valid reason for being there.

Naomi looked mildly surprised. "No, Hayley, it's fine, come in."

"I thought I should talk to Ms. Faber," Clara said in a rush, tucking a strand of hair behind an ear. "About what facilities are available for the opening-night gala. I'm compiling a report for you that will include bids from three caterers."

At that moment, the opening-night gala seemed even further away than the actual exhibition, which made no sense. "Thank you, Clara—that's a topic we hadn't even started on. I appreciate your thinking of it." *Who has scared her so? Was it Naomi?*

"I should get back to Mr. Berryfield now," Clara said, and slipped past me.

"Clara," I said, and she stopped. I moved us a few more steps away from Naomi's office door and asked quietly, "Are you all right?"

She nodded. "Oh, yes—super."

"It takes time for those left behind to recover after a death. You'd been working with Oona the better part of a year, and I'm sure this is hitting you particularly hard."

Clara's eyes filled with tears. "No, I'm fine," she said. "It's only, I keep thinking about the last time I saw her—I had no way to know I'd never see her again."

That's right—Clara was the last person to see Oona alive. "Can you recall how she seemed on Thursday morning?"

"What?"

"Was she happy or annoyed or worried or—"

"I don't know," Clara replied with a shrug. "I suppose she was all those things—she was Oona."

I understood what she meant.

"Perhaps," Clara said slowly, "she was a bit more annoyed than usual when I came back with our coffees that morning."

"On Thursday? But I thought you hadn't left the office except to get lunch at Pret and then later, for sketch pads."

"But I'd gone out for coffee, didn't I say that?" She frowned. "Ms. Faber stopped in and asked if I was going, and if so, would I get her cappuccino, but the café at the Assembly Rooms wasn't open yet, and so I went around to the Boston Tea Party on Alfred Street."

"How long were you gone?"

"Only about fifteen minutes. Ms. Faber was still in our office when I returned."

"That's when Oona was annoyed? And you told this to the police?"

Clara's eyes, now void of tears, grew large. "Yes, I did. I must've. I'm sure I mentioned it."

I knew what that meant—it meant I needed to give Detective Sergeant Hopgood a ring.

When Clara headed for the spiral staircase, I turned back to stop again in Naomi's office.

"Everything all right?" I asked.

"She seems to be a bit highly strung, don't you think?" Naomi shifted the papers on her desk.

"I'd think that's to be expected after what she's been through," I said. "Finding Oona like that. Had you seen much of her on Thursday? Oona, I mean."

Naomi tapped her pencil on her lips and said, "Mmm. I put my head in that morning."

"And after that?"

"Crisis with the watercolorists. It took hours to get sorted—I missed my lunch—and then suddenly the police were here, questioning everyone. Terrible, really. So, Hayley, I've had a few thoughts about the focal point display for your exhibition, and if you have a minute, I could just—"

"Sorry," I said as if I actually meant it. "I must be off. We'll talk later. Bye!"

I would call that more than a little presumptuous, thinking she could stick her nose into our exhibition as if she were the manager and not Zeno. Zeno, who had come up with not one single good idea.

I continued down the stairs and to the event space and met with a beehive of activity as the Druids—all dressed in white coveralls—moved in. Two fellows passed me carrying several wide, flat stones tucked under each arm.

"Cairns to the right, dolmen to the left," Tommy King-Barnes called out, waving his hand one way and a clipboard the other.

"Aren't those awfully heavy?" I asked.

"Prop rocks," he said. "One hundred percent post-consumer recycled plastic. When you've been around for six thousand years, you learn to take care of the environment. Howerya, Hayley?"

"Fine. Move-in going all right?"

"A breeze," Tommy said, ticking an item off his clipboard list. "Zeno said as much, told me Naomi Faber runs a tight ship. You wouldn't believe some of the cock-ups we've had to endure—and only because people don't take Druids seriously."

"Naomi and Zeno have worked together before?" I asked conversationally, but with a flutter in my tummy.

"Mmm, some oasthouse museum in Kent, I believe. Last year or year before."

From somewhere nearby came the sound of a Celtic tune—Enya, I thought, singing about Middle Earth. Tommy began patting pockets until he came up with the correct mobile, then held a finger up to me and turned away as he answered in a breathy whisper.

So, Naomi and Zeno had acted as if they'd never met. Incorrect, according to Tommy. Perhaps I could pull a few more details out of him when he finished his call.

From behind me, I heard, "Sorry, could we—"

I turned to find three bigger-than-life mannequins wearing togas, their feet not touching the ground. Then I saw the live arms round their middles, and one of them waved a hand.

"Do you mind?"

"Sorry!" I said, and stepped out of the way, backing up straight into the stack of faux stones. They shook as if the earth had trembled. I moved again, into a short corridor that led to a small storage area. Really just an alcove where a few folding chairs were resting against the wall and, behind them, something large and flat, wrapped in brown paper with a label that read *Greg Renshaw, artist* with a colorful swish and his phone number.

I remembered the watercolorist who had told Naomi he would leave a framed piece behind to collect later. Although Naomi had claimed that no single person had managed the watercolorists' exhibition, this fellow had spoken as if he had been in charge. Perhaps he could confirm Naomi's alibi for all of Thursday afternoon. Of course, she had told everything to the police and they had naturally followed through and checked it, but after Zeno had lied about seeing Oona, Clara had forgotten she'd gone out for coffee, and Naomi was trying to push exhibition ideas on me—I would be hard-pressed to trust even my own alibi.

I snapped a photo of the artist's contact details and left.

18

DS Hopgood, please. It's Hayley Burke."

I phoned this time, because who knows where these police officers got off to during the day, and I didn't feel like waiting in the lobby at the station on Manvers Street.

Kenny Pye came on the line. "Ms. Burke?"

"Yes, here I am again, turning up like a bad penny." When he didn't argue, I went on. "There are a few things I'm not sure you know about. Should I come down?"

"How about I meet you for a coffee?" he asked.

"Oh, yes, all right—where?"

"The café on the Pulteney Bridge?"

I started walking in that direction as I said, "An excellent idea. I'm not too far away."

"Ten minutes, then."

I stepped up my pace, arrived in seven, and waited on the pavement for DC Pye, who arrived not a minute later. We scanned the offerings in the window, went in, and ordered before nabbing a table that looked out on the weir. Now, this was a civilized way to conduct a police interview.

"Am I beginning to annoy everyone at the station with my frequent appearances?" I asked.

"Are you saying you'd rather be in Interview number 1?"

I laughed as it occurred to me that Kenny Pye was really a nice, well-rounded fellow. Probably in his late twenties, a police officer, and a writer of 1920s detective stories starring a PI named Alehouse. I wondered if he was married or had a partner. I wondered if I could get Dinah to come down for a visit and I could introduce the two of them.

Our coffees arrived along with my rock cake and his sausage roll. Kenny got his notebook out, and I remembered my business. First, Clara and her coffee excursion the morning of the day Oona was murdered.

"I believe she's still suffering shock," I said, "and may not be aware of the importance of telling you every single detail of that day." Difficult to remember that had been only the week before, it seemed like ages.

Pye bit off the end of his sausage roll and chewed while he jotted something down.

I proceeded with caution. "Are you suspicious when someone forgets to tell you about where they were and when?"

"Witnesses withhold information for different reasons," Pye said, and stuck out a thumb as he listed them. "They don't think it's relevant. They're afraid it is relevant, and don't want to get themselves or someone else in trouble. Or they truly don't remember. At first. If someone said to you, tell me everything you did a week ago Monday, would you be able to that? Down to the last detail—on the first go?"

I couldn't even have given him the high points, much less the detail. I understood what he meant and was happy that Clara wouldn't be in trouble.

"Now, about Naomi Faber and Zeno—" and I passed along what I'd learned.

Pye flipped pages back and forth, chewed, jotted, and nodded once or twice.

"Did you know that already?" I asked. "Because I keep

finding out these things and turning them over to you without knowing what you will make of it. If I'm repeating myself, if you and Sergeant Hopgood know all this, then I'm only wasting your time."

The DC flipped his notebook closed and stirred what was left of his coffee before he spoke. "It can help to have someone else—that is, not the police—ask a few questions. You can get an entirely different sort of answer that way."

"Detective Constable Pye," I said, "are you saying I am actually a useful part of this enquiry?"

He grinned. "Don't tell Sarge."

The quiet over the next two days got on my nerves. My visits to the Charlotte became unannounced to find out if anyone was actually working on the exhibition. Once, I caught Zeno banging on about some event in County Durham at which he'd re-created the Lambton Worm. I hadn't a clue what he was talking about, but didn't dare ask. Twice he had abandoned the office to chat with Tommy the Druid downstairs, but most often he would be in Oona's office flipping through pages of detective stories while Clara tapped into her tablet.

At Middlebank, I sat in the library and examined the books in the last few cartons that had come from secure storage, making notes about how they might be used in the exhibition. I came across a pristine edition of Sayers's *Gaudy Night* and carefully opened it to read the first line. Before I knew it, I had finished two chapters, and had to force myself to put the book down and return to my search. But nowhere did I come across a first edition of *Murder Must Advertise* signed by members of the Detection Club in 1933.

I reread Lady Fowling's draft letter to Dorothy L. Sayers, hoping to find a clue I'd missed. Adele said her ladyship would've loved to set a puzzle that needed to be solved. What puzzle would that be? I walked out on the library landing—

Mrs. Woolgar had gone to lunch with Mr. Rennie—and had a chat with Lady Fowling.

She could be quite blunt about what she thought or wanted me to do—yes, it was a painting, I remember that—but today, her ladyship kept schtum. I'd heard Sergeant Hopgood use that word and knew what it meant.

"All right, fine," I said to her after asking a few pointed questions. "I'll change the subject." I gazed at the figure of Lady Fowling, full length on a larger-than-life canvas, and wearing a backless, burgundy-satin, halter-top evening dress. Cut on the bias, it draped elegantly to the floor. The artist showed her half-turned and looking over her shoulder, her hand resting on an empty wingback chair. I knew that enigmatic smile by heart. I fancied she had been about my age when she sat for the portrait. Or, more correctly, stood.

"Did you keep that lovely dress you're wearing? Because, on top of everything else I have to worry about, I need a fancy frock for the opening-night gala. And, you know, if you did and if I came across it and if it fit and if you didn't think it was too presumptuous of me . . . do you think I could wear it?"

I heard the front door click closed, and I broke out in a cold sweat. I went to the railing and looked down.

"Mrs. Woolgar?"

"Yes, Ms. Burke. I'm just in from lunch." She said it in all innocence, but she'd already hung up her coat, so she must've been standing there a minute or two. I blushed. "I'm sorry if I've disturbed your meeting," the secretary added.

I cleared my throat. "Yes, well, it's all right. I was only on the phone." My phone lay on my desk downstairs. I prayed it wouldn't ring and give me away.

Thursday at the Charlotte, I'd had to sit through another session listening to Zeno's inane ideas for displays. A map with pins showing where each book in Lady Fowling's collection had been set. Mildly interested, I had asked what we would do about all those imaginary places authors had invented, but he had gone straight on to another one of his so-called brainstorms. He suggested we show the many kinds of locks involved in a locked-room mystery—rim lock, rotating bolt, lever lock, slide—was ironmongery that fascinating?

Exasperated, I gathered my things together to leave, but paused in the doorway and ginned up my courage. "I feel there is a certain energy lacking in the ideas we"—a charitable use of the word *we*—"are coming up with. We need a bit of drama, you know. Something to grab the imagination of those attending. Let's leave it there for now. See you in the morning."

Val rang after his evening class and let me witter on about my frustration.

"We could explore Lady Fowling's affection for each of the main writers of the Golden Age of Mystery," I said. "We could group books appropriately, and the signage could contain quotes from letters and inscriptions—personal things written to her ladyship. What about a whole investigation into her own detective? 'Who Was François Flambeaux?' One of those screens where detectives were listed on one side and attributes on the other, and people would have to match them up? We could get a mannequin and dress him in character. What did Flambeaux wear?"

"I don't know," Val said, "but those sound like the ideas of an exhibition manager to me."

"Silly," I replied, but smiled. Then I remembered the problems with displaying fragile items without damaging them. Light, humidity—Zeno knew about those concerns. But what would he do with my ideas if I handed them off to him?

Val and I fell silent—listening to him breathe was a comforting pastime on the phone, as we had had precious little time together since Tuesday. The week wouldn't end any other way. He had a day full of meetings at the college on Friday, and I would be off early Saturday to visit my mum. We were back to needing time, and not having any until something broke free.

"Have you heard from the girls?" I asked.

"Bess is being slippery, and I don't know why. Becky has a plein air session this weekend at the site of an Iron Age fort in Dorset."

"Plein air in winter?" I asked. "That's dedication for you."

"Says the woman who'll spend half the day poking round tide pools in November," he replied.

I laughed. "That's because I knew you would warm me up after."

"I would do now, too." We fell into a moment of silent longing punctuated by my heavy sigh.

When I arrived at the Charlotte Friday morning, Clara sat alone in the office.

"Mr. Berryfield has gone to carry out more measurements of the front entry," she explained. "He seems to have an idea."

At last.

"Good. Now, Clara, I hope you don't mind my asking, but are you going back to Shepton Mallet for the weekend? I'm sure your nana is eager to hear how your job is going."

Before she could answer, there came a clanging and rattling from the spiral staircase. Zeno, on his way up and in a hurry.

"Ms. Burke—excellent. Delighted you've arrived. Would you mind?"

He held out a tape measure and I took it.

"What are we measuring?"

"The stairs," he said. "Come out, now, and I'll go to the next landing, and you can reel the tape down."

I followed him out and he ran round and round and down, and when he'd arrived at the lower landing, he looked up and said, "Fire away."

I obeyed but, as I did so, asked, "Mr. Berryfield, why do you need these measurements?"

"Confirmation, Ms. Burke—all shall be revealed! What do you read just to the top of the railing?"

"Fifteen feet and—"

"Yes, that's fine. Just as I suspected," he muttered, then let go of the tape and ran back up the stairs and into the office. "Come in."

Clara had stayed put in her chair in the far corner. Zeno took a flip chart—the kind that usually sat on an easel—from behind the desk and looked at us both with a gleam in his eye.

"I give you," he announced, "your focal point display— the offices of Pym's Publicity, Ltd."

He opened the flip chart with a flourish and held it in front of him, like a man wearing a sandwich sign. I saw a large sketch done in pencil with shadings and distinct lines, and my first thought was to wonder if Zeno had started out as a draftsman or architect. But that first thought lasted no more than a second as the subject of the sketch hit home.

It showed a spiral staircase and a landing at the top with several figures looking over the railing to the floor below. Two others stood with their hands against a wall, as if backing away in horror. At the bottom of the stairs, sprawled at the feet of three other people, lay a body outlined in chalk.

I couldn't speak. Zeno glanced from me to Clara and back, his face lit with enthusiasm. "Don't you see? We will replicate the iron staircase from *Murder Must Advertise* at the entry to the exhibition. It will be full size, in the middle of the room, and visible from anywhere in the exhibition, drawing visitors to it. It will be as if they had just walked into the murder scene themselves!"

Beside me, Clara whimpered.

"Put that away," I whispered fiercely to Zeno, and when he didn't move, I added, "Now!"

He flipped the cover closed.

"Ms. Burke," Zeno said with a hurt tone, "you wanted an

idea for the most prominent display in the show, and I have given you one. I must say I expected a different reception for a visual that not only embodies the puzzle of a murder mystery, but also ties into what you tell me is the most significant find—or, that is, nonfind at the moment—in the history of writing detective fiction. What have I done wrong?"

"Clara," I said, putting my hand on her arm. I felt her tremble. "I hope you don't mind if I take you away from the exhibition today. It's only that Mrs. Woolgar and I are barely keeping our heads above water with so much work. We're trying to get out the Society's newsletter and . . . there are all sorts of other things we need help with. So, I am going to take you back to Middlebank with me. All right? Why don't you go on down and let Naomi know, and I'll be right behind you."

I doubted if Naomi cared one whit where Clara worked—I only wanted to get the young woman out of this office so that I could have a word with Zeno.

"Yes, of course, Hayley." Clara popped out of her chair, snatched her coat, bag, and tablet, and fled.

I closed the door. It always took Clara extra time on the spiral staircase, and after what Zeno had just shown us, she still might be hovering on the landing when I'd finished. I looked round at him now as he dropped the flip chart behind the desk.

"Was there something wrong with Ms. Powell?" he asked.

"Did it not occur to you—" I had caught Clara's trembles. They'd gone to my throat, and I coughed them away and began again. "Did it not occur to you that your sketch represents how Oona was killed? That Clara was the first person to find her after she had been pushed down the stairs? Did you not think this would bring that horrible moment back to her? And how in the world could you think this an appropriate display for the exhibition? It would be seen as an advertisement for murder—real murder, not a story in a book! How would it look for the Society to condone such violence?"

My ears rang. I took a deep breath.

Zeno's face had gone white and his hands shook. "But it *is* a story—that's all. I wanted to tie in this exciting discovery and . . . oh, dear God, what have I done?" He sank into a chair. "I would never make light of Oona's death, you must believe that, Ms. Burke. I assure you, it could be the one defining moment in my life. The watershed where I look behind at what I've lost as well as ahead. I face my past failures and hope my future actions will atone."

Could he be that thick? Yes, I believed he could.

"Of course, now I see." He nodded. "Why, I suppose my brazen idea would even shock the murderer, wouldn't it?" He cut his eyes to the closed door. "I'm so terribly sorry."

"Well, regardless, Clara needs to step away for a moment. I've plenty for her to do at Middlebank. Obviously, your idea won't do, and you will have to try again. I'll be sure to check in at the end of the day, and if you've got nothing else, you may need to shift into a more technical role."

Would Naomi buy that? Would she insist that she become the exhibition manager—I'd seen that desire in her from the first meeting after Oona's death. No, I may need to keep Zeno as the figurehead, disguising his demotion from both Naomi and himself.

"If that happens, you and I will work on each and every display together," I continued, although the thought of spending hours and hours with Zeno felt too much like a harsh self-imposed punishment. "You have time and you know the subject. Look for something that connects the women authors to Lady Fowling—a quality, a passion."

Zeno showed no emotion and only murmured something unintelligible. I thought it best to leave without asking him to repeat it. I paused at the top of the spiral staircase and looked over to the landing below, and with a sick lurch in my tummy, imagined Oona tumbling down. Even without Clara's admonition, I held tightly to the railing.

Naomi's office door was closed, but I heard the clattering of construction downstairs and so followed it, and spotted Clara with the Druids, looking quite chipper.

"Ms. Faber wasn't in her office," she explained, "and Mr. King-Barnes said it would be all right for me to observe their move-in. Did you know, Hayley, that the Druids never wrote anything down?"

"That must make it difficult to come up with signage," I said to Tommy.

"Contemporary sources," Tommy said, "and later, blokes such as Pliny the Elder helped us out a bit. We'd have much more, if it hadn't been for those damned Romans." He shook his head.

Clara laughed. "Mr. King-Barnes says he actually likes the Romans and mounted an exhibition on the Fosse Way."

"Actually *on* the Fosse Way," Tommy said with a grin. "Also known as the A46 in the East Midlands. We put installations in lay-bys along the highway with actors in Roman togas." He spread his hands out as if sweeping across a roadside sign. "'Have a Cuppa with an Emperor!' People loved it."

I wonder, did Zeno work on that one?

Mick Jagger started up, and Tommy patted his pockets until he'd come up with the correct phone. He answered as he stepped away, sounding a bit like—

"Hayley." Clara stood in front of me, her shoulders thrown back. "I want to assure you that my reaction to Mr. Berryfield's idea was only momentary. And it wasn't his fault. We should never try to blame another for our actions—it makes us look weak. We should take responsibility no matter what. I'm all right now, so I can stay and work. You don't have to take me away."

"Nonsense," I said. "We need you at Middlebank." I'm sure I could find something for her to do.

19

Early Saturday morning, I boarded a train to Bristol Temple Meads and then, twenty minutes later, changed for a train to Wolverhampton, where I would change again for Liverpool—my normal weekend visit to my mum. On the last leg, I settled with a cup of tea and a bun, and texted Val.

Wish you were here

He rang, and when I answered, he said, "And you here. Although I quite look forward to going up to Liverpool to meet your mum."

Another hurdle we hadn't jumped yet—meet the parents. Even at our age it mattered.

"Bess is stopping by today," he told me now.

My heart fluttered. "Is she? I'm sorry I can't be there."

"She wants to go through a few old boxes, she told me, but—it's a bit odd. I don't know what she's looking for."

Her mother, no doubt.

"Give her my regards," I said.

It wasn't enough, but would have to do for now. Still, the remainder of my journey I stewed about what else I could've said. "Regards" sounded cold—is that what she would think of me? Finally, having worried myself out on that subject, I picked up my worn paperback copy of *Murder Must Advertise*.

At my mum's flat, I deposited my bag and gave her home health-care worker an envelope with her pay. Once she'd left, Mum put a plate of shortbread on the seat of her rolling walker and took it to the kitchen table. I switched the kettle on, and we began to dissect our weeks.

"Any word on your surgery date?" I asked.

"No, still on the list. I don't mind that," Mum said. "I just hope it doesn't interfere with your exhibition, because Dinah and I are coming down for it."

"Oh, Mum, you don't need to, but—I'm awfully glad you will. Dinah will be a good traveling companion for you, and you know how accommodating the train staff are." I measured out coffee into the cafetière and, when the kettle went off, poured in the water. I was awfully pleased Mum would see the exhibition. She had not been to Bath since I'd started at the First Edition Society, and I so wanted to show it off to her. And now, to introduce her to Val. I did not forget that I lived on the second floor at Middlebank—up two flights of stairs—but I would work something out.

"Tell me more about Val's daughters," Mum said, reaching for mugs off the counter and uncovering the jug of milk. She and I had talked only briefly during the week. I had tried to cover everything—dinner at Val's and the girls' visits the next morning—but my account had been inadequate, to say the least. Now I could give it my full attention.

"And so," I said after Mum had given me a thorough interrogation, "I think what it is, is that they're worried I'll leave him and he'll be hurt, and they believe it's their job to prevent that from happening. At least, that's what Bess seems to be worried about. Becky may have other ideas, but her sister has taken charge of the matter." I wrinkled my nose. "Still, there's something that doesn't ring true."

"Mmm," Mum said. "It does sound a bit off. As if Bess were . . ." She reached for another shortbread finger and tapped it on her plate. "No"—under her breath this time—"I'd say there just might be something else going on."

I ate my shortbread and we drank the rest of our coffees in silence, until Mum picked up on what sounded like an altogether different topic.

"Do you remember the time a few years ago, when Dinah became so dead set against me selling my little house?"

That was an odd time in all our lives. Years after my dad died, Mum had married again and moved to Liverpool from Ross-on-Wye. Shortly thereafter—when her husband moved to Scotland, taking part of her pension with him—she realized the marriage had been one of those bad decisions. At the time, I'd been so caught up in the drama of my own marriage's disintegration and trying to protect Dinah, Mum had been divorced almost before I knew it. She decided to stay in Liverpool, and a few years later, when Dinah had turned seventeen, sold the house in Ross-on-Wye. My daughter had thrown a fit.

"I do remember that," I said. "She kept going on and on about how you were giving up a lifetime of memories and your independence and—well, I can't remember what all she said."

"Dinah remembered that little house from her summer holidays. We thought she was worried about losing her memories. Turned out to be nothing of the sort."

"That's right—what upset her the most was that she wanted to take a gap year and work on the Isle of Mull in a pub and have time to think about what she wanted to do with her life."

"But she didn't know how to tell you," Mum said, "and so she latched on to something entirely different to be upset about. She was quite adamant in her protests, as I recall. 'But, Gran, how can you do this to us?'"

I stared at the plate of shortbread. "Are you saying what Bess is upset about has nothing to do with Val and me?"

"I'm saying you should put your detective mind to work and see what you can discover."

I snorted with laughter, and it took several minutes before I could speak. "Detective mind—good one, Mum. If I had one of those, couldn't I point the finger at Oona's murderer and save everyone a great deal of trouble?"

"Early days yet," Mum replied with a grin. "How's the book?" She nodded at my paperback.

"Nearly finished," I said—or would be by morning, so that I could give a good report.

On Sunday, over a late breakfast—so late it could've been called lunch—we discussed Lord Peter Wimsey.

"I loved it!" I said of the story at Pym's Publicity, Ltd., as I smeared butter on a slice of toast. "It must be the first thing police thought about Oona, too—that it was an accident. But as Lord Peter says, 'Some accidents are too accidental to be true.' It was true of Oona."

"Lord Peter has Inspector Parker, you have Detective Sergeant Hopgood."

"And Kenny Pye," I said. Should I bring up my idea about introducing him to Dinah?

"What about the wordplay?" Mum asked.

"What a wit," I said. "And Lord Peter made a fine copy-writer, didn't he?"

"Because Sayers had been one herself. And there are all sorts of things a mystery writer can do with words, aren't there?" Mum asked. "Codes. Anagrams."

"Oh dear," I said. "You aren't going to start in on that, are you?"

Mum had been at the kitchen table that morning with

her phone open to a wordplay app. Anagrams had become her latest craze.

"Silent," she said, and I knew it to be a challenge.

"Sss . . . wait, I need something to write on." I scribbled, tried once or twice, and said, "Listen!"

"Tosser," Mum said.

I wrote, rearranged, and jabbed my pencil on the paper. "Stores!"

"Repetitive mole rolls."

"What? Oh, Mum," I said, "I'm being taken here, aren't I?"

"You've got to keep those little gray cells working."

"Well done, Ms. Poirot. Repetitive mole rolls." I wrote it down and wrinkled my brow in mock concentration. "All right, what is it?"

"Liverpool Lime Street."

"Really?" I copied that out, too, and ticked off each letter before I conceded. "But Sayers didn't use anagrams, did she? She used—"

A door in my mind flew open, and I had one of those blinding revelations just like a real fictional detective in which, suddenly, a puzzle becomes incredibly clear.

"I've got it—I've got it! It was right in front of me the entire time, but I didn't see. Do you remember I told you that Oona had me transcribe Lady Fowling's notebooks from the 1950s?"

"I do remember—and you weren't best pleased about the assignment, thinking it was busywork."

"True, it did seem a rather useless task at first, but she is, after all, the exhibition manager."

"*Was*, dear," Mum reminded me.

"Yes, right. Well, I came across an odd list of phrases her ladyship wrote and I dutifully copied them out even though I had no idea what they meant. She did have a tendency to go off on tangents and hop from one topic to another in her notebooks. Sometimes even on the same page—detective stories, recipes, shopping lists. Makes for entertaining, if confusing, reading. So, I printed the transcriptions out and gave them to Oona, who went through the pages scribbling comments and jotting down ideas for the exhibition."

"What did Oona make of those odd phrases?"

I slapped my hand on the table. "You may well ask! When she was found, dead, the papers were scattered everywhere. The police took them in as evidence, and Sergeant Hopgood asked me to take a look, hoping I'd find a clue to her murderer. I've gone through them twice and there was not a clue—about anything. And do you know why that is?"

Mum leaned forward. "Tell me."

"Because that one page with Lady Fowling's odd phrases on it is *missing*. Gone! And now that I've read to the end of *Murder Must Advertise*, I know why. The phrases must be a word puzzle her ladyship made up, and Oona must've cracked the code."

"And what do they mean?"

I slumped back in my chair, exhausted from this sudden burst of vision. "I think she learned the location of the book from the code—the signed first edition. She texted me seconds before someone threw her down the stairs. Here now, let me find it." I grabbed my phone and brought up Oona's last message.

I know where it is! Death is the clue. Murder must

Mum studied the text and then nodded slowly. "Death Bredon—I can see that. Yes, she must've known the book's whereabouts."

"All along I had the feeling that I was missing something."

Mum took a sharp breath. "*You* weren't missing the *clue*—the *clue* was missing!"

We sat in silence for a moment. It had been the book all along. The murderer had taken the key to finding the first edition and that left us . . .

"Well," said Mum brightly, patting my hand. "It looks like you'll have to go back to the original and break the code yourself, then, won't you? It may not be first letters, remember that—could be any sort of wordplay."

If I couldn't even get the name of the local rail station out of an anagram, I'm not sure how I was to—

My phone pinged with a text. It was from Dinah—the three words that could strike terror in the heart of any mother.

I'm all right.

20

D inah, sweetie, it's Mum."

"Mum. Hi. I didn't mean for you to . . . I didn't want to worry you. The fire's out now."

"Your house?" I could barely breathe.

"No, only the mudroom, where the electrics are—and then, a bit of the kitchen."

The word *electrics* rang a bell—a deep and foreboding clanging.

"What's happened, sweetie?"

"It was an accident." Her voice trembled and my heart ached. "We told the fire brigade that. They didn't mean to, it was only that—"

"They? Who are they?" An arsonist? An old boyfriend with a grudge? A gang of looters targeting aging Victorian semidetacheds?

"Dad and his mate, Crowdey. Remember Dad said he could upgrade the electrics and you said we'd need a certified electrician. But Dad said Crowdey has done loads of electrics for other people, and so they just sort of showed up today and got to work."

She had me at "Dad." I laid my phone down on the kitchen table and with a shaky finger pushed a button.

"Sweetie, I'm at Gran's and I've put you on speaker, because she wants to hear, too. You go on."

"Hi, Gran," she said, her voice quavering. "Well, I'm not sure what happened, because Ginny and I were upstairs, but we heard a loud pop, and after a few minutes, I smelled smoke . . ."

I listened, and while Mum kept up our side of the conversation and Dinah told her story, I dashed back into the spare room to shove my belongings into my overnight case and grab my toothbrush from the bathroom. I was back out in the kitchen as Dinah wrapped up the tale of woe.

". . . and the fire brigade was here and they said it was mostly smoke. It was a lot of smoke. And the power was cut to four houses on our side of the road."

"You and Ginny are all right?"

"Yeah, we're okay," she said in weak voice.

"Dinah, sweetie, I'm on my way. It's only an hour to Sheffield on the train and we'll have the rest of the day to sort this out. Wait until I arrive and we'll ring your landlord together. And listen"—I stopped and took a breath—"is your dad still there?"

"Yes, they're downstairs packing up their gear, but I came back up to my bedroom to ring you. Dad said I didn't need to tell you and that he would take care of everything. It's only I thought—"

"Never mind, sweetie," I said in a soothing voice. "Of course you did the right thing phoning. I'm going to give your dad a ring right this minute. Just to have a chat. Now, look, have the fire brigade left yet?"

"Not quite. Downstairs is a disaster, Mum—there's water and foam everywhere."

"We'll soon put that to right," I said. "I'll text you to say which train I'm on, and I'll get a taxi to your house. See you soon, sweetie."

Mum came to the door with me. "You tell Dinah she could come and stay with me for a few days—her winter half term is coming up."

I gave her a kiss on the cheek. "Thanks, Mum. I'll phone you later."

As soon as her door closed, I took off like a shot for the rail station, at the same time phoning my ex. It rang long enough to go to his voice mail. I hung up and tried again—same result. The third time, he must've realized I wouldn't give up, and answered.

"Look, Hay"—he knew I hated that nickname—"did Dinah ring you? Because I want you to know Crowdey and I are going to put this to rights and—"

"Get out of that house," I demanded, my voice thick. "Do you hear me? *Now!* Haven't you done enough to your daughter for one day? Get out and take your cowboy electrician friend with you. What in God's name got into you? Electrics? Will you not rest until you've had your daughter turfed out of her house because of the damage you've caused?"

I strode into the station as Roger offered a feeble protest. "Shut it!" I told him. "Who knows how much this will cost to repair and how much of it the landlord will require them to pay. But know this—*you* are the responsible party, and *you* will come up with the money. I'll see to it. I will get every penny you've got even if I have to wring it out of your—"

I hadn't realized I'd been shouting until a security guard approached me with his hands loose at his side, as if he might need to use his truncheon on a violent commuter. The crowd near the platform barrier stared at me.

"I'll let you know about the cost," I muttered, and rang off. I smiled at the guard and walked meekly to the nearest ticket machine.

* * *

I stewed about Roger all the way to Sheffield, and continued in the taxi from the station. Every time he did something like this—it wasn't always setting fire to a kitchen—I
threatened and shouted, but he always seemed to be able to
work his way round any responsibility. He would come up
with lame excuses and poorly thought-out solutions, wearing me down until I would give up the fight. Not the best
pattern, but one that I hadn't yet had the energy to break.

Like a slap in the face, it hit me—my relationship with
Zeno mirrored the one with my ex. He created chaos, I
exploded, he groveled, and we started again. How could I
not have seen it?

The taxi pulled to a stop, and I pushed aside those
thoughts to concentrate on my daughter. The old brick Victorian where Dinah and her housemate, Ginny, lived had
seen better days, but it was ideal for two uni students, and
after all, you can put up with almost anything when you're
twenty-two. They'd briefly had a third housemate, but she
had moved on to London, and now Dinah and Ginny sol-
diered on together, each with spotty jobs that earned them
barely enough to live on most weeks. I helped Dinah out, of
course, and Ginny's parents, who lived in New Zealand,
did what they could, too.

When I got out of the taxi, I thought the house looked
worse than usual, but it was my imagination, because the
damage from the fire was at the back. Dinah met me at the
front door, hollow eyes, disheveled hair, and wearing only
shorty pajamas and a shapeless cardigan even on this frigid
day.

"Dinah, sweetie." I put my arms round her and felt her
body relax against mine. Even at the door, I could smell the
smoke. It had drifted out into the front hall and still hung
heavy in the air.

"It's a bit of a mess," she said, and took me straight back

to the scene. The mudroom and half the kitchen looked as if they had been hit by that marshmallow man in *Ghostbusters*, and puddles of water dotted the floor like a miniature fen. The firefighters, now departed, had added to the mix by tracking in mud, and now dirty, foamy boot prints could be seen going in and out. If it had been a crime scene, there would've been plenty of forensic evidence.

A man stood in front of the fuse box in the mudroom humming to himself, an open toolbox on the counter at his side. For a moment, I thought this might be Crowdey, and I was poised to attack, but Dinah grabbed my arm and said, "He's an electrician, Mum—the real kind. Next door rang our landlord, and he got this fellow out straightaway. Said we'd sort out the cost later, not to worry."

Not to worry about an electrician called out on a Sunday afternoon? I shuddered to imagine the bill. Because, although I did my best to threaten Roger, I knew we'd see little if any compensation from him.

The fellow slammed the metal door shut. "There you go," he said cheerfully. "Power restored."

"That's grand," Dinah said. "I'll run up and tell Ginny."

"So," I said, "not too much of a job? I mean, considering the damage."

"The problem was," the man said, straightening up the contents of his toolbox, "they got their wiring colors switched round and the cabling—"

And therein began a detailed description of basic electricity that I'm sure I should've understood, but didn't. I smiled and nodded as he nattered on about voltage and breakers and residual current and earthing.

". . . and after that," he concluded, "well, Bob's your uncle."

"I can't thank you enough for coming out on a Sunday afternoon to help the girls," I said. Not that he wouldn't be well compensated, I was sure.

I led him to the front door and bade him good-bye and

then rested my forehead against the doorpost for a moment, gathering my strength. I heard a rustle behind me. The girls had come out of hiding and stood at the bottom of the stairs.

"Hello, Ms. Burke," Ginny said, pulling down the sleeve of an enormous woolly jumper that looked as if it were held together by a wish and a prayer. "It's awfully good of you to come and help. Would you like a cup of tea?"

"I would indeed," I said. "I'm gasping."

"Right," Dinah said. "I'll just go down to the corner shop for milk."

"Lovely, but, sweetie—put some clothes on first."

Scrub, mop, dry, polish, repeat. Once we'd got the kitchen and mudroom back in order, I moved on to the front room and then up the stairs to the bathroom, because why not? Dinah and Ginny disappeared not long after we'd finished the ground floor, but I kept it up, and at the end of five hours, I felt as if we'd got the old girl—the house—in better shape than she had been in before the fire. The only reminders of the disaster were the blackened wall around the fuse box and the plug sockets in the kitchen. I was admiring my work when the landlord stopped in.

"Not too bad, is it?" he asked. "But the smell of smoke really hangs in there, doesn't it? On the walls and such."

"A fresh coat of paint would go a long way to getting rid of that," I said, and then suggested that Dinah and Ginny repaint for him to help offset the cost of the electrician.

The landlord confessed that the electrician was his brother-in-law, who would give him a deep discount. "And these two"—he nodded to the girls, who had crept out of hiding—"are the best tenants I've had in years. I wouldn't want to lose them over someone else's mistake. So, yeah, I'm sure we can work something out."

That called for a bit of a celebration. When he'd gone, I said, "Right, you girls, shall I cook us a meal?"

"Mum," Dinah chastised.

"You young women," I corrected.

Whatever they were, they had nothing in their fridge but that one small jug of milk, and so I walked down to the shop, came back, and made a quick pot of chili with frozen pre-formed beef burgers, a tin of tomatoes, an onion, and a bottle of some sort of hot sauce—its label was in a foreign language. That and the box of Magnum Double Caramel ice cream bars for afters did the trick—their spirits bounced back, and we soon landed in a discussion about what color the kitchen should be. Ginny leaned toward orange and Dinah campaigned for dark blue. My suggestion for white went unheard.

We were clearing the table when I looked at the time.

"You could stay the night, Mum," Dinah said.

"Sweetie, I'd love to, but I need to be at work first thing in the morning."

When my taxi arrived, Dinah and Ginny followed me out the door with many thanks. I got to the station in time to sprint for a train, which pulled out just before eight o'clock. Finally, I relaxed—I wouldn't have to change trains until Bristol Temple Meads. I pulled out my phone to text Val and could hardly read the screen, I was that tired.

I had sent a message on my way to the fire with the barest of details and he had responded, happy that Dinah and Ginny were safe. Now all I could manage was:

Leaving Sheffield. Late home. See you tomorrow.

Just after I sent it, I realized my error—tomorrow, Monday, Val taught all day and into the evening. But I had no energy to correct myself, and so put my phone away, set my bag on the table in front of me, and rested my head on it. A lumpy pillow, but all I had.

* * *

The train came to an abrupt halt, jolting me awake. I peeled
my cheek off my bag, rubbed the indentation it left behind, and blinked the sleep out of my eyes. Where was I? The
handful of people remaining on the train stood, retrieved bags
from overhead, and made for the exit, leaving behind empty
teacups and sandwich wrappers.

A voice announced: "This is Bristol Temple Meads.
This train terminates here. Please remove all your belongings and make your way to . . ."

Right, time to find my next train. I scooted out of the
seat, heaved my case onto my shoulder, and caught sight of
myself in the carriage window—the band on my ponytail
had pulled half out, and I'd buttoned my coat wrong, so one
side of the collar stuck up under my chin. How had I managed that? I dragged myself off the carriage and stood
squinting at a departure board, unable to focus well enough
to see from which platform I would catch the next train to
Bath.

"There she is!"

I whirled round at the sound of his voice, threw myself
off balance, and stumbled. Had I imagined it?

"Hayley!"

Val stood at the ticket barrier, talking to a guard and
pointing my way. The guard nodded, allowed him to pass,
and he ran toward me. Fear froze me to the spot.

"What's wrong?" I said, a sob in my throat. "What's
happened?"

The smile on his face vanished. "Nothing's happened,"
he said. "I drove over to save you the last leg of your journey. I sent you a text."

My brain was still in a fog. "Oh, I fell asleep on the
train." I pulled my phone out and saw his message.

Look for me at BTM

"I thought you needed a break, after the day you've had."

For a moment, I could only stare at him. A worry furrowed his brow, and he looked as if he might speak, but before he could, I dropped my bag on the platform and threw myself into his arms, almost knocking him over. As he held me tightly, I nestled my head against his neck. "That's the nicest thing anyone has ever done for me," I said, my voice muffled by his coat. "Ever."

"Ever?" he asked.

I looked up at him. "I love you."

The corners of his eyes crinkled as he smiled. "If only I'd known it took a thirty-minute drive to get you to say that." He brushed the hair out of my face. "I love you back, you know."

"I do know."

Nothing like a three-hour train nap to revive a person. On the drive to Bath, I filled Val in on the Sheffield excitement, the aftermath, and how I would hold Roger's feet to the fire until he paid up. At one point, I sniffed the air.

"Do you smell smoke?" I asked.

"Yeah, love, I do," Val said. "I'm afraid it's you."

"Oh, yes, of course. But at least I left Dinah and Ginny with a clean house. And speaking of daughters—how is Bess?"

Val negotiated the curve on the Weston Road and sighed. "I don't want you to think this is about you," he started.

"Oh, I know it isn't," I replied. "I talked to my mum about it—that was all right, wasn't it?"

"Of course. I like your mum."

Which is funny, really, as they'd had only two brief phone conversations when I'd been indisposed and asked Val to answer my mobile for me. But Mum said the same thing about him.

"I don't want you to think you have to . . ." Val said, and

started again. "I should be able to find out . . . it's just that she's got something she won't . . ." He grabbed my hand for a moment.

"Would it be all right if I talked with Bess?" I asked, a touch apprehensive. I didn't want to annoy her or step on any parental toes. "What do you think?"

"Would you?"

He pulled to the curb a few doors down from Middlebank and switched off the engine.

"If you stay, I promise I'll get you out the door in time for your first class."

He leaned over and kissed me. "It's a deal. Here now, give me your bag."

I handed it over, but as soon as I'd opened the front door, I had to take it back again. Bunter sat on the glove drawer of the mahogany hallstand with a pained expression on his face that I'm sure was meant to make me feel as if he'd been waiting there for hours and hours.

"Yes, cat, never fear, I didn't forget." I rummaged in my bag until I located his peace offering—a fresh catnip mouse. He jumped to the floor and began his circle eights round both my legs and Val's. I dangled the newest offering, he batted at it a few times, and our ritual complete, I tossed it across the front entry. It landed just inside my office door, out of sight. Bunter began the hunt.

In my flat, I had a shower, and while my hair dried, Val and I drank mugs of hot cocoa, played with each other's fingers, and smiled. But my burst of energy had not lasted long—it was, after all, close on two in the morning—and before our mugs were empty, we went to bed.

The next morning, I was true to my word, sending Val on his way after tea and toast and a kiss in plenty of time for his nine o'clock class. Ten minutes after he'd left, I remembered what the fire at Dinah's house had managed to push out of my mind, and I sat over a second cup of tea as I thought through the matter and decided on my course of action

One page of transciption from Lady Fowling's notebooks had as good as vanished. The police had taken all the scattered papers from the crime scene and put them in the three fat binders—evidence masquerading as ephemera in a scrapbook. But they didn't have that one sheet, which held the key to the location of the signed first edition of *Murder Must Advertise*. Oona had spotted Lady Fowling's clues and had broken the code and crowed about it in the text she sent me—she mentioned "Death," which must've referred to Death Bredon, Lord Peter's undercover identity.

Someone else knew the worth of the book—a one-of-a-kind—and had killed Oona for the clue to its location. That made sense. She had the paper in her hand, and once she was dispatched, the murderer had taken it. But if the murderer had the key and he knew the location of the book, had he found it and taken it away? Impossible—wherever the book was, it had to be under the control of Middlebank and the Society.

I had no way of knowing how Oona had arrived at the answer, and so I would turn to the original clue—Lady Fowling's page of funny phrases—and decipher the code myself. And I would do that, just as soon as Mrs. Woolgar and I agreed on the menu for the exhibition's gala opening.

That took the better part of our morning briefing. I could barely sit still while we discussed the drinks menu, the finger food, and how to limit the numbers at an event sure to draw a crowd. One second, I teetered on the verge of telling her my theory, and the next, caution overtook me and I determined to keep quiet.

"I don't care to eat soup while standing," Mrs. Woolgar said, perusing a bid from a caterer. "The probability for a mishap is far too high."

My mind continued to argue with itself while I glanced

down at the list of finger foods. "Oh, arancini—those little Italian rice balls are easy to eat. Actually, do we need to decide now?"

"As Ms. Powell took it upon herself to gather the information from three caterers, I thought we should show some interest."

"Yes, of course. When did you last talk with Clara?"

"She rang late Friday to ask for the board members' contact details. She plans to interview them about her ladyship. I believe she's spoken to Jane Arbuthnot and Maureen Frost as well as the Moons. Ms. Babbage was away for the weekend."

Clara seemed intent on furthering her career, I must say. Taking over Oona's flat, assuming the responsibility for publicity, and now contacting the board members without even running it past me first. A bit presumptuous. How far would she go to—

"It sounded like a fine idea to me," Mrs. Woolgar said.

"Yes, of course it is."

I blushed. If anyone wanted to further a career, how about Naomi? Or Zeno? No, not Clara.

The secretary glanced at her notes. "And how are plans for the displays progressing?"

I had deftly put Zeno's callous and bizarre suggestion— to put a spiral staircase in the entry—out of my mind for the weekend, circumstances being what they were, but now the horror of it hit me again with full force.

"We continue to gather ideas," I said.

"Well, then, is there anything else for this morning?" Mrs. Woolgar asked.

All at once I was certain I didn't want to say anything about Oona's discovery that may or may not have revealed the location of the missing rare book, because I had not one shred of hard evidence.

"Yes, I believe that's all."

I would settle down immediately to study the code—but first, I'd better check on things at the Charlotte,

Zeno sat hunkered over his laptop in Oona's office. I eyed the flip chart tucked behind the desk and thought about the spiral staircase sketch. His gloves lay at his feet, as if he'd rushed in only a moment before I arrived and shed his winter outer layer. He turned to me with nonchalance, put an elbow on top of a stack of papers, and gave me a mild and pleasant smile.

"Ah, Ms. Burke. A lovely weekend, I hope? Did you say you went to Liverpool to visit your mother? I've spent a bit of time there myself. Where in the city does she reside?"

"It was lovely, yes. She has a flat . . . Zeno, that reminds me. I don't seem to have a physical address for you. And I really need one to complete the paperwork."

"An omission on my part, Ms. Burke, forgive me. I'll send the particulars to you by email, if that's all right?"

"Fine."

"Heigh-ho."

"Mmm. Now—"

"Before you ask, let me just say that Ms. Powell is off on a legitimate errand this time. She has gone to print out some sort of background material for ease of access, not only for you, but for . . . others. When it's appropriate for you to . . . utilize it."

In other words, he didn't have a clue what she was up to. "And what do you have for me today, Zeno?"

He held up a finger. "Books, Ms. Burke."

"Yes, books."

He lifted the top page on the stack, and gave it a quick perusal.

"How much does a book cost?" he asked.

That sounded rhetorical, so I kept quiet.

"Or more to the point, how much did a book cost in the 1930s or those editions during the war? You see, what I envision is a chart." He turned the paper toward me. He'd drawn a square and divided it into columns and rows, each one containing squiggles. "This chart will tell us how much a book cost to make and how much it was sold for. Because—books. We're all about books."

If we didn't have at least one display decided on soon, I would go mad, so I tried to look at this effort as not as boring as the others and certainly not as sensational as the entry idea he had put forward.

"You would focus on the mystery genre, right?" I said. "And, what about using one publisher as an example—Victor Gollancz would be good. After all, they published most of Sayers's work in Britain. And also, you would need some perspective—was the cost of a book in 1932 a great deal of money or pocket change? Show us who bought the books and a sampling of incomes from various fields. That might—"

"Brilliant, Ms. Burke," Zeno said. "Absolutely brilliant."

Not brilliant, but it might be turned into a vaguely interesting bit of information for one small display.

"And then perhaps a tie-in," I said. "Those books that cost a few shillings then—what are they worth now?"

"Of course." Zeno nodded. "There we are again—that book. Ms. Powell brought up the topic just this morning. What would that signed edition be worth today?"

Nothing if we can't find it, I thought, but was saved from replying with Clara's return.

"Hello, Hayley, good morning. How was your weekend?" She set her satchel in the corner and chatted away as she hung her coat over mine on a peg behind the door.

"Well, may I leave you two to it?" Zeno asked, standing, pulling on his coat, and retrieving his gloves from the floor. As he wriggled his fingers in, he said, "Thought I'd nip out for a coffee. Can I bring you one?"

"Not for me, thanks," I said. Clara declined, too.

Zeno tapped the stack of papers and then picked up the lot and thrust it into Clara's hands. "Here you are, Ms. Powell, all you need to know and more about the exhibition I mounted with Oona on the Wars of the Roses. Visitors were encouraged to throw red or white rose petals at each other in mock battle." In response to my raised eyebrow, Zeno hurried on and said, "Ms. Powell did ask me for details. But, of course, you're right, Ms. Burke. Now is not the time for this." He took the stack of papers back, slipped them into his satchel, and slung it over his shoulder.

Zeno left for his coffee, and I replied to Clara's question. "I had a lovely weekend with my mum and then took the train to Sheffield to see my daughter yesterday afternoon. And how was yours?"

"Oh well, that is—" She hauled her satchel onto her lap and pulled out a file folder. A single sheet of paper came loose, and I bent over to catch it before it hit the floor, but Clara got to it first. She stuffed it into her bag. "Fine. My weekend was fine."

"But you didn't go home to Shepton Mallet?"

Her hands went still and her face went pink. "My nana has quite high expectations for me. I can't let her down." She looked up brightly. "And, after all, February is here. February, Hayley. That means the exhibition on Lady Fowling is less than three months away. Mr. King-Barnes told me he started on the Druids last year. There's no time to lose, and so I stayed over in order to interview the First Edition Society's board members. I began with Mrs. Arbuthnot and Ms Frost. And then spoke with Mrs. Moon and Mrs. Moon—"

"Yes, I heard. Clara, I'm delighted you are coming up with all this inspiration, but you cannot take things into your own hands. You need to talk with me first."

"But, Hayley, it was your idea."

"Was it?"

"Yes, you said we should take advantage of primary sources—the people who knew Lady Fowling. Then, on Friday afternoon, when I was helping you map out the library shelves because you thought it might be a good idea to rearrange according to date of publication—"

I had wanted to get Clara away from Zeno, and it was the only project that had come to mind. Yes, busywork.

"—you were telling me about how Lady Fowling and her friends would take tea at the Royal Crescent. And so, I thought it would be good to interview those friends."

Yes, I remembered now—that had been my idea. What surprised me was that someone had listened.

"Well, I hope you heard a few interesting stories."

"Oh my, yes," Clara said. "Also, I consumed a great deal of tea—and a fair amount of sherry."

I chuckled. "That must've been at the Moons'."

Clara giggled. "Mrs. Sylvia Moon and Mrs. Audrey Moon. I wasn't sure I should ask them, but—how are they related?"

"They married brothers, and are now both widows, so they decided to combine households."

"Ah. Well, I wanted Lady Fowling's friends to read through what I'd written, and so I offered to email my notes to them."

"That's very thoughtful of you."

Clara didn't look up. "It was Mrs. Arbuthnot's idea— she said she needed to give final approval, but she would have to read it in print."

"I can imagine she did—Jane Arbuthnot can be a bit contrary."

"I still want to talk with Ms. Babbage," Clara said.

"Adele teaches at the girls' school, and she will give you an entirely different view of Lady Fowling—from a younger perspective. In fact, her ladyship would sometimes visit Adele's class, and I think some of the girls formed a François Flambeaux fan club. You know that her ladyship's detective wasn't really French—he was from Dorset."

We both laughed, and at that moment, the office door flew open so abruptly that Clara's coat fell off the peg onto the floor. Zeno looked at us both, his smile frozen, and then he said, "Heigh-ho, you two—having too much fun without me? Tommy's invited us down to take a look at the show before the grand gala. Interested?"

21

Interested in seeing the Druids exhibition? Yes—perhaps
I could pick up a few pointers about shows.

Clara, Zeno, and I trooped down the spiral staircase,
through the door to the other part of the Charlotte. We
reached the landing for the stairs that led down into the
exhibition space, and I saw a dozen or so people milling
about with glasses in hand, including Naomi.

"Come down," Tommy said, gesturing to us. "It's our
unofficial blessing." When we arrived on the ground floor,
flutes of prosecco were pressed upon us. "Have a wander,"
he told us. "Tell me what you think."

I sipped my fizzy wine and examined everything, starting with the exhibition title—*Druids Then and Now*—
printed on a banner that hung over the entrance. It had a
drawing that suggested figures in flowing garments and
circles of stones protruding from the earth. In the bottom
corner of the banner, in smaller letters but quite readable,
were the words *Brought to you by Timeless Productions*.
If we had a banner with *Lady Fowling: A Life in Words*,

would Zeno insist we include *Brought to you by Make an Exhibition of Yourself!*? I shuddered at the thought.

I continued through the show, studying the signage font, the size of displays, and the angles at which objects were shown. I stood in various spots in the rooms and observed what could be seen, what was hidden, and how new views were revealed by walking around a tall display or a toga-draped Druid mannequin. Along the way, someone kept refilling my glass.

Electric leads across the floor from wall outlets had been carefully covered as per Health and Safety rules— no cowboys here—and this led me to take note of the number of plug outlets and their location. From there, I began a general analysis of illumination as part of the exhibition's art. The intensity of a halogen lamp inside one of their Perspex boxes made me blink. How much light was too much? Naomi must have guidelines for the Charlotte that detail such things. I scanned the room for her and noticed the crowd had grown. When I stepped around a massive and quite realistic trunk of an oak tree, I saw Naomi and Zeno in a serious chat back by the kitchen, each of them with glass in hand as they surveyed the room. Naomi saw me, said something, and Zeno looked, too. They smiled.

I acknowledged with a wave. Did I look as if I had been spying on them? What were they talking about? Could Oona's murder have been a conspiracy? I turned away to be met with a fellow who refilled my glass. I needed food.

But Tommy, standing with a few others at the entry beneath a dolmen made from those faux rocks, had started an impromptu explanation of the importance of continuity within an exhibition, and I lingered to listen. When the group broke up, I approached and said, "Thanks for letting us have an early look."

"Drop in anytime, Hayley," Tommy said. "We exhibition managers need to work with each other, not against. We're a brotherhood—and sisterhood," he added quickly.

"Well, I'm not really—"

He didn't listen, but turned to greet several newcomers. I looked round. If this was the pre-event, what would the actual gala be like?

Time for me to be on my way, although—my mind fuzzy with fizz—I couldn't quite say where I would be going.

Setting my empty glass next to others on a table with a stack of leaflets titled *Druids of the Twenty-First Century: Join Us*, I made my way back to Oona's office to collect my bag, gripping the iron railing as I worked my way round and round and up. I pushed open the office door, heard a *flump*, and saw Clara's coat had come unpegged and landed on the floor.

Zeno, standing over his desk, whirled round as he pulled off his gloves and tossed them aside.

"Were you looking for me, Ms. Burke? I confess to slipping away for a much-needed coffee. There's just so much prosecco one can drink in the morning, wouldn't you say?"

Clara came in behind me as I took my coat off the peg and replaced hers. "Aren't they a fascinating group of people?" she asked. "And Mr. King-Barnes has experience on many fronts, not only Druids. I heard someone ask him about Henry the Eighth."

"Yes, Ms. Powell," Zeno said, "but let us not forget we have our own exhibition to mount. We'd best get back to work."

"I have a project waiting for me at Middlebank," I said. "Clara, would you like me to set a meeting up with Adele? How about this evening?"

"Oh, yes, Hayley, that would be lovely."

I pulled out my phone and, as I sent Adele a text, said to Zeno, "Clara is interviewing the board members, because they were all good friends of Lady Fowling's. We'll have bags of material to use from her sessions, I'm sure of it. Plus we've loads of photos."

"Clever of you, Ms. Powell," Zeno said.

"Oh, not me—" Clara began.

I interrupted. "Here's Adele now. She says seven at the Minerva—do you know it? Northumberland Place, just off Union."

"I'll be there! Ms. Babbage won't mind me recording, will she?"

"Certainly not—and you call her Adele."

And I was away, off to the café at Waitrose, where I sobered up over a chicken-and-stuffing sandwich and a pot of tea. And an iced cupcake, because—just because. Fortified, I returned to Middlebank and the task ahead, which I both desired and feared: cracking Lady Fowling's code.

I printed out a clean copy for myself. At the top of every page of the transcription, I'd put the month and year in the header, and if her ladyship had written an exact date, I included that, too. This page had only September 1950, and apart from the phrases, it held nothing else. They'd occupied their own page in her notebook, and I wanted to retain what she'd written just how she had written it.

> *Quiet Anticipation Despite*
> *Wiley Detective Beckons Death*
> *Betrayal Deemed Quintessential Appraisal*
> *Marvelous Merchants Appropriate Quietly*
> *Authentic Deception*

Bunter kept me company in the wingback chair. The important thing about detection, I decided, was to take things slowly and with a clear method so as not to overlook an important clue. Step one, take the writing at face value. So, I read the phrases aloud over and over again, forward and backward, and with different voice inflections. The cat occasionally twitched an ear, stretched, or had a sudden fit of washing, but otherwise gave me no feedback. After an hour, my eyes were out of focus and my voice tired, so I moved on to step two—first letters of the words.

QAD. WDBD. BDQA. MMAQAD.

Jibberish.

Right, next up—anagrams.

What could be made of the word *detective*? *Cede. Deck* without the *k*. *Video* missing the *o*. I felt betrayed by the letters—where were they when you needed them? Fine, how about one entire line. I pulled my laptop over, searched for an anagram website, and tried *Quiet Anticipation Despite*. The top result was unintelligible and the dozens that followed just as useless.

I emailed the phrases to my mum, hoping the Anagram Queen could make something of them. She promised to get started first thing the next day, as she had a committee meeting for Cats Rescue People followed by an awards dinner for her local library society.

Perhaps a change of scenery would help. I decamped to the library, accompanied by Bunter, who hopped up to the corner of the table and did his impression of a ceramic cat figurine, closing his eyes to slits. I took down all the François Flambeaux books, starting with *Flambeaux and the Purloined Poison*. Perhaps these phrases of Lady Fowling's had a direct connection with her books. But after another hour I was no further and rather overwhelmed by her ladyship's florid prose.

> *Flambeaux watched in abject horror as the murderer's chest heaved, his wheezing breath akin to the ear-piercing whistle of the steam locomotive that bravely made its way down the lines at daybreak every morning in June delivering its treasure of fresh strawberries from the fields of Kent to the kitchens of the Ritz in London.*

The cat yawned and that set me off. I changed venue one more time—up another floor to my flat, where the two of us stretched out on the sofa.

After my nap, my clothes felt as if I had them on backward, and I reminded myself never to fall asleep in a skirt, jacket, and tights. I changed into denims and a jumper, and with a cup of tea in hand, I texted Val. He had a short break before his next class and rang me immediately. As he ate a sandwich, I told him everything I'd forgotten to say the evening before and then caught him up on the day's activities. I ended by whingeing about Lady Fowling, her so-called secret code, and what Oona could possibly have made of it.

"What did she write before and after?" he asked me.

"Oona?"

"Lady Fowling. Sometimes it isn't just the code itself, but how it's set up in the story."

"I'll have to look at the original notebook for that. How did you get to be so smart?" I asked.

"Years of practice, my love."

I smiled into the phone, forgetting about detectives and codes for a delicious moment.

"We could take a look at it together tomorrow afternoon," Val added. Tomorrow afternoon, my flat, a bottle of wine. "Before our next speaker arrives," he added.

"Oh, yes, Tuesday. Literary salon." I sighed. "How about coffee in the morning?"

We ended our conversation on a wistful note, after which I phoned the watercolorist whose name I'd copied from the wrapped painting left at the Charlotte for later pickup.

Early on, Naomi had told me the watercolor exhibition did not have a manager, but instead had been run by committee, creating a headache for her. It was always good to get another point of view on a matter. After all, the Society had hired the Charlotte for its upcoming exhibition, and we should be aware of any difficulties on either side of the relationship. It was a perfectly good excuse for ringing the artist.

If, in our conversation, I learned details of Naomi's whereabouts the afternoon of Oona's murder, all the better. Yes, this was a police matter, and I felt certain DC Pye had followed up on the information I'd given him about Naomi and Zeno, but I held out little hope that either he or Sergeant Hopgood would tell me what they'd learned. Didn't I have a right to know?

When the artist answered his phone, I identified myself in great detail and then asked a few general questions about mounting an exhibition at the Charlotte. It didn't take much to segue into discussing Naomi.

"She tended to hover a bit," he said. "I don't think she trusted us."

"So, you're saying she was there with you all afternoon— the day of the murder? She mentioned some disaster that she needed to deal with. What was the problem?"

"That's a bit much, that is—I wouldn't call it a disaster. Easel malfunction. Someone tripped over it, and then fell onto it and broke one of the legs. Snapped it in two. The easel, not the person."

"Dreadful. Was the painting damaged?"

"Corner of the frame cracked, but it was mendable. So, I asked Naomi if she had some sort of stand we could use temporarily. Anything to get her out of the middle of things. She said she might have an easel in storage. She was gone for more than an hour."

"What time was that?"

"What does that matter?"

Don't push, Hayley. "It's only that I thought she might've become involved talking with the police when they arrived, and that kept her away." That couldn't be true—didn't I remember that the police couldn't find her that afternoon?

"No," he said. "This was before the police arrived. She'd gone off to have a poke round storage, but by the time she finally returned, she came in the main entrance. Said she'd nipped out for a coffee. Cheeky of her, as she left the artist standing there acting as his own easel for all that time."

"You told the police this, of course," I said, as a way of excusing my nosing in. "About Naomi."

"The police didn't ask about Naomi, did they?"

A dele stood at the end of the bar in the Minerva when I arrived, cleaning off laminated menus with Dettol and a towel while chatting with Pauline.

"Oh, look, you've got a new job," I said. "Hiya, Pauline, how are things?"

"Good! Yeah, good." She nodded toward Adele. "Did she tell you we're moving in together?"

"I might've heard the rumor," I replied. "I've some empty cartons if you need them."

"We're not taking your collection of wine corks," Adele said, shaking a finger at Pauline.

Pauline laughed. "But I wanted to make a lampshade with them."

The pub door opened and Clara walked in. She had dressed halfway down for the evening, still keeping her Oona bun in place for that professional look. After introductions all round, we ordered food and drink and settled in the corner for a good long while.

Even the arrival of food didn't stop the stories from flying—Adele knew not only a lot about Lady Fowling, but also about the other board members. "Jane Arbuthnot refuses to talk about it to this day," Adele said, "even though we have photographic proof. Now you won't say anything to her about this, will you?" she asked Clara, who shook her head, her eyes wide as an owl.

I came up with a story or two of my own—about Adele and how we'd first met seven years earlier when, instead of her long mane of curly red hair, she had a shaved and well-tattooed head. "Still under there, isn't it?"

Adele parted her hair and revealed a streak of green on her scalp. "It's a Celtic knot design," she explained.

"Stuart Moyle has a stack of books on his neck," I said, suddenly reminded of Bulldog's tattoo.

"He's the collector?" Adele asked.

"Yes. Clara, do you remember meeting him last week at the salon?"

She nodded. "He told me about a first-edition Anthony Berkeley he found at an Oxfam shop for two pounds."

"He's the one. Listen, I don't suppose you recall seeing him around the Charlotte . . . while Oona was still alive?"

"I'm afraid I don't. What sort of a collector is he—does he have his own bookshop?"

"No, I believe he's the sort that doesn't like to share."

"He can't be the only one who wants Georgiana's first edition found, can he?" Adele asked.

Couldn't I leave the subject of murder alone for one night?

"Adele, tell Clara about the time you and Lady Fowling went to Greenway and it was so muddy walking that steep bank, you slipped and sprained your ankle and her ladyship had to go the rest of the way alone to find help, and the two of you ended up having tea in Agatha Christie's actual library."

L eaving the Minerva that night, I walked Clara as far as the Pulteney Bridge. "Are you all right in the flat?" I asked. "I don't believe the police have anywhere to send Oona's things, but it doesn't seem right for you to have them there."

"Oh, I don't mind. I've just left everything as it was."

"Are you still sleeping on the camp bed?" I asked.

"It's quite comfortable."

It was as if this one-bedroom, short-term flat had become a shrine to Oona. "I tell you what, why don't I stop in one day and bring a few cartons, and we'll pack up whatever Oona left behind? Then we'll ask DC Pye for his advice."

"That would be lovely, Hayley, thanks so much." My eyes pricked with tears at the gratitude in her voice. Poor girl. Young woman.

I set my sights on Middlebank and my bed. It was dark, but general foot traffic made it so that you were never really alone. Still, one should always be aware of one's surroundings, and so I surveyed the pavement and doorways and, against a streetlight, saw the silhouette of a hulking fellow wearing a shapeless hat. Hadn't I seen him when we'd come out of the Minerva? Now he ducked into the doorway of the Old Green Tree. I paused to stare into the gloom, heard the pub door open and close and a few people spill out onto the road. On his own pub crawl, evidently.

I began my Tuesday morning by making an unorganized but necessary list of assorted tasks for the exhibition—staffing, coatracks, name tags, removal services. The latter because, although I would bar the front door before I let anyone take Lady Fowling's portrait out of Middlebank, I was not averse to shifting a few pieces of furniture over to give the exhibition a certain ambience. Her ladyship's desk, for example. Yes, that's what I needed to do—take stock of the furniture in the cellar. I jotted this down.

The next twenty minutes I spent fussing over a text to Bess.

Hi, Hayley Burke here. That sounded as if I were soliciting funds for a charity, but she didn't have my number, so how else would she know? **I'd love to get together for coffee next time you're near Bath. Or—how about lunch? Let me know—anytime is good.**

Friendly, unpresuming. Pushy? Would she feel cornered? I sent it before I could second-guess myself to death, and then sent the same to Becky, just in case they compared notes.

I lit the fire in my office and set the kettle to boil just before Val arrived with a pink box. He'd stopped at the Bertinet.

"Coffee?" I asked Mrs. Woolgar, who had come out to the entry. "Val and I are going to examine Lady Fowling's notebooks looking for clues about *Murder Must Advertise*. You're welcome to join us. He's brought along pastries."

"No, thank you, Ms. Burke, I'm afraid I must attend to other things. I do wish you luck." She retreated into the sanctum of her office and closed the door.

Mrs. Woolgar had taken her own look at the notebooks that morning, but had handed them back to me almost straightaway. "Her ladyship's mind was an intricate machine always seeking challenges that were beyond me. She once became enthralled with Morse code and decided we should both learn it, and so installed those tapping machines between our offices. How she could interpret a string of beeping noises as letters, I could never understand."

I couldn't help thinking the secretary might be a wee bit annoyed that Lady Fowling hadn't outright told her about the book and where it was—but if it had been put away decades earlier, perhaps even her ladyship had forgotten all about it.

"Right. We'll be in my office if you need me."

W e dispatched the coffee and croissants first. I brushed flakes of pastry off my desk and carried the tray to the kitchenette. When I returned, we took the notebooks and photocopies of the notebooks and began our study.

"Listen to this," Val said.

"'The housekeeper crept up to the desk with a bottle of oil preservative in one hand and a worn flannel in the other. Glancing over her shoulder to make sure she was alone, she turned out the oil onto her cloth and drew nearer and nearer until . . . *"Stop!"* Flambeaux called out. "Never use oil on wood furniture! Instead, rub in a good paste wax and you'll preserve your pieces for generations to come.'" Val looked up. "Not many writers would put their main character into a tale of household cleaning."

"Remember the story she made out of a grocery list," I said.

"She should've lent him out for adverts. 'Flambeaux recommends Brixon's Brooms for Cleaning Up Clues.'"

"François says, 'Always lay the table with Norfolk silver— it's burglarproof!'"

An enjoyable hour later, we had learned nothing new.

"I have class," Val said as he stood and stretched. "Not much use, was I? But do you get the feeling the answer is right under our feet?"

"You mean, under our noses."

As we gathered up pages, Val held up one sheet and asked, "Is this you trying to work out the code?"

I glanced at my own shorthand. "No, it's only a list of bits and bobs for the exhibition."

"So," Val said, "I'm collecting the speaker at one. Do you want to meet us for lunch later?"

The title of that evening's literary salon—"Were Charles Dickens and Wilkie Collins the Same Person?"—did not exactly pique my interest. We'd booked the speaker because he'd had a string of successful books taking two contemporary historical figures and making the same claim. Also, he was a theatrical producer and Maureen Frost had recommended him, so my hands were clean.

"No, I'd better not commit. But won't Maureen be there? You can let them natter on about the theater. I'll need to spend the afternoon with my lot at the Charlotte."

* * *

My lot were about to break for lunch.

"Oh, Ms. Burke, I daresay we expected you earlier," Zeno said, in an effort to make me feel the slacker. "Shall we stay? I could reschedule my lunch appointment, and Ms. Powell could—"

"I don't need to go, Hayley," Clara said. "I'll stay."

Zeno dropped his satchel. "As will I."

"No, both of you go to lunch." I waved them off. "I'll see you back here in an hour."

I didn't need lunch yet and so wandered down to look in on the first day of the Druids show. Perhaps two dozen people milled about—not a bad midday attendance for early February. The exhibition manager himself leaned on the ticket table at the entrance, chatting with the woman selling.

"Hello, Tommy," I said.

"Hayley." He opened his arms wide. "We've launched! It's like giving birth, isn't it?"

"Of a sort," I replied graciously. "So, Tommy, if you've got just a second, I wanted to ask you again about Zeno and Naomi. You mentioned to me that they'd worked together on that . . . er . . . oasthouse exhibition. Did they not get along?"

"I wouldn't say it was quite that," he replied. "They're both ambitious, so perhaps there was a bit of competition. You know how it is; you want to work with your peers, and yet you need to be just that little bit better than they are to get on to something bigger. I'm sure that's all it was."

A pipe band sprang to life playing "Scotland the Brave," and Tommy began his pat down, coming up with the correct mobile on only the second try. He stepped away, and although I could not hear exactly how he answered, it didn't sound like "Timeless Productions." Also, he seemed to have overlaid his London accent with a Scottish lilt. A different phone, a different . . . A thought snagged in my mind.

Tommy King-Barnes had three phones. Some people couldn't keep up with even one—look at Clara, she had lost hers. Bulldog had said he'd lost his, but that wasn't true. According to Arthur Fish, Stuart Moyle had more than one phone, a different one for each of his various pursuits. Why did Tommy have three phones?

He had his back to me, and so I crept closer and pulled my own mobile out, scrolled through recent calls, and tapped one. As he ended his conversation, Enya began singing about Middle Earth. He reached in a pocket, pulled out one of his other mobiles, and answered in a breathy, high-pitched almost whisper that I heard not only in the room, but also through my phone.

"Exhib, Ltd."

"Hello, Tommy," I said. "Gotcha."

22

❧

Tommy spun round and stood with his mouth agape and his mobile to his ear as he realized I had discovered the ruse. He was not only Zeno's reference from Timeless Productions, but also from two other exhibition companies with different names and each with its own particular voice.

I steeled myself for denials, bluster, fake outrage. Instead, Tommy burst out laughing.

"This is a joke?" I shouted at him, and someone peered round a Druid mannequin.

"No, not a joke," Tommy said, sobering up in an instant. "Come this way."

I followed him down the corridor but made sure to keep my back to the wall and have a good view of both the exhibition area and my closest exit.

"That's quite a scam you've got going!" I whispered furiously.

"Not a scam and not a joke." He pulled all three phones out of his pockets and placed them on his open palms. "I have three different exhibition management businesses, and each one caters to its own demographic."

It took me only a second to see the gaping holes in this explanation.

"You could have twenty companies, I wouldn't care. What I care about is that Zeno lied to me. Again," I muttered. "He offered three references but in fact they are all one—you."

"But from quite unrelated events," Tommy said.

"What does that matter?"

"Entirely different skill sets were required of each production."

"Then, why not say that from the beginning?" I demanded.

"That was not my secret to tell."

"Ah, yes—you see, even *you* think it was a secret."

"What I said about Zeno was true. Perhaps I should've let you know that I owned each of those businesses, but I didn't." He tipped all three phones into one hand and placed the other one over his heart. "Mea culpa."

And this from a Druid.

I could see no point in arguing with Tommy. No, I should save my fury and aim it elsewhere. I went to lie in wait for Zeno.

When I passed Naomi's office, she looked up from her computer and gave me a brief nod. I traveled on for three or four steps before I stopped. It occurred to me I had enough anger to go round, and another appropriate target right to hand. I backtracked and paused in the door as she finished typing. I told myself to remain calm, but I trembled nonetheless.

Her fingers hovered over the keyboard as she cut her eyes at me.

"Hello, Naomi," I said. "I hope I'm not disturbing. I

know we had that early look at the Druids exhibition yesterday, but I wonder did you attend the gala last evening?
Must've been quite a do—Tommy's eyes are bloodshot today. Listen, Naomi, here's an odd thing. You said you and
Zeno had never met before, but Tommy said you and Zeno
had worked on an exhibition together in Kent. Oasthouses?"

Naomi had kept stock-still while I blathered, but now
dropped her hands in her lap. The color came up on her
cheeks and I saw her jaw working.

"'Worked together'?" she repeated with derision. "I
could hardly call it that. I'm a faceless entity, aren't I? Oona
never remembered me—neither did Zeno. Am I that forget-
table? Did I not work on those events as much as any other
expert in her field?"

"What exactly was your job?"

"I see," she said with a huff. "You're just like them,
aren't you? Saying I contributed nothing?"

"No, I'm asking what it was you did. Design? Construction? Publicity and promotion? Tickets? Did you carry
around samples of dried hops for visitors to smell? What?"

"Traffic flow," she said, jutting her chin out. "It is a vital
yet underappreciated responsibility in any public event to
provide not just an adequate path for visitors to walk, but
one that will enliven and enrich their experience while
maintaining the Health and Safety standards that ensure a
trouble-free experience."

"Traffic flow," I repeated. I filed that topic away for later
consideration and our own exhibition, before focusing on
Naomi again. "Is that why you were so annoyed with the
watercolorists the afternoon Oona was killed?"

Naomi rolled her eyes. "Where do I begin? Idiots.
They'd set an unsecured, flimsy easel in the middle of the
room at the very spot where people would want to take a
sharp left or right. They were inviting trouble—I'm surprised it hadn't happened before that."

"You left them," I said, hoping I wouldn't have to name my source. "You said you spent the entire afternoon with the watercolorists until police arrived. That isn't true."

"Well, aren't you the little detective?" Naomi snapped.

Lord Peter knew the importance of knowing where everyone was and at what time. And Kenny Pye said people don't always tell the whole truth the first time they are questioned. No wonder police had to go over the same events again and again with a potential witness. Or suspect. This was the truth of detection—plodding and relentlessly pushing forward.

"Did you think the police wouldn't find out?" I asked.

"I didn't think it would matter," Naomi said, and shifted uncomfortably in her chair. "And afterward, I suppose I felt too ashamed to admit it. That afternoon, I was up to here with the watercolorists. I told them I might have a substitute easel for them to use and that I would go and look, but what I really did was march straight down to that café at the bottom of Bartlett and have a coffee and catch my breath. I must've been there for an hour or more, and when I returned, there were police everywhere. So there—satisfied? I'm not proud of my action. What sort of an exhibition manager gets fed up and scarpers? No wonder I'm only here doing bookings."

"Booking managers are a vital part of any public event," I said with passion, for I had suddenly thought of Bess. "Why, any exhibition or performance would be chaos without guidance." Had Bess's job as booking agent for three performance groups in Cheltenham become too much for her? Is that what was wrong? She hadn't replied to my text yet—neither twin had.

"Well," Naomi said as she searched up her sleeve for a tissue, "you'll be happy to know I've told the police all about my past association with both Zeno and Oona."

But not voluntarily, I'd wager.

* * *

Clara had her tablet tucked under one arm and a hand holding firmly to the railing as she reached the bottom of the spiral staircase.

"I've returned a bit early, Hayley," she said. "I had an idea you might be looking at the Druids and thought I'd come and find you. Wasn't it awfully nice of Mr. King-Barnes to invite us down anytime we want? Shall we go back to the office now and we'll get down to work?"

She'd made it to the landing by then and so was able to look at me. I considered what sort of a task I could give her and thought perhaps the two of us could start on a few simple displays, seeing as how most of what Zeno had come up with was rubbish. Then another thought occurred to me.

"I think it's time we take a look at the floor plan—look at the built-in display cases. We'll need to source freestanding units. I realize we don't know how many, but we can count up what the Druids have and estimate. Also, we need to consider how best to accommodate the public. These are things you always need to keep in mind in an exhibition even if we don't have the displays chosen and designed yet. Traffic flow—did you know that's Naomi's specialty? Let's see if she has a few minutes for us."

In the absence of inspiration, we may as well focus on the practicalities. And, yes, I did feel a bit bad about Naomi and how she'd been treated, so this might cheer her up.

"I'd be happy to help," she said when I asked, and immediately launched into an explanation of the theory and function of traffic flow. Clara took a chair and began tapping away into her tablet while Naomi searched for an article titled "The Study of Footprints." Traffic flow, not detective work.

I left them to it and went back downstairs to count plug outlets. I counted once and then, to be sure, counted again and came up with a different number. I started on the third time, my eyes on the floor, when a pair of high-shine black oxfords appeared.

"Well, Ms. Burke."

Zeno stood over me, his face giving away nothing, but his eyes were small and dark, telling me he knew that I knew. I stopped counting outlets. Out of the corner of my eye, I saw Tommy drift off into the back and out of sight.

"Who told you I'd found you out?" I asked. "Was it Exhib or Tartan Affairs? Or could it have been Tommy himself with Timeless Productions?"

"I hope you will allow me to explain. Shall we withdraw to the office?"

I wouldn't want Clara walking in on us. "No, let's go across to the café."

Zeno glanced in the direction of Oona's office and then out the door and across the road to the Assembly Rooms. "In public, Ms. Burke?"

"This isn't a flogging, Zeno. Come on."

I even bought him a coffee. Although he ordered a drink so complicated he had to repeat it twice, reminding me of how Oona liked her Earl Grey.

We sat near a window and I idly stirred my cappuccino, waiting for him to begin. He rearranged the salt, pepper, sugars, and sweeteners on the table, smoothed his Smarties tie, and shifted his cup a quarter turn to the right and then back again. If he didn't start talking soon, I would throw my coffee at him.

"You are upset at the references I offered."

"Yes, I am. Because you represented them as three different references, but in fact they were all the same person."

Zeno lifted his shoulders and his eyebrows followed suit. "Ms. Burke, I fail to see my sin here. Yes, Tommy has several distinct businesses, but I have legitimately worked for all three separately. They stand alone as individual projects, each with its own trials, tribulations, and glories. It is not my place to tell him how to handle his affairs or to reveal that one is the same as the other. Because they aren't. And regardless, my work records speak for themselves."

"You lied, Zeno," I said, sounding like a broken record.

"But for a good cause," he said.

"Good cause? You mean, paid employment?"

"To create something for Oona."

Across the room, dishes clattered and the espresso machine hissed, and I looked round and realized we were sitting at the same table where I'd seen Oona that first day. I said nothing and Zeno continued.

"When you came to me after she died"—after she had been murdered, he meant—"and offered me this post, it was the last thing I wanted to do. How could I begin to measure up to what she might've created had she been given the chance? I tell you, I wanted to turn tail and run, but I didn't. I knew I had to do this for her. And so, I hid my grief, put my best face forward, and gave you references that reflected the breadth of my talent as well as my connection with literature."

Literature? Oh, that's right—in Tommy's Scottish persona, Zeno had worked on an event called *Dr. Jekyll, Mr. Hyde, and Me* about Robert Louis Stevenson.

"What else are you hiding from me?" I asked.

"Ms. Burke," Zeno said, and I could hear the confidence return to his voice as he cottoned on to the fact I was relenting. "My life is an open book." He grinned. "Heigh-ho."

Damn you, Roger.

Zeno left from the Assembly Rooms for an appointment to "pursue a notion of some significance," and as it was well past lunchtime, I was too weak from hunger to ask any further questions. I bought myself a sandwich from the café's cold case and ate it as I returned to the Charlotte by way of the side entrance.

I met Clara on the first-floor landing coming back from Naomi's office, having learned surely all there was to know about traffic flow, and I started up the spiral staircase ahead of her.

"She called it manipulation, but really it's only guiding people," Clara explained. "Ms. Faber says you can predict which way a person will turn in the room just by—"

Clara broke off as I opened the office door and her coat fell off the peg, *flumping* to the floor. A crumpled paper tumbled out of one of the pockets, and I set my sandwich on the corner of the desk and bent over to retrieve it.

"No, don't!" Clara shouted. She shoved me, grabbed the paper, and clutched it to her chest. But she was too late, because I'd seen the date printed in the corner—September 1950—and I knew it to be a page of transcription from Lady Fowling's notebooks.

23

❦

"lara, what do you have there?" I asked.

Red blotches had appeared on her face, and her breathing was ragged.

"Nothing. Sorry, it's just something I'm working on."

"No, it isn't."

My heart pounded in my chest, and it took every ounce of my strength to stay calm.

I held my hand out. "Let me see."

"But it's mine, it is," she insisted, and then thrust it at me. "Oh, all right. Here."

I took the paper, smoothed it, and saw that it was the page I'd printed out of Lady Fowling's coded phrases along with Oona's adornments—wild scribbles and doodles.

For a moment, all I felt was enormous relief. Here it is at last! Now we would find the book, that elusive signed first edition of *Murder Must Advertise*, because Oona had broken the code, and what she had written would lead me to it.

But my elation did not last long, because this page—long sought after and last imagined in the hands of a murder victim—had been found in the coat pocket of her personal assistant.

"Clara . . ." I held out the paper, unable to ask the question that needed to be asked.

Clara craned her neck to look, and behind her glasses her eyes grew large. "What's that?"

"You know what it is—it was in your pocket."

"No, that's not what—"

"You snatched it out of my hands. Clara, where did you get this?"

"I don't know—it isn't mine."

"This is one of the pages I transcribed from Lady Fowling's notebook—you remember I brought them over to Oona. Just moments before she was murdered, she sent me a text. She knew where that valuable first edition is stored. I believe she'd looked at these phrases and figured out that Lady Fowling was using a code to tell us the book's location."

"Oona didn't say anything to me about it."

"She didn't have the chance, did she? Someone hit her over the head, pushed her down the stairs, and she died. Police gathered up the papers that had been scattered all over the floor and the landing and took them in as evidence. Except this page—it was gone. Stolen."

Clara recoiled against my unspoken accusation, backing up to the wall, her face so pale she looked translucent. "No, I don't know about that." Her voice wobbled and I saw tears in her eyes. "What do you mean? You think I could . . . it's nothing to do with me. I didn't do it."

She sank to the floor in a swoon.

Where's a cup of tea when you need one?

With my arm round her shoulders, Clara managed to get off the floor and into a chair, but she kept her head down and turned away from the paper. Although I longed to study it, I also needed her attention, and so I folded it up and stuck it in my bag. Once it was out of sight, a bit of color came back to her face. I sat across from her, our knees almost touching.

"So, Clara," I said, using my soothing mum voice, "that wasn't the paper you thought it was."

She shook her head.

"You didn't pick it up accidentally that afternoon when Oona died—perhaps thinking it was yours?"

Another shake.

"But then, how did it get in your pocket?"

Clara shrugged.

"You realize, don't you, that you're going to need to explain this to the police."

"Yes," she said, and swallowed. "I will explain that I don't know how it came to be in my pocket." Her head came up. "Will they put me in prison?"

"Clara, no one is accusing you of anything." Yet. "But this is evidence. Look, I'll go with you."

Because the police had never heard of this paper before. I would need to explain that I hadn't realized it was missing until two days ago. They would need to be made to understand its possible significance as a piece of evidence.

We pulled on our coats. I cinched the buckle on my bag and then clutched it to my chest as if that one page might form itself into a paper airplane and fly out of the office of its own accord. I had barely glanced at it—was it evidence or was it nothing? I longed to take another look. Clara had her back to me, repairing her bun, and so I turned away, opened my bag, and slipped the paper out.

Oona had been lavish with her words—or symbols or sketches. Whatever they were, they looked like hieroglyphics to me. She had drawn one circle round the entire list of phrases and then lines from each word out to the margins, making the thing look like a wonky wheel with too many spokes. To the side floated a square with smaller boxes inside and dots inside those. The box sat on four legs. What I could read quite clearly were two names. One came from *Murder Must Advertise*: "Death Bredon."

The other name was mine.

W e walked with purpose and in silence to the police station, my mind teeming with conjecture and confusion, while Clara's—well, who could say what filled her thoughts?

"Hello, Sergeant Owen," I said.

"Ms. Burke," he replied. "How are you?"

We'd be asking after each other's children soon.

"Fine, thank you. I hope you're well. We're here for Detective Sergeant Hopgood or Detective Constable Pye—whichever, it doesn't matter. But it's quite important."

We hit the jackpot—both detectives came out to the lobby.

"So, Ms. Burke, Ms. Powell," Sergeant Hopgood said. "What do you have for us?"

I drew the paper out of my bag, unfolded it, and handed it over. Before I could begin an explanation, Clara jumped in.

"It was in my pocket. I don't know how it got there. I've never seen it before that I remember." She frowned and glanced at me. "But I suppose I must've seen it before Oona died, because Hayley brought it over to us at the Charlotte."

Hopgood kept his brows in neutral, but his eyes cut to me.

"It's a page from the transcriptions of Lady Fowling's notebooks," I said. "I have them on my computer, but I'd printed them all out for Oona. That's what those papers are that you took from the scene and put in binders. I've been looking through them for a clue. But this page was missing until today. And I think it might be possible that it has something to do"—I noticed how cautious I had become in my declarations—"with that rare first edition."

"It was in my pocket," Clara repeated. "I don't know how it got there."

I sensed a new version of "I lost my phone," and now wondered if she truly had.

"Right," Hopgood said. "Pye, why don't you have a chat with Ms. Powell while Ms. Burke and I discuss a few things."

Clara flinched. "But, Hayley—"

"Yes, that's fine," I said quickly. "Clara, I'll see you in a few minutes. You wait for me—or I'll wait for you."

She nodded, a barely perceptible movement, and we followed our escorts behind the desk and through the door that remained locked to all but us precious few. Hopgood paused at Interview #1 and handed the evidence to Pye, moving aside for them to continue to #2.

DC Pye asked Clara if she wanted tea, and I heard her say, "Yes, please. Thank you. Two sugars."

Hopgood opened the door for me, and with uncomfortable familiarity, we settled across the table from each other.

"Now, Ms. Burke—why hadn't you informed us of the missing paper?"

"Because it hadn't occurred to me it was missing. I only realized it Sunday." And then I'd held on to the information for two days. But in my defense, I had been distracted. Still, I was one of those people Detective Constable Pye talked about— someone who withholds information. But not on purpose.

"And," I added, "I really didn't know what I could tell you that would help, so I spent yesterday afternoon trying to decipher those phrases. But perhaps now that we have Oona's notes, we'll know more."

Before he could react to my all-inclusive *we*, a knock came at the door. DC Pye walked in, handed Hopgood a paper—a photocopy of the evidence—and left again.

"Could I have a copy of that, too?" I asked. An eyebrow jumped. "It will help me find the book, I'm sure of it."

"Do you mean to say you understand what these phrases

mean?" Hopgood asked, studying the page. "Looks like a load of nonsense to me. Except for your name here, Ms. Burke"—he tapped on the page—"and this other name. And, of course, the word 'Death.'"

"Death Bredon. It's the name of a character in *Murder Must Advertise* by Dorothy L. Sayers."

"She named a character Death? A bit obvious, don't you think?" he asked.

"Lord Peter Wimsey's middle names."

"Oh, him," Hopgood muttered. "The Oxford man who had nothing better to do with his time." He pushed the paper toward me. "So, Ms. Burke, can you sort this out?"

I studied the page as a whole and then ran my finger over each of its parts. Silly phrases, squiggles, and boxes. And my name.

"Oona texted me just before—well, you know that, you've seen her phone. She must've had this brainstorm and wrote my name down because she wanted to tell me about it."

"Who might gain by taking this paper from the hands of a dead woman?"

He's good, that Sergeant Hopgood—knowing just how to keep a witness on her toes by changing the subject.

"I thought that Bulldog was the most likely, because of his book collecting. It would be quite a prize, a first edition signed by every member of the Detection Club." I paused and gave Hopgood an encouraging look. *Go ahead, tell me his alibi.*

"Car boot sale, Colchester," he said. "Mr. Moyle was very obliging with the details of his whereabouts, and we've followed them up."

This time, it was Hopgood's turn to wait. Eventually, when I'd arranged my thoughts, I said, "I suppose you want to know about Clara and Naomi and Zeno."

"You do seem to be working in close quarters with them, Ms. Burke. Is there anything you know about them that might help the police enquiry?"

"Clara's a g—" I sighed. "A young woman who is just starting off in the working world. What would she gain by murdering Oona? She'd only be out of a job."

"But she wasn't out of a job after Ms. Atherton died," Hopgood pointed out. "You've kept her on."

"Yes, true."

"And I understand that she's living in the flat Ms. Atherton had let for her time in Bath."

"She seems reluctant to commute from Shepton Mallet, and Oona had signed a lease and paid for the flat through . . . I don't know. May, I think. But, Sergeant, Clara is small. I can't see her throwing Oona down the staircase."

"That staircase is dangerous—wouldn't take much of a push, especially if Ms. Atherton had been cracked over the head first."

"Naomi and Zeno each have a history with Oona," I said, relieved to change the subject and guilty at pointing the finger elsewhere. "Naomi feels slighted, professionally. She wasn't where she said she was that afternoon."

"Well done on that account, Ms. Burke—sussing out Ms. Faber's movements. However"—I hadn't even had a second to bask in the glow of his compliment—"it would be better for you to come to us and not take it upon yourself to question suspects."

I assumed a look of being duly chastised. "Yes, sir."

"Once Ms. Faber amended her statement and we talked to one of the watercolorists, we were able to find her sitting in the café at the bottom of Barlett for that hour."

"So, she's accounted for?"

Hopgood's eyebrows danced a jig. "Is she?"

"She isn't?" I whispered.

"It takes three minutes to walk from the Charlotte to that café. Piecing together her stated departure time and comparing it with one of the watercolorists as well as her appearance on CCTV along Bartlett Street, we find she had a good ten minutes to spare."

My heart was in my throat. "Are you going to arrest her?"

"We are going to question her again."

And again and again, most likely. I calmed down.

"And you'd already confirmed Zeno's story," I said.

"Yes, Bristol. Mr. Berryfield traveled by train to and from."

That took care of my suspect list, and it left me unsatisfied. "And, of course, CCTV doesn't lie. But twice now—or it might be three times—Zeno has lied to me about something. He said he hadn't seen Oona in Bath, but he had. He gave me three references, but it turned out they were all the same person. He withheld the fact he and Oona had been married—although, I suppose that doesn't have anything to do with the job, actually. Still."

"Are you looking for a reason to remove Mr. Berryfield from his post?" Hopgood asked.

"I don't think I could lose another exhibition manager—it was one of the restrictions Naomi put on our booking the Charlotte, that we have one. No matter how irritating he can be, I've got to stick with him. But I've got the measure of him now, and I will force him to toe the line." How many times had I said that about Roger? "Where did you say he went in Bristol that day?"

"We've got it in the notes—I'll check with Pye. Well, Ms. Burke, and how is your exhibition going?"

Tick, tick, tick.

I waited for Clara in the police station lobby, checking my messages. Val had sent a text to say that although our speaker for the salon may play fast and loose with facts, he would be sure to hold everyone's attention. And it might be a good idea to keep the sherry decanter away from Maureen Frost for the evening.

"Thank you for waiting," Clara said when she emerged, "but you don't have to walk me back."

"Only to the bridge," I said. "It's practically on my way."

We buttoned up our coats and headed out, making it to the Grand Parade before we spoke again.

"Did everything go all right with DC Pye?" I asked. A gust of wind blew up off the river and sent an icy chill down my neck.

"I suppose. Did they keep the paper?"

"Yes, they are looking at it for fingerprints."

"They'll find mine, won't they?"

I shivered. "And mine. Along with Oona's, probably. And maybe . . . others."

"Constable Pye asked me if I could read what Oona had written."

"You mean there was more than just my name and Death Bredon? Nothing else looked like actual words to me."

"Oona had her own version of what my nana calls joined-up writing. Next to your name—"

"Hang on." I stopped just past the steps leading down into the Parade Gardens and pulled out the photocopy that Hopgood had given me. "You mean these squiggles?"

"Yes," Clara said. "That's *said* and *it*. She wrote: 'Hayley said it.'"

"Hayley said what?" I asked.

She shrugged.

"Clara, when that paper fell out of your pocket, you thought it was something else. What?" I asked.

She glanced at me and away and fiddled with the top button on her coat. "Oh, it's nothing. Only an idea or two. Nothing useful. And now it's gone."

"Gone—you've lost it? One paper turns up and another goes missing—it's like we have a poltergeist in our midst."

We had reached the Pulteney Bridge, and Clara straightened her shoulders. "I won't go to the literary salon this evening, Hayley. I don't want to be a distraction."

"Don't be daft," I said. "Of course you should be there.

We must carry on with our work, and your presence at the lecture is part of the routine."

"I didn't kill her."

Above the frame of her glasses, her brow furrowed. She'd pressed her lips together, but it didn't keep her chin from quivering.

"Oh, Clara," I said, patting her on the arm. "I know you didn't."

But somebody did. It's just that they all had such good alibis.

Our literary salon lecturer didn't actually claim Charles Dickens and Wilkie Collins were the same person, and neither did he offer an excuse for such an outrageous assertion. Instead, he compared the authors' styles and encouraged a discussion. "What if Collins had, in fact, finished *The Mystery of Edwin Drood* after Dickens died?" he asked. "There is some evidence that . . ." There apparently was no evidence, but the suggestion sparked a lively debate.

I had kept a worried eye on Clara throughout the evening— she appeared listless and distracted—and when Adele said she was giving Audrey and Sylvia Moon a lift home, I asked if she would also take Clara.

"That's kind of you, Ms. Babbage," Clara said as they wrapped up and left.

Adele turned to me and asked, "Is she all right?"

"Just tired, I think."

Zeno pulled on his sheepskin coat and immediately became three times larger than normal. He glanced out the front door at Adele and her group departing.

"Everything all right with Ms. Powell?" he asked. "She did seem a bit preoccupied this evening. Nothing bothering her or you about the . . . enquiry?"

"The enquiry is a police matter," I said. "And I must say,

they seem to be moving at a rapid pace." Yes, it was a lie, but I wasn't about to tell him what we'd really been up to during the day—that Clara had been caught with an incriminating piece of evidence in her pocket. "Clara is working on a fabulous idea for the exhibition."

"Is she now? Splendid."

Zeno left, and he was replaced by Stuart Moyle.

"Tell me, Bulldog," I said. "If you had that signed first edition of *Murder Must Advertise*, what would you do with it?"

"Well, I wouldn't lose it."

"It isn't lost," I replied crossly.

"Is that why she was murdered—for that book?"

"The police do not share details of their enquiry with me, but I believe they are . . . closing in on the truth."

My head hurt from putting up a positive—and entirely false—front.

O f course, Southend-on-Sea is the longest pier in Britain," I said, "but we wouldn't have to go all the way to Essex just to walk on a pier."

Val and I were tucked up in bed, my head resting on his chest and his arms wrapped round me.

"Wouldn't you like to see Clacton again?"

Clacton-on-Sea had been our holiday spot when I was young—Mum, Dad, and I would travel east straight across England from Hereford to Essex. Those happy times had molded my lifelong love of the seaside.

"I might be disappointed," I said. "After all, I was twelve last time I saw it."

He pulled the duvet up to our chins and kissed my temple.

"How about we go clockwise around England starting at Woolacombe. Or if you like, we could begin at Margate."

I looked at him. Val had grown up in Margate on the southeast coast—I took this as his offer to share with me his childhood. I accepted.

"You can show me the shell grotto," I said. "And we can take the cliff walk from Margate to Broadstairs. But I suppose we'll have to hold off until after the exhibition. May— at least it'll be warmer."

"In theory."

We were quiet. Sleep seemed a long way off, and I considered getting out of bed to make a cup of tea, but out there, beyond the duvet, it was cold, and in here, it wasn't.

"You're all right with Clara staying on?" Val asked.

"Who put that paper in her coat pocket?" I asked in response.

"You don't think it's obvious that she did it herself?"

I frowned. Was I so gullible that any twentysomething young woman could trigger sympathy in me instead of suspicion?

"I believe she was truly surprised to see what the paper really was. She thought it was notes she'd made—ideas for the exhibition, I think—and she was distressed at what it turned out to be." I pressed my hand to my forehead. "But maybe what she was distressed about was being discovered."

Val took my hand and kissed it. "If not Clara, who else had the opportunity?"

Sergeant Hopgood had presented me with that question as I'd left him.

"The people already inside the Charlotte are the most likely," I said. "We keep the street door on Circus Place locked now, and so anyone coming in the front entrance would be spotted on CCTV. Zeno, Naomi, the Druid. But Clara had been out this morning. She'd gone down to George Street to make photocopies. Of course, the way she's been forgetting to report her movements, she might have stopped off for coffee, gone shopping on Milsom, or taken her clothes to the launderette along the way. Loads of opportunities for someone to slip the paper in her pocket."

"So," Val said, "the question isn't only 'Who killed

Oona?' but also 'Where's the book?' 'Who took the paper?' 'Who put it back again?' Do those questions have anything to do with each other?"

"If we answered one, could we answer the others? Or will the questions continue to pile up until my head explodes?"

I'm going down to the cellar this morning," I told Val as I walked him to the front door Wednesday morning. I wore only my short silk robe and hoped Mrs. Woolgar wouldn't get it in her head to come upstairs two hours early.

"You won't get lost?" Val asked. It was a little joke. I'd spent a quiet afternoon the previous autumn down in the cellar unaware that everyone in Bath—it seemed—thought I'd been kidnapped.

I kissed Val on the nose. "I thought I'd poke round the furniture to see if there are any small pieces we could use in the exhibition. While Zeno continues to fuss over a central display—or any display, for that matter—I'm going with Oona's entry idea using Lady Fowling's Queen Anne desk."

The shred of a frown crossed Val's face, and he cocked his head as if listening to some other voice. He drew breath and seemed about to speak, but I heard a noise from the lower-ground-floor flat.

"Mrs. Woolgar emerges!" I whispered. "Have a good day!"

He left, and I scampered back upstairs, followed by Bunter, who dashed past me into my flat and to the front window, where he took up a pigeon-watching position.

I made a second cup of tea and dropped another slice of bread into the toaster. I heard my phone ping and went in search of it, to find a text from Dinah.

Dad's offer—£200 or Crowdey would paint/replace outlets for free

I held my breath as I replied.

Which did you take?

Her answer came quickly.

£££

"Ha!" Bunter flinched. "Sorry, cat," I said, and texted Dinah.

Smart girl

I caught myself too late, and followed up immediately.

Sorry—smart woman!

I hope she'd asked for cash.

24

꧁꧂

"Must the invitations to the gala opening be online only?" Mrs. Woolgar asked at our briefing. "A properly printed request sent through the post carries so much more weight."

"Let's do both," I said.

"We will indicate it is formal attire, won't we?"

"Yes, I suppose so," I replied with little enthusiasm. My heart sank at thoughts of my wardrobe. Back to the charity shops—my income may have blossomed in the last six months, but not so much as I could spend a few hundred quid on an evening dress. Mrs. Woolgar, on the other hand, could probably whip hers up on her sewing machine in an afternoon.

"Shall I begin on the invitation design?"

"Yes, why don't you," I said. "Wouldn't it be lovely to have the invitation look like the cover of a book? Perhaps one of her ladyship's own books, as they are that exquisite tooled leather with gold lettering."

Mrs. Woolgar watched me for a moment, enigmatic behind her thick specs, before replying, "It's worth a try."

A ringing endorsement.

I heard the distant pinging of my mobile, left on the desk in my office.

Ping ping ping

Three pings, three texts. And then it began to ring.

"If that's all we have," I said, "I'd better see to that."

I caught the phone on its last ring before going to voice mail and had no time to look at the caller.

"Hayley." It was Val, and he sounded as if he'd been running a race. "Listen, your list—"

"Aren't you in class?"

"Yeah, just stepped out into the corridor. They've got five minutes to critique their partner's first lines. About the list you made."

"What list?"

"Things to do for the exhibition. I saw it the other day when we were going over the printout of Lady Fowling's odd phrases—do you remember?"

"Yes." That seemed ages ago. I gazed down at the detritus that now covered my desktop. It would be under several layers by now.

"When I left this morning, you said something about the Queen Anne desk."

"Did I? Oh, yes, for the exhibition." So far, nothing made any sense to me, but I would go with it regardless.

"Lady Fowling's. I was thinking we might use it."

"Queen Anne desk," he repeated. "Look at your list."

"Hang on." I put him on speaker, set the phone down, and searched through notes on the Society's newsletter, printed out articles on curation, a recipe or two I wanted to save, until . . . "Got it!"

"What did you write?" Val asked. "Read it exactly as you wrote it."

"About the desk? Well, it makes no sense when I read it that way, it's just my own shorthand, but here goes. 'LF— space—QAD—space—cellar.'"

"QAD. Now, look at Lady Fowling's phrases. What does the first one say?"

Another search. With more urgency, I pushed papers left and right, littering the floor. "Here!" I slapped my hand on the page. "The first one is 'Quiet Anticipation Despite.' Despite what?"

"First letters—QAD. What does that stand for?"

"Queen Anne desk?" I could manage little more than a whisper. "Queen Anne desk? Is that where it is?"

"Bingo."

"My God!" I'd found my voice, but it came out an octave higher than normal. "She did leave a clue, she—"

"I'll be there as soon as I'm finished here. We'll have time to look at it before my afternoon class."

"You're brilliant!" I shouted.

"You're the one that wrote it down that way," Val said. "See you soon."

When he rang off, I stared at my phone, absorbing it all. I must phone Mum and tell her she'd been on the right track all along. But then, three texts popped in.

From Clara.

Feeling unwell. May I take the morning off? See you after lunch.

From Detective Sergeant Hopgood.

Berryfield's Bristol day: TKB Events

From Bess.

Am in Bath. Will stop by soon. Thx

Thoughts of bounding to the cellar, locating Lady Fowling's Queen Anne desk, and ransacking its every nook and cranny flew out of my mind. Although I had a fleeting thought for Clara's health, I skipped over Sergeant Hop-good's report entirely, because the third message sent a shot of adrenaline through my system, and for one second, I did not know whether to flee or stand my ground. Bess, here, soon.

The front door buzzed.

Bess here now.

I opened the door to the formerly put-together twin, look-ing as if she had begun to unravel. She wore denims close to being in shreds and worn trainers, a patchwork cardigan over a roll-neck sweater, and a heavy coat, unbuttoned. She stuck her bare hands in her coat pockets, drew them out, and stuck them back in again as she said, "Hello. This is a bad time, isn't it? You're at work."

I caught one of her hands as it came out of a pocket and pulled her over the threshold. "This is a pleasant surprise, Bess—I'm delighted to see you. It's not a bad time at all."

On closer inspection, I saw an empty look to her eyes and the suggestion of dark circles.

"Why don't you take your coat off? We'll go upstairs to my flat, shall we? Would you like a coffee?"

With these bits of pretense and a gentle tug on the collar of her coat, I got her out of it and up one set of stairs. She stopped on the library landing and gazed at Lady Fowling.

"Is this the woman who started the Society? Such a life-like portrait. I didn't notice it last week. She's lovely."

"Lady Georgiana Fowling," I said. Hadn't I told her this already? But no, that had been Becky. "She was a kind and intelligent woman who loved people and books. I never met her—she died four years ago—but I feel as if I knew her. I'll tell you a secret"—a badly kept secret, but nonetheless—"I talk to her sometimes."

Bess turned hollow eyes on me. "Does she answer?"

"I imagine that she does, but actually, I believe I answer for her. Come on." I took her hand.

We made it into my flat, where I set her free while I

switched on the kettle and got out the coffee. When I brought the tray to the front room, Bess whirled round from the window.

"Do you like living in Bath?" she asked.

"I do, yes—I've been here for ten years or so. It certainly feels like home."

"I've lived here my entire life. Until I went to uni and moved to Cheltenham."

"Then it'll always be home, won't it?" I asked.

A brief turbulence crossed Bess's face. I looked away to pour our coffees and offer shortbread. She sat on the sofa, stirred milk into her cup, and said, "I've never read any Agatha Christie, but I've seen a few stories on television."

"I'd never read any, either, not until a few months ago," I said, leaning toward her and dropping my voice into a conspiratorial murmur, "but I try to keep that under my hat."

Bess smiled. We fell into chatting about the Golden Age of Mystery, books in general, and more specifically, her dad and his teaching.

"He loves it—you can tell, can't you?" she asked. "He writes, too. He even had a book published ages ago. Not long before Mum died. Did you know?"

"Yes, he told me, although I've never seen it."

"He says that no copies exist. I'm not sure I believe him." She took a shortbread finger and turned it over and over in her hand. "I'm glad he told you about it."

That was a hurdle cleared, wasn't it? Still, another subject lurked in the room like a silent guest, waiting to be introduced.

Bess rose and went back to the window, but instead of the Bath skyline view, she looked down at her nails and picked at a cuticle. "Can you be sad to leave a place and excited to go to a new place at the same time?"

Careful now, Hayley, don't startle her. "Life is full of mixed emotions."

"I'm sorry about how I acted last week."

"It's all right."

"You and Dad—"

I held my breath.

"You and Dad look really happy together. And I'm glad of that, I really am. It's only I feel as if I'll be missing things." Her voice broke and she coughed. "And then there's Becky. She's like a sausage dog nipping at me from all sides because she suspects something. I haven't even told her yet."

"Are you leaving?"

Bess looked up. Her eyes swam. "New York."

Tears cascaded down her cheeks as her face crumpled. I jumped up and took her in my arms, which precipitated wailing. I let her go, cooing a bit—"it's all right, there you are," that sort of thing—and when the storm had subsided, I offered a box of tissues, and we went back to the sofa and our coffee.

"I've been offered a job as a booking agent for a theater company." She hiccuped a last sob and blew her nose. "I'm good at what I do. With a company, it isn't all dates and times, I'm often everyone's agony aunt. Plus, you have to know a lot about so many things—the technical side of the show, the cast, the crew. It's a great deal of coordination. The next thing to being a producer, actually. In an assistant sort of way. This is a bigger company than Cheltenham, and so it's an advancement."

Far too much effort had gone into that explanation. "Is there some other reason for New York besides the job?"

"Adam." She smiled when she said his name, and dropped her head. "He's not only an actor, he's one of the founding directors of the new company. He's American, but he's been working with us in Cheltenham."

"You're moving to New York with him?"

"We've known each other for a year!"

"And you've been afraid to tell your dad?"

Tears threatened. "I don't want him to think I'm deserting him—it wouldn't be fair."

"You're a young woman with a wonderful future, Bess. Your dad will miss you, but he would never deny you a chance to live your own life." I prayed that Dinah would never, ever meet and fall in love with an American. Or Canadian or Australian or . . .

"He also works in IT, and he's got a job in New York doing that. To help tide us over, you know."

"New York's rather an expensive place to live, isn't it?" I ventured.

"Yes, but I've worked it out—I've always been good with budgets."

I should ask her to work up one for my personal finances.

"And you and Dad can come to visit!" Bess said brightly. I'm sure she'd worked up a good few ways to convince her dad the whole thing would be a success.

"That sounds wonderful—"

I heard the front door buzz.

"Bess, that's your dad." She clutched my arm, and my cup and saucer rattled. "He doesn't know you're here—he's come about the exhibition—but don't you think this is the perfect time to tell him? Don't you?"

"Yeah," she said, drying her face with the back of her hand and sniffing loudly. "I'll do it."

"Right, dash into the loo and splash some water on your face. I'll bring him up." I moved to the door, but paused for a moment. "And listen—when you tell him about Adam, why don't you lead with the news that he has an IT job in New York. After he gets used to it, you can tell him he's an actor."

I hurried down the stairs, catching Mrs. Woolgar coming out of her office.

"It's all right—I'll get it."

The secretary retreated with a nod.

When I yanked the door open, Val jumped.

"Hiya," I said. "Come in."

"Have you found it?" he asked, shedding his coat and giving me a quick kiss.

"Found it?" Wait, now I remembered—Queen Anne desk, *Murder Must Advertise*. I'd moved that off center stage, and it took me a moment to come back to it. "Oh, no, I haven't had the chance. Look—" I put my hands on his shoulders. "Bess is here."

The excited spark in his eyes vanished, to be replaced with a cloud of worry. He glanced round the entry and up the stairs. "Is she? Why?"

"Well, I asked her to stop by, didn't I?" I said with great cheer. "She's in my flat and wants to have a chat with you. C'mon."

I took his hand and gave a tug, and he followed me up one staircase, and as we turned to go up the next one, he pulled me to a stop.

"Is she all right?" he asked.

"She's fine."

"Are you two . . ."

"We're fine." I got him going again, and we arrived at the second-floor landing. The door of my flat stood ajar. "I'll leave you to it," I said quietly. "Take as long as you need. I have a couple of things to see to, including looking in at the Charlotte. Let's go down to the cellar later. I'll text you."

I had great sympathy for his look of sheer panic—his face had drained of color and his green eyes had faded to hazel. I took his face in my hands and said, "Stiff upper lip. And don't worry—she isn't pregnant." I gave him a little push.

He slipped in the door. I waited for just a moment, and then left them to themselves. I gave Lady Fowling a nod as I went past and descended to the ground floor, where I would hear nothing from my flat, even Val's anguished cries. Good Georgian construction, you know.

I went to my office and instituted a search for my mobile, patting all the loose papers on my desk and finally spotting it on the seat of the wingback chair, where I had dropped it as I ran out to answer the door. *You see how easy it is to lose a phone, Hayley.* Is that what had happened to Clara's? Covered over by a stack of papers and tossed into the recycling bin or inadvertently dropped through the slot in a postbox? I'd seen a phone someone had left charging at an outlet on a train platform—poor sod when he discovered it missing. I didn't know if police considered Clara's phone evidence, but if they did so, had they tried tracking it down?

Thinking about Clara, I called up my messages, reread hers, and sent a reply.

Feeling better? Do you need anything?

I took another look at the text from Detective Sergeant Hopgood—Zeno had spent his day in Bristol at TKB Events. I couldn't remember why I'd asked. Just being a nosey parker, I suppose.

I went to the entry, pulled on my coat, and looked in on the secretary. "Mrs. Woolgar, I'm off to check on Clara— she's feeling a bit peaky—and then to the Charlotte. But I'll be back here in the afternoon, because I want to go down to the cellar."

"You won't lock yourself in, will you?"

Will I never live that down?

Clara didn't answer when I pushed the button for Oona's flat. I waited a couple of minutes and tried again. I sent another text and then turned to go. Perhaps I would find her already at work at the Charlotte, and if so, I would impress upon her the need to answer a text when I sent one, because otherwise, I would worry needlessly. An image crept into my mind of her lifeless body, sodden, at the edge of the weir. With a quick breath, I banished the thought, but it left a residual echo, and before I crossed the Pulteney Bridge on my way to the Charlotte, I made sure to walk down the steps by the Boater pub and scan the riverbank. If she was unwell, perhaps I should contact her nana in Shepton Mallet.

The Charlotte lay quiet apart from a smattering of visitors in the Druid exhibition. I didn't see Tommy King-Barnes, Naomi wasn't at her desk, and Oona's office was empty, signaling to me that Zeno must be working on some fresh idea. I disliked it out of hand.

I chastised myself for my bad attitude. Surely, Zeno could come up with a reasonably interesting suggestion that would not leap the bounds of decency and common sense while at the same time would catch people's interest and show Lady Fowling in the light she deserved?

No Clara and no sign she'd been there recently. I glanced down at the desk—as much in need of a tidying as mine had been. I put a forefinger on the top layer of papers and slid them round, looking for something of use. Oona had not been a good artist, but she had come up with brilliant ideas. Zeno, on the other hand, lacked inspiration but was good with pencil and paper. Here, he'd sketched an overflowing bookshelf with the last volume held in place by a knife stuck through its cover. Hmm. Another, he'd drawn what looked like an old-fashioned doctor's bag with vials and bottles peeking out, some of them with a skull-and-crossbones warning.

Creepy, but not bad, although I couldn't quite see what the actual display would be about. I must remind him that the subject of the exhibition was the life of a fascinating woman, not murder methods.

My eyes went to the flip chart, safely tucked away behind the desk. I thought of that rendering he'd done of the spiral staircase. An enormous mistake on his part—it still beggared belief that he would suggest such a thing after Oona's death. But perhaps he'd drawn larger versions of other ideas. Perhaps one of them held an iota of possibility as an entry display. I pulled the chart out and sat down, propping it against the desk.

The first page showed only a few pencil lines, but there was no mistaking the shape that wrapped round and round like a loose spring. The spiral staircase. The horizontal line at the top might've been the landing. But he'd scratched this attempt out with a large X. The next page looked almost the same, but a few more details had been added. It was that way page after page—the risers and treads on the next, the handrail after that until, at last, a figure appeared on the landing with a doorway behind. Still mostly suggestion, but I felt sure it was Oona. I could make out the bun on the top of her head.

The background had been shaded heavily with dense, horizontal pencil scratchings, creating a harsh, shadowy effect, and so I almost missed the second figure that lurked behind Oona in the office doorway. A person with indistinguishable features and a face thrown into darkness by the brim of a shapeless hat.

I heard the clanging of footsteps on the stairs, and my heart thumped in my chest. I leapt up, grabbing the flip chart before it slipped to the floor as Clara walked in.

"Oh, Clara," I said, sinking back into the chair. "How are you feeling?"

She didn't unbutton her coat, she didn't put down her bag, she didn't move. "It's a very odd thing," she said, her brows drawing up into a peak. "But my phone's turned up."

"Your lost phone? Well, good. That's good. Isn't that good?" Because I've got to say, it didn't look as if she were reporting happy news. "Where was it?"

"In my bag."

She paused to great effect. I'd seen inside Clara's bag—it was quite organized and bare of the ever-increasing number of bits and bobs that take up too much room in my own.

"But you'd looked in your bag."

"I looked in my bag. The police looked in my bag. I turned it out again and again that day. And yet this morning, it was where it should've been all along."

"Are you saying it was taken out and put back?"

"What else could it be? I didn't do it! I can swear to that—will they ask me to swear to it? Because I will."

"You mean the police? I'm sure they'd appreciate knowing it has returned," I said, as if the phone had taken it into its head to go on holiday and now felt rested enough to get back to work. "You're certain it is your old phone?"

Clara got out the phone and held it so that I could see the thin edge. "It's etched with my name."

"Well, I suppose that settles it. Do you want me to ring the old number, just to make sure?"

"The SIM card is gone."

Hang on, this was no lost phone—it had been interfered with. Would removing the SIM card erase any trace of Clara's calls and texts? And if so, who would want to do that?

"My," I said with a lightness I did not feel, "this is a puzzle. You'll tell the police, won't you? You should probably go right down there this minute. I'm sure it's something they would want to know."

I hoped to gauge Clara's guilt in the matter by her reaction, but her eyes had fallen on the flip chart that lay across the desk.

"Did Mr. Berryfield have another idea?"

"No." I picked up the flip chart to put it away. "I don't know why I looked inside. Morbid curiosity, I suppose."

"Let me see it again." She set her jaw firmly. "I shouldn't have reacted that way. I should be more professional. This is a decision about the exhibition, not my personal feelings."

"All right. But you don't need to look at all of them."

Clara took the flip chart and took charge, going through each page from the beginning until she paused when she arrived at the highly shaded, gloomy scene with the figure at the top of the staircase and the shadowy form in the doorway behind. She squinted, and then removed her glasses and got quite close to the drawing, her nose almost touching it. She twitched an eyebrow.

"What do you see?" I asked.

She straightened up with a sniff. "Why did he draw it

that way? Put a real person in the picture? Is that supposed to represent the actual crime?"

So, she thought the figure on the landing looked like Oona, too.

I moved the flip chart back behind the desk. "Zeno has a vivid imagination." Except when it comes to exhibition displays. "There's no need to concern ourselves with this. I'm going back to Middlebank—sorting through old furniture to see what we might be able to use. Let me know how you get on with the police, won't you? Because you're going to the station directly to tell them about your mobile, aren't you?"

Clara promised she would and I believed her—although I'd left her standing in the middle of Oona's office looking a bit at sea. I would follow up later.

At Middlebank, I ran up to my flat to change clothes—the cellar was not the place for a skirt and blouse and tights. I rummaged in the fridge and the pantry for a bite of lunch and ended up with buttered cream crackers and a morsel of cheese even a mouse might overlook. I searched for signs of Val and Bess's morning meeting. They had tidied up the coffee service. I took this as a sign that the conversation ended well, and he would resign himself to losing a daughter to the big lights of New York City. And to a man. Now all Bess would need to do was explain it all over again to her identical twin.

Val had a class later in the afternoon on Wednesday, but I thought we'd still have time for the cellar. I sent a text.

Ready when you are.

Five minutes later, the front door buzzed.

I listened at the landing and heard muffled voices below. Then Mrs. Woolgar came as far as the first floor, saw me leaning over the railing above, and said, "There's someone here to see you, Ms. Burke. A Mr. Kilpatrick. I've shown him to your office, but he didn't stay there."

Dom?

"Yes, thank you, Mrs. Woolgar. I'll be right down."

Dom waited for me in the entry, arms locked at his sides and his hands flapping in a more agitated fashion than usual.

"Hello, Dom. Lovely of you to stop." Unusual, too— Dom broke his routine only reluctantly.

"I saw his shoes," Dom said.

"You saw his shoes?" I repeated. I was reminded there were times when the subject of a conversation with Dom had to be discovered in an oblique fashion, because a direct "What the bloody hell are you talking about?" would get you nowhere.

"Whose shoes did you see?"

"Zeno Berryfield. I saw Zeno Berryfield's shoes. He went into the Charlotte. On Thursday."

The most curious feeling came over me—a queasy sensation in my stomach combined with a lightness in my head as if I stood at the precipice of a great abyss, my toes hanging over the edge.

"Which Thursday, Dom? Last week? When Zeno was working at the Charlotte?"

"No, Thursday the week before. The day Oona was murdered."

25

"Mrs. Woolgar, I'm going to the police station with Dom. I'll return . . . er . . . I'll let you know when I'll return."

"Is everything all right, Ms. Burke?"

Did I look as if I was about to be sick? Because that's how I felt.

"Fine. It's . . . I'll let you know."

I almost took Dom's arm as we hurried out the door and down the pavement, but I caught myself in time.

"The thing is, Dom, Zeno wasn't around on that Thursday. He was in Bristol. Police have confirmed that. So, couldn't it have been someone else you saw who wears the same sort of shoes?"

"I saw his shoes."

High-shine black oxfords—an integral part of Zeno's overall persona.

"And he was wearing that teal suit?" I asked.

"No."

My heart sank and my steps slowed. We had reached

Upper Borough Walls and would pass the abbey and soon be on Manvers Street.

"But that's all he ever wears. How do you know it was Zeno?"

"His shoes," Dom insisted. "And . . . it's a clue. Like on *Midsomer Murders*."

"Oh, do you like that program?"

Dom launched into a description of his and Margo's television viewing habits, which included watching countless reruns of the long-running *Midsomer* as well as the old American program *Murder, She Wrote*.

I respected Dom on so many levels, and he'd saved me from more than one computer disaster during my time as assistant to the assistant curator at the Jane Austen Centre. But he'd never been as aware of people as he had machines, and now—as we marched our way to the police station—I feared that his love of television murder mysteries had led him to believe he might hold the key to the case.

But there was no turning back now. At the station, I hurried up the ramp after Dom and into the lobby.

"Ms. Burke," Sergeant Owen said in greeting.

Dom looked at his surroundings and leaned over the desk to peer at the sergeant's computer screen.

"Hello, good afternoon. This is Dom Kilpatrick. We're here to see Detective Sergeant Hopgood about the Oona Atherton murder enquiry." Stating the obvious, but I wanted to set a good example for Dom. "Detective Constable Pye would be an adequate substitute. It's quite . . ."

"Important. Yes. Let me see what I can do for you. Would you like to take a seat?"

We sat in chairs along the wall. New situations often threw a spanner in the works for Dom, so I thought I'd best prepare him. "When you tell the police what you saw, they might ask the same questions over and over again," I said.

"In an attempt to break my story," Dom said, nodding.

"No, only to find out if you might remember anything

else. DC Pye says that happens often—witnesses don't remember all the details the first time. Asking again can help
to jog your memory."

"Because of his shoes. I didn't remember the first time
you asked me. Well, I did remember, but I didn't." Dom
frowned at what he'd said—too subjective for his own taste.

Introductions had been made, and we'd settled across the
table from the police officers. Dom didn't begin until DC
Pye had his pen poised over his open pocket notebook.

"On Wednesdays at eleven o'clock and on Thursdays at
three o'clock, I go to the Fashion Museum inside the Assembly Rooms to run a virus check. On Wednesdays, I
have coffee and a McVitie's Penguin, and on Thursdays, I
have tea and a fruit scone."

He paused and watched Pye write in his notebook. Hopgood nodded and said, "Go on."

"Hayley has told you about my sighting on last Wednesday week. That's when I saw the man I know now as Zeno
Berryfield walk down Circus Place and into the side door
of the Charlotte. That door leads to offices and storage. We
used that area five years ago for an exhibition called *Jane
and Siblings: The Austens at Home*. We reported rising
damp in the storage areas."

Another pause while Kenny Pye wrote.

"It still smells a bit musty," I said, filling in the silence.
Dom continued.

"Last Thursday week, I walked up Gay Street as I always do and turned right at the Circus and right again on
Bennett Street." Dom shoved his glasses up the bridge of
his nose and watched as Kenny Pye wrote in his pocket
notepad. "It was ten minutes before three o'clock. The
courtyard in front of the Assembly Rooms was empty and
there was no bus, and so I could see him across the road.
He walked into the same door."

"This was Zeno Berryfield—the man you'd seen the day before? The man Ms. Burke introduced you to yesterday?"

"Yes."

This was the sticking point, because the police had confirmed Zeno's alibi—he'd traveled by train from Bath to Bristol in the morning and returned that evening. They'd caught him on CCTV.

"And what made you think it was Mr. Berryfield?"

"I didn't think that when I saw him, because he was wearing other clothes—brown trousers, brown coat, and a hat pulled down low. But his shoes are shiny, and the sun hit them when he walked. Those are dress shoes. Don't wear dress shoes with everyday clothes. That's what Margo says."

Silence. Hopgood's fingers drummed on the table. His caterpillar eyebrows crept closer and closer to each other— a movement so slow it was difficult to see—until they met in the middle. DC Pye jotted in his notepad. Dom cleared his throat.

"A witness often doesn't remember everything the first time he is interviewed. When Hayley questioned me"—I did my best to look innocent of impersonating a police officer—"about seeing Zeno Berryfield the day before Oona was murdered, I did not associate it with the second time I saw him."

"Mr. Kilpatrick," Hopgood said, using his kindly-uncle voice, "We'd like you to take a look at CCTV footage of both Bath Spa and Bristol Temple Meads rail stations and see if you can find this person. I'm afraid it might take a while, and it could be rather boring work."

"Will you do an E-FIT of my description?" Dom asked eagerly.

"An E-FIT of a fellow in a hat that covers his face and who is wearing high-shine oxfords? We'd better hold off on that—if you see him on the film, we can lift that and have an actual photo, not just a computer mock-up."

Hopgood went off to set up the CCTV viewing. Dom

rang the Centre to say he needed the afternoon off, and then he rang Margo, and his voice became more animated. "CCTV!" he told her. "I might be a vital witness—the one that no one knows about, just like in the episode last evening with . . ."

I stepped out of Interview #1 and caught Hopgood returning.

"Dom's very observant," I said. "He isn't making this up."

"I believe he's telling the truth as he saw it," Hopgood replied. "But we have quite clear evidence of Mr. Berryfield coming and going that day. And regardless of a person's talents at computers and that sort of thing, it doesn't mean he is the best witness. Still, I'm willing to give Mr. Kilpatrick the time to find this out himself. Pye will stay with him to go through the CCTV."

"Will it take long?"

"They'll have to look at the entire day again," Hopgood said. "I'm not sure how quickly Mr. Kilpatrick can work through it."

Dom was a perfectionist—if he could, he would take half a day to explain a software update before he ever installed it. I looked at the time—gone two thirty already. The immediate excitement at his possible sighting began to fade.

"Will it be all right if I go now? Will you text me if Dom sees anything familiar? I'll be working in the cellar at Middlebank, but I can come straight back. Wait now—did Clara ring or stop by?"

"Ms. Powell? Not that I know of. Why?"

"She found her phone—the one she lost the day Oona was killed."

"Where?"

"In her bag. The bag she carries every day and the one she had with her the day of the murder." I didn't need a detective sergeant to tell me how dodgy that sounded. "The SIM card is missing. She has no idea what happened."

"Is that so?" Hopgood muttered. "That reminds me, Ms. Burke, about that paper in Ms. Powell's coat pocket yesterday. We found fingerprints."

"Hers? But you would, because she touched it yesterday—so did I."

"Yes, quite a few partials due to the paper being crumpled up. But no, these were quite clear. Let me show you." Hopgood cast his gaze round the corridor, spotted a paper recycling bin in an open office, and rummaged round until he came up with a single sheet of paper. "I'm going to give you this paper, and I want you to take it with both hands. Right?"

He held it out, and I did as I was told.

"There now, describe how you're holding the paper—where would your fingerprints appear?"

I looked down. "All four fingers on both hands are touching the back side of the paper, and my thumbs are pressing on the top side. Clara's fingerprints were the same?" I knew how bad that would be. Clara hadn't wanted to touch the paper yesterday, so the fingerprints would've come from an earlier time.

"We found Ms. Powell's fingerprints on the back side of the sheet, but nothing on the top side—no thumbprints at all."

I lifted my thumbs off the sheet. "How would she do that?"

"If the page had been at the bottom of a stack—"

"Ah! Her thumbs would've landed on whatever the top sheet was—she wouldn't've seen Oona's notes at the bottom. These could've been planted!"

"Planted or planned, Ms. Burke." Hopgood's phone went off. "Now, mind—"

"Yes, mind how I go," I said.

I walked out to the pavement buttoning my coat. What could I do now? I could get back to work—my own work, I resolved, but before I moved, Sergeant Hopgood came out the door of the station. "Ms. Burke," he called, and stuck his hands in his trouser pockets against the cold. "One more thing. About that office Mr. Berryfield said he'd gone to in Bristol—any joy there?"

"Oh. What was it called . . ."

Hopgood took his phone out and checked. "TKB Events. Sound familiar?"

"Not really, but I'll give it a think."

TKB, I repeated to myself as I left. TKB, I repeated as I nipped into the newsagent at the top of Manvers for a packet of crisps. I crossed the road, turned my collar up against the cold, and stood looking over the Parade Gardens. TKB.

As I crunched on crisps, TKB changed themselves into another trio of letters—QAD. QAD—Queen Anne desk. I tossed my empty packet into a bin and continued on my way to Middlebank. QAD—Lady Fowling's code for where the first edition of *Murder Must Advertise* lay. Soon we would know that for certain.

My feet took me the long way round. Clara had not gone to the police about her mobile, and so I would look for her in Oona's office. I cut over and turned up Barton Street, which became Gay Street, turning right at the Circus and right again on Bennett.

QAD. Queen Anne desk, I repeated to myself. QAD. TKB Events. TKB.

From the other side of the road I saw him at the entrance to the Charlotte. Tommy King-Barnes. TKB.

"*You!*" I shouted, pointing at him.

Tommy looked round in bewilderment and then saw me striding toward him.

"Hayley?"

"Are you TKB Events?" I accused.

"Ah, now," he said, his hands raised defensively, "that wasn't one of Zeno's references."

"Do you have an office in Bristol?"

"TKB is an umbrella company for my many and diverse businesses that—"

"Did you let Zeno use your Bristol office on the day Oona was murdered?"

That shut him up—at least for a moment.

"Hang on, what are you asking?"

"You heard what I asked."

"There's nothing wrong with giving a mate a place to work that isn't in a sea of hot desks." Tommy lifted a forefinger. "He wasn't working for you then, was he? So, you've no cause to complain where he spent his time."

"He was in Bristol the whole day?"

"I'm not his minder," Tommy said, holding up his hands as if to ward me off.

"In other words, you have no idea where he was." My gaze swept the surrounding area as if a man in high-shine oxfords and brown trousers might be lurking behind one of the bollards. "Have you seen him today?"

"Zeno's never one to hold still long—not when he's possessed of an idea." Tommy stepped aside to let a small group into the Charlotte. "Welcome to *Druids Then and Now*, I do hope you enjoy your visit."

He watched them enter, and when he turned back and saw me, he flinched, as if he'd forgotten my presence. I kept my eyes on him and took a step forward. "Have you seen him today?" I repeated.

Tommy glanced at the scene behind me and screwed up his face in concentration. "Oh, wait now, he said he needed to nip up to London."

"London?"

"For the exhibition. A good price on flat-pack display cases. They're all the rage—but you probably know that."

Tommy's phone rang—Enya, Middle Earth. He looked down at it and gave me a sheepish grin. "Sorry, Hayley," he said, and backed up into the Charlotte. I was about to follow, but a text pinged on my mobile.

From Sergeant Hopgood.

CCTV results. Can you take a look?

I began a shaky reply as I broke into a trot.

On my way—

My phone rang—Val. I sent the text and answered his call.

"Hi," I panted, and held up by the postbox at the top of Gay Street.

"I've been caught," he said. "The department head wants to talk about the exhibition—he has a few ideas for us. I've got my class at four. I won't be free until close to six. You go on to the cellar if you're ready."

"Something else has come up. Dom has information about—"

I heard Val's voice, turned away from the phone. "Yeah, I'll be right there." He came back to me. "I'm sorry, but as the college is a sponsor, I thought I'd better do this."

"No, that's fine." My mind overflowed with important questions and vital details. I caught the first one I could get hold of and asked, "Wait—how did it go with Bess?"

A moment of silence followed.

"My girls. I don't know how they got to be twenty-four, I can tell you that."

"How dare they grow up on us," I said.

I heard a laugh—a small one.

"And why isn't London theater good enough for them?" he demanded.

"Perhaps Bess and Adam will make their marks across the pond, return home, and start a theater company in Bath."

He mumbled something, and then said, "She was glad to talk with you."

That was my bright spot, and I basked in it for a moment before saying, "You go on. I'll see you later."

At least it was downhill to the police station.

* * *

Well, Ms. Burke," Sergeant Owen said. "This time they're waiting for you." He picked up his phone, and in a moment Kenny Pye appeared. I followed him back to the inner workings of the station.

"Is it really Zeno?" I asked as I trotted behind him. "Wearing brown trousers and the like?"

Kenny turned to me and his dark eyes held a gleam. "He's quite observant, Mr. Kilpatrick." He opened a door to a room with several desks and wide screens. Dom leapt up from a swivel chair, sending it spinning off to a far wall.

"All right, Dom?"

"He's there, Hayley. I've seen him. Come and look."

I approached the screen and stood at Dom's side, Sergeant Hopgood on the other.

"Now," Dom said, controls in hand, "we can go directly to the images because I've marked the specific frames by first adding a . . ."

It's possible I didn't absorb Dom's complete and thorough description of how the technical side of CCTV worked, but a terrible thrill ran through me when he went directly to an image of a platform at the Bristol station.

"There." Dom pointed to a tall man in drab, shapeless clothing and wearing a fedora that looked as if it had been left out in the rain. The film had been slowed so that the man's every move could be examined. He kept his head down and his face in shadows, and yet he was oh so familiar.

"Must've changed his mufti at this office in Bristol," Hopgood said, and Dom snorted.

"Mufti means ordinary clothes," Dom explained to me with obvious delight. "Detective Sergeant Hopgood is referring to the suspect's usual manner of dress—that blue suit. Teal. And the tie with the large colored dots on it."

"They look like giant Smarties to me," I said, and Dom

laughed again. At least someone was having a good time here.

"He forgot to change his shoes," Dom added.

He forgot to change his shoes, and that's what had sunk him. For want of a nail, so to speak.

"Can you be sure it's Zeno?" I asked.

"Watch, Hayley," Dom said, raising the controls again. "Watch."

The scene on the railway platform jumped and here he came again, the tall man in the floppy fedora. A child ran by, disturbing a pigeon, which then flew toward the man. He flinched as the bird barely cleared his head, lifting his arm as if to ward off the attack and looking back over his shoulder in the camera's direction for an instant. Dom froze the frame and there he was—Zeno Berryfield.

My arms broke out in gooseflesh, and I shivered as if I'd been doused with ice water. "Oh my God." He had lied and lied and acted the fool, and all the while Zeno had murdered Oona.

"And it's the right time?" I asked.

"Oh, yes," Hopgood said. "In these frames, he's returning to Bath midday. Mr. Kilpatrick has offered to look through the rest of the footage to find Berryfield heading back to Bristol, where, we presume, he switched out his clothes."

"Back to the teal suit and Smarties tie," I said.

"Why would he do it?" DC Pye asked. "Only to get her job?"

"To get her everything," I said. "Oona was all that Zeno wanted to be but wasn't. She had talent, skill—"

"She scared me," Dom said.

I laughed. "Yeah, she scared me, too. But she was good. Zeno is none of that. He comes up with lame ideas and talks big and does nothing. Apart from once electrocuting a fellow."

"Time we had another chat with Mr. Berryfield."

"He's gone up to London," I said bleakly. Had Zeno

done a bunk? "But I'll tell you who told me, and you could talk with him. It's the person Zeno used as a reference, the man who is TKB Events. You asked me about that earlier, and I finally made the connection. Tommy King-Barnes—TKB."

"TKB—the Bristol office where Berryfield said he'd spent his day?" Hopgood asked. "Do you have a phone number for Tommy King-Barnes?"

"I have three."

The police left to have a word with Tommy at the Charlotte. I intended to follow on foot, but stayed to keep Dom company as he waited for Margo. He had dearly wanted to ride along with Hopgood and Pye, but I reminded him that he might've cracked the case and wouldn't his girlfriend want to know everything? She arrived only minutes later, and I listened to Dom's entire story again. At last, the couple left, discussing the fact that Dom looked a great deal like the detective sergeant on *Midsomer Murders*. I bade Sergeant Owen good afternoon and hoofed it up to the Charlotte.

Had I expected the road to be lined with blue-and-yellow-checkered police cars with their blue lights flashing? Had I hoped to see Tommy King-Barnes being dragged off in handcuffs? I don't believe I had any particular expectations, but the utter lack of activity stunned me.

The exhibition perked along with a handful of visitors and a cluster of ten-year-olds ogling the display on human sacrifice. The woman at the ticket table said Tommy had left a bit ago. On his own? I asked in all innocence. She couldn't quite remember, as the school group had arrived at that moment, and she'd been busy.

Naomi's office stood open and empty. I had nowhere else to go but up to Oona's office, where I sat uncomfortably at the desk chair and thought what to do next. Val would be in class, and I shouldn't distract him by texting that Oona's

murderer had been found and he had an accomplice—a
Druid. No, I'd hold on to that news until later.

A few papers from the desk had slipped to the floor, as
if they'd been caught in a breeze. I collected them and
looked for clues to Oona's murder or, at the very least, ideas
for exhibition displays. Nothing—only a receipt for duct
tape from Homebase.

My eyes fell again on the flip chart behind the desk, and
I remembered the shadowy figure in one of the drawings. I
had recognized Oona on the landing, and I believe Clara
had, too, but now I remembered the shadowy figure who
wore a hat with a floppy brim that covered his face. I took
the chart out and paged through, looking for that sketch.
Had the murderer drawn a picture of the crime scene and
included himself? Was he that self-obsessed? Or that thick?

But although the other sketches he'd started and abandoned were there, the drawing with the man in the hat was
missing. It had been ripped from the chart, leaving behind
the top inch or two of pencil marks that filled in the darkness of the scene.

Had Zeno torn it out? Was he belatedly trying to cover his
tracks? Or perhaps he had blithely traveled up to London
carrying the sketch in his satchel to show it off to the British
Library, where he hoped to co-opt the post Oona had expected to take. That, I would believe. But something—
someone—was missing.

Where was Clara?

26

Feeling all right?

For five minutes, I stared at my phone and waited for a reply from Clara. When nothing came, I sent another text, which took me twice as long because my finger shook.

Let's meet for coffee. Free now?

Two minutes later, I left, by way of Naomi's office.

"Have you seen Clara?" I asked her.

Naomi replied with a frown. "I looked out the window earlier and saw those police detectives. When I went downstairs, they were leaving with Tommy, but they stopped long enough to ask if I'd seen Zeno. He's your problem—I knew you'd have trouble with him. The cowboy. I hope he hasn't dragged Tommy into anything, because the Druids have been one of the easiest bookings I've had."

"Have you seen Clara?"

"Yes, but that was late morning. Why?"

I didn't answer, but hurried down to the ground floor, out the door, and headed for the Pulteney Bridge, keeping my mind in neutral and my nerves under control. I arrived at the block of flats on Williams, breathing heavily, and pressed the button for Oona's flat. The door unlocked, and I went in. Lift or two flights of stairs? The indicator told me the lift was on the fifth floor, and so I took the stairs and arrived at the second floor still breathing heavily. The door of the flat stood ajar. I knocked and then pushed it open with one finger.

"Clara? It's Hayley—are you all right?"

No movement, no sound. The place looked deserted and untouched.

"Clara?"

I didn't like the silence. I realized what a terrible idea it was for me to be there, and how much better it would be to leave and ring the police. But at that moment, I heard a faint clanging. The sound reminded me of footsteps on the spiral staircase. Perhaps I'd imagined it, but I shivered nonetheless. Then came a muffled voice—no words, only "Aaaahhh" like the wailing one might expect from a ghost.

But would a ghost haunt a bathroom?

I dropped my bag and ran into the pass-through from bedroom to kitchen, and flung open the bathroom door.

Clara sat awkwardly in the tub, knees up to her chin, her hands and feet bound with duct tape. Her mouth had been stuffed with what looked like a tea towel and secured with more duct tape wound round and round her head. Her arms extended forward over her knees, and her wrists were attached to the hot and cold taps with more loops of tape. Her bun listed to one side, her face blanched of color. She shook her arms, and the taps, slightly loose, clanged.

I rushed over and knelt by the tub. "Are you all right?"

She nodded. I searched for the end of the tape round her mouth as she began speaking. Although she was completely unintelligible, I could pick up from the intonation that she was telling me the whole story. "Hang on," I said. I picked and picked at the tape and at last began to unwrap her gag.

"It's Zeno, isn't it?" I asked.

Her head bounced up and down and her bun wobbled. She continued her tale, her voice leaping in register and then dropping down as she said I knew not what.

Finally, I reached the last layer of tape. "Sorry, Clara— this will sting."

She shut her eyes tight. I ripped the tape off her face, but I didn't have the heart to pull it off her hair, and instead let it hang in a long, silver curl down her back. I pulled the tea towel out of her mouth, and she coughed and worked her lips and tongue.

"Is he gone?" she asked quietly, her voice raspy.

"Yes. But where?"

"He wants to get away. He said he only needed time to get away."

"Did he follow you here?" I asked as I started to pick at the tape around her wrists.

"He wanted that drawing, and he followed me from the Charlotte. You see, after you left, I took the flip chart out again. There was something about the one with the figures in it that looked odd. Familiar, but odd. And then I knew it—I recognized the man in the hat. He had stood close behind me at Pret A Manger on the day Oona was murdered. I thought hard about those few minutes, and realized that there had been some jostling in the queue, and I think he took out my phone then." She turned large, watery eyes at me. "It was Mr. Berryfield."

"Yes, it was. But if he took it out, why did he put it back?"

Clara shook her head. "'Obfuscation.' That's the word he used. He said it would confuse the police." Her voice dropped to a whisper. "I think he only confused himself."

I snickered in relief at this show of good spirits. I was

getting nowhere with the tape on her wrists, and stopped. "I've got to phone the police. I'll be back to help you, and we'll get out of here. Hang on."

"Look," Clara said, nodding to a cosmetics bag at the sink. "In there."

I took the bag and turned it out on the floor and riffled through until I came up with a pair of nail scissors. I cut through her wrist restraints. "Here," I said, handing over the scissors, "you do the rest." It looked as if Zeno had used half the roll of tape on Clara's feet alone—that would take her a few minutes.

I left her to it, ran out to my bag, and dug for my phone, always at the bottom when it's most needed. When I'd closed my hand round it, I moved to the window to ring Hopgood, but before I could hit a key, an arm went across my throat, and I was wrenched back and held fast.

"Ms. Burke," Zeno said, "what a surprise to see you here."

27

❧

Choking out a cry, I struggled, trying to get a good angle to elbow Zeno in the stomach, but he had the advantage of height and weight, and the pressure on my throat made me both faint and nauseated.

"There's no need to put up a fight," he said, his voice strained. "I won't hurt you. But you must not ring the police. Calm down and give me time to make my exit."

It was what he'd said to Clara. I stopped fighting. Zeno produced the roll of duct tape from a pocket, wrenched one of my arms back and then the other, wrapping my wrists behind me and to the drawer pull of the built-in sideboard. I took a step toward him, yanking the drawer open. Dishes rattled, but the piece of furniture didn't move.

Zeno backed off slightly and straightened his suit jacket. "There," he said with a nod. "That should hold until I can leave."

"Did you set a trap for us here?"

"Nonsense," he replied. "I merely followed Ms. Powell, because she'd taken something I needed."

"The sketch you'd made of yourself as murderer. Good move, Zeno."

He didn't take the bait. "When I saw it was you who rang the bell," he said, "I didn't think you would just go away. So I stepped down the corridor until you were safely inside the flat so that we could all three—"

"Why did you kill Oona?"

His dark, beady eyes flickered to me as he adjusted his cuffs. "She asked for it," he said, his voice full of acid.

"Because you wanted her job?"

"Oona took everything," he said, checking his watch. "She didn't want only this job, she wanted all of them. And she got them, too. She had merely to point and say, 'I'll have that,' and it was hers. Everyone else was invisible as the great Oona Atherton took over. And I swear it was her idea for me to flood that entry on the Isle of Man where the fellow was electrocuted. Dropped me in it. It wasn't fair."

I heard a faint clang of metal and, beyond Zeno, in the pass-through, I saw a shadow of movement in the bathroom. Had Clara broken free?

Zeno cocked his head. "Is Ms. Powell all right?"

Such concern. I raised my voice to cover the noise.

"Oona's flat, Oona's office, Oona's exhibition—the nerve of her! You couldn't stand it, could you? The truth is, Zeno, Oona was very good at what she did." *And you aren't.*

"She never gave anyone else a chance," he snapped.

"You went to the Charlotte in disguise—you planned to murder her."

Zeno grunted. "I went to talk to her about a compromise."

"You stole that paper from Oona, didn't you?"

He glanced out the window behind me. "I had no idea what she was crowing about, but I knew that paper meant something, and so I took it, certain it would come in handy. And so it did. It bought me time, pointing the finger at perfect Ms. Powell."

"You failed there. You planted Clara's fingerprints on the paper in a way that made it clear it was faked."

And speaking of Clara, a thin line of her slight figure appeared at the corner of the pass-through. I tried not to look and continued to goad Zeno, to keep his attention focused on me.

"You put on such a show when I told you about Oona's death—you laughed in my face when I offered you the job. And then the next day, you were contrite and practically in mourning."

He smirked. "Good, wasn't I? Always making it clear that Oona had been the love of my life. I tell you now, being married to her was sheer torture. But I knew if I cast doubt on others, I would be in the clear."

"But nothing you tried worked, did it? Pretending you hadn't seen Oona, trying to make me think Clara was usurping power, planting evidence. Police have a witness who recognized you in your disguise and saw you on the day Oona was murdered going into the Charlotte. You see, Zeno, you forgot to change your shoes. Bad luck."

He pulled a cosh out of his satchel and squeezed it—the same one he'd knocked Oona out with, no doubt. "Just a precaution, Ms. Burke," he said when I eyed it. "I promise. Not to worry."

I thought of that weapon cracking Oona's skull and worried regardless. I wondered if he would truly leave both Clara and me alive and well and able to point police in his direction.

Zeno tapped the cosh in the palm of his hand and, as if he'd heard my thoughts, said, "I will be out of your life soon. I have friends, you see. True friends who have agreed to assist me in leaving my current situation and starting afresh elsewhere. There'll be no trace of Zeno Berryfield left."

"They are looking for me. They are looking for Clara." My heart tripped along and my skin felt clammy. I leaned back against the sideboard to keep from dropping to the floor.

"Ms. Powell didn't feel well today," he said. "You probably passed along that news to any relevant person. And as for you—"

They think I'm in the cellar, but I wouldn't tell him that.

"Well, if you're going," I said, "you'd better hop it. Police will be here and you will be caught."

"*I am waiting for word!*" Zeno loomed over me and pointed to the cosh. "And it would do you good to shut it for a few minutes."

Behind him, on the other side of the room, Clara crept out of the pass-through, the duct tape still stuck to her ankles. She had the kettle in her hands. I began to shake as she crept forward, and disguised it by pulling on my tether and rattling the dishes in the sideboard. "I hope it isn't Tommy you're waiting for, because he's already spilled everything to Sergeant Hopgood."

I gave a ferocious yank and the drawer came flying out, casting forks and spoons across the floor. Zeno lifted the cosh to strike just as Clara rushed forward, raised both arms as far as she could, and pivoted as she took a swing. Water spewed out in an arc as the kettle came down on the back of Zeno's head with a solid *clank*.

He whirled, and—brandishing the cosh—staggered toward Clara, and then crashed to the floor, where he lay motionless and moaning.

Someone pounded on the door and Clara shrieked, but I heard the voices and yelled, "Police, Clara—it's the police."

They didn't wait, but burst in—Detective Constable Pye and Detective Sergeant Hopgood followed by four or five uniforms. The DS nodded to Zeno and the PCs surrounded him where he lay. One of them pulled the cosh from his hand.

"Are the two of you all right?" Hopgood asked.

I grinned at Clara. "We are."

"Well done, Ms. Burke," the DS said.

"Oh, no," I said. "I didn't save the day—it was Clara."

Clara, her Oona-bun demolished and with trails of duct tape hanging off her as if she were a silver-gilt ancient mummy come to exact revenge, looked down at the kettle in her hand.

"Would anyone like a cup of tea?"

28

Police took the kettle away, and so Clara boiled water in a saucepan. I kept her company in the small kitchen while the officers busied themselves with telling Zeno his rights. An ambulance came—Hopgood insisted for legal purposes, although I'm sure we all knew that Clara couldn't've hit Zeno hard enough to cause damage. And wasn't that too bad.

"You were amazing," I said to her as we leaned against the kitchen counter.

She giggled—a disconcertingly high giggle that quickly turned to tears. I made her sit at the table, and I saw to the tea bags, biscuits—oh, look, Maries—and milk and sugar.

"I miss Oona," she said, sniveling and using a fresh tea towel to wipe her face and blow her nose. "She would always know what to do and what to say. And I know she could be difficult and bossy, but she could be unexpectedly kind, too. She was very much like my nana in many respects."

I leaned over and gave her a hug. Although I'm sure she did miss Oona, I thought that perhaps Clara missed her nana, too. "Look, we'll need a few days to sort through all this," I said. "You still have a job, but for now, won't you please go back to Shepton Mallet?"

"Yes, of course, I will do that, Hayley." Clara glanced at me in an oblique manner. "Tomorrow?"

"I'd be happy to drive you over this evening." Kenny Pye had appeared in the kitchen doorway. "See you safely there."

Clara's cheeks turned a lovely shade of pink. "Thank you, Detective Constable Pye. That's very kind of you."

Sergeant Hopgood put his head in the door. "All right if I have a chat with Ms. Powell in here? You'll be up after that, Ms. Burke."

Kenny carried the tea tray out to the sitting room. We settled on the sofa while a couple of uniforms milled about talking into their radios.

"Tea?" I asked them.

"Ta," they said, and I poured theirs as well as ours.

"If her nana is like Oona," I said to Kenny, "it's no wonder Clara didn't feel as if she could give up on the exhibition no matter what happened."

The DC nodded. "She told me that her grandmother came from Portugal. She married a sailor from Southampton, and when her daughter died in a boating accident, she took Clara in. Her nana has high expectations. Children—and grandchildren—of immigrants need to be super-achievers to satisfy their families."

"Sounds like you have firsthand knowledge."

He grinned. "My granddad was a boy when he came from India to Manchester in 1956. He worked in the textile factories all his life, and my dad after him, but I was supposed to be a Harley Street doctor, or at the very least, a barrister."

"Or a famous writer?" I asked.

Kenny glanced toward the kitchen—and the inspiration for his PI Alehouse—and his dark eyes glittered. "I'm saving that for my retirement," he said.

When Hopgood had finished interviewing Clara, I took her place. I asked as many questions as the detective sergeant did, and—miracle of miracles—received a good many answers.

"You'll stop in tomorrow to sign your statement?" Hopgood asked as I heard my mobile ring.

"Oh, yes," I replied. "Wouldn't miss it."

I followed the ringing of my phone—I'd dropped it when Zeno attacked—and discovered it on the floor in the corner under an aspidistra. It was Val.

"I'm all right," I answered.

"What?" he said. "What's happened?"

I winced—I'd done the same thing to him that Dinah had done to me.

"Nothing. That is, lots, but really I'm fine. We're at Oona's flat on Williams. They've arrested Zeno—he murdered Oona."

Silence on the line. "Are the police there?"

"Yes, and they've taken him off. So you see—I really am all right." I looked at the time—five o'clock. Was I supposed to be somewhere? "Where are you?"

"I was just leaving for Middlebank, thinking you were in the cellar."

Yes, that's what I should be doing now.

"I'll see you there."

At Middlebank, Val answered the door. Behind him, Mrs. Woolgar hovered near the hallstand with Bunter at her feet.

I gave Val a quick hug—and a squeeze that promised more later—and asked, "Did Val tell you, Mrs. Woolgar? About Zeno?"

"A sketchy account," the secretary said. A mild reproof, but her face looked drawn with worry.

"I told her all I knew," Val said. "Do you want to tell us the rest, or should we wait until you're—"

"No, I'm fine, really." I was knackered, but also washed with relief and, in an odd way, energized and ready to talk. "But I could just do with a cup of tea." And a proper biscuit.

The three of us trailed off to the kitchenette, where Mrs. Woolgar put the kettle on, Bunter settled in Val's lap, and I popped the lid on the biscuit tin.

"Thank God," I said, "custard creams."

In as clear and concise a manner as possible, I told them the story of my Wednesday—a day that seemed to have many more hours in it than it should.

"Oona came to Bath, and Zeno followed her—although he had made out he'd been here for a while. She let that flat across the Pulteney Bridge for five months, but Sergeant Hopgood said that Zeno spent his nights in a series of cheap lets—sleeping on sofas here and there."

"He kept himself remarkably well, considering," Mrs. Woolgar commented.

"He's vain," I replied.

"Your Mr. Kilpatrick broke the case, didn't he?" she asked.

"He did, and he's justly proud of himself."

"And the Druid?" Val asked.

"Tommy King-Barnes is still at the station. Sergeant Hopgood said that Tommy told them that Zeno told him the reason he needed to leave Bath was because I was trying to hold him—Zeno—accountable for a broken glass case here at Middlebank." I stopped and frowned. "Does that make sense?"

"No," Val said, "but go on."

"Tommy swears he didn't know anything, was only doing a mate a favor, and will tell police anything they want to know—according to Sergeant Hopgood."

"Well, Ms. Burke." Mrs. Woolgar stood and collected cups and saucers. "I'm sure you are looking forward to a quiet evening, and perhaps you'll take tomorrow off in order to recuperate?"

"I'll take the morning off. I don't think we can afford to have me wasting time lying about on a fainting sofa when I should be—oh, Mrs. Woolgar, we've found it! At least, we think we have. Val figured out what Lady Fowling's odd phrases meant, and we believe the signed first edition of *Murder Must Advertise* is within reach. Won't you come down to the cellar with us and find out?"

The cellar presented what looked at first to be a solid front of furniture stacked from floor almost to the ceiling. It had been a wooden puzzle I'd taken apart a few months ago, and then had to fit back in; otherwise, we would've been left with an odd lot of occasional tables and chairs lining the corridor. But the door to Mrs. Woolgar's lower-ground-floor garden flat lay at the other end of the corridor, and so that would never have done.

The secretary stood in the open doorway. Bunter sprang up onto a console table with a marble top and from there worked his way deeper into the room without ever touching the ground—he loved cellar expeditions. It took longer for Val and me to make the trek, shifting a highboy this way and a love seat that way, until at last we'd worked our way to the back of the room and arrived at Lady Fowling's burled-walnut Queen Anne desk with cabriolet legs.

It had five drawers—one center and two on either side, but we had to move more furniture before we could actually get the drawers open, and we did so with some ceremony. The central drawer was empty. The two top drawers were empty apart from a program for the 1982 grand reopening of the Theatre Royal. Nothing in the bottom right-hand drawer. Val and I stared at the last unopened drawer.

Mrs. Woolgar watched. Bunter observed from a nearby fern stand.

"Go on," Val said with a nod.

I pulled open the drawer, and found a small, acid-free— I recognized the type—book-sized box tied with twine. Dangling from the twine was a monocle.

Lady Fowling had such a way.

We weaved our way to the door and, under the light from wall sconces in the corridor, loosened the twine and opened the box. Inside, a clean and vivid yellow dust jacket proclaimed:

DOROTHY L. SAYERS'

NEW DETECTIVE STORY

MURDER MUST ADVERTISE

We opened the cover with reverence—not too far, no need to break the spine—and saw an array of signatures.

"Anthony Berkeley," Val said with a nod.

"G. K. Chesterton." Mrs. Woolgar pointed without touching.

At least I could recognize Agatha Christie.

We had found it—and then some. Under the book, Lady Fowling had left a newspaper clipping dated June 1950. It was a photo of Sayers. She wore a floral frock and a lively hat that seemed to dance even on the static paper. The caption explained that the author of the Lord Peter Wimsey books had been invited back to her former place of employment—S. H. Benson's Advertising, Ltd.— to unveil a plaque near the spiral staircase, and that both staircase and business had been inspirations for *Murder Must Advertise*.

"Such a treasure," Mrs. Woolgar whispered.

I replaced the clipping and book and retied the twine. "Mrs. Woolgar," I said, holding out the box, "would you keep this safe for us until tomorrow? We'll need to tell Mr. Rennie about it and ask his advice."

"Thank you, Ms. Burke, that's quite . . . Yes, I will." She gently took the package and added, "Would you like me to ring the board members this evening and explain events? Apart from Ms. Babbage, of course—I'm sure you would like to talk with her. And perhaps I won't wait until tomorrow to talk with Mr. Rennie, either."

"Yes, please do—and tomorrow we'll sort out what to do about the exhibition."

We left Mrs. Woolgar at the door of her flat and—Bunter trotting up the stairs ahead of us—we climbed the stairs. The cloud of Oona's death had been lifted, but the uncertainty of how we could move forward remained.

"What do you say," Val offered, "we don't talk about books or mysteries or exhibitions or murder this evening?"

"Agreed." I checked the time—gone seven o'clock. "Pizza?" I asked as we reached the entry.

The buzzer sounded.

Val and I stood there, staring at the door, until I sighed with great effect and said, "Oh, all right. This better be good."

It took me a moment to recognize this young couple on the doorstep. Clara had abandoned not only her business suit, but also her Oona bun and now was dressed in corduroy trousers, boots, and a large woolly jumper. Her dark, straight hair hung past her shoulders. Behind her, Detective Constable Pye—or rather, Kenny—wore denims, shirt, sweater, and a dark jacket with a faint tartan to it.

"Don't worry, Hayley, we're not stopping," Clara said with a wide smile. "I rang my nana and asked if Detective

Constable Pye could stay to dinner to thank him for driving me over, and so we're on our way to Shepton Mallet."

"How lovely," I said—and meant it, although I realized I would need to give up the idea of introducing Kenny Pye to Dinah.

"Also," Clara said, "Sergeant Hopgood has been in touch with Oona's solicitor, and as she had no family, they've asked me to help sort through her possessions. Apparently, all she had was in two lockups in Taunton and it's mostly hardware, display cases, and drapes for exhibitions. Wouldn't it be lovely if we could use a few things and so put Oona's name in the program?"

I had a feeling Oona would be all over this exhibition. "Yes, if we're allowed, that would be lovely. Now, you enjoy these days off, Clara, and I'll see you on Monday—why don't we begin our day here?"

"Kenny," Val said, "see you tomorrow evening in class. Do you remember the topic?"

"I do," Kenny replied, and even in the dim light I saw his dark eyes shine. "How the end of one story is the beginning of another."

Val and I had the laziest of Thursday mornings, but eventually we readied ourselves to face the world. He had an afternoon class to teach, and I had to sort out what the First Edition Society was to do about the exhibition. I no longer felt apprehensive about what Naomi would allow and what she wouldn't, but concerned myself instead with what the board would say and whether they would want to form a managerial committee to run the event. If that happened, I wondered how many bottles of sherry we'd get through before April came.

"Time I looked in with Mrs. Woolgar," I said to Val, who was checking his email on his phone. "I'll see you downstairs before you leave."

The secretary's door was open. I took a deep breath and went in.

We exchanged good mornings in the nick of time—only a few minutes before afternoon began—and I dived in.

"Thank you for explaining our situation to the board. I'm sure you were able to discuss the need to name a new manager, and although I realize that I have no qualifications, I believe it would be best if I at least put my name down. For appearances' sake, only. Of course, if the board members felt that we should continue to search for a . . ." I was running out of steam. The computer screen reflected in Mrs. Woolgar's glasses and I couldn't see her eyes, and so I gave up. "I know you had great faith in what Oona could do, but—"

"No, Ms. Burke," Mrs. Woolgar cut in. "My trust was not in Ms. Atherton."

"But her ideas—the way she could bring Lady Fowling and her life to people today."

"Ms. Atherton talked a good show at the board meeting," Mrs. Woolgar said. "But what did we know of her follow-through? No, Ms. Burke, it's you I trust. I know you have come to treasure her ladyship's reputation and would never put it in jeopardy. You trusted Ms. Atherton and so I trusted you."

"You did?"

"The board has all agreed, and Mr. Rennie, too, has voiced his confidence in your ability to carry off the exhibition to the credit of the Society and her ladyship's memory. And so, over to you, Ms. Burke."

"My." It took me a moment before I could speak without choking up. "Well, first things first—we'll need to finalize the menu for the opening-night gala."

We had a brief exchange about crab puffs and then I excused myself and went out to the empty front entry, quivering. I dashed up the stairs and met Val coming down. We stood on the library landing at Lady Fowling's portrait.

"Well, what do you know—here I am, the exhibition manager."

Val grabbed me round the waist. "Well done, you," he said, and kissed me.

I put my arms round his neck and grinned. "I'm just where I thought I would never be. And would you credit it—Mrs. Woolgar said she trusted in my judgment and thought I could do it."

"Oh, and you don't remember me saying the same thing?" Val said. "That you would be a great exhibition manager?"

"You said that because you love me."

His eyes crinkled at the corners as he smiled. "I do love you—but can't both be true? I love you and you'll be a great exhibition manager?"

Modesty overtook me. "I don't think she said 'great.'"

"I'm sure she was thinking it."

"Well, here we are in February. We've a great deal of work to do, and very little time," I said. "I've decided we'll go with Oona's suggestion for the entry—and give her full credit—using Lady Fowling's desk."

"We'll have to move everything out of the cellar to get to it."

"Yes," I agreed. "Also, remember my idea to add audio to the exhibition? Clara has interviewed board members and wants to pull quotes for signage—I believe we should combine the ideas. Then, last night, Adele told me she remembers Lady Fowling recording one or two of their afternoon teas at the Royal Crescent and also reading aloud some of her François Flambeaux stories. Mrs. Woolgar remembers, too, but they don't have any idea where the recordings are. They've got to be here somewhere. I'm going to search."

"Perhaps," Val said, "Lady Fowling left a clue to their whereabouts."

I gasped. "Yes! I'll need to go through the notebooks again. Wish me luck."

"Luck." And a kiss. "I'll see you this evening—here, or would you rather meet for a meal?"

"The Raven?"

"Pie and a pint it is."

I saw him out and went back up the stairs, stopping on the library landing to take in Lady Fowling's portrait—just in case she had anything else to tell me.

"Ms. Burke?" Mrs. Woolgar stood at the bottom of the stairs.

"Yes?"

"When you have the time, would you come down to my flat?"

Surely I hadn't heard her correctly. *To* her flat? To *her* flat?

"It's only that," she continued, "I have a length of fabric, a lovely deep, dusky purple. It's quite enough for an evening gown cut on the bias, which would give it an elegant drape. I thought it might just suit you. Are you interested?"

ACKNOWLEDGMENTS

Many thanks to my fabulous editor, Michelle Vega, as well as Jennifer Snyder and everyone at Berkley Prime Crime for cheering on the First Edition Library Mysteries. And when a writer has a question about any little thing regarding the business or creative side, who's she gonna call? Her agent, of course. Thanks to Christina Hogrebe of the Jane Rotrosen Agency for knowing the answers or finding them out in short order.

My other "editors"—aka the weekly writing group— keep me on my toes, helped along, no doubt, by the wine and chocolate. Thanks to Kara Pomeroy, Louise Creighton, Sarah Niebuhr Rubin, Tracey Hatton, and Meghana Padakandla. And grateful thanks to family and friends who cheer me on.

All Bath buildings and businesses mentioned in *Murder Is a Must* are real—except for the ones that aren't. I have inserted Middlebank House into one of those grand Georgian terraces that rise above the city center. There is no Charlotte (although I'm sure it would be a popular exhibition venue if it did exist), but you can certainly have coffee at the café inside the Assembly Rooms. Maybe I'll see you there.

The Golden Age of Mystery continues to intrigue. This book, the second in the First Edition Library series, was inspired by Dorothy L. Sayers's *Murder Must Advertise*. If you have not read it, I highly recommend you do. It is my favorite Lord Peter book by Sayers—too bad it wasn't hers. She dashed it off to meet a contract obligation, relying heavily on her own experience as a copywriter at S. H. Benson's on Kingsway in Bloomsbury (the offices had a spiral staircase and all). I confess I am a sucker for her snappy patter and will reread sections of this book for the banter alone. Such inspiration!

KEEP READING FOR A SNEAK PEEK AT

THE LIBRARIAN
ALWAYS RINGS TWICE

THE NEXT FIRST EDITION LIBRARY
MYSTERY BY *USA TODAY* BESTSELLING
AUTHOR MARTY WINGATE.

S hall I be mother?"

Charles Henry Dill didn't wait for a response, but reached across the library table for the pot, the sleeve of his baby blue linen jacket pulling up and exposing his hairy arm. He poured, managing to splash tea into the saucers and onto the highly polished walnut surface before, at last, hitting the cups.

Beside me, Mrs. Woolgar flinched and leapt up to get a towel—either that or she was about to go for his throat, a prospect I found not all that unappealing.

I stood. "No, let me."

Mrs. Woolgar sat down again as I retrieved a small towel from the trolley by the door. I mopped up the spill as Charles Henry distributed tea round the table, after which each of us poured the excess from the saucers back into the cups before adding milk. I noticed he had handed board member Maureen Frost, sitting next to him, a saucer with no spills.

"Well, now," Dill said, with a smirk of self-importance, "let me just say I'm ever so glad to be joining you here at

Middlebank House and the First Edition Society, and I look forward with eager anticipation to working with our esteemed curator, Ms. Burke, in my new role as her assistant and, I daresay"—he chortled—"general dogsbody."

How had it come to this?

It had started on Monday. My boyfriend and I had returned from a week in Deal—a lovely seaside town in Kent—and I was ready and rested for the First Edition library's inaugural public open hours in two days' time. I believed it to be the logical next step to increasing the awareness of the Society, gaining new respect and members, and contributing to the overall knowledge base about those wonderful women writers from the Golden Age of Mystery.

But a library open to the public had been a shocking proposition—at least to the Society's secretary, Mrs. Glynis Woolgar. It took a fair bit of song and dance on my part to convince her that our founder, the late Lady Georgiana Fowling, had intended for her impressive collection of first edition books—as well as rare and unusual printings—to be enjoyed, not hidden away. The secretary had agreed, but with reservations.

On my first day back at work, I had expected to find Mrs. Woolgar with her knickers in a twist about the launch of the Wednesday afternoon opens, but instead, at our morning briefing, I had been met with an ashen face across the desk from me. Even before we had exchanged "Good mornings," she made the pronouncement: "It's about Charles Henry."

Rarely was any news that involved Charles Henry Dill, Lady Fowling's lout of a nephew, good news, unless it was that he was out of the country. Because when he wasn't, he applied himself to his life's goal of trying to get more, more, more money out of his aunt's estate.

Mrs. Woolgar had told me his latest scheme was to become my assistant, and when I could find my voice again,

I said, "But surely the board wouldn't allow it? Mr. Rennie wouldn't allow it?"

Duncan Rennie, the Society's solicitor, did his best to keep Dill and his machinations at bay. Sadly, as Mrs. Woolgar had pointed out, "Asking for a job isn't nefarious unto itself."

The board members' reasons for acquiescing had been another matter. The board comprised four dear old friends of her ladyship, plus a young one. Mrs. Audrey Moon and Mrs. Sylvia Moon—they had married brothers—and Jane Arbuthnot were in their eighties; Maureen Frost, in her early seventies; and my friend Adele Babbage, several decades younger than the others and ten years or so my junior.

Dill had worked his subterfuge quickly while I had been away, and he had kept under the radar of Mrs. Woolgar, aided and abetted by Maureen. First, he had worn down resistance from the Moons by "stopping in for a cuppa" every afternoon the week before. Under the guise of sharing stories of his aunt, he had revealed to them his wistful hope to be a part of the Society as a way of honoring her. Jane Arbuthnot had been easily swayed by Maureen. But I had been shocked to learn that Adele –the turncoat—had agreed to Dill's proposal, too.

The meeting had been arranged for Tuesday, the next afternoon. When the attendees, including Mr. Rennie, had arrived, Mrs. Woolgar had taken them up to the library. I had stayed on the ground floor in the kitchenette to get the tea tray ready, and so when the front-door buzzer went off with the last in—Adele—I answered.

"Are you still speaking to me?" she asked, slapping a sweet smile on her face.

"Barely," I said.

Adele stepped in and stopped. "Is that his?"

A large white Panama hat hung on the hallstand.

"I'm afraid so. He's cut off that dreadful ponytail, probably so the hat would fit on his head. He must've taken scissors to it himself—it's all one length, and he has to tuck it behind his ears."

Adele wrinkled her nose. "Eww. Look, Hayley," she said, following me into the kitchenette, "I know hiring Charles Henry sounds dire, but the Moons as well as Jane have had to endure four years of his trickery in his attempt to get hold of Georgiana's fortune."

"And house," I had added as I arranged pastries on a tray.

"And house."

"What about Maureen?" I asked. "What does she see in him?"

"Yes," Adele said. "You'd think she'd have better judgment than this. Perhaps all those years ago, he wasn't quite so . . . Charles Henryish."

Nearly twenty years ago, Maureen, a local actress, and Charles Henry Dill had been involved. He had been in his forties and Maureen, married at the time, in her fifties. The affair had ended, and a few years later, Maureen's husband had died, but it had been only in the four years since Lady Fowling's death that Dill and Maureen had picked things up again. Those were the only shreds of the story I could tease out of Mrs. Woolgar, who probably knew much more.

"And," Adele said, "it just seemed that a half day a week as your assistant would be a small price to pay to keep him quiet."

Possibly, but who would pay that price? Me.

I had handed Adele the tea service, taken the pastries, and headed upstairs to meet my doom.

It was done and dusted, and now Charles Henry reached out to nab the last blackcurrant macaron, holding it aloft for a moment between a stubby finger and thumb. "I'm sure my dear aunt Georgiana would be so pleased to know that the *only living member of her family*"—he carried that description like a badge of courage—"is once more involved in her great undertaking."

Pairs of eyes darted round the table. No one attempted to contradict this outright lie. Even I, who had never met Lady Fowling in person, knew that "pleased" was not a word that would've described his aunt's reaction to the situation. Not after he had absconded with that set of eighteenth-century silver basting spoons. During her funeral reception. He had best watch his lies or the late Georgiana Fowling, founder of the First Edition Society and its library, might just rise from her grave and set her nephew straight.

"And now, Ms. Burke," Charles Henry said in his oleaginous fashion, "to the particulars of my employment. Shall we set our day and time now while we're all gathered? What about Monday mornings?"

"No," I said quickly, "I'm sorry, that won't suit." Did he think I wanted to spend my weekends dreading the start of the workweek?

"Friday mornings?" he offered with what he might have thought looked like a polite smile.

"Sadly"—*happily*—"that won't work with my schedule, either. I have a local adult-learning student starting on a special project Fridays."

"Well, then," Dill said, his voice practically gurgling with pleasure, "what is left but the middle of the week? Shall we say Wednesday afternoons?"

He had tricked me. He had wanted Wednesday afternoons all along, so that he could be present during our public openings. What sort of devilry might Charles Henry get up to during those four hours when he could mingle with the public? Whose ear would he try to bend in the process—reporters, bloggers, academics—to support him in his desires? No, I would do everything I could to keep the proverbial bargepole between Dill and the public.

"You know," I said, "now that I think about it, Monday

mornings just might work." *There go my worry-free days off.*

"Lovely," he said with some resignation. "Now as to the particulars of my employment."

"No need to drag the board and Mr. Rennie through the details, Mr. Dill," I said, smiling innocently. "The two of us can sort all that out on your first morning. I'm sure the others need to be on their way."

They couldn't get out fast enough, offering quick good-byes along with weak congratulations to Charles Henry and quiet asides to me.

"Arrivederci, mon ami!" Adele whispered. "I'm stopping at the Minerva for Pauline. We have an evening class. We'll talk later."

"You're young," Jane Arbuthnot murmured as she left. "You'll survive."

"Dear Hayley," Mrs. Audrey Moon said, patting me on the arm. Mrs. Sylvia Moon added, "It's so good of you. I suppose we should've been stronger and not let him in, but he is Georgiana's only relative. Do let us know how you get on. Stop in for a sherry, why don't you?"

I noticed Dill had cornered Duncan Rennie before he could get out the door. Maureen Frost gave them a quick glance, leaned toward me, and said, "He deserves a chance."

Mrs. Woolgar ushered the group, including my new assistant, downstairs to show them out. I remained in the library, propping my elbows on the table and sinking my head in my hands. She returned a few minutes later to find me unmoved—not an inch.

"Ms. Burke."

"Yes," I said, stretching my shoulders and then slumping back in my chair, "I know I must buck up. I'll tidy in here, and we can discuss this tomorrow at our morning briefing. You go on."

"Thank you. Mr. Rennie and I do have a few items to go over. But I want you to know that in no way will Charles Henry

Dill be let loose to do as he pleases in Middlebank House. He remains as he always has been—not to be trusted. He will be watched."

The secretary left, and I followed her out as far as the landing, dragging one of the Chippendale chairs from the library behind me. She continued to the ground floor, but I stayed, placing the chair across from the full-length portrait of Lady Georgiana Fowling.

I sat down, heaved a great sigh, and said, "Well, now what?"

Even though I had never met her ladyship, I felt as if I knew her through this work of art. It had been painted in the 1960s, but in it she was dressed in retro fashion from the '30s in a burgundy satin evening dress with a halter top. The gown was cut on the bias and draped elegantly to the floor. She was turned, slightly revealing a low back, and had a hand on an empty chair—representing her late husband, Sir John.

I confess that on the rare occasion I talk to the painting, but only in the sense that I use Lady Fowling's image as a sounding board. It isn't as if I thought she'd answer back—although the artist had done such a wonderful job of capturing the spirit of his subject that there were times when I felt as if her ladyship seemed about to reply. Needless to say, no one else knew I did this.

Today, she offered only her enigmatic smile, but I detected a steely glint in her look as if to say *beware*.

Ready to find
your next great read?

Let us help.

Visit prh.com/nextread

Penguin
Random
House